Finding Dignity

Finding Dignity

J. MARIE DARDEN

STREBOR BOOKS

NEW YORK LONDON TORONTO SYDNEY

Strebor Books
P.O. Box 6505
Largo, MD 20792
http://www.streborbooks.com

© 2005 by J. Marie Darden

Cover design: www.mariondesigns.com

ISBN-13 978-1-59309-051-7
ISBN-10   1-59309-051-X
LCCN 2005920191

First Strebor Books trade paperback edition January 2006

10 9 8 7 6 5 4 3 2 1

Manufactured in the United States of America

For information regarding special discounts for bulk purchases, please contact Simon & Schuster Special Sales at 1-800-456-6798 or business@simonandschuster.com

Acknowledgments

This book is dedicated to all of the people who helped me to find my own dignity: To Christ, who strengthens me.

To my Honey Husband and Handsome Kissy Son—I love you more than anything, and I always will, no matter what.

To Mrs. Hubble, Mrs. Buckwalter-Robey, Mrs. Ahearn, Mrs. Silver, Mrs. Frick, Mrs. Levine, Ms. Clayman, Mr. Davis, Mr. Grooman, Mrs. Knox, Ms. McManus, Mr. Berkowitz, Ms. Almand, Mr. Brisco; thanks for taking on the noble profession of public school teaching because what you do makes a difference. You may never remember all of the names of the many lives that you touch, but hurry up and believe that they remember you!

To Dr. Sheffy, Dr. Bayton, Dr. Jackson, Professor Tyler, Professor Taylor, Dr. Lupton, Dr. Jeremiah (who was a bullfrog), and the late, great Dr. Carter—professors at the greatest college on earth, Morgan State University—the knowledge you pass on, the discipline you instill, the excellence that you demand, and the effort that you give to students is life-altering, and I will never forget it.

To the students and alumni of Morgan State, especially the English Club and class of 1993, residents of Blount and Northwood—HOLLA, HOLLA! This book is all about you!

To all of my friends from the Montgomery County Public School System, especially Estelene—I wish you peace, mad props, and "big ups" because you do the impossible every single day for not nearly enough pay or recognition.

To my friends and coworkers at The Community College of Baltimore County because you are the smartest and most dedicated people that I know, and to all of my students, who work and raise babies and go to school and still find time to read my books—you rock!

To the Columbia Alum Chapter of Delta Sigma Theta because your work in the community changes the world, and because your support is overwhelming; y'all are my heroes!

To the book clubs who have supported me, especially the Heavenly Honies and The Pages of Life—hugs and kisses to every last one of you!

And to Jonathan Westbrook, who had the good sense to dedicate the song, "Sweet Melissa," to me whenever he performed it. See you in the next life, bro.

And don't be late.

[PART ONE]

Deal

Breakers

IN MEDIA RES:
JUST AFTER FINALS, JUNIOR YEAR
[MORGAN STATE UNIVERSITY 1994]

[THE PREMISE]

Dignity Jackson

S trong as the bond is, much as you might love and cherish someone, and even though you might need an anchor to cling to in this hostile portal called life, there are deal breakers. You can know someone for so many years that the two of you can play "remember when" all day every day and never run out of material. And you can come through for someone again and again in intangible ways that require something other than language to express—distant drums, gossamer bubbles, or the beating of dragonfly wings on cool summer lakes—and even still, even still! There are deal breakers. The concept of deal breakers is the hardest lesson I have learned so far in college.

Eventually, inevitably, loved ones come to a blockade, a forceful wall that neither can penetrate. When that happens, and you can no longer walk forward, the obvious choice is to go backward. Cut and run. Happened to my mom, Sister Rebecca, with, well, practically everyone that she was close to, including me. To my Ain't Angus and her sister, my Grandma Pearson. And now to me and my estranged, Italian boyfriend, Sal. I wonder if there is any way to overcome this dilemma.

Either way, this deal-breaking is a good reason to leave town. Because bonds, living bonds, the ones that people read about and dream about and leave about, these are the only things in this life that really matter. They are safe harbors against incompatible truths. I'm beginning to realize that breathing brings paradox, that to exist is to contradict, so close relationships, then, inevitably end in escape. That's why I am going back home to Kentucky.

This morning, right after finals, I couldn't stop to pack up the whole apartment. There'd be time for that later. All I knew was I had to get the hell out of Dodge. I had already called Ain't Angus to tell her I was coming, although I didn't have to. Ever since I can remember, Ain't Angus' door has always been open. Literally. Any time, day or night, I can show up at her door and just walk in. She is always glad to see me and encourages me to stay, and very often I have taken her up on it. Before I left for college at Morgan State in Baltimore, back when I was in high school and got bored over winter break, or if I had a tough time with Aunt Lette and her "holiness" rules about church all day every day, and always for the majority of the summer, I would pack my bags and go stay with Ain't Angus. She is the closest thing I have to a mama, next to Aunt Lette, the woman who raised me.

Of course, I talked to Mercer that morning. He's been my best friend since I was three years old. He's always had my back. He is one of those extraordinary people. Couldn't wait to see him, tell him all about me and Sal. I also wanted to hear about his latest antics at Kentucky State. He'd be able to tell me what to do about Sal. When I talked to him, he said he had some interesting news to share. Tried to pump him for details, but he said I'd understand when I saw him in person.

Once I found out my final grades (four A's and a B, just enough to blow my 4.0, son of a biscuit!), I called Sal and gave him my Ain't Angus' phone number and address. I didn't want to totally cut him off, just in case I was making a mistake. Then I packed two suitcases, stopped at the 7-Eleven on Cold Spring and bought two bean pies, a huge container of Gatorade and a pack of Capri menthols, and I headed for Route 70 West to get some serious road before dusk. By 10:30 a.m., I was well on my way. It would take me eight hours to get to Lexington if I drove non-stop. If I played it right, I'd get there well before dark.

Junior
Year

[MORGAN STATE UNIVERSITY 1994]

1

[QUIET REVOLUTION]

Dignity Jackson

I t was our junior year at Morgan State University, and I was nominated by *The Quiet Revolution (QR)*, a group of passive-aggressive anarchists who thought globally and acted locally, to run for Ms. Morgan during senior year. At first I was only flattered by the group's show of support, counting it as proof that they accepted me. And I thought it would be groundbreaking to have an "independent" candidate, someone unaffiliated with a sorority, in the running. Soon, though, my obligatory neurosis set in. I began to strangle myself with a subconscious "what if" pattern that I could not turn off.

What if I run but I lose? What if the race gets ugly? What if they find out that I am a fake? What if they finally see that I am a completely neurotic quasi-wannabe revolutionary with a bag of compulsions the size of east Baltimore?

Yet, my friends thought I was the obvious choice. We had some capital saved up from our fund-raisers. I actually stood a chance of winning. In my mind, I wanted to take a shot at it, to make a statement that you don't have to be a right-wing sorority girl to make a name for yourself at Morgan. But, in my heart, I felt nauseous, weak, and confused. Still, I officially accepted the nomination, so that meant I would have to be ready to speak at the rally that coming Friday. I would have to stand on stage, announcing my platform and intentions, with a world of judging faces before me. I swallowed down my anxiety and felt it mix with my intestines to create a thick rope in my middle.

By this time, Salmon and I had been together since the middle of freshman year, and we were still going strong. Unless you count the fact that I literally went into conniptions whenever he tried to touch me. Or the fact that his family had practically disowned him for choosing a dark-skinned girl of questionable lineage rather than a wholesome Italian one. The family dissention gave him nightmares. Between my intimacy issues and his nocturnal freak-outs, neither of us was sleeping at night. But we did it together, and we did it lovingly.

I spent at least a portion of most evenings with Sal, unless I had a meeting with The QR or the Art Club. I had a million acquaintances but no really close friends. I carried a steady supply of emotional bricks in my countenance and built invisible walls whenever anyone tried to get close. There were only two people that I confided in: Sal and Kiko, the Japanese girl upstairs who did my hair and nails.

After I accepted the nomination for Ms. Morgan, I walked across the campus to my apartment in Northwood. Sal wouldn't be around until after basketball practice, so I went upstairs to visit with Kiko. I felt like I needed to talk.

That's when I ran into Stacy Smithe. We used to be girls back in the day, but then she played the backstabbing ho card. Went after a dude that I was supposed to be seeing. If that wasn't bad enough, she tried to front and say that she did it because I am a redbone. "You must think you're all that," she said. In other words, she took my man to protect the purity of the black race. To me, *she* is the one who thinks I'm all that, because *she* is the one who always has something to say about it.

For real, she is underhanded. Ever since that whole thing with Khalil, the guy she skeezed from me back in freshman year, she had it in for me. When I was rushed during sophomore year, she went around badmouthing me to the sorority sisters to tell them I was not worthy to pledge, meanwhile kissing their behinds so that she would get online. I didn't pledge because I wasn't the type for sororities. Then she tried to get Khalil to bad mouth me to Salmon so he wouldn't want to be with me. Khalil and Sal have been thick for years, even after Lil started seeing Stacy. Finally, she tried to get Khalil to stop speaking to Sal, saying she didn't feel comfortable doing things with Sal if I was going to be around. That girl has been taking witch pills since early freshman year!

That day she greeted me with the usual grimace and scowl.

"Dignity! What you into these days?" She put on a fake smile that she pressed in my face on her way down toward the parking lot.

"Minding." I can't stand somebody who tries to sabotage and hate on your life behind your back, then wanna grin up in your face later.

Stacy walked two more steps closer. "Umm. I see you still got that nasty attitude! So unbecoming for a girl like you. Did you hear about the Greek breakfast on Saturday? Oh, that's right! You're not a Greek, are you?" She ran her fingers through her freshly permed hair.

"No, Stacy. I guess I don't need a circle of elephants around me to feel secure. But eat some eggs for me, huh?"

"To be sure. I guess you heard that I'm running for Ms. Morgan. Can I count on your vote next term?" Stacy looked over her shoulder at me, like she hoped to see envy in my eyes.

"That would be silly, Stacy. Only a moron would vote against *herself!*" This time it was *my* turn to see her jaws drop.

"You? Oh, really? Did you pledge sometime and I didn't know about it? I didn't know you were one of us!" She oozed with fake enthusiasm.

"No. It's all Greek to me. I was nominated by an independent group. So let's wish *each other* luck!" I tossed my wavy mane, a feature that I knew she envied, and continued toward Kiko's apartment.

Stacy did not turn around as she continued through the lot of parked cars. "Good. Then I'll see you at the rally on Friday! Good luck! I know independents can have a hard time!"

When I finally reached her apartment, Kiko did her best to console me, although she didn't badmouth Stacy, one of her clients. But she did reassure me about my nomination for Ms. Morgan.

"You beautiful, Dig. You much prettier than many other girl! You do fine; you see! I do your makeup—remember how we do with gold and brown? Eyes look like sunset? And pile your hair up like model—you be beautiful!" Kiko patted my hand while we sat at her table drinking green tea, sweetened with honey.

I tried to explain to Kiko, and to myself, why the whole thing was so scary for me.

"It's complicated, and I haven't completely figured it out. Maybe, maybe it's that Ms. Morgan stands for something that I'm not sure I can be…" I looked into my green tea, and my reflection was distorted—how fitting.

Kiko broke off a corner of the toast she was eating and nibbled. "Why? Ms. Morgan—she a queen, right? Smart, pretty. You perfect!"

"No! That's just it. I don't *feel* smart or pretty! I feel… like a fake!" I played around with the loose leaves that had eased around the bottom of my cup and pouted.

"Silly! You no fake, Dig. I know you, and you not no fake. See, Mother use to say, feelings is funny. You no can trust feelings. They change like quick silver! You make decision, and you go, you do, but no trust feelings all the time!" Kiko finally swallowed the toast corner she'd been gnawing.

"What do you mean? Don't trust my feelings?"

"Feelings change, okay? Decisions you make, they don't change. See, one day, I wake up, look in mirror, I feel like the pretty goddess. Hair feel shiny, skin feel pink and full of color. Next time I see mirror, I feel like the monster! Why I got sunken cheek? Why my hair seem brown instead of black? No. Feeling change too much; you can't keep track. So, I make decision: Me, Kiko, I am beautiful. Inside I shine, so outside I shine, too. No feeling, Dig. Decision."

What she said seemed so simple and made so much sense that I rather believed her. Or, at least, I wanted to. I swished my index finger through the tea to see if it was still hot. It was tepid, but I took a sip. "Ah-hah! So, if I just ignore my feelings, maybe *I* will feel beautiful, too!"

"You almost see but not all the way see. You say you ignore *feelings* and *feel* beautiful—no! You ignore feelings and *be* beautiful. Beautiful mean smart, Dig. And sweet in the heart. And wanting to work for good. That's why maybe you win!" Kiko ate the last of her buttered toast, scraped the crumbs from the table into her hands, and took both of our cups to her kitchen sink. Kiko was forever eating buttered toast. It was her favorite thing.

While Kiko was rinsing out our cups, in those moments while I didn't have to look into her simple face or splinter her trusting eyes with my fearful truths, I cut to the center of what I was feeling.

"You have pictures all over your apartment, Kiko. Your mother, even though she is passed to another plane, your grandparents, sketches of Okinawa. I love all the jewelry you kept from your paternal grandmother and the kimonos from your great-aunt! I mean, even if you live here in Baltimore, and many of these people are still in Japan or gone on before, I look around here and I know you're connected. Me, I have nothing. No real clues as to who I am!" I had to blink away tears quietly, quickly, before she finished rinsing and came back to the table.

"I mean, I have Ain't Angus—that's a nickname for my Aunt Agnes, and Aunt Paulette and Uncle Sam, who raised me, but it's like all this messed-up patchwork that doesn't make any sense together. At holidays, I would see all of these folks that looked just alike. Same hair, same skin color, same eyes. And then me, like the one patch of blue in a basket of red cherries. I don't seem to belong to any of them. They're always so careful around me, like they are hiding the fact that I am completely different. They don't have any stories to pass down to me, and I won't have anything to pass down to my children. I feel like I have no identity! It sucks!" I wiped the wetness from around my eyes, but there was no way to erase away the red puffy pillows that formed around my lids whenever I started crying.

Kiko sat down at the table and pulled the silver chain from around her neck. She passed it to me. I noticed the silver and jade locket on the bottom, and I opened it up. Inside there was no picture, no trinket like what I am used to seeing. Just an inscription in a straight, Roman font. "Kiko." I looked at the locket with a puzzle in my voice and questioned, "Okay…?"

"It is me. It is who I choose to be, the name I choose for myself. Not Papa. Not Mama. They hold their share in picture, in memory. But, me, Kiko, I keep inside my own heart and decide every day and choose every night who I will be. You the only one who can decide that. You alone have power to decide who you will be."

Sounded like a plan to me. I just had to decide who I would be, make a decision about it, and stick to it. With this revelation in hand, I went down to my own apartment to write my nomination acceptance speech and to wait for Sal to come.

[Ms. Morgan]

Salmon Rinaldi

When Digs was nominated to run for Ms. Morgan. That's when it started to unravel with us. It wasn't just us, neither. Seemed like everywhere you looked, folks were coming undone. Mommy and Pops were fighting like mad dogs, about me and my love life with a black girl, about Pop's brother, Uncle George Sr. and his dead sons, Georgy and Darryl. Khalil was beginning to get wise to Stacy and her trick ass, and they were getting shaky. Everywhere you looked, it was turmoil.

And I told Digs that this whole Ms. Morgan thing, the whole beauty queen popularity gig, was for the birds. But, she didn't wanna believe that's what this one was about. She wanted to make it a political thing, an indication of the revolution on campus. I kept trying to explain to her that there WAS no revolution on campus or anywhere else, for that matter. We were all too busy trying to make sure our senior audits were correct so we could walk up out of that trick bitch. Because everybody knew administration was famous for sending an audit claiming that you still needed, like, thirty-six more credits to graduate just before your senior year, just before you were ready to take those last few classes and shake. And if you weren't careful keep records of everything you did on campus, administration could get away with keeping you one or two extra semesters. I had seen it happen before, and for me, I wasn't having it.

But Digs didn't want to let her idealistic talk group, The QR, down. And she thought if she could win this prestigious title that she could make some significant changes on campus. I told her to look at the changes we needed to make in our own lives and worry about the campus revolution later. But she wouldn't listen.

About two weeks before finals, they had the nomination rally at Hill Field House. Each of the nominees, male and female, was going to read an acceptance speech. They were going to let the crowd know where they were coming from in terms of their views and all. That's where all the spit really hit the fan. Where Stacy and Digs had at it so bad that both nearly got suspended.

Now granted, by that time, Stacy Smithe had become a real witch—way outta hand, so I can't say I was surprised at the way Digs reacted to her. But I would like to have seen Dignity practice a little more restraint.

There were three candidates for Mr. Morgan and four for Ms. Morgan. All of them were upper classmen. There were two people who seemed to have the audience's favor—Michael Wayland and Tiffany Jamison. Michael was the campus comedian, associated with the Kappas, and he had the crowd going with jokes before he even read an acceptance speech. He could be corny, but you hadda admit that some of his jokes were on. Especially when he cracked on Professor Wexler, saying she was so old that she was around when the Dead Sea Scrolls got sick. Had me howling. Then Tiffany had this "skee-wee" thing going with her sorors; all of them waved their pink and green flags until the whole place looked like flying watermelons. These two were obviously the popular candidates, so you hadda really be saying something to keep the crowd's attention after they spoke.

Digs, man, she was up to the task! Even I was a little surprised by her eloquence or whatever.

The thing was, you were supposed to accept the nomination and explain what your platform, or your focus, would be. One of the functions of this pageant thing was tied to public service. Mr. and Ms. Morgan worked directly with an organization of their choice to contribute something positive to the community.

Michael wanted to work with Special Olympics, since his little cousin died from Multiple Sclerosis. Tiffany was interested in AIDS prevention, since the virus was becoming more prevalent among African-American youth. But Digs, she came from out of nowhere with her idea to form an organization rather than to just align herself with an existing one. Her idea of forming an organization was unique, but it sounded conventional in comparison to the theme she wanted to focus on.

Dignity used well-researched quotes and realistic, hypothetical examples to explain how black people cannot hope for equality and unity with other races until they can get along with each other. Dignity, God love her, announced that her platform would be in-house racism. She announced that afternoon, in front of thousands of Morganites, that she would be spearheading a new organization called ColorKind, "to educate students about the insidious and dangerous effects of black-on-black discrimination, and to promote cultural pride and self-love." She confessed that she had been the victim of this kind of discrimination and knew first hand how damaging it could be. She told the students that she had already acquired some funding from some local organizations, including 3 major Greek organizations, that she had a committee that would be creating brochures to alert the community about the organization and its mission. Oh, she had it all down! The real trip, though, was what she said at the end of her speech:

"Some say that this election is nothing more than a beauty pageant. I guess that could be true because every single candidate here has a unique idea, a cause to fight for, and a reason why they deserve to represent our 'Fair Morgan' next year—and that's beautiful. But my platform, and my reason for standing before you this afternoon, is a little different. I want to let you know that beautiful thoughts, unique ideas, and the willingness to contribute something positive to society, are ideas that belong to everybody. Like many of you, I have the insight to recognize a problem that plagues my people; thus, I have a responsibility to contribute to the solution.

"Fair Morganites, I cannot be with you when you choose your candidate next fall. I cannot be sure that I will win. But I do know that we have a host of wonderful, beautiful candidates this year, that each one has something special to offer to Morgan and to the world, and, in this respect, I know that I cannot lose. Remember to love each other. My name is Dignity."

The whole gymnasium fell silent, no joke. She caught the campus off guard. Because, for one thing, most people had never heard of her, and there she was speaking like Sojourner Truth or something. And for another, she was so tiny and wild-looking, with her small, oval glasses and her fire-engine hair. And, she was well-spoken as all hell. Nobody had expected her to be so classy, so informed, so mature up there. She didn't sling any mud and she didn't talk about silly things. From her whole spirit, you could tell that she was being sincere. Shocked the socks off of Morgan, myself included.

And the applause—oh man. That clapping was no joke! You'da thought Dignity was Mariah Carey or Janet Jackson, the way they carried on. Dignity just stood on the side of the stage and said thank you. She was such a classy chick and didn't even know it, with her neurotic self. So after that, Stacy was the next, the last candidate, in fact, to speak. But she had to wait what seemed like a lifetime for the folks to stop clapping and screaming Dignity's name. You could see the heat rising up in Stacy's face, like inside of that red and white suit she was sporting she had a mean fire going on. She stood at the podium looking like the zookeeper when the monkey house has gone mad.

Stacy must have ditched the speech she prepared and opted to free flow her acceptance. Bad move. She explained how she was concerned about domestic violence. She was doing all right until she realized that no one was listening to her. Folks were squirming in their seats and talking loudly to one another. Many folks simply got up and left. Morganites can be like that—rude as an Apollo audience on a Saturday night if they are over the event and if you aren't saying what they wanna hear.

Well, any idiot would have just wrapped up and called it a day. But Stacy kept at it, telling a sketchy, make-it-up-as-you-go-along story about a cousin who had been beaten up by her husband so bad that she no longer could talk. That's when it turned ugly.

"If I come up there and knock you up side the head, will you shut up, too?" Some dude hurled this insult up from the audience, and the whole gymnasium fell out. It was cold, but it was also funny. Stacy was trying so hard up there, but it just wasn't happening. So, Stacy got back to her roots, got loud, and let the ghetto out of the bag. She pointed her finger into the audience and told them they were not right, that abuse was not funny, and that they all needed to grow up. It was getting uncomfortable. The same dude who had insulted her before stood up and started imitating her, shaking his neck and pointing his finger. Half the crowd was howling at him, and the other side was beginning to side with Stacy, telling him to grow up and sit down.

The whole time this was happening, I could see Dignity getting more and more frantic. She had this thing where she couldn't stand to see any kind of violence—she'd go nuts. She gave the term "peace loving" new meaning. Any kind of dissention used to make her crazy, and she'd do anything to stop it. The gymnasium was loud with all the hoo-ha, and it really did seem like we were on the outskirts of a riot. Next thing you know, Dignity comes flying over to the podium next to Stacy, grabbing the mic, and giving her best peace-keeper act:

"Stop it! Stop it this instant! This woman has something to say, and each and every one of you had better listen!" But before Dignity could really get started defending her, Stacy knocked Dignity to the floor and started cussing her out.

"Oh, please! The day I need your help will be a cold day in hell, red bone! Witcha Pollyanna shit about all colors of the rainbow! This madness is *your* fault anyway! If you hadn't a been so long-winded with your Little Mary Sunshine shit, these people wouldn't have been so tired and ready to go!" Stacy used the side of her foot to soccer-kick Dignity to the side, like she was some kind of trash.

That's when I got up and headed for the podium. I didn't care if she was a woman; Stacy was not going to drop kick my girlfriend and get away with it. I was seeing red, I was so angry running up there.

But Dignity surprised me. Much as she loved peace, she must have had a temper, too, when she was threatened or when her principles were at stake. She came up swinging, ready to draw blood. I already knew that she loved Martin Luther King, Jr., that she thought about his "I Have a Dream" speech, which she'd memorized in 10th grade, whenever she needed strength, but I did not expect her to draw strength from that speech *that* day under *those* circumstances.

I was a few feet away when I saw my Dignity pulling herself up by the boot-straps of Stacy's hair. "Naw, Stacy. I have a dream today! You're not gonna turn it into a nightmare…" Stacy's bottom lips turned down in discomfort, nearly covering her chin with a grimace of shock, pain, and surprise.

Dignity didn't miss a beat. She had Stacy in a death grip; Stacy's hands were pressed behind her back, as Dignity propelled herself and her victim toward the podium. "Oh, we're gonna work together, Sister! Not because of the color of *your* skin, but because of the content of *my* character—I have a dream today, Stacy!"

"What is the matter with you?! You crazy bitch, let go of my arm! Security!" Stacy was struggling with all of her weight, but she couldn't get loose from Dignity's grip. I had never seen my girlfriend in that light before. I wasn't sure whether I was turned on or scared of her. I remember I just froze like a deer caught in headlights and watched her like a soap opera.

The crowd was hooting and yelling as Dignity strong-armed Stacy and made her walk apologize for her ugly words to Dignity. But those few steps to the podium were filled with drama.

"We may not get there together, Stacy, but I can promise you—we as a people will reach the Promised Land! Now you say you're sorry! Say it!" It took all of her strength to keep Stacy from breaking free and running out of that gym like the chicken shit she was.

"Girl, do you know I work for lawyers? I will sue your ass, big time! Let me go, you crazy, yellow heifer…"

"Oh, you're gonna apologize, Stacy! You're not gonna deface this whole rally with your hateful ways! Blacks and Whites, Jews and Gentiles…" Dignity continued with her disjointed quoting of "The Dream."

"Mad Cow! Mad Cow!" Stacy tried her best to pry loose, but she couldn't. The spectators were watching her, watching Dignity, not sure about the high tone that Dignity had taken, but appreciating the idea of a catfight. But, by that time, Dignity had worn her victim down, and Stacy visibly deflated. You could see the fight go out of her as Dignity prompted her with what to say.

"Apologize to the student body," Dignity said.

"I am sorry, Morganites, fellow sorors, and frats for this nasty behavior." Stacy spoke softly into the mic while the crowd cheered and laughed.

"Free at last! Apologize to the faculty for wasting their valuable time," Dignity insisted, somehow maintaining her hold on Stacy's arms.

"My apologies to the faculty and staff for, ahh, this misconduct…" You could see Stacy's cheeks pulsing, like the words she was saying were draining her face, her brain of all of their energy.

"Free at last!" Dignity squealed. "Now, apologize to *me* for your ignorant act of violence." I could see that my girlfriend's strength was wearing thin, and I was ready to jump in whenever necessary.

Stacy coughed and sweated and nearly choked on the words. "I am sorry, Dignity. I lost my temper with you, and I am sorry." Stacy closed her eyes with those words, maybe to avoid seeing the crow she was being made to eat.

"Thank God Almighty, we are free at last!!!" Dignity let go of Stacy's arms, her own upraised in victory and praise.

You shoulda seen those college kids, clapping, cheering, laughing, going nuts over a scene that they probably only partially understood. But by the time I approached Dignity, security had shown up. And two days later, I was right there with Digs when she and Stacy had to explain their behavior and appeal their disciplinary probation to regain the right to run for Ms. Morgan, and plead to the dean not to suspend their sassy asses in the fall.

Well, to make a long story short, Dignity got what she wanted: an apology from Stacy, a nomination for campus queen, and the right to come back and finish senior year. Me, I got the chance to see my Dignity in action. She was a force to be reckoned with, that girl.

But, along with a subtle victory in terms of Ms. Morgan and the chance to see what she's really made of, we both got something else: a serious lover's quarrel that nearly cost both of us our dignity.

3

[DARKER PERSUASION]

Stacy Smithe

I don't know what got into me that day. Nerves I guess. And that green-eyed monster. It's just that I looked out there into that sea of black faces, and I saw most of them screaming her name, and everything I'd ever had to live down or try to overcome came flooding over me. Felt like I was bathed in hate.

Even though I was surprised to find out Dignity was running for Ms. Morgan, I don't think I was all that surprised to hear how beautifully she spoke that day. She has a gift, that girl, something special in her. Maybe that's why I had such a problem with her. I mean, she was like a golden child, or something—who needs it? Everybody always raving over Dignity like she's the greatest thing since cheese grits. And is it any coincidence that she's got all that good hair waving down her back and no darker than a minute past morning? I don't think so! Those kind, they always get all the breaks. Just like my half-sister, Helene. Me and her have different daddies.

My daddy is coal black and locked up until some far-off day in the twenty-first century. Left me nothing but a hard way to go. Must be every time my mama looked at me, she saw Nigger Charlie. That's what she called my daddy. Said that's the name of a well-known dog, or something. She said it was well-known that he was a dog, so the name suited him.

Real name was Henry Harrel Smithe. Hank for short. He'd been on lockdown since I was six, but I inherited a few things from Hank Harrel: two pictures of him and my mom taken in the late '70s, both of them looking like something out of *Cotton Comes to Harlem*, a rain hat he used to wear, his dog tags from the Vietnam

War, skin the color of black strap molasses, and a ruthless temper. Sometimes that temper gets the best of me. Apparently it runs in the family.

According to the legends passed down by my grandmother, Melba, and my aunt and her children, my daddy was a drinker and a gambler. He stayed drunk so he wouldn't have to think. They tell me he had a lot of brilliant thoughts but no money to put them to use. So he stayed drunk. He took up with my mama in late '69. He'd done a brief stint in Vietnam and came back injured in his body and in his mind. That's when he met Mr. Daniels. Got along with Mr. Daniels so well that he began calling him by his first name—Jack. Daddy and Jack were inseparable.

But according to Big Melba, my granny, he didn't mean to shoot that officer. He meant to shoot the deputy, the one who looked like the gooks, the enemy. He thought he was doing the right thing and protecting his platoon. Only reason why he didn't plead insanity was because he didn't want to go down in family history as a crazy man. He'd rather be known as a straight-up thug. Judge probably wouldn't have gone for it anyway. Daddy had a drunken delusion. That ain't a matter for the psychiatrist; that's a matter for Alcoholic Anonymous.

Not long after that, Mama took up with her current friend, Willy Moseby. Been together, unmarried, for nearly as long as I've had breath. Looked like that old guy, Cab Calloway. He and my mom were about as light as you could get without being white. And my little sister, Helene, was the same way—bright yellow. Ever since she showed up, with her tiny little self, Mama hasn't wanted much to do with me. Especially since she claimed the only reason why Willy wouldn't quit his first wife, Denise, and marry her was because of my black behind. Doesn't want to be linked with a crazy murderer's dark-skinned child.

And Helene was always trying to prove how much she loved me, how much she recognized that Mama was wrong. Jumping to my defense whenever Mama went off on her "you're just like your father, never gonna be nothing, never gonna have nothing" routine. But I don't need Helene's sympathy. Words ain't worth much. I didn't see her turning down the clothes Mama bought. I worked all up and down Security Mall to earn money for mine. Never saw her turn down the modeling lessons or the dance classes or the private school education at Archbishop Keough even though we ain't Catholic and haven't stepped foot in a church since precious little Helene was baptized. Helene can save the sympathetic drama for her mama. The two of them can have each other.

My sister always caused me conflict. Because she was smarter than me, she never had to work as hard at school, and she did have a sweetness about her. But, shoot, I might be sweet, too, if I had a mama that doted on me. Shoot. I wanted to be spoiled, too.

And Dignity put me in the mind of Helene. Smart, pretty, and light enough for everybody to spoil and shower with affection. Made me angry. I tried hard to hide what I was feeling; I planned to make my speech, accept my nomination, and feel good when my sorors. But all I could hear was them screaming out Dignity's name. So, I snapped. I wanted to take her yellow ass and her prayer for peace and pound it into the dirt somewhere behind Hill Field House, where rats the size of small cats come out when it is quiet and dark, and let her feel, for one moment, what I feel every day of my life—beaten down and buried just for being someone, something I cannot change. All this equality and peace and sunshine— it was easy for her to preach that mess, cuz that's all she'd ever seen. Me, I live on the dark side where it ain't so easy to see the sun.

[CALLING IT QUITS]

Khalil Towers

J unior year was a trip. They say many people don't make it through junior year. I can see why. That third year is no joke! That's when you're done with all the general ed courses and you get deep in your major. Half the time, students have picked a major blindly, having no idea what it's really like. Plus, poverty sets in, and students get antsy, wanting to get out there and earn money and live life again. For real, niggers is so broke in college, they can hardly pay attention. It can wear on a brother.

But, not being faint of heart, I had made it through that infamous third year. I was looking forward to the summer, going to work for my dad, earning some money so I could chill during my last year.

I was involved with this chick, Stacy Smithe. She was fine as all hell and crazy about my narrow ass. I guess that's why I put up with her shit. She was always involved in high drama, ever since I met her chocolate behind. We started kicking it back two years before, during freshman year. The way it happened was kind of messed up. Originally, me and my homie, Sal, were interested in Stacy and her friend, Dignity. I was feeling Dignity, and Salmon was gonna get with Stacy. But then, some shit we didn't anticipate went down, and I ended up flipping the script. So, Sal ended up with Dignity, and I ended up with Stacy. I didn't mean to play my homeboy foul, though. It just happened that way.

Stacy must have looked at me and seen a white picket fence and two-point-five children or something because she clung to my ass like stink clings to raw chitterlings—she was all over it! I told her I was a free spirit, not ready for any heavy commitments, and she went for it. Being as though she accepted my stipulations—she allowed me to see whomever I wanted whenever I wanted; she could only see me—I stayed with her. Women can really accept some ridiculous shit.

But even though she put up with my one-sided rules, she still started to trip and pitch fits, and we was starting to have issues. Stacy had this phobia of redbones, as she called them, always afraid that light-skinned people were stepping on her, or getting the stuff she wanted just because they were light. Stacy was a deep bluish-black, skin just as smooth and shiny as a baby's butt. She was gorgeous, with her dark self. But she was also paranoid as hell, thinking everybody treated her differently 'cause she was dark. The girl had issues.

I had a plan, though. I figured I'd finish the semester and lay low with her, turning my cheek to her craziness, then I'd go work for my dad in Virginia and drop her ass over the summer. Come back for senior year with my wallet on swoll, ready to roll.

That was the plan, but as they say, plans don't always go smoothly. When Stacy showed her ass at the Ms. Morgan rally, showing her deep-seated need for intensive, on-going therapy, I knew I had to bounce right then. I mean, I knew that contest was important to her, but the way she acted with Dignity was uncalled for. Digs and me were cool—I always liked the girl. And, hell, her boyfriend, Salmon, was one of my top dogs. Nah. I couldn't put up with Stacy's stunts no more. Tricks are for kids.

Soon after I called it quits with Stacy, Salmon and Dignity got into it big time. Even though we was way down, Sal didn't talk to me much about his large, Italian family or his relationship with Digs, at least not on that deep tip. But he did mention that his father was old school, kind of backward in his ways. He implied that maybe his pops wasn't cool with the darker persuasion, that he wasn't down with Sal and Dig's love gig. Didn't seem like his pops was big on Sal's stint at Morgan State, neither. Used to be the situation with his pops didn't bother him much. But by junior year, I guess it started to bug him, and he started to talk to me about it.

Salmon is from one of these Italian, Catholic families, like *The Godfather*, or some shit. Originally from Brooklyn, they lived out in Silver Spring, close to Washington, D.C. They was forever having these family reunions, dinners and what not, that Sal never wanted to mess with. I could count on one hand the times he went home during our first two years at MSU. Most holidays he either stayed at his apartment and let my moms slide him a plate, or he came home with me. One Christmas we drove down to Norfolk and chilled with my dad and his girlfriend for a hot minute. But Sal never really went home, and he didn't go deep into why.

That year, though, he began to toy with the idea of going home for Easter, a big deal holiday for his family. He went, and when he came back, he wasn't the same Sal. I don't know what happened, but whatever it was must have really messed him up. And soon after that, right around finals, homeboy started to really trip. Told me he was having nightmares and was missing sleep. Said he had to work this thing out with his dad cuz the madness was messing with his dreams and his stomach. I remember telling him to do what he gotta do and that I had his back, regardless.

Cuz I remember when me and *my* pops had got into it, when he played out on Moms and took the job in Virginia. When they divorced, I didn't want to forgive him, didn't want nothing to do with him. But the separation messed with me. I was relieved when he showed up during the playoffs when I was balling during senior year of high school. It wasn't the simplest thing, but we did manage to improve our relationship.

So, one night, two days before the end of the semester, the day before me and Sal had that killer final in Physics, I had crashed over at his crib up Northwood. By that time, I had moved into the frat house, and damn if you could study in all that madness. With the dogs, it was non stop chaos, 24-7. So I had went to Salmon's so we could study and ace that final. Much as we both loved to play, we both kept a decent GPA.

I was in thick z's when I heard Salmon mumbling and crying in his sleep. Tossing and throwing punches like something was after him. Freaked me out. So, I went in the kitchen and called Dignity. Told her to wake her ass up and come see about her man. Cuz I'm his homie and I got nothing but love for him, but a psychiatrist I ain't. Let his woman comfort his troubled ass, and let me get my beauty sleep.

Digs came over and climbed into bed with Sal, put her arms around him and started rocking. Looked like he got quiet for a minute, so I took it as my opportunity to get dressed and roll out. It was almost two in the morning, and if I hurried, I could still get five hours of shut eye before our 8 a.m. final.

But when Sal showed up to take the Physics test, looking like the walking dead he was so pale and washed out, he told me that he and Digs had called it quits, that she was going back to Kentucky and may not come back in the fall. That he was going home for the summer. Messed my ass up. In a matter of days I'd ditched my bitch and Sal and Digs had called it quits.

Oh yes. The end of junior year was no joke.

5

[THE BROTHERS RINALDI]

Salmon

Dig trips, simple as that. I said to her, "Dignity, you can't be sweating the small stuff," but she don't wanna listen. Nobody gets a perfect deal, and she oughtta know that already. I mean, her mom, my dad—our families are messed up. But she knew that when we first started college. I told her I didn't care about any of that stuff, but, like I say, Dig trips. She kept saying she wanted to go home with me for Easter or later in the summer. Can't happen.

When I got this scholarship to study at Morgan, I knew I wasn't gonna be able to bring my "father drama" up in this bitch. See, I wanted to go to school, and this was gonna be my only chance. Pops wasn't feeling it. For many reasons. Bottom line, Poppy wasn't gonna pay for school. Maybe he couldn't have, even if he wanted to, and mainly he didn't want to:

"My poppy didn't go to college, and I never went to no stinkin' college, and somehow we turn out okay! Enough of this college stuff already! In our family, we don't do that, and we still make it. So it's settled! You learn the business along with your brother, Frankie! Next thing ya know you're a self-made man, just like me!"

Yet, I was never good with that stuff like Pop and Frankie. I couldn't look at a blank wall and figure out what was going on behind it. I mean, cripes, if the light's not working, I say make sure she's plugged up, change the bulb, and beyond that, ya got me! Hell if I know! So this whole family electrical business idea never truly worked for me.

I am good at other stuff—Pops don't wanna see that. I mean, I could crack a bat with the best of them, and I could shoot hoop like a brother, believe that. I mean, I wasn't no sissy, alright? But I liked to think, too. I don't know. Build. Plan. Read about the world. History and Art and that kinda crap. Always, from since I was just a twit in elementary school. The stuff fascinated me is all. Especially buildings in Italy and all that. Guess it's the Italian in me.

So, I already knew that me and the family had parted ways some when I took the scholarship to Morgan. Everybody knew the place was historically Black. Everybody knew Pop didn't trust Blacks. Everybody knew Pop didn't like colleges and books and all that kind of fancy stuff, as he said. So, right away, I knew I was putting a wedge between me and the family by going, and I knew it might never be the same with me and Pops, but I knew I had to do what I had to do. So. I skipped the "father drama" from the day I got here. Didn't tell anybody but Khalil, my best bud, about how Pops trips. As for Mommy and Frankie, I knew we could still be cool if we kept on the low. But Pops, I didn't know if he'd ever come around. Although I guess I sort of hoped that he would.

Pops is kinda out of place, anyhow. Where we come from, Washington, D.C., nobody really cares what your background is. So, I just skipped telling my friends that my family is strict Italians who don't wanna mix up with no dark-skin people. To me, we are dark skin people, especially since Mommy is Latin. To me it's so much foolishness I can't be bothered with. So, I didn't tell most people.

I had been here for three years, and this hush on the family hate thing was working just fine. Next thing you know, with graduation around the corner, suddenly Frankie and Mommy thought Pops might want to come to graduation. Pops might want me to come home for Easter. Pops might want his youngest son in his life after all.

Three fricking years, and I'm busting my ass over here! Work study this and financial aid that! Hadda plan for how to have books and pay for housing, since the scholarship only paid for tuition. Then, when we all knew I was gonna do it, when I was about to graduate at the top of my class, suddenly heeeeere's Poppy!

Yo, where was he when I had to do my advisor's yard work, for cripe's sake, so's I could make enough to pay for my dorm room the next semester, huh? I'm struggling, and he's nowhere to be found. I graduate, and suddenly he wants his son back. Bite me.

But somewhere behind that, my spirit smiled. That's something I heard Digs say a lot—what will make your spirit smile? At first I didn't get it, but now I do. It's when you feel really happy and peaceful inside. And when Frankie came one Sunday, so we could go to afternoon mass and then to Happy Hour to knock some back and watch the game (the Italian Paradox, as Digs calls it), he started in on me about whether I was going home for Easter.

"Mommy really wants it, Sal. You know how it is. She's got all the stuff for Italian gravy at home, a shit load of her vegetables, and next week she'll be cooking and canning. Aunt Celia's coming, bringing the kids. I hope her fat-ass husband stays home! We're gonna play soccer and all that. Ya gonna make it, Kid?"

Frankie was two years older than me, and he'd been working with Pops since he was fifteen. He was a fricking genius or something with wiring and engineering. He could do anything with his skills, but he chose to work with Pops. Go figure. With him in the business, they had hired fourteen new people and opened a second office in Silver Spring.

But I didn't appreciate the way he was looking at me. Or, rather, not looking at me, serious and casual all at the same time. He had this way, see, since he was a kid. Where he'd be sucking back the drink and looking up at the ceiling, but really he had his mind all over you. And, if you disagreed with him, suddenly he wasn't so cool anymore, and you had a fight on your hands. With Frankie, fights were all gestures and punches, no words really. He was a real fricking hot head. With me, it was more words as bullets. So, I knew I hadda be careful or this weekly brother-bonding ritual could turn really foul.

I slurped the meat from my spicy wing and threw the bone to the side of the plate. Sunk my lip into the foam of my mug to get down past it, where the beer was. And I weighed my words and measured my feelings.

"Frankie, it ain't that easy. Where I'm sitting, Pops is an asshole about this whole thing! I mean, I'm busting my ass over here, and I done good *for* myself, *by myself*. I ain't exactly the same Sal that left for Morgan a few years ago, alright? I mean, cripes! You don't know what it's been like, all this time, him not talking to me, me not coming home for Christmas and everything else. I got a hardness around me now is all; I don't know."

Frankie started to jiggle his leg some and looked over my head at the screen. It was halftime. The cheerleaders were dancing to Madonna and showing a lot of ass. It had his attention, but only half of it. Frankie was like that. Half focused on a million things at once. "I gotta take a piss, Sal. Get us another pitcher, alright?"

My brother hopped up from the table and strutted his way through the crowd at Uno's Pizzeria, which wasn't as bad as it could be sometimes when you could hardly get a seat. But we'd gotten there early. I watched Frankie, with his black boots, black jeans, and black leather jacket work the crowd as he walked to the can.

5.2

[EASTER IS RISING]

Salmon

F rankie slid through the restaurant, giving lots of attitude. A small wink and a warm smile to the red-haired waitress. He was a nice guy, Frankie. Paid his bills, loved his mommy, but he was a player for real. A heart-breaker. And, even though he's quick to gesture and punch, later on, when he's calmed down, he usually makes smart decisions.

I wasn't surprised when the waitress came back and looked disappointed to see that Frankie was not there. He had been working her over since we got there, and she was buying it. She was the type he went for: short and busty with a candy ass. Long dark hair. Brown eyes.

"What happened to your friend? He gone already?" She looked at me from under long eyelashes, trying not to seem too pressed.

"Na. In the john. Say, can we get another pitcher? And some pretzels or some-thing? These wings are burning hell outta my mouth!" I pushed our empty plates toward her and gave her a look to help her remember she wasn't an old friend; she was the help, so quit hanging around. I get that way when people hang around waiting for my brother. Take a number, ya know?

"Sure thing. I'll be back in a sec." She switched toward the back, and I could see why Frankie was working her to begin with.

But this Easter thing was hanging over my head. On the one hand, I did want to see Pops. I had seen him all of four times since I started school. And inside it hurt me that he held so strongly to his mixed up point of view about school and race, to say nothing of the whole Darryl/Georgy situation, when it meant he had to sacrifice me. But, cripes, he was my father!

He used to sneak me books from the library when he knew I had fines on my card. Mommy wanted to punish me, you know, teach me a lesson for not returning the books on time. I mustta been about ten. I had a stack of, like, twelve books on Roman structures and the Rococo period next to my bed one summer. I got so engrossed in the pictures and the plans for these buildings, that I wasn't done with them in two weeks when they were due. Then, I started drawing scale models of some of the stuff that I saw, so I really couldn't return the books. Next thing you know, it's the end of the summer, and I owe the library thirty-two bucks in late fees even though I returned the books. They wouldn't let me borrow until I paid.

Mommy said it served me right, that I would have to use my allowance to pay, and until then, no books. But Pops would sneak me books. Just stack them under my desk and wink at me. He'd whisper, "From me to you. Now shush!" I remember one was about gargoyles. I checked it out again and again once I got my fines paid off.

Poppy was also funny as hell, and everybody knew it. We'd come in to the office early, back in the summers when Frankie and me helped out around there. When the guys were getting their assignments, everyone would get quiet to hear what Poppy had to say. He was a riot. Always a story about the guy at the Sunoco or the woman who owned that building he just wired. And he did voices like you can't believe! If you closed your eyes, you could picture the people he was describing—he was that good. I missed Poppy. The old Poppy. The one who loved me no matter what.

But I didn't wanna catch hell about the choices I made and the lifestyle I lived. He didn't know yet that I was accepted into grad school, and that, if I could pay for it, I was going. Let alone my semi-black girlfriend, Dignity Jackson.

So, the jury was still out on Easter when Frankie came back and slid in on his side of the booth.

"Shucks, I missed her! Did she ask where I was at?" Frankie ran his fingers through his curly black hair and adjusted his collar. He was vain as hell, but I guess it paid off. Chicks were crazy for him. He had dimples and a cleft in his chin, and he was six feet four, easy. Filled out his jeans, Dignity said. We looked alike, but I was just six feet and more slight.

"Actually she did," I said, burping from the last gulp of beer, "but you know she'll be back. She's gotta bring the check sometime." I started to drum my fingers on the table. I could tell that I didn't have Frankie's full ear, and it bugged me. I didn't want to have an argument with him, but I did want to talk about Easter. I couldn't stand to have stuff hanging over my head.

"Yea, so. This Easter thing. I know you gotta point, Sal. Pops is nuts about this whole college thing. I know that. Mommy knows it. But, I don't know. I mean, we get one mom and one pop, okay? He ain't gonna be around forever, alright? You gotta see him, stand your ground, and dare him to love you anyway. Might as well do it this Easter, when Mommy makes her famous ziti. Ya can't miss that!"

I checked my watch. I had a midterm tomorrow, and I needed to study. I also wanted to clean my clothes before the eleven p.m. dash to the washing machines that happened every Sunday at the laundry. When I looked up, Frankie was looking me dead in the eyes, demanding a response from me.

"So, can we count on you, Salmon? It means a lot to Mommy. Hell, it means a lot to me." He had his mug tipped toward his mouth like he was waiting on an answer before he could take another sip.

"I guess I better. Otherwise, you'll have to listen to Aunt Celia's stories about almost being a Rockette for the fifty-millionth time all by yourself. Is she still telling those lies?" I belted back the last sip of beer and reached for my wallet.

Frankie pushed back my hand and took the check. "Turns out, they ain't lies! I seen pictures of Mommy and Aunt Celia from high school. Celia's got legs from here to Chicago! Let me just get this, alright? I wanna talk to candy ass over there, anyhow." Frankie stood up, stamped his foot to adjust his pants leg, and headed over to the register, looking for our waitress, and probably a little action later on. I gathered my jacket and slid out of the booth, thinking about the commitment I had just made. It scared me some. But mainly I felt my spirit smile.

Freshman Year

[MORGAN STATE UNIVERSITY 1991]

6

[THE WELCOME BRIDGE]

Sal Rinaldi

I can remember coming out of McKeldin most days and heading over the bridge to the other side of the campus. Checked out the Library and the Gym before crossing the street and heading home to Northwood. They had a shuttle that you could take from the yard to the apartments, but when the weather was good, I'd walk.

Funny how different things could get when you weren't even so far away from home. I grew up in Silver Spring, and there were plenty of Blacks where I was from. Here it was like a rainbow of chocolate, and I was. I liked the way the brothers walked, ya know? They hadda certain style all their own. And the chicks? Forget about it! Hot as hell is all. Sassy, you know? Curves and hips and butts all over the place, and attitude galore. Made me interested. Not that I didn't dig chicks from my own background. They were hotties, too. I guess I just liked chicks, period. Tall, short, light, dark; I was all over it, regardless.

The way I looked, I didn't think people knew right away that I wasn't black. Maybe they just assumed I was one of those light, bright brothers. Especially since my hair is tight and wavy, cut close, and my skin is dark olive. Or maybe they thought I was one of those international students. Either way, nobody never gave me no beef here. When I first came, I spent a lot of time on the yard, as we say, just checking things out. They got these benches all over the main campus, and sometimes I'd sit there, but mainly I would hang out on the Welcome Bridge. It was this concrete bridge that connected one side of campus to the other. Get there before class in the morning, and you could get a total feel for what was happening on campus. Tickets to frat parties, the word on house parties and games. The latest gossip, if you're into that kinda thing.

I wasn't. I just liked watching the ladies tipping over from Blount, wearing their high heels and tight pants. What a trip! It was like a fashion show most days. You wouldn't believe! They wore their hair piled high on their heads, full face paint, and skinny four inch heels, even in the snow. I loved that stuff! I had my favorites, too. Got so I could pick them out from way far away by the way they walked. Then they'd get closer, and I'd pat myself on the back for recognizing them.

There was a chick named Brenda. She was real heavy on the bottom and tiny on the top. She messed me up. She'd wear these form-fitting pants in animal prints or wild colors and blouses that crisscrossed over her tiny tits. But it was her walk that was so sexy. One foot directly in front of the other and a whole lotta jiggle in the middle. Smelled like flowers. She was nice.

Then there was Tia. She was in my Poly Sci class during my first semester. She was what they called "redbone." Kind of a yellow complexion with short, slick hair. She was really skinny, but she had a balloon ass. Real nice. She had this smooth slide when she came across the bridge. Reminded me of melted butter. Loved it.

By the third week of classes, I had made a few friends, and one of them was a kid named Khalil. To this day, he is my number one homie. Excepting Darryl. Dead or alive, Darryl will always be my best friend, regardless. Lil and I ran track together, and he lived across the hall from me.

This one Monday, we Khalil and I were on the bridge, and these two chicks came toward us from the Refectory. The Refectory was the dining hall where all the kids who had meal plans and, therefore, no choice ate. I never messed with it since I lived in the apartments. I could tell by the way Lil squared his shoulders that he knew these girls. One was big-boned with rounded hips, dark skin, and short, curly hair. The other was a wild card. Her hair was kinky and waving all over her shoulders and winding down her back in springy, orange curls. She was barely five feet two inches, and she had a cute face, tiny hands, tiny feet, and a wide full mouth. Plump behind.

"Yo, here come Stacy and Digs, Man. I been trying to get up in that since the summer! Dayuuum! Is she fine or am I half blind?" I didn't know which one he referred to. Khalil swatted me in the side as he watched them come closer. He started licking his lips, and I knew he was preparing his rap.

Their voices got louder as they approached and they sounded like a brass duet—Stacy kinda loud and low and Digs kinda high and loud. They were talking over each other. Words flying a mile a minute. At first I thought they wouldn't stop walking or talking at all, even though Lil was flagging them down. But at the last minute, Stacy turned around, grabbed Digs' hand, and glided over to us.

"What's up, fellas? What chou know good?" Stacy let the words curl out of her mouth and hang over our heads like smoke. She was dressed in stone-washed jeans, tight in the behind with straight creases down the center of the legs. The pants were a little short, and you could see she was wearing short leather boots with a buckle and a square toe. Too mannish for me, but the rest of it looked okay.

"Oh, hey! Aren't you the one from Dr. Miller's class? You kept asking him what color was Jesus, and all that? What a riot! What's your name again?" The short one was active and used her whole body when she spoke. Her eyes sparkled when she looked at Khalil.

"My bad, my bad. My name is Khalil, Baby. And this is my top dog, Salmon." He reached for the short one's hand, but the whole time he was looking over her head at Stacy. He kissed the short one's hand and said, "And you would be…?"

I looked down at my shoe out of embarrassment. He told me he'd been sweating these girls for a while, so I figured he knew both their names. His Mr. Charming act could backfire on him, you never knew.

She looked up at him playfully. "Dignity. My name is Dignity, but most people call me Dig or Digs, ya dig?" She swatted her knee with her free hand and did a fake belly laugh. Right away I almost hated her. She seemed like she was putting on some kind of a show. I'd wait 'til it came out on video. "And who's your friend again?" She turned her attention on me.

"I know that guy! His name is Salmon, as in croquettes! I didn't know you was tight with Khalil. How you doin'?" Stacy stuck her hand out to me like she wanted the Prince Charming treatment. She was cute, so I obliged her.

"Yes, I am Salmon, but friends call me Sal." I kissed her gently in the middle of her hand. "Pleasure is mine, Baby. All mine." I retracted my hand and stuck it in my pocket. I narrowed my eyes and looked at Stacy's friend.

"Salmon, huh? I knew something fishy was going on here! Say, don't you sing in the choir?" Dignity cocked her head toward me and looked at me like I was hiding something.

"Na. I ain't much for singing. Maybe you're thinking of somebody else." I leaned against the rail and checked my watch. My class was starting in twelve minutes.

"Huh. Maybe. Anyways, what are you folks up to?"

Khalil jumped in. "'Bout ready to head to Soper myself and do some reading for my first paper. The effect of Colonization on American culture." I saw Dignity's eyes light up then, and it made me laugh inside. Khalil has been "reading for his first paper" since the day we met. That paper routine seemed to get him a lot of play.

"Wow! Sounds deep! I might be able to help you. There's this book I read by Beverly Shif…" Her voice trailed off as I caught Stacy giving me the once-over. I pretended I didn't notice and gave a half-smile from the corner of my mouth. She was hot.

"Hate to break up this party, but I gotta jet. Humanities starts in a few minutes." I hitched my backpack up and turned to leave, but Stacy caught my arm.

"Ah, hold up, home slide. Let me walk with you. I got a class in Jenkins, too." Stacy shifted her bag up on her back and got ready to roll with me. No problems there!

"Wait! Umm. I was hoping we could go over to Soper real quick and see if they got this article I heard about…" Khalil had a sound of despair in his voice as he gestured toward me and Stacy.

I never broke my stride, and Stacy was right there with me. "I got class, Man. Let me catch you after, alright?" Stacy just smiled a knowing grin at Digs and kept walking.

"Hey! I'm going to Soper, too! I'll go with! Meet us later at our spot, Stacy. And Salmon—swim on by!" Dignity spun Khalil around and half trotted, half ran to Soper. She jogged along like a puppy or something. Khalil just shook his head and went along with her.

[THE DARKER THE BERRY]

Dignity

The day I met him, during our first year at "The Black Yale," I was wearing a sweatshirt that listed all the historically black colleges in America on the back. On the front it said, "The Blacker the College, The Sweeter the Knowledge." I wore it all the time. It was a way to stop the questions people had about my race and nationality. I couldn't very well wear a T-shirt that said, "My race is all mixed up and I have no idea who I am." So I wore that sweatshirt and hoped that people would assume something about me that would make them accept me.

That's all I wanted at first—to be accepted. I wasn't all that interested in Khalil so much as what he represented. But, he did have a decent reputation. He was a deep, dark chocolate brown, which I liked, plus we had a few things in common. So, I decided to respond when he kissed my hand and gave me his best American Gigolo that first time on the bridge. Of course, I didn't buy half the stuff he said about colonization and all that. Even though he seemed to know what he was talking about, I doubted seriously that he was writing a paper on that topic. Assigned by whom?

When we were walking over to Soper, I had one thing on my mind: The Ques' Two Tongues in Your Butt Bring It On Jam. Everybody on campus was talking about it. The Omega Psi Phi fraternity, the guys who barked, called themselves dogs, and wore purple and gold (simultaneously!) were infamous for their jams. This one was happening on campus, and we knew we'd better get tickets fast before the Ques did something to get themselves in trouble and wound up having to cancel on-campus activities and move underground. Stacy told me that most time the frat wasn't active on campus because they did outrageous things and got suspended. I wanted the chance to attend at least one jam on campus, and I didn't want to go there alone. So, I figured Khalil could prove useful.

I was right. Even though he was more into Stacy, I ignored that and monopolized his attention. Back then, I needed a dark brother. For validation or something. To prove that I was "down," so to speak.

I was tripping unnecessarily. My people know what the deal is, that we got all kind of spit locked in our background to give us that rainbow effect, honeysuckle to purplish black. So, I never got flack, exactly, for being light, bright, and damn near white. Except from my ex girl, Stacy. Yet, somehow I was uncomfortable in my own skin.

Not because I wasn't attractive. I knew that I was at least sort of good-looking. People told me I looked like Mariah Carey, only with wild red hair. And I was led to believe that was a good thing. Still, when I would hang out with my friends, black and white, I felt like I was somehow suspended, less grounded than the others. Like they had some secret that I didn't that kept them comfortable, optimistic, confident. Inside of myself I was always so uneasy and unsure. My light complexion somehow added to my discomfort. So, to create some sort of a balance, I made sure to hook up with the deepest, richest-toned brothers out there. In college, Khalil was my first ebony find.

As was my practice back then, I went into chatterbox mode and kept talking, my words yelping at Lil's heels like an anxious poodle. I didn't let him get in a word edgewise. And when he did manage to eke out a few words, I was right there to finish his sentence and segue into my own. I think I must have worried him to death.

Stacy and I had just come from lunch, and I guess I might have had too much caffeine. My heart was racing, and I could feel the lettuce, eggs, and cheese from my salad tossing around in my stomach. I was more nervous than I should have been. I so wanted Khalil to like me and ask me to the Two Tongues Jam. I knew that if he found out that I was a mixed bag of tricks with a lifetime of queer history, he would drop me like a spaghetti sandwich from the Refectory. Actually, I never saw them serve spaghetti sandwiches in the Refectory, but it was a campus-wide legend that they did.

My hair was flying behind me. I was gesturing like a wild woman, laughing urgently at my own stupid jokes, batting my lashes every time Khalil spoke. He must have thought I was crazy! Yet, he didn't show it, as we angled across the bridge and over to Soper. I was running out of witty things to say, so I was relieved when Khalil ran into a guy he knew.

"Oh, hi ya! I mean, WHAZZUUP?! Sorry I can't stop and talk!" I said to Khalil's friend. "Khalil, I gotta go potty. Meet me inside, okay?" I gave a cheerful wave and hightailed it inside. In the bathroom, I chose the second stall, hung my pack on the door, and leaned against the wall. I did not have to use the toilet. I very rarely used public toilets, which was ironic since I spent so much time on campus. It got tricky sometimes, but I managed to mostly use my own toilet in my apartment. But just in case, I carried a roll of TP in my backpack so I could cover the bowl if I really had to go.

College kids are funky. Who knew what kind of germs and infections they brought up in there! Yeeck. I couldn't put my butt up against that!

I twisted my wild hair up from the middle of my back and held it in a bunch on top of my head. I fanned the back of my neck with my hand and did some aerobic breathing. "Easy, easy." I breathed to myself. "Stay calm." I said a silent prayer to the Creator and asked Her for strength. I had a little bit of an anxiety disorder going back then.

I knew I had to go out there and meet Khalil—I didn't want him to think I ditched him. I pressed my eyes shut, summonsed up the energy to open the stall door and leave the restroom, my backpack swinging from my left shoulder. Blam, right into another student's face.

"Whoops—my bad! I best watch where I'm going!" I said, trying too hard to sound like the sistah I already was.

"Dat's alright. Is you Dignity? A boy out there looking for you." She dropped her bag in a stall and slammed the door shut.

I heard Khalil saying goodbye to his friend as I approached.

"I'll get back, Kid," Lil's friend said, giving his friend the brother's knock of knuckles.

"Do dat shit!" Khalil said, as he turned toward me. "Girl, thought you got sucked down somewhere up in that joint! Look here, you trying to go to the party this weekend?" I watched him slide two cardboard slips into his wallet and struggle to return the wallet to his front pocket.

I didn't want to appear too anxious, so I said nothing. So I played dumb. "Hmm. Which party is that?" I adjusted my pack and stroked myself for such a brilliant comment. This way he would think I was invited to, or at least aware of, so many parties that I couldn't be sure which one he was talking about.

He cleared his throat as he barely managed to get his swoll back in his britches. "Got all kind of shit going on up in here, can't hardly hold all this bank! Ha ha! Tayvon just comped me two tickets to the Que Jam this weekend. Thought you might want to roll with me?" He diverted his eyes for a minute and then looked straight at my nose.

"Yes! I mean, you know, I am down with that! If you have a ticket you're not trying to use and all that, I can help a brotha out!" I was not successful at hiding my approval. I was just too lucky that day, I thought. Meeting Khalil in the first place and then getting a date for the Que Jam, too? I was batting a thousand! Now I just had one more mission to accomplish this weekend, but that one was going to take a little more doing.

"Ah-ight, den! We gone get into it come Friday! I'mma get my swerve on!" Khalil started doing the white boy dance, swinging his arms and moving from side to side.

"I can see I'mma have to school you first before we get up in there and you make me look stupid! I wish you would be up there dancing like that!" By then we were walking upstairs to find a place where we could put our books down and chill. We talked back and forth with me in front tossing silly comments over my shoulder while he checked out my ass. I hoped he approved. My behind is the one clue that I really am a sistah.

Once we found a table, we put our books all over it so we wouldn't have to share. Plus, we wanted to have enough room in case Stacy and Salmon showed up. We had about given up on ever finding the article we came looking for (Soper didn't actually have any resources; it was just a place where you could hang out in the *attitude* of study), when we finally sat down at the table and started to talk.

"So, Dignity. Where you get a name like that?" Lil leaned in with his elbow on the table and his chin in his hand.

"Long story…," I said.

"Yea? I got time. I'm curious."

I cleared my throat and told him a combination of lie and truth because I didn't know the whole truth. "Well, when I was born, my real dad was already dead, and I lived with my mom and her auntie, Paulette. Mama wanted to give me a name that would give me protection, so it was either Smith and Wesson or Dignity. She didn't know how to spell the former, so she chose the latter." I gave him a half-serious, half-silly grin and hoped he would laugh. He did not.

Khalil shook his head and held my eyes with his own. "Coo," he said, dropping the "l" on the word. "Always interested in names, why people call themselves what they do. Like, my name, for instance." He leaned back in the chair and crossed his legs in his Timberland boots.

"Tell me about your name." I clasped my hands and leaned forward.

"Well, you heard of Kahlil Gibran? Eastern Philosopher? Named after him. Mine is spelled differently, but still—same idea. He was s'posed to be a real sharp dude."

"Are you sharp?" I asked.

"I get by. I mean, I don't know everything, but that's what I'm here for, right? To learn."

He licked his lips in a semi-suggestive way, and I responded like a sex kitten.

"What's your favorite kind of lesson, Khalil? And who is your favorite teacher?" He never had the chance to answer because Sal and Stacy came pounding up the stairs with a lot of loud talk and outside air. I was disappointed. Then, I saw how Stacy kept putting her hands all over Salmon, and I knew that I had to work fast or she would win.

8

[THE BET]

Khalil

I guess I knew what the deal was by the end of that first day. Didn't say nothing. Both of them was fine, so it made me no never mind. Granted, I had been sweating Stacy. But Dignity, with her neurotic self, she was fine, too. So I didn't mind.

Seemed like the right thing to do asking her to that first Que Jam. Everybody was going. Tay came through with the tickets, so hey—it was on. I'd give her a free ticket, and she'd give up a little sumpin-sumpin, too. Fair and square.

But all this gabbing shit and calling me at night and riding with us to the yard? Wasn't trying to have that. I didn't like to have babes hang too tight. Only good thing was she must not a been a morning kinda sistah, cuz she would come out to the bus stop looking evil. And when she was evil, that's when she shut up. Hey, praise God for morning. Cuz Dignity would talk your ear right off your head if you weren't careful.

But I put up with it that first week, cuz actually I liked her crazy ass. She was funny and smart as shit, too. She lived in the building right next to ours with a girl name Lisa. Sal had a place by himself, and me and Tay lived across the hall. We all could get into some crazy conversations sometime. Like, can you tell which flavor Kool-Aid it is with your eyes closed. Once we was up on the bridge waiting for Stacy, and Dignity started with her craziness. She had us rolling.

She claimed she could tell how a brother was hung by the way he walked. I said, now that's some messed-up shit, if it's true! But she would point somebody out, like this kid Wayne who played for the Bears. He came lumbering out of the science building one morning, clumsy as an ox, and she said she knew he had a tiny package. Said he was making up for it with this super masculine walk. Then, Reg came up from Cummins, and she said she could tell he was hung like a horse. That didn't seem as funny.

So, Sal was like, "How do ya know this stuff, Digs? What, are you some kinda ho or something?"

I chimed in, just to mess with her. Anybody could tell she hadn't been with nobody really, except third base in high school. "True. How you know? Take Reg, for example. How you know about him?"

Dignity flipped her flaming mane over one shoulder and explained, "Easy! See how he's built? Long and lean like that? Narrow through the hips? Those types are always huge!" She nodded her head like she was sure of what she was saying.

I couldn't resist. I pimped around a little bit and asked, "So, what about me? What chou think?" I sniffed and wiped my nose and then held my package like one of those street kids.

"Well-endowed, I'd say. Extremely well-endowed, but I'd hate to guess with something that seems so important to you! I could be all wrong!" She was teasing me.

"Na. I think you got it right the first time. But if you wanna be sure, you have to see for yourself!" I said this with only a half-smile, and that shut her up, I think.

"Oh, woh! You heard that? Sounds like a fricking challenge to me, Digs. You up for it?" Salmon slapped me five and waited for Dignity's answer.

She just smiled and shook her hair, like women do when they trying to be all mysterious or something. "Treat me nice on Friday. We'll see what happens."

Stacy came over wearing a one-piece navy leotard kinda thing with orange pumps and an orange jacket. She killed me with that! What in the world she wanted to dress like that every day for, I don't know. Like she was always on display. But I wasn't complaining cuz she was fine as I don't know what! She and Digs got to talking about what they was wearing Friday and all this, and me and Sal was planning to meet before dinner and shoot some hoop. He could hoop for a white boy, almost as good as me. But ain't nobody that good!

Stacy made a point to stay up close to Sal, brushing her hand on his arm and backing up close so she'd touch his side. That's how come I knew what was going on. Nobody I knew talked about being with Stacy last year. So that let me know where she was at in terms of the game. And then she kept making a point to drop something and stick her booty in Sal's face. She also walked with him to class and stuff. So, that tipped me off, too. But Digs would follow check what Stacy was doing with Sal, and then she would do some version of it with me. Like I say, she was fine, so I sure didn't mind.

It was Thursday, and I had French in a few minutes, and Dignity had a class in the same building, so we walked over to Holmes together. Sal and Stacy had planned to talk later that night because he had to work until late that afternoon, and then he was shooting hoop with me. Digs and Stacy were hanging out at Dig's place that night, so I thought I might see her later on, but I went ahead and put on the lovey-dovey act before I went into class. Made sure I was in there for Friday.

We was on the steps one Thursday afternoon. I pulled her close to me. Gave her a big old bear hug. Chicks love that shit. Makes them feel safe and whatnot. I saw the panic that came through her eyes real fast when I grabbed her, but I ignored it. If she was gonna play this thing, then she couldn't get nervous when I played along.

"So, what we gonna do tomorrow night? You decide yet?" I said this in her ear, in my best Barry White voice.

Dignity kept her hands against my chest and looked up at me with a fake-ass smile. "Hmm. I sort of thought we would go to The Jam, you know. Shake our groove thangs, yea, yea."

"Yes, and what else? You trying to take me home for a late-night snack?" I caught one of her fingers in my mouth and sucked gently for a second before letting go. I saw the slight burn in her cheeks when I did that, and I knew it was a smart move.

"All I can say is, if you dance real well tomorrow, I might have something for you to eat later! I'll holla!" She ducked under my arms and ran inside. I watched her ass jiggle when she ran; then I went in the opposite direction to my own class.

9

[IT'S ON]

Dignity

I was flying around the apartment, cleaning up from whatever it was Lisa had done at lunch. It looked like some kind of striptease from the front door to her room with a quick stop in the kitchen for honey and peanut butter sandwiches straight from the counter.

That girl, I swear, was a female pig. Always sticky stuff on the counters and clothes all over the living room and the bathroom. Great Day in the Morning! I hated sharing that space with her. Really, I hated sharing a bathroom with anybody. Ever since I was little, I've had this thing about bathrooms. If they aren't clean and sanitary, I am a basket case. I gotta get everything just right—the toilet, the sink, the floor, the bathtub—before I can even think about using them. And, once I've done all the groundwork, the last thing I need is to have someone come in and spoil it. So, most mornings I took almost two hours in the bathroom. First, cleaning up after Lisa and then cleaning myself.

Stacy was coming over, and we were gonna do some homework and then watch *Martin* and *Living Single* while we made plans for The Que Jam. But, before I could let homegirl up in there, I had to make sure the place was neat and presentable. I wasn't having her coming into my apartment and then heading back over to Tubman saying I was a skank-type ho.

Stacy and I would have some time to talk privately because Lisa had an ROTC meeting. I had socked away a little cash so I could order pizza that night and have a little spending change over the weekend. That first year, I didn't work at all and lived off the stipend that Aunt Paulette sent me up there with. Taught me a lot about being frugal.

I met Stacy over the summer, before school even started. I'd gotten an internship at the Baltimore Museum of Art. It didn't pay much, but it allowed me to get to know Baltimore before starting classes. Mainly, it gave me the chance to get the hell out of Kentucky. Aunt Lette didn't want me to worry about cooking, so she bought me a meal card for the whole year. When I first got to Morgan, I didn't have sense enough to starve rather than go to the Refectory. That's where I met Stacy, at the Refectory.

They only opened weird hours during the summer, and it was never really crowded in there. Stacy was walking toward a table by the side door. She was wearing a very short leopard-print skirt and matching pumps. She looked sharp. But, before she sat down, she put the tray she carried on the table, took a cloth out of her purse, and swept her chair before sitting down. Made me chuckle because I used to do the same thing.

Once during my sophomore year at Central High School, I was so busy running my mouth that I failed to notice that somebody had left a cup of barbecue sauce in the cafeteria. I dropped into the chair, and all this red stuff started shooting from between my legs. Seemed like the whole cafeteria had its eyes on me, and they rolled about that. Next thing you know, everyone was saying that Digs got her period. Then they said I had an abortion on the spot. I went to the school nurse and asked to go home and change, but she wouldn't let me. I had to walk around the rest of the day with a sweater tied around my waist to cover the big red spot on the back of my pants. It was so gross! Ever since then, I don't dare sit down before checking the chair.

So, when Stacy was busy wiping her seat, and I went over and asked if I could join her.

I found out that she was from Baltimore, that she worked in a law office downtown to earn money for the semester, and that she was taking a remedial math class as well. I also found out that she loved to draw and hoped to become an art major. She lived in Tubman, and she knew her way around campus. We clicked right away. It wasn't until the Fourth of July, when she invited me to a cookout at her cousin Trina's house, that I found out we had something else in common. We were both virgins and wanted to lose our virginity that semester. We had a bet to see who would lose it first.

I was spreading my books on the dining room table and setting out two cans of Diet Pepsi, when I heard Stacy come up the stairs. I yelled for her to come in. She had changed and was now wearing a nylon sweat suit that had a yellow and purple print down the side. She was classy even when she was slumming. I felt tacky in my worn gray sweats and dingy Tracy Chapman T-shirt. The singer came to Rupp Arena during my junior year at Central High School, and I still wear the souvenir.

"What up, Girl? I see you already got your nose up in the books! You shoulda told me you was one of those bookish types when we first started to hang. I might have told you about yourself back then!" She slammed her backpack on the floor and sat at her end of the table. She brought out her sketch book, three sharp pencils, a large rubber eraser, and a sharpener. She was working on a sketch for one of her classes, and I had homework in American History.

"Well, I wanna party, but I also gotta keep my GPA up, or I will lose my ride up in here. Don't worry, girl! I got plenty time for fun!" I swigged some of the Pepsi and flipped to the worksheet I had started in class. Dr. Phillips gave us a list of terms we needed to look up in the textbook and define at the beginning of the unit. It was busy work, but it did help me to understand his lectures.

"I hear that! Speaking of fun, girl, you talk to Khalil yet? Y'all straight for tomorrow?" She got this sheepish grin on her face as soon as she mentioned his name.

I didn't want to admit that he'd been really forward with me before class that morning. Somehow it seemed private. So I said, "He's gonna call me when he gets back from playing with Sal. But, ah, he did say he wanted to come over after The Jam!" I had to giggle. This whole thing was getting so exciting! In a way, I wanted it to happen, and in a way I didn't think I was ready. "How about you and the fish? Straight?"

"Girl, please! He's eating out my hand, he so anxious to get with this. Plus, I think he's Latino or something. And you know what they say about Latino brothers!" She looked at me with devilish eyes.

"No. What do they say?"

"Can't half tell, cuz they say it in Spanish! But I bet you it's all good! Aye, Papi! I tell you tomorrow!" She spoke in a Spanish accent while she lifted her hand and gave me a high-five. We laughed like she was Eddie Murphy.

"But you know, they say that once you go black, you never go back, so I'll give you the fill when I'm done with Khalil! We both gonna have something to talk about!" I gave my best impression of Lil. Back then, Khalil had this way of talking in rhymes when he was making a point about something. Even though it was corny, it was kind of funny.

Me and Stacy didn't get much work done. She told me about the little black dress she was going to wear and helped me pick out an outfit, too. I agreed to wear a short gold dress, but I refused to wear pumps. I just knew I'd be falling all over the place if I wore pumps. The gold flats were going to have to do. I promised I'd wear my hair pinned up in order to look older and more sophisticated.

Me and Stacy decided that we would all walk back to the apartments together after the party. If it was warm out, then Sal would probably want to sit outside and smoke a little. He never smoked in his apartment. Then, I would ask Khalil if he wanted to see my apartment, and Salmon would invite Stacy over to his. We promised we'd call each other that night if anything went wrong and first thing in the morning if everything went right.

10

[SHOOTING HOOPS]

Khalil

Me and Sal got into it on the court that day. Nobody planned on it. We was doing one-on-one since most of the brothers wanted to make it back in time for dinner. They was having fried chicken that night, and if you didn't get there early, you might miss out. Folks came up in there armed on the days the dining hall served something edible! Foil packs in they backpacks and what not, so they could take away whatever they could carry. It was standard procedure to carry away cartons of milk, loaves of bread, and small boxes of cereal. Brothers got hungry at night and didn't always have no cash. To them, it was part of what paying tuition guaranteed—the right to snag whatever they needed from the Refectory.

Sal is funny when he plays. Turns into a different person. Way more aggressive and on. Normally, he's ice, shows no emotion whatsoever except the occasional wisecrack about this or that. But, I learned that day that he does have a temper.

I said that it seemed like Digs and Stacy were hot for us. Then, I made the mistake of mentioning how I was especially interested in Digs since she is, well, multicultural. I went on to explain how me and my buddy Gabe, before he left for Fisk, made a pact. We wanted to sleep with women from as many ethnic backgrounds as possible before graduation. We called the pact, "Operation Rainbow Acquisition." O.R.A. for short. When we did have the time to talk, usually during winter and summer breaks, we would give each other the details on our progress. At least up until junior year when Gabe got with this bright-yellow sister and stopped messing around. Or so he said. Far as I can tell, brothers don't never stop messing around 'til they dead.

I told Sal that I wanted to bag Digs so I'd have something to share with Gabe that Christmas.

Sal got pissed. "That's like, reverse discrimination or something. That don't sit right with me." At first I thought it was because he was against interracial ecstasy. I attacked him on that point without thinking.

"Oh, so you one of them front like you right and only date white kinda dudes, huh? All yo hoes gotta be in the blue book, am I right?" I blocked him on the left and stole the ball from him with my right hand. Dribbled back some to buy space and time.

Sal snatched the ball back and turned to shoot. It bounced off the rim and into my hands. "You're full of shit, Lil. What do I look like here? Was it me that was underneath Stacy's ass all day the other day in Soper, or was that somebody else? You could be so stupid!" Sal blocked me solid for a few seconds, and I had no choice but to shoot. Doosh—straight in the center. Sweet shot.

"True—my bad. My bad. But, speaking of that, why you all up Stacy's behind anyway? For all I know, you and your homies got a similar thing as the O.R.A., and now you fronting about it." As the words left my mouth, Salmon faked right and snatched the ball, started prancing around with it.

"Wrong again. My homies and I don't make bets like that—it's childish, alright? Chemistry don't work like that, man. If it heats up when you meet up with someone, and if the time is right and the mood is right, well, hell, it's on. Don't matter what color she is long as she's red hot!" When Sal shot this time, the ball bounced off the backboard and dropped straight through the hoop. He scooped the ball again as it came down and tried another basket, but I swatted it down before it took.

True. It didn't seem like he was really too pressed about color. "Easy for you to say, man. Nobody worried about you making it with somebody, even if they ain't from your hood. A chick see you, black or white, and all she see is a white man, owner of the entire universe or some shit. Can't lose with you. She see me, and she see a potential problem. All I'm saying is it would be nice to get to know some other chicks, too, dig? See what all we got in common."

"That ain't exactly true, Lil. Brothers ain't the only ones that gotta worry about race. Speaking of Digs, was it *you* who was saying you think she's hot for you and that garbage? Wasn't it *you* saying she had such a luscious butt? Were ya really digging on Digs, as you claim, or were you just preoccupied with making your racial quota? Cripes, you're so full of shit!" He was so busy making his point and using his hands to do it that he didn't bother trying to take the ball. I quick made three shots while I thought about what he was saying. Sal wasn't thinking about balling no more, so I dribbled to the side and picked up my water bottle.

"Cripes! Cripes? What kinda shit is that, Cripes? What are you, Vinnie Barbarino over here?" I did a Brooklyn Italian to melt the ice and make Salmon laugh.

Salmon picked up his jacket, and I could tell by the way his shoulders sloped that he was laughing. "I don't hassle you for your native tongue, so you don't hassle me, alright? Where I'm from, you don't use the Lord's name in vain. Deal with it."

"Touchy! Mad true, Bro, I feel you. You keep your talk and I keep mine. But for real, haven't you noticed how the two of them act with us? Just seem like maybe they want us worse than you think. O.R.A. aside." I slung my bag over my shoulder and started walking. Sal was right behind me.

"Yea. I guess so. And I am all over it, okay? I think Stacy is like, dayum! But, ah, it ain't cuz she's black or nothing. It's cuz she's classy and sharp, and, and,…"

"Delicious?"

"Exactly. And Digs? I think Digs is sweet, in a group-home kinda way. She's complicated or something, maybe vulnerable. I don't know. I just think, if she knew you wanted to bang her cuz of your O.R.A. or whatever, she wouldn't like it. That's all."

"Consider using bone, Man. Bang is like, I don't know. Some 1950s *Grease* type shit. Let me stop—I feel you. PWT, point well taken."

Once I got home, I threw some hot dogs on and got in the shower. Read some psychology. Shot shit with Tay. But I didn't call Dignity until real late. I told her we was still on for the next night, but I didn't fill up her head with my sexy machinations. I was beat. Even though I technically won the game with Sal, he sort of wore my butt out. And that whole thing about Digs—had to think about it. Seemed like she was a sure thing, and I wasn't about to give that up. I just had to figure out a way to get the drawers without causing no flaws.

11

[BAD DREAMS]

Salmon

I only had one class on Fridays, and then I was in the Financial Aid office all day, working. I usually got done at two p.m., and then I would either see who was on the yard or head back to the apartment to get ready for the weekend. If I had some cash in my pocket, I might stop up at the Northwood shopping center and get a couple of egg rolls or something. I was crazy for those things. Ate them all the time on the way home.

A lot of times on Fridays after work, I just slept. In college, sleep is a hot commodity. You don't get much of it, so if you have an opportunity, you go for it. That was my plan that day. Go home, stretch out on the couch, flip around and see what's on the tube, and catch some Z's. Stacy was walking over to Digs' sometime after classes, and then me and Lil were gonna walk over and pick them up around nine p.m. I already knew what I was wearing. I didn't keep a lot of clothes, so it was easy. The olive suit. Without bragging, I was at my best in that suit. Sometimes I wore it with black accessories, and sometimes I wore it with navy. It was my last girlfriend, Elaine, that hipped me to navy. I never would have thought about it. But once, when we was going to her sister Charlotte's engagement party, Elaine bought me all this stuff to go with an olive suit Poppy got me back in high school. I still got the suit and the accessories to this day, but I can't wear them. I sort of bulked up a bit in college, but I look healthy, or so Digs says.

I turned the hanger around that had the new olive suit on it, and I decided on the black accessories. Seemed like bad luck to start out with Stacy wearing Elaine's colors. Then, I pulled off my shirt and threw it on the bed, grabbed a can of nuts from the kitchen, and flopped my six-foot frame on the worn, tweed couch. I found a western on, put down the remote, and no sooner did Wayne say "Pilgrim" than I was fast asleep.

I dozed off for a little while, but I didn't sleep well. Mainly just restless dreams.

I slid off the couch and gave a big stretch to show off my six-foot wing span. I flew down the hall to my bedroom, and when I opened the door, there was Darryl and his little brother, Georgy. Darryl held George's head in his lap, and the blood was soaking through his jeans and straight through the mattress onto the floor. George's head was broken open, almost disconnected from his neck, and Darryl was rocking him and sobbing.

"Christ, no! Oh my God, no! Jesus, Georgy, not you, not you! You never done nothing to nobody. Breathe, Georgy! God damn you!" He was squeezing his brother's head, like he wanted to keep the blood from gushing out, the life from pouring away.

I was flying over the two of them, my wings touching from one end of the room to the other. I reached down to take Darryl and his brother under my wing, but the blood from Georgy's head was slick, and the two of them kept slipping out of my grasp. I reached for them both again when I saw the gun in Darryl's hand.

"I'll help you, Darryl. You don't gotta do this. Leave this alone now and let God…" I heard a gunshot, and it felt like it struck me right in my eardrum.

I woke up sweating with a pounding headache. I kept my eyes shut to get rid of the bad dream, and it took me a few minutes to realize that the phone was ringing.

"The fish! My man! You down for some home cooking? Moms made us some baked chicken, some lovely vegetables and rice and whatnot. You tryin' to eat?" I could hear from the muffle in his voice that he had already started. His moms was a good cook, and I was lucky that he shared the stuff with me at all.

"No doubt! I'll be right over." I stood up and shook the sleep out of my ass as I walked, cordless still in hand, to the bedroom to get my shirt and walk across the hall to Khalil's.

"Eh! You got any hot sauce? Bring some with you!" I heard him gulping, Kool-Aid probably. Seemed like all we used to drink those days was Kool-Aid.

"Hot pepper sauce? I don't got any." What in the world would he want with that anyway?

"Man, you can be so Anglo for somebody who call himself hanging with brothers. Bring your own plate, cuz the three we got is dirty." Khalil shut the phone down, and I grabbed a plate and headed over to get my grub on.

12

[HIGH ANXIETY]

Dignity

Since I was a little girl, I had been dreaming about what my first time would be like. I never pictured anyone specific, but whoever he was, he was dressed in a tuxedo and was carrying a bouquet of wildflowers. He scattered them all over the bedroom floor, and then he swept me up and carried me to the bed. With one touch of his finger, my clothes would fly off in eager layers until finally I lay there, completely naked, breathing up at him and waiting.

My dream never got any further than that. I just couldn't picture anything specific with this mystery lover. I used to try to put a face on this guy, someone I was sweating in high school, or someone from my old neighborhood. Or even Mercer, my very best friend in the whole world. He was hot as hell. And every girl I knew wanted to do him. But for me, he was more like a brother or something. We did get into it this one time, two days after the prom. But that was kind of a disaster—he seemed even more nervous than I was. Since I couldn't imagine doing it with just anybody, and I couldn't attach a sexual image to Mercer, I just settled on this faceless stranger. But after the mystery guy got me naked, he always sort of disappeared.

It was a good thing, too, because quite often this fantasy was followed by a real-life panic attack. Just before the stranger would try to get physically close to me in the fantasy, my throat would close up, my chest would clench, and I would grasp for breath in real life. I would have to lift my hair in the back and fan my neck vigorously to stop the perspiration and the panic, and all of this was because of a *fantasy*. There's no telling what I might have felt if I'd gotten intimate with someone for real! It was weird. I never recognized that these panic attacks indicated a deep-rooted fear of intimacy.

This idea of sleeping with Khalil was part mystery, part fantasy, part rite of passage. I had turned eighteen back in March of that year, and I still hadn't lost it. Everybody I knew at home had already done it, some of them several times since the beginning of high school. I don't know what happened with me. I just didn't like the idea of getting that close to anybody in Lexington. The place was too small and full of too much history.

Plus, I grew up with Aunt Paulette and Uncle Sam. They were really my great aunt and uncle. I called them Aunt Lette and Sam the man. They were very strict Pentecostal. I moved in with them when I was three, right after Mama got depressed and left with Mr. Edward, her husband. I call him her husband because he's not my dad. He made that very clear. I don't really know who my dad is, but it sure isn't him. Some dead white guy that nobody wants to talk about. Aunt Lette and Uncle Sam always clammed up whenever I asked about him.

But Aunt Lette and Grammy, my mom's mother, were avid church-goers, and they turned their noses up at anyone who wasn't. When I was little, they always alluded to the bad things that would happen to me if I took up with one of those little boys I hung with. That I'd wind up in "a world of trouble." Whatever that meant, I was scared to find out. Then, Aunt Lette fell out with Grammy, and she stopped coming around.

And my mama, on those rare occasions when she came home from her tours, back when she was still talking, always made a point to explain that sex was bad. She was hung up on it. She'd go off on her long tours, singing in dumps all over the South with her funktified band, and then she'd have the nerve to come home and lecture me. She'd get on me about my grades and my plans for college and warn me that sex would surely be my downfall. She had a lot of nerve. She barely sent me so much as a note while she was off somewhere singing, but she'd pop into town now and again and want to play the mother act. Too late for that.

Yet, some of what she said, about sex and about boys, really did stick. I could tell by the way her eyes fell under blank pillows and her shoulders tightened as if pulled together by invisible strings when she lectured me. I didn't know what had happened that made her know, but I knew she was telling me the truth. That I should be careful in choosing a partner, that sex could change your life. Even though I resented the absentee messenger, I still believed the message.

And that's how I made it through Central High without being deflowered. I had a steady boyfriend all through school, but if he pressured me about that, if he couldn't get satisfied with what I had to give him, I drop kicked and moved on. There was all kinds of stuff that I would do to have fun, but when it came to the actual deed itself, I couldn't get there. Between Mama's lectures, Aunt Lette, and the panic attacks, I guess my virginity was no surprise.

Then I went to college and felt like I was missing out or that I was ready. Hormonally or something. I was having hot flashes all over the place. I'd look at all those fine young specimens on the yard and get all steamed up. I really wanted to do it, but I also didn't want to admit that I hadn't done it before. So, when I hooked up with Stacy, and when she told me that she was in the same boat, we started brainstorming. Somewhere along the line we made a pact with each other that we would "do the do" before midterms. Soon after, we took up with Salmon and Khalil, and it just seemed natural to single them out as "the ones."

I hadn't completely decided how I felt about it. Of course, Khalil was dark chocolate cream, and I thought I wanted me a scoop. He had these really warm eyes, and he was way more intelligent then he wanted people to know. I knew that he liked me by the way he acted with me that first week, once we broke the ice over in Soper. But, it also seemed like he was overly anxious, like maybe he thought I was one of those girls who always wanted to get their freak on with the next available brother. I didn't want him to see me like that.

But then, isn't that what I was? A girl who had decided to get her freak on with the next available brother? Wasn't I just using him to get rid of this label that I had been wearing, to pass into that circle of women who "knew?" Sort of. But it was more than that. I did like Khalil, and he did seem sweet, and it did seem like he would know what he was doing, so he seemed a logical choice.

With that, I checked my purse once more to make sure I had the condoms Stacy and I got from the Infirmary. I went through my shower ritual, and when I got out, I spent some time in my bathrobe with the strings open in front so I could see myself in the mirror.

Not much to comment on. I wasn't bad-looking. Five feet three, average sized chest, swell hips, and a big behind. Flatfooted and sort of knock-kneed, if I wasn't careful. I had hair down to the tip of my butt back then, and I had it permed with a body wave. My hair was wild red and limp for real, stuck to my head like cellophane, so I started doing home body waves back in tenth grade. Fluffed it up, made it wild and unruly, but it gave me character, I felt. I usually clipped it back or just let it hang, flipping it to the side or scooping it all up in a scrunchie.

My skin was so pale, though, and it bothered me. I had to wear blush to even get a little yellow in my cheeks. And, I wasn't good with the sun. I didn't tan to a warm brown like Aunt Lette or turn brownish-orange like Mama. I just burned and peeled and freckled. And, if I stayed out there too long, the skin under my eyes would pucker like a popped balloon. Full lips and a tiny nose. I looked like who I was: an interracial coed with an identity crisis. I thought about the girls that I went to school with, how we were all struggling to figure out who we were, and wished that this race card was one thing I didn't have to worry about.

I closed the robe up and began my lotioning ritual. I had three bottles next to me on the nightstand. One to exfoliate my heels, one to moisturize my arms and legs, and one especially for my face, which was oily, especially when I got my period. I had a lot of steps to go through before I could go upstairs and let Kiko do my nails. In some ways I was tired of the procedures I had to go through before going out, but it just seemed safer this way. I was always afraid that people were laughing at me. If I got out there, and everybody laughed at me, then I would absolutely know that it was because I had skipped some of the steps—not flossed my teeth enough, not spent enough time on my hair, not chosen the right clothes, the right soap, the right emollients. But, when I left the house and found nobody laughing, it only confirmed the necessity of my rituals.

Except that I was relatively certain that some people were laughing at me secretly, indiscernibly. Oh well. You can't please all of the people all of the time.

I knew there was a lot at stake for me, more than for some of the other girls I went to school with. Because I was different, I was in an impossible situation. If I didn't talk the right way, then they would say I was trying to act white. If I admitted to some of the things that truly interested me, I feared, they would say I was a geek. If I admitted that I wasn't sure exactly what I was doing, then my honesty would get me blackballed. So, I walked a fine line in college, hoping I was coming off the right way to the right people and all the time wondering if I'd ever understand what I wanted and who I wanted to be.

I finished the moisturizing process and pulled on my gym shorts and a T-shirt. I'd been listening to Bob Marley all afternoon since I got home, and the vibe he gave me was so sweet and encouraging I almost wanted to stay in my room, read Zora Neale Hurston, and leave this Que Jam to the folks who knew what they were doing. Then, I thought about Khalil, with his fine self, and I felt a flush of fever. I knew it was time to quit belaboring the obvious. I called Stacy, told her it was time, and I headed up to Kiko's.

13

[FLIP THE SCRIPT]

Stacy

Digs rang me up just when I was about to get my nap on. It was all good, though, cuz I probably wouldn't a slept no way. I'd been waiting for that night most of my life, and I was excited. Like a kid before Christmas.

I wanted everything to be perfect. I had my dress laid out and ironed, the panty hose and pumps, too. I'd had my hair done earlier that day, and it was all hooked up with some sexy spiral curl tracks in the front and piled up in the back. I had my bag packed to take over to Digs' apartment. Change of clothes, toothbrush, all that kinda stuff. Because hopefully I would not be coming back to that tired dorm that night!

I had packed my best nightgown, a lavender one that came just above the knee, with lace around the sleeves and the neck. Some extra Paris perfume (actually, it was a knock-off called Continental). I doubted that Salmon would be able to tell the difference. I tucked a whole roll of rubbers in there and some scented oil that I borrowed from my roommate, Candice. Everyone knew she was a freak! You shoulda seen the stuff she had in her desk drawer—oils, edible panties, pornographic magazines—I didn't think she would mind if I borrowed her bottle of Mango Mojo. S'posed to heat up when you blow on it. I wanted to make sure I got hot that night.

When Dignity called, I was ready to roll out.

Kiko hooked us up that night. I got a French manicure with diamonds on the pointer fingers, and Dignity got this tannish-gold to match her dress. Kiko did a special design on Digs' pointers, and she didn't charge her for it. While Kiko did our nails, I was steady thinking.

I didn't say nothing to Dignity, but I had been sort of looking at Khalil a little differently lately. With his fine behind. I know I was all set to be with Sal, but at the last minute, I started looking again at his friend, Khalil. When I thought about us together, it made more sense anyway. Me and Khalil were both, well, on the same side. Digs and Sal, now who could tell with them? Maybe they wasn't some of "them," but they sure wasn't some of "us" neither.

Take Dignity. Something about her didn't sit right with me. I hated how people were always looking twice at her, like she was so fine or something cuz of all of that hair and pale skin. She had a way about her that I didn't understand. She was always so particular about everything, like if everybody didn't treat her real careful she might melt or go off or something. Had to have her hair a certain way. Always taking two and three hours in the shower before she could meet somebody in the Refectory or at Soper. And that nervous thing she had of laughing so loud at her own stupid jokes—in some ways she was starting to bug me. Reminded me of my worrisome little sister.

Maybe it was the fact that she looked so white. When we went around together, people were always looking at her, especially brothers. It felt like a violation to have her going after Khalil. I know it's crazy to say, seeing as how I was the one who was running after Salmon before, and he ain't exactly a brother, much as he act like one. So, it ain't like I was against the interracial thing. Not exactly. But, it just seemed like with the bet on, and with Digs going after Khalil, that maybe it was all just a game to her. And, quietly, it was a game for me, too, but I was in it to win it. I already knew that the college thing might not last for me. I could run out of money or ruin my grades if I wasn't careful. I wasn't all that into the books. Really, I wanted me a husband and some babies. So, I couldn't afford to let Dignity play games with a potentially good catch. That was my rationale.

I never intentionally set out to hurt Dignity, but I guess I was looking out for myself. Shoot. I had to work hard for everything I got in my life. I'd been buying my own clothes and paying for my hair and my nails since I was fourteen, upkeep that my mama implied was essential for me. She always told me, with my plain face and my dark brown skin that I would have to work hard to get noticed. Girls like Dignity, and like my little sister, Helene, with their long, slick hair and pale-ass skin, people would always be sticking out their hands to help people like them out. And Dignity thought she was prettier than she was cuz she talked proper and had those European features. Me, I was not so special to look at unless I worked hard at it. No offense, but Dignity wouldn't die if she lost one man to a dark sister friend. There were bound to be plenty more for her anyway. But Khalil was a fine brother, so I decided I best go after him.

[QUE JAM]

Salmon

The way Stacy was dancing, I couldn't keep up with her. She was freaking and running and jumping and all this, like somebody off MC Hammer's wish list. I liked watching her, but all that heated action and movement, that ain't my style. I could hold my own, believe that. Loved to dance. But, for me, it was more subtle and mellow or something.

Khalil was the same way as Stacy—a big show-off. I'll admit, the brother could move. He danced like he had something hot in his pockets he needed to get rid of, and if he wasn't so, I don't know, graceful or something, it would have been comical. Khalil was six feet two, muscular, and lanky as all hell at the same time. Feet the size of a Lincoln Continental. But, with all that jumping around, he was still smooth. I had to admit.

So it wasn't long before I started sitting out and Khalil started dancing with Stacy. Me and Digs would take our drinks over to the table we shared with about a zillion other people, where Stacy had stashed an overnight bag that was hogging up leg room, and just watch them get their grooves on. You'dda thought I'd of gotten pissed about Lil edging in on my date, but it didn't bug me. Not really. It was a riot watching them dance, and me and Digs were keeping each other company. She had this gold thing on that barely covered her ass, and her hair was pinned up and falling around her face in little rings. She looked good. And for the first time ever, she had a sort of a quiet spirit about her. I mean, she was still talking, but not as frantically as she usually did. At first I thought it might be because Khalil was busy freaking with Stacy.

"They got a lifetime of energy, those two. You wanna go over and cut in?" I was drinking Cokes like they was going out of style. The place was so crowded and hot it was pathetic.

Dignity was sipping bottled water, and she kept looking at her nails. She had these flowers or something painted on her first fingers. It was pretty. "Na. Not right now, anyway. Maybe in a few minutes." She kept the beat of the music with her head and sort of looked around the room.

They had purple and yellow balloons everywhere and posters of bulldogs with their tongues hanging out of their mouths. They had two big square tables near the door, and the other exits were blocked off so they could control who came in. There was a bunch of security guards hovered around the door, too. Next to that, they'd set up a concession stand where they had all kinds of refreshments. There was supposed to be food, too, but I heard the hot stuff was totally gone by eight p.m., and we didn't get there until close to ten p.m. By then, all that was left were chips and drinks.

I kept thinking how the whole event was disorganized. I mean, if we paid for food, then there shoulda been enough for us, regardless of when we came. And, those square tables took up a lot of useless space. One long rectangular one would have done the job better and taken less space. And, if it were me, I'd have put the refreshments on the other side of the room. That way, when people gave their tickets and went in, they'd be forced to disperse all over the room. That would take care of the bottleneck clutter at the doorway. And if you got rid of the bottleneck, I'd make the security guards' jobs a lot easier, the dance a lot safer.

I was always thinking about that kind of thing—how to plan things out so they'd work better. How to design rooms, events, buildings so that they would run smooth. I was in the middle of my master plan when I noticed that they were playing a slow jam by Keith Sweat. Folks were busy doing a slow belly rub all over the floor. The whole vibe had changed in there, and it made me a little nervous. I searched the room for Khalil and Stacy, but they weren't around. Probably in the can.

"So, Digs. You alright? You seem kinda quiet tonight." I didn't want to look a gift horse in the mouth, but if she was upset…

She spun a ringlet of hair around her finger before she spoke. "I don't know.

I guess the day just hasn't gone as I expected." Dignity shrugged and sighed. "But I'm not gonna die or anything. I'll be alright." She looked me right in the eye when she said that, and it seemed like I could see a part of her that I hadn't seen before. Like maybe she was a little vulnerable or something, and maybe in that moment she was willing to admit it.

"Hey, let's dance, huh? You wanna dance?" It was more a command than anything else. She looked cute to me just then, with her hair piled up like that, and I thought it might feel good to hold her a little and glide her across the floor. Her eyes narrowed and smiled at me when I took her hand and led her out to the middle of the floor.

I remember they were playing that old song "Whip Appeal." Used to be the song back in the day. Dignity was resting her head somewhere between my stomach and my chest, she was so short, and I could feel her singing along, the words vibrating against my skin. Felt real familiar for some reason. I had my hands in her hair at the back of her neck, and both of us had our eyes closed, floating along there.

The song stopped, and I realized that the two of us had shared a moment. She knew it, too. She just looked at me and didn't say anything. I put my hand on the small of her back to lead her over to our table, and that's when we saw Khalil and Stacy playing tongue darts in the corner. For some reason, at that moment it cracked us both up. Dignity was laughing and shaking her head, as if she couldn't believe her eyes. Couldn't tell if she was mad or what.

"Oh well—there goes that idea!" Dignity gave this full belly laugh that she only did when she was laughing at her own jokes. I was laughing, too, but I didn't really get the joke.

"What idea? Were you, ah, really interested in him?" I tried sounding casual. But I knew it would have hurt a little if she said yes. Which was completely hypocritical, I know. The way I'd been handling Stacy's merchandise all week. But, I'm a man, alright. Shoot me.

"Nothing. Let's not go there. Let's go... there!" She pointed toward the bathroom door. "I'm gonna go to the ladies, and you come up with a plan for us. How's that?"

Now she was commanding me.

I waited for Lil and Stacy to stop kissing, and then I went over there. I saw Khalil adjust himself and prepare for a confrontation or something. Must have surprised him when I came out with an unreadable grin. I wasn't sure how I was feeling, but I knew I had to talk to him.

"Nothing like Babyface, huh? That kid can sing! You alright over here? Cuz *your date* and me just wanted to make sure you was having a good time." I took on a sarcastic tone. Not because I was especially angry about what was going on. But because he didn't know that. He didn't know what my feelings were for Stacy or Digs. Hell, I didn't even know. So, it was borderline disrespectful, what they were doing.

Stacy didn't look at my face. She put her little beaded bag on her shoulder, turned on her heels, and said, "I'm going to the bathroom. I'll be back."

15

[DOG EAT DOG]

Stacy

What in the world was I thinking, carrying on with Khalil Towers like that? Right in front of Dignity? I beat myself up the whole way to the bathroom. It's just that he was so, so, I don't even know! Fine as all hell. He was like a premature Denzel Washington. Tall and muscular, but thinner than my favorite actor. All this vivid brown in his face. And he was wearing the hell out of that suit that night. The pleats hung just right, and the shirt underneath was the perfect shade of blue, shoulders broad and well-developed, and lips like red licorice. And I love me some licorice.

I couldn't help myself. He could dance, too. We had so much fun out there. I hadn't danced like that in such a long time. And when they played that slow jam, and I could smell his Cool Water cologne on his neck and on my own hands, I wanted to kiss him. Bad. I didn't stop to think, just let him do it. Then, I was all confused. I knew that I had decided to go for Khalil, but I hadn't planned on doing it that night, in front of Dignity, in front of my own date, Sal.

I thought I'd go into the bathroom and freshen up, buy some time, think of what to do. I knew it could turn out really bad if Digs was really into Khalil or if Salmon was really feeling me.

I took a breath and pushed into the bathroom. Nearly knocked Dignity down.

"Well! If it isn't Little Miss Hoochie Mama! What, did my date eat your lipstick off, and now you need a fresh coat?" Dignity had her arms crossed in front of her, and something around her temples was pulsating.

I cleared my throat and looked at her, then around the room. The small room was chock full of people, and all of them had their eyes on me. I spoke softly, in my professional "legal offices, how may I direct your call" voice. "Ah, can we talk outside, please? I'd be happy to discuss this further out…"

"Why? You afraid these sisters will know that you a date-snatching, bet-breaking, smile-in-my-face-and-stab-me-in-the-back-type ho? Call it public service, Stacy—I ain't going *nowhere!* Inquiring minds want to know!" She had a calm look in her eyes that didn't make sense with what she was saying. I knew I deserved a tongue lashing, but I didn't expect this drama. She was really loud and everybody in the bathroom was all up in our business.

"Girl, listen! I didn't plan this. I swear. We was just feeling each other, that's all. But it's over now. I'm going back out there and dance with Salmon soon as I get out the bathroom. And, you know Khalil is still after you!"

"Hmm. Feeling each other, huh?" She looked in the mirror and messed with her hair. Sisters who had waited ten minutes for an empty stall were hesitating before going to do their business, trying to see what we was gonna do next.

"Look. We just hit it off is all, but if you want him back, Girl… And this bet, we could just scrap that." I pleaded with her with my eyes. Truth, I wanted Khalil, but I didn't want an embarrassing scene to get him.

"Oh, *hell* no! The bet is on! And I don't want Khalil. I been hanging with Sal, and I'm all up in *that* now!"

She ticked me off, trying to imitate Lil's flow and challenging me and what not. I didn't care who it was, I had never backed down to a challenge, and I sure wasn't gonna start that night.

"Aah-ight! You think you Burger King—have it your way! The bet is on, and come tomorrow we'll see who done won!" I gave a regal snap in the air, and I flew up out of there. Dignity was just standing there fuming, but from what I could tell from their comments and whispers, she had the girls in the bathroom on her side.

When I got back out to our table, Khalil and Salmon were sitting there drinking Cokes and talking. Didn't seem too strained, but who could tell. After what I had just experienced, I didn't know what to expect. Sal stood up when he saw me coming, and Khalil reluctantly stood as well, not sure what to do.

"There she is! I was waiting on you to dance—they been playing all my favorite songs out here." Sal extended his hand and poured on the charm, acting as if he hadn't just seen me sucking his homeboy's face.

Dignity pushed me out of the way and snatched Salmon's hand. "Good! I been wanting to dance all night." She gave a sneering smile to Khalil. "Thanks for asking." The DJ had this Gloria Estefan salsa-type music going, and the two of them slid out to the dance floor. He was dipping her and oiling his ass all over the floor, smooth as taffy. They looked really hot together. But they left me and Khalil in an awkward silence at the table.

"Look. I guess I owe you an apology, too. I put us both in a crunch when I, ah, kissed you before." Khalil had his hands in his pockets, and since I knew he didn't have a gun in his pocket, I figured he must have been glad to see me.

I extended both hands to him for a hug. "I accept. I guess I sort of wanted you to do it, anyway." We shared a warm embrace, and I pressed in a little, giving him something he could feel. I hadn't forgotten Dignity's challenge and our bet to see who could lose their cherry first before midterms. It seemed like I might be on my way to winning, even if it was with the wrong man.

Khalil backed up some so he could look at my face. I kept it as innocent and alluring as I could. "Stacy... You and Digs are friends, and umm... I talked to Salmon and me and him are straight, but, you and Digs..." He let the sentence trail off somewhere, half confused and half hopeful.

I gave him a kiss near his collar. I knew I couldn't tell him about our bet, and I knew that Digs had already claimed Salmon, so, I just figured I'd let what happened happen. "You worry too much. Digs will be alright. She's a big girl." I slid my hands down just above his butt. "And you're a big boy."

"Okay. I hear that. Let me tell Salmon, and then let's roll out. You down?" Khalil walked back a few steps toward where Salmon and Digs were dancing.

"I'll be outside waiting." He helped me slip on my jacket before he headed over to Salmon and Dignity. I licked my lips while I waited for him, blocking out the fact that me and my girl had just got into a fight and concentrating on finally doing what I had never done before. And with Khalil, who looked like the love language of women.

16

[THAT ZING THING]

Dignity

I'm not sure what all I felt, but I was a bundle of tender emotion. I felt violated or something. I knew that I wasn't in love with Khalil or anything, not by a long shot. And, when I thought about it, I really had been having a good time hanging out with Salmon. Nevertheless, when I saw Khalil kissing Stacy, both of them with their eyes closed like they wanted to savor the moment, something inside snapped. It was like that back then, even sometimes now. All of a sudden I just see red, and then, well, whatever comes next is off the heezy.

I was tripping. I spent all that time daydreaming about Khalil, trying to rustle up some real emotion for him, knowing that emotion would enhance anything physical we got into. I knew it wasn't really there, that "zing" feeling you get when you think about someone that you are really feeling, but I wanted it to be there. And I was willing to pretend that it was there that night, to help make my first time special.

But, there was Stacy, all up in Lil's face, and neither of them looked like they were faking that "zing." Looked like it was for real. And that made me angry. Our bet was to see who would lose her cherry first. It had nothing to do, technically, with cultivating a "zing" type thing, as far as Stacy knew. Still, with one deep kiss, Stacy had stolen all my plans for that night: sleeping with Khalil and creating a fake but satisfying "zing thing" with the brother. And I was ticked off about it.

At first I didn't want to focus on the emotions I was feeling. For me, passion was passion, regardless of the source. So, if I started feeling really passionate about something, I could flip a switch and go in a different direction with it. That night I was really angry and disappointed, but I redirected those heightened emotions and poured them into dancing with Sal. Fortunately, he was right there to receive my drama. During the dance and, unfortunately, afterwards.

Aunt Lette taught me how to do the Hustle when I was a little girl. She and my Grammy used to take these dance classes at the Y, where they'd learn all these couple dances. Salsa, Rumba, Fox Trot, Hustle—they knew all the moves. Uncle Sam never wanted to practice with Aunt Lette, so she would teach me. I used to love that. She'd put on the radio, and we would dance all over the living room. We'd drink lemonade after. It was fun.

At first I wasn't sure that Salmon would be able to follow me when I started to Hustle, but he was right there. Smooth as hell, too. He didn't use a whole lot of unnecessary movement with his feet or with his body. Mainly he just led me around, allowing me to spin and dip when I needed to, knowing when to turn and when to stand still. We were like something off of *Saturday Night Fever*, and before long, I forgot that I was dancing out of anger and disappointment. I was just having fun watching Salmon watching me, both of us a little bit surprised by the other's skills.

The DJ switched after a few fast Latin songs and played another slow jam. This time it was Stevie's "Overjoyed."

Salmon caught me close around the middle and pulled me against his chest. I was sweating a little, but he was cool as a metal bucket. I rested my head just above his middle and felt his heart beat, smelled his cologne. He was making soft circles on my back with his hands. The mixture of his hands on my back and our slow rhythm on the floor made me feel comfortable and sleepy.

I must have been half asleep and dreaming when he kissed me. Without my detecting his movement, Salmon had moved his hands up to hold my face in his hands, twirled a lock of my hair with his finger, brushed my left eyebrow softly, which made my eyes close in reflex, and kissed me so deeply, so softly, that I heard myself breathe a sigh of relief, as if he had knocked me unconscious and resuscitated me simultaneously. I gulped at him, as if his mouth held the breath of life, and I felt his hands move down to my hips and anchor me as he led me into round two.

We stayed that way, our bodies moving imperceptibly, for a long time. We never noticed that the music had changed until we heard the room crack open with howling and barking as the DJ played "Atomic Dog." The lights started to come up, and people started milling around the exit, asking each other what was going on next. I rubbed the print of my lipstick from Salmon's mouth before allowing him to lead me back to our table, where I had left my jacket. He was holding the small of my back as I walked. The feel of his hand there made me weak in the knees.

I felt stoned as I put on my jacket and fussed with my hair. Like his hands and his tongue had given me a buzz. I didn't know what to say. So I said nothing. Wish I could have done the same thing that night at his apartment, when he wanted to extend that wonderful soft full tingle without having to deal with a big freak-out.

"That was nice, Dignity. Thanks for dancing with me." Salmon reached for my hand and squeezed a little when he said it.

"No, thank *you*. Who knew you could dance like that? The pleasure was mine, Salmon."

"Listen, I know this didn't exactly go the way that you planned, but, umm, I still had fun." Sal looked at me like a child, hoping that I would agree that I'd had a good time.

"I think it went just the way it was supposed to go, you know? And I had a ball." I was being sincere.

"Good. Good. You wanna walk back over to the apartments? I ain't sleepy yet, and we could, I don't know, watch a movie or something. Talk."

I slipped my evening bag on my shoulder and reached for his hand. "That sounds good to me. And I'm starved!" We walked, hand in hand, out the door and headed across the street. They had a shuttle going over to Northwood, but it was warm, the stars were out, and we decided we would walk. I said, "I got some pizza at home—let's go get it."

"Yeah? What kind you got?" Sal adjusted his jacket as we walked.

"Pepperoni."

"You like pepperoni, huh? I'll keep that in mind. So, where did you learn to dance like that, anyway? You're like Rita Moreno over here!" Sal looked at me like he was equally curious and impressed. Made me feel good.

"I don't know. Watching other people I guess. My Aunt Lette. Musicals and stuff. How do you know Rita Moreno? She is one of my favorites!"

"Easy. She used to be on *The Electric Company*. And she did *West Side Story*. My mom loves that movie; I seen it about a million times."

"Me, too! You know that scene where they're dancing on top of the building, and the boys are all teasing the women? Anita does this one step where she's on one foot and bends over backwards and kicks straight out in front. She's incredible."

"From what you just described, she's a double-jointed circus act or something! What the hell was she doing?" Sal started to laugh at my crazy description.

"Stop! I'm not describing it right. But she is just so talented. I love to see her dance."

"Yea. I know what you mean. Bernardo is pretty smooth, too. You think he was gay?"

"Bernardo??! He was practically *married* to Anita!"

"No, the actor. The way he danced and all, you think he was sweet or something?"

"No. Not necessarily. I mean, I don't think you could tell about someone's sexuality by the way they dance."

That started a heated but friendly debate.

"Get outta here! You think you can't tell a fairy by the way he moves and what not? *You*, who claims to tell a the size of a man's package by the way he walks?" He was teasing me, but I knew that he wanted a better explanation.

I had to think about that one; the two ideas did contradict. "Well, it's like this. When someone is dancing, usually they are putting on a show, performing. Some of what they're doing is real, but some of it isn't. But, when you walk, you're getting from point A to point B. You're not acting, so it's more real. I think you can tell about a man's package that way, from his walk. But sexual preference, I don't think dancing is a reliable form of judgment for that." I was proud of myself for breaking it down so quickly in a way that halfway made sense.

"Let me get this straight. Back there, when we was dancing just now, we were putting on a show?" He stopped for a minute so that he could see my reaction to his question.

"Sort of..." I had a half-smile and wouldn't look in his eyes.

"And all that other stuff, that came after, were we performing then, too?" He had the smile then. He knew he had me cornered.

"That wasn't dancing."

Salmon put his arms around my waist and kissed me again, softly, on the lips. "It wasn't an act, neither."

17

[GOOD BLACK DON'T CRACK]

Khalil

I don't know how we got away with that one, swapping dates and leaving with the wrong girls. It just happened. Somehow, when Stacy and me started running The Que Jam, sirens started going off. I was feeling all this heat and energy from her. Like electricity. She would start one move, and I would follow, and then I would go in this direction, and she'd be right there with me. It was synchronicity. So, I had to kiss her. When two people are vibing off each other, part physical, part mental, hey, you gotta kiss. It's obvious.

I didn't know what to expect from any of them—Sal, Dignity, even Stacy. For all I knew, Stacy could have kissed me back and then slapped me or some shit. Women do crazy stuff like that, supposedly in the name of friendship. But, even if she had slapped me later, I seriously doubted she would turn down the kiss. Call it a gut instinct that turned out to be right.

Even though she did kiss me, I was surprised when she wanted to come to my crib after. But again, hey, if she had game, with her fine self, I said let me play. She was all over me on the way home. I was going to walk, but I guess she figured like Digs and Salmon were walking, and she didn't want to run into them. We ended up taking the shuttle. She pressed herself up against me in the seat, so close that I could smell her perfume.

Back at the crib, she started to come on real strong, which I didn't really like. I mean, a chick needs to leave some stuff alone, dig? Wait and let it happen rather than pushing so hard. So, I pulled back. Clicked on the tube, poured two Burger King thirty-two-ounce cups full of grape Kool-Aid for us. Leaned back on the couch and chilled.

Next thing I know, she goes into this routine about Dignity, how she never trusted her no way, how Dignity probably wanted Sal all along since he was "closer to Dignity's style." The rattle bugged me, but I wanted to know what she was getting at, so I questioned her.

"Her style? What chou mean by that?" I was careful not to have attitude in my voice. Didn't want to upset her and ruin the vibe. Since I'd gotten her in the door, I figured I might as well score.

Stacy flipped off one of her black pumps, crossed her legs, and dangled the other pump on the end of her big toe. She licked her lips before answering, as if each one had a drop of honey on it and she had a sweet tooth. "You know. Dignity is, umm, one of those fence straddlers. Can't tell if she's, uhh, one of *us* or one of them. Kinda hard to trust that type…"

I knew she wasn't saying what I thought she was saying. Not in the 1990s. "So, you think Digs is with Sal now because she is light-skinned?" I was about to sip my juice, but I needed to hear her response first, had it tipped toward my mouth midair.

My sultry ebony company stuck her index finger in her own grape juice, pulled it out, and sucked a moment before explaining, "Come on, Khalil—don't front! We all know that the ones who are light, bright, and damn near white will do anything to keep that color line from tanning! They always stay with folks who look like them! Even if they have to go back to the other side." Stacy set her cup on the coffee table before stroking my arm with her middle finger.

I coughed and looked over the girl's head, toward the doorway to my bedroom, toward the front door. I was stuck with what to say. If I spoke my mind, then she would be out the door, and I would a missed the bodacious ebony boat on this one. But if I shut up, she might think I agreed with her ignorant ass. Or, being true to the path of least resistance, the average brother's duty and obligation, I could simply avoid the subject entirely by trying to change the subject. "Yo, it's getting stuffy up this joint! Let me go change out these rags and put on something more comfortable." I hopped off the couch and bounced to the bedroom, closing the door behind me. "I'll be right back," I called from behind the door. "Make yourself at home."

I guess that must have satisfied her for a while. When I got back, she had put on this luscious lavender thing, her thick thighs the color of morning coffee. I could see something black and lacy peeking from underneath. Before she could start talking smack again, I pulled her face to my own to encourage her to use her tongue for a more useful purpose. I had her lavender thing off, and I was down to my shorts. I could feel her reaching for her purse, and next thing I knew, she came out with a raincoat for Charlie. I leaned up on one knee to put it on, keeping my eyes on her as she removed her black lace bra and panties. I licked my lips when I saw her release the twins, with their stiff, purple peaks. I circled my hand against one and my mouth around the other. She opened up and welcomed me in. She was tight and tender, and we created a rhythm together that was sweet, sharp and sweet.

She had her legs up around my ears, her arms around my shoulders, and a fevered pitch in her cheeks. I was in there like swimwear. I was about to crack the nut fantastic, with Stacy right there with me. Uh oh. Uh oh.

"Tell me I'm beautiful, huh? Prettier than *her*. You like it, right? Let me hear you say I am more beautiful, Khalil!"

I felt myself slam shut against Stacy's sugar walls when she started to screeching like a tight violin. What the hell was she talking about? I responded only with the obligatory groan. Let her interpret it whatever way she wanted. I didn't say a word.

Kinda spoiled the moment, though. I kissed Stacy before she went in the bathroom to clean up. I jumped off the couch, butt naked, and stood in the middle of the floor. Stacy came out of the bathroom, and I was standing there, with my package swaying in the breeze. Stacy smiled at Charlie like she had just won the lotto.

"You alright? I mean. Uhhh…" I was gathering up my clothes and heading to the bathroom. I thought I'd get dressed and get ready to walk Stacy home.

"I'm alright—a little new at this, but it didn't stop us from doing what we needed to do." She smiled at me wide and bright. I don't know what she did with her clothes, but they were gone, and all she had on was that lavender thing again, with the black bra and panties underneath. She plopped down on the couch and started chugging her juice.

"True dat, true dat. Mighty nice. Let me get dressed, okay?" I didn't wait for an answer, just went to the bathroom and shut the door.

"So, umm. Is your roommate coming home tonight?" Stacy called into the bathroom. Which I hate. I don't want nobody to talk to me while I'm in the toilet. It's private. You never know what I might be doing in there. It just so happened I was only getting dressed, but she didn't know that.

"Uh, I don't know. I assume so. Why do you ask?" I hoped she wasn't getting at what I thought she was getting at. Because to get busy is one thing, but spending the night at the crib, I wasn't ready for all that.

"Well, it's just that it's late, and I wouldn't want to disturb my roommate, and I thought..."

I came out of the john to find Stacy easing back on the couch, pulling the faded yellow sheet with orange daisies over her fine frame.

I sailed down slowly onto the other end of the couch, like a feather losing its flight. I wanted to tell homegirl to get dressed so I could take her ass home, but once again I could not find my voice. I tried to think of a good way to say I didn't want the chick to stay. But it wouldn't come.

I heard Stacy say, "Well, I guess I won, didn't I?"

I said, "How's that? What did you say?" I rubbed my temples to off-set the migraine that I felt coming on.

Stacy, a phat black cat curled comfortably on the couch, pawed the fur on her arms and purred, "Oh, nothing. Just reminds me of this thing my Grandma Melba used to say. She said black women are blessed because their dark pigment makes them age slowly, beautifully. They never look old. But the white women, and those light ones like 'you know who,' they ripen quicker than a banana in a dark paper bag. Big Melba says those light ones age quickly and poorly, but good black don't crack."

Laid up on my couch without an overnight invitation and still tripping about Dignity. I should have dropped her ass right then.

18

[CONNIPTIONS]

Salmon

Shoulda known the night was destined for weirdness when I ended up with Dignity and Khalil ended up with Stacy. I'd been sweating Stacy all week. All that work for nothing. No, I didn't love her, but I would have done her, and we both would've had fun. Believe that.

I couldn't tell at the time how Dignity felt about the situation, whether she was really disappointed at how things turned out. But judging by the way we danced and the kisses and stuff that came after, I figured she wasn't exactly mourning or nothing. But I started to question it again when she showed out at my apartment that night.

We were cool at first. I mean, way cool. We were waxing the dance floor like you wouldn't believe, dancing to salsa and house and disco for, like, five straight songs. She was sexy as hell, too, the way she moved. She was more sure of herself, less spastic and jumpy. I liked it, that confident side of her. And we shared some kisses and what not on the floor and on the way to her house. Stopped by her place and picked up some leftover pizza and Cokes to take over to my place. We headed to my apartment and set up camp in the living room. No problems, I thought.

While I went in the bedroom to change into some sweats, Dignity went in the kitchen to find plates and cups. I explained to her that I didn't have much, didn't need much, but she went ahead and looked anyways. She found these two chipped wine glasses I had bought at a yard sale that summer. A guy in my math class was having this sale at his parents' house, over in Roland Park. Real fancy area. Said he was sure to have some stuff for cheap that I'd want.

Well, this guy and his folks must have been crazy! They had all kinds of crap—paintings from dime stores and old appliances, clothes and dishes—priced as if they was new. Right! Like I'm gonna pay twenty bucks for an old wilted poster of *Starry Night* they must have gotten at the museum gift store eighteen years ago. Wasn't just me, neither. Nobody was buying the crap. People would stop by the tables, pick up an item, and offer some reasonable price—a dollar or two. And these guys would wrinkle their noses and say, "Oh, we can't let it go for that!" I say, if you don't want to part with your crummy shit, why have a yard sale? Why bother? But Chris, that was this guy's name, I felt sorry for him. He looked sort of embarrassed, too. So, I bought these two old wine glasses, and he gave them to me for one dollar. They weren't worth fifty cents new.

Dignity came back in the living room with two saucers and the wine glasses. She made a production of pouring the Cokes in the glasses and serving us each a slice of the pizza, which had gotten a little rubbery in the microwave. She pulled the coffee table up close to the couch, and both of us sat on the floor on either side of it.

"Let's have a toast! To friendships that last forever, and to classes that don't!" Dignity raised her glass and held it up to mine.

"Yeah. And to successful date swapping and to Rita Moreno and her infamous circus kicks…" I said, clinking my glass with hers and remembering the conversation we'd had about *West Side Story* on the way home. I silently said grace then, crossed myself, and started to eat. As usual, I folded the slice in half lengthwise and devoured it, finishing it in three big bites. Washed it down with Coke and then burped loudly.

Dignity laughed at that and took her time eating her slice of pizza. Seemed like she chewed each bite like thirty-six times or something. Later on, I found out that she *did* count the number of chews and tried to keep each bite at thirty or so. She'd read an article once that said for better digestion, to prevent choking, and to promote weight loss, we should chew each bite a certain number of times. Counting chews and stuff—that was typical Dignity action.

After about fifteen years of waiting for Dignity to bite and count and chew, both of us climbed up on the couch to veg. Digs had changed her clothes when we went to her place for the pizza, and we were both comfortable, full, and happy.

Felt natural to me when she leaned her head over and rested on my shoulder. Felt natural when I put my arm around her shoulder and gently fingered around in her hair. It was like petting a dog, fingering that hair. Soft, fluffy, fly-away hair. I loved touching it. She seemed to love it, too. I could hear her breathing settle and slow down.

We started kissing, and her hands were all over my back, my chest, my abs, and I reciprocated. She felt so soft and warm, and I could feel tingles and electric bolts going up my spine. It was weird. But I knew what that tingle was about, and I assumed she was having it, too. So, I'd had my hand under her shirt, rubbing her back, massaging her naked breasts. Her tits were small enough that she didn't always have to wear a bra, and I could feel the tension from their center, could see the tingle from it in her eyes. That's when I took my hand from her breasts and slipped it inside her orange, MSU sweats. Like our mascot, boy did she ever turn into a bear!

At first I thought she was trembling out of sheer excitement. A girl will do that sometimes, start to vibrate, and all. It's a good sign. So, I dipped a little further down, past her belly button, just to the tip of her magic kingdom. I stopped there for a minute, listening to hear her breathe, wanting to make sure it was quick, agitated, excited. I licked the inside of her ear and felt her move closer to me. When I heard her panting softly, I saw it as a green light and tramped down to her tangled bush. That's when I felt the worst cramp I ever had in my life, like my hand was caught in a fire-lined vise.

"Shit! What the hell...?" I tried to pull my hand quickly from her pants, but her thighs wouldn't let me. She had her knees clamped together like she was trying to hang onto a hundred-dollar bill. My fingers were her thighs' new fortune. "Let me go, would you? Cripes!"

Dignity had her eyes clamped shut and her knees clenched like fists. She'd put her hands over her mouth and was suppressing her own screams, which were escaping quietly, sounding like the yelps of a wet puppy and the crazy laughter of a mad clown mixed together. She had tears streaming down her face. And the more I tried to get my hand free, the harder she smashed her thighs together. In that short time, in that short travel from her navel to her nookie, she'd gotten completely hysterical.

"Dignity, calm down, Baby. Calm down. I ain't tryin' ta hurt you, alright? Relax your legs and let my hand go—you're really giving me a cramp here." I looked at her face and tried to wipe away the streaming tears with my free hand, working quickly because I was in so much pain.

Still rocking, still shaking, still yelping, she did manage to release my hand from her death grip. But she didn't open her eyes at all. I took my newly freed hand, blood-red from pressure and pain, and shook it vigorously for a minute; then I put both arms gently around her shoulders. I whispered "shhh, shhh" into her ear, and she finally stopped yelping, eyes still slammed shut.

"Look, Love. I thought we was on the same page, but apparently I was wrong, okay? I apologize. You hear me? I'm not trying to go anywhere you're not willing to go here, alright? Calm down, Digs. Please try to calm down." I rocked her gently in my arms, and spoke in my lowest, coolest tone to soothe her.

After a while, Dignity did open her eyes and use my sweater to wipe away her tears. Then she hopped off the couch and went into the bathroom for damn near forty-five minutes. Again, as I would later learn, standard Dignity. She spent more time in the bathroom than you could ever imagine. Hours sometimes. I knocked on the door after a while to make sure she was okay. Finally, when she came out, we watched *On the Waterfront*, an old flick with Marlon Brando. Love that guy. Both of us had seen it before and knew some of the lines. When it got to that part, we looked at each other and said, "I coulda been a contender!" Then we both burst out laughing. It felt so cool and natural with her, except for that freak-out part. I wanted to ask her what that was about, try to help her work through it, but something told me to leave it alone. I had my own nocturnal freak-outs to think about. I was in no position to complain.

IN MEDIA RES:
JUST AFTER FINALS, JUNIOR YEAR
[MORGAN STATE UNIVERSITY 1994]

19

[GOING HOME]

Dignity

I had a huge bag of cassette tapes next to me in the passenger seat. There was a CD player in my red '91 Nissan Sentra, but I was too paranoid to use it. I was always certain that I would lose my favorite CDs or that they'd get stolen. People were always breaking into cars around Morgan, and Khalil told me about how he lost his whole Stevie Wonder collection in one fell swoop last year when someone broke into his car. After I heard that, I made copies of my favorite CDs on cassette to carry in my car, and I kept the real CDs on lockdown in my bedroom. Music is too crucial to take a chance losing. Can't imagine what would become of me if I couldn't block out the world and listen to my trademark tunes.

I started to pop in James Taylor's greatest, but the whole second side felt like winter, so I chose Sly and the Family Stone instead. I learned him from my Uncle Albert, my estranged mom's brother. He was barely ever around, either, but when he was, he made a point to spend time with me. Taught me all about classic rock, soul and funk music, even odd stuff like Jimi Hendrix and Creedence Clearwater Revival.

I tried to let the tension roll off of me, bopping my head to "Dance to the Music," but I kept flashing on the other night, when me and Sal decided we "needed some space." My mind kept moving like a newsreel, running movie clips of memories that Sal and I had created together. Sometimes I'd get to one that was too real, too painful. The clip would melt down, my brain would short-circuit, and I had to shake or cry or smoke. Sometimes all three.

It started when Khalil called me over one night saying Salmon was talking in his sleep and acting crazy. He asked me to come over. I pretended to be scared and concerned while I spoke to Lil, but really I wasn't. Sal had been having these weird nightmares for months at that point. Always the same thing: flailing his arms like he was fighting, calling his father, calling on God. And when he woke up, he never wanted to tell me what he was dreaming and why he was so upset. After a few weeks of it, I got tired of asking. I'd just rub his back or whatever until we both could go back to sleep. But I didn't want Lil to know all this. I just told him I'd be right over, not to worry.

By the time I got over there, Khalil had gone back to the Que house and Salmon was sitting on the grass in the courtyard outside our apartment buildings smoking a cigarette, a habit he helped start me on last summer. You could tell from the way he was sitting that he was troubled, had something heavy on his mind. I sat down on the grass beside him, lit a Capri, put my hand on his left knee, and gently squeezed. We didn't say anything for quite some time.

Salmon flicked his cigarette far ahead of him in the damp grass, a thing I hate to see him do, and he turned to me with a puddle of something troublesome in his eyes. He had a longing there, a need for…something that made me very nervous. I get that way when it seems like a gig is getting too emotional, too personal.

He reached out and put my hand inside of his. He wouldn't let me lose his gaze, which instinct had me avoiding. "Baby, I…I wanna talk to you about something. I know how you hate to get heavy, as you say. But, ah, this one's really messing with me, and I think I could use your help. Or at least it would make me feel better for somebody besides me to know." He looked at me earnestly, his eyes penetrating into my own. I began to sweat.

"Sure, Sal. What is it? You can talk to me." I said these words mechanically and without a convincing timbre. I didn't mean any of it. Quite the opposite. I knew good and well that I could not, would not listen to anything extremely personal, painful, or wrought with meaning.

Sal is no idiot, and above that, he knows me, so he blanched and blinked before he continued. But somehow, maybe out of need or hope, he pressed on.

"Babe, you know my folks are, like, way backwards, alright? Like, ignorant about contemporary values and what not. Hating on anything that isn't a part of their culture…" He hedged around the obvious, the fact that his parents are openly racist and against our relationship, a fact that we have discussed briefly, but not since earlier this year.

I used a finger to smooth my eyebrows, a gesture I do incessantly when nervous. "Yes. I know that." I tried to sound like I was urging him on, but in my heart I was begging him to stop. Just stop.

"Uhh. Yeah. Did I ever tell you about my cousin Darryl and his little brother, Georgy?" By now Sal realized my apprehension and had gone in another direction. He took his eyes, his emotion away from me and directed them toward the midnight blue sky.

I suddenly went into a late Romantic moment and became taken with the blades of grass surrounding me, fingering and gazing at them with a forced sense of interest, and tried to think only of Coleridge, Wordsworth, Whitman. "Georgy? I don't believe you have." Uh-oh. Where was he going with this?

"My dad has a brother named George, and he had these two sons, Darryl and Little George. They called him Georgy. Darryl was a little older than me, and Georgy was three years younger than both of us. Uncle George is older than my father, and they are the only two left in their immediate family. Pop's parents died when I was eleven, and he had a sister I never met who died of leukemia when Pop was little. So much for the family tree. The thing is, me and Darryl were thick, alright? Like two peas in a pod thick, like peanut butter and jelly thick. Even more so than me and Frankie at one point. Because when Frankie was in the last years of high school, he didn't have time for me no more—always pimping the chicks and what not. But Darryl—me and him would always hang! I was in eighth grade and he was in ninth, and we were tight."

I was listening to Sal, but I was purposefully remaining detached. Caressing the blades of grass, seeing which parts, if any, I could remember of "Cristobel," a Coleridge work that I wrote a paper on once. Because any time now, Sal could change his tone and get into something sad, something serious, and I needed to stay prepared.

"Now Georgy, he wasn't like other kids. You know that disease people get where they have an extra chromosome or whatever? Down Syndrome? Leaves them with a distinct look with their large heads and all. Well, Georgy had that. It wasn't nobody's fault, you know. He was born that way. And we all loved him to death, especially Darryl. You'dda thought Georgy was his son instead of his brother, the way Darryl went on about him. Good ole Georgy. Had a simple sweet way about him." Salmon was chain smoking, something he only does when he is studying something difficult or when he is really upset.

I wanted to hurry Salmon along, make him get to the point, but I was afraid. Seemed like a simple thing he was telling me, about his cousins. But, his being so upset let me know that there was more to this story than met the eye. So I just sat tight and listened.

Sal cleared his throat. Two opaque veils fell over his eyes. "Well, Georgy didn't make it." My boyfriend inhaled his Salem, allowing the smoke to form a chain from his mouth to his nose.

I remember thinking *oh dear. Here it comes.* "What happened?" I wanted to know but I didn't know how I would react when I did hear.

"Uncle George lived around the corner, but he figured his was a sort of bad neighborhood. On accounta the African-Americans and all. So he kept a gun. He kept it loaded, but it was supposed to have a safety latch, or whatever. Me and Darryl knew where he kept the gun, and being half-grown, we was curious, you know. Cripes, you see the movies and all, and the guys are always packed, and no one wants to mess with them. Bad-ass mofoes. Seemed glamorous is all. So, we had the gun out from this cabinet Uncle George had built into the wall behind his bed in the master bedroom.

"We weren't gonna do nothing with it, you know. We weren't stupid. Least we *thought* we were pretty sharp. Figured we'd pull it out and each of us hold it, just to see how it felt. To be strapping bad ass mofoes for once instead of two young teenagers that hadn't grown into their deep voices and long legs. But I guess we weren't so smart after all."

I was afraid to hear what would come next. Already felt the sympathy, the fear, the panic at how this story would end and how it affected my Sal tonight, the night before his last final, in the still moonlight of the pre-dawn sky.

"You can guess what happened. Georgy was supposed to be in the front room watching cartoons, but he came back looking for us, asking for another drink box. He loved those things! Could drink a whole carton of them in a day, if you'd let him. We tried putting the gun away quickly, but he must have seen it, seen where it was kept.

"Two days later, me and Darryl are up in his room trying to get the nerve up to call Donna Wheeler and her better half, Rhonda Rablicci. Both of them were stacked and lived in the neighborhood. We wanted to see if we could get something going with the two of them. And we didn't want Georgy around, with his crazy, childish questions and all.

"So, Darryl locked the door and told his little brother to watch *Oprah*, and by the time it was off, we'd be back downstairs. *Oprah* was one of Georgy's favorites..." Salmon wanted to light another cigarette, but his hands were shaking too bad. He had pulled his knees up against his chin, and he had his arms around his legs, rocking himself, like the motion might keep him from flying completely off somewhere. I looked at him from the corner of my eyes, never extending a hand or giving him full attention with anything more than my ears.

"Then, oh my God, Jesus! What happened! We heard the gunshot coming from Darryl's folks' room. Darryl slammed down the phone, cutting off his smooth rap with Donna. I just kept hoping the shot had come from outside. After all, Uncle George said it was a bad area. But in my stomach—Cripes! In the pit of my stomach. I knew. That shot hadn't come from the outside.

"Next thing you know, we're racing down the hall to Uncle George's room. Before we get there I can smell this stinging, pungent odor, like blood and licorice and Old Spice Cologne. So thick you couldda swallowed it..." He started to cough and choke with the memory, his tears and rocking adding inflection to the kind of diatribe that nobody wants to hear.

"Oh my gosh, Honey! Oh my Lord!" All I could manage to say, now focused on the sky, now looking for an escape from this horrible revelation.

Salmon gulped for air. "It was him alright, little Georgy. Got his hand caught on the trigger and blew a chunk the size of his fist right out of his own head. And the blood was pouring out, and Darryl was shrieking. Can't forget his shrieking. Felt like his head, his heart, every piece of his spirit was caught in that shrieking. I can still hear it. Always hear it..."

I finally turned to face Salmon, who looked at me with the urgency of a burning cat trapped on a hot tin roof. My face was blank and expressionless. I could not allow myself to live or feel what he was relaying to me. Just couldn't.

By this time Salmon was panting and crying, barely able to catch his breath. "Jesus, Darryl, it wasn't his fault! It wasn't anybody's fault! But he done it anyway!

He tried rocking little Georgy and holding his head together while I dialed 911. But Georgy couldn't make it. He went limp before I even connected with an operator. And as quick as that, before I could say something or do something or pull him away, Darryl took the gun from the carpet, shoved it in his mouth, and ate his daddy's bullet." Salmon was rocking, shrieking, crying, almost as if the wrong word, the wrong piece of wind, would completely tear him apart. "In front of me! In front of me! His head flying out on the wall, all over the carpet, next to his little brother, my little cousin! Oh, Jesus! God help me! God help me!"

I knew that I should say some comforting words, maybe engage us both in prayer. Put my arms around him and rock with him, cry for him, cry for Georgy, cry for Darryl. And In my heart I wanted to. But something else, a thing I could neither specify nor overcome, had its grip on me, and instead of showing this man how much I felt his pain, how much I wanted to support him and comfort him, I showed him nothing. Kept my arms folded, kept my eyes diverted, kept a poker face. And so we sat there: me staring ahead as if in a coma, and Salmon wrapping his arms around himself, rocking himself, nurturing himself…

I hit West Virginia and I snapped out of my reverie. Sly was singing "Family Affair." How fitting. I thought about my family. What family? I know I shouldn't say that. After all, Aunt Lette and Uncle Paul love me like their own, and I never want for anything. At least nothing material. And I also have Ain't Angus, and good friends. But I always feel like something is missing. And, quietly, I feel worthless because of it.

Let's face it, something *is* missing. My parents. My mama isn't dead; she was just too spiritually dead to raise me. I never could understand why, and I was never sure that it wasn't something I did that she just couldn't forgive. The woman can't look on me, and I don't understand why. And my father, whoever he was, actually *is* dead, although his spirit is alive and well and has haunted me since as long as I can remember. What did he look like? Who are his people, and how come they don't claim me, either? Nobody wants to claim me. It hurts.

I guess when it comes to family, nobody has it easy. I know Mercer and his folks have been at it since the day he was born. They are what you call bougie people, affluent and upwardly mobile. Put Mercer in Jacks and Jills and went to the one Black Episcopalian church in our neighborhood in Lexington. Groomed Mercer to follow in his daddy's footsteps, go to Kentucky State, his parents' alma mater, and then to Medical School at Howard. And Mercer still fights them tooth and nail. Says he doesn't want to live in their conventional boxes.

And Salmon doesn't have it easy with his clan, either. That whole thing about his father and his Uncle George is bugging. And here I thought their worst problem was accepting my black face in their lily white circle. But the thing with Georgy and Darryl makes me pale in comparison. Pardon the pun!

I slipped past mountains, past the University of West Virginia as the Family Stone crooned "Que Sera, Sera." I had to agree. Nobody can control or even predict what will happen, what will be. My mind rewound back to the last night with Salmon.

I had felt so bad for him. The idea of seeing his little cousin dead and seeing his older one, his running buddy, dead, all in the same day, well it was too much for me to take. The feeling it gave me was a kick in the middle, a prickly pill that got caught in my center and died, unexpressed. I couldn't say or do anything.

And when he explained how it made *him* feel, how he nearly failed eighth grade and almost didn't make it to high school, how he'd struggled with a bad crowd, dabbling in drinking and drugs to overcome his memories, I said nothing. That thing about his father telling him never to talk about it and to stop crying about it. How was I going to deal with that? And the part that was most like a serrated knife on my gums was when he said that his father had never really been the same since. That his uncle resented his father for still having children. That both Uncle George and Salmon's father blamed Salmon for his cousins' deaths. And for being alive.

Family can be so fucked up.

But I didn't expect to have to lose Sal. I mean, I've been pretending not to feel and not to care for so long that I forget I even have any emotions. I know he was looking to me for something that night, and I gave him all that I could. My physical presence. But when we finally went to his bedroom, as the sun was just beginning to rise, I thought I could lie next to him and somehow offer my emotional support through telepathy and mind melding. It didn't occur to me that he'd even think of making love to me again. We both knew that I wasn't ready, that it just wasn't going to work, with all my hysterical episodes…

The sun was at its most hot, glaring at me and blaming me from on high, scorching me with what I thought might be the truth, which was that maybe this break up was all my fault. I wanted to feel the mountain air on my face as I drove, but as the afternoon progressed, there wasn't enough to breathe. I turned on the air conditioner and left my window cracked while I smoked a cigarette, my sixth so far that day.

It hadn't seemed unreasonable to me, my ultimatum. I told Salmon from the beginning, when I lost the bet with Stacy during freshman year because I couldn't have sex, that intimacy was a problem for me. I didn't change my program or become someone that I had not always been. He was there with me all those times when I tried, when reflex had me crunching his hands between my knees and shrieking. I don't know why. I honestly have tried not to react this way to him. I love him. But something about his touch, anyone's touch, feels like a violation.

We both seemed happy enough cuddling, kissing, holding hands. I honestly believed him when he said that intercourse was not the most important thing. I hoped that telling him that I just couldn't, that I couldn't explain why, would be enough of an explanation for him. Truth is, I didn't really know why I had such a sexophobia. I guess it was because of my mom, how she said it could really spoil your life. That and Aunt Lette's Pentecostal, "Sinners in the Hands of an Angry God" mentality.

So, a few weeks before, when he started pressuring me to explain, to tell him why I freaked out and panicked like I was being raped whenever his hand ventured below my waist, I clammed up. Like I said, I didn't really know what was at the root of my phobia, and I didn't think I was ready to find out. I had a ghost of a memory or a terrifying something in my subconscious, and I didn't know where it came from, and I wasn't ready to look on it and figure it out. He told me that he loved me more than anything, that one day he wanted to marry me. Said I should trust him enough to confide in him, that I should want to work through my problem. For our sake.

Rather than admit that I was afraid and that I never truly believed that he actually loved me, that anybody loved me except maybe Ain't Angus and Mercer, I gave him an ultimatum. He'd been making noise about his family's Easter celebration, that his brother Frankie had been urging him to go. I said fine. Take me with you. If I was gonna work out my intimacy issues, than he oughtta have been willing to confront his racist father and let him know that my black behind wasn't going anywhere. But he said it wasn't time yet. That he knew his father. That they had a lot of trouble to work through, not just the race issue. And it wasn't going to happen overnight. I wasn't buying it.

But the time came when he needed desperately for me to be emotionally available to him. He was ready to confront some of his deepest fears. He knew he would have to in order for us, for anything else, to work. In return, he wanted me to get therapy to work through my intimacy panic attacks. He had seen me freak out a time too many and thought it was serious enough to look into. At the time I'd given it, I didn't think my ultimatum was empty, but turned out it was. I couldn't imagine myself going to a shrink, a complete stranger, and telling her my business. Couldn't imagine looking in Salmon's dad's face knowing he saw me as the enemy. And, mostly, I couldn't imagine becoming so emotionally close to Salmon, or anyone, that I would share my feelings and my body with him.

I told him that I needed more time. He said he didn't have any more time. He told me that he needed space, wanted to take a break. I told him I did, too, that I wanted to go home, that I might transfer and stay there. Which was a lie. I didn't *want* to go home; I felt like I *had* to. How else was I gonna face the fact that I had lost the best thing about my life due to my own neurotic foolishness? But he didn't want to budge, and neither did I.

We said we'd always be friends, another lie. I knew that seeing Salmon and not being with him would break my heart, and that's why I decided to go home to Kentucky. Maybe I did need to figure out why I was so freakish about being close to anyone, even someone that I loved and trusted almost more than myself, like Salmon. And if I did confront my issues, what better place to do it than in the (discomfort?) of home…

When I got back from the yard that last day of classes, he'd boxed up the stuff that I kept at his apartment—my sweats, my toothbrush, and other odds and ends, and placed the box in front of my apartment door. I brought the box inside, packed my suitcases. Then, after three long years at Morgan State and without even a degree to show for my trouble, I left an hour later for my old Kentucky home. I'd have eight hours to think about why I went to Morgan, why I had to leave, and if I had any reason to go back.

PART TWO

Home to Glory

DOWN HOME:
SUMMERTIME AFTER JUNIOR YEAR
[LEXINGTON, KY 1994]

20

[BLACK ANGUS]

As soon as I got into town, I stopped at Leiger's Eatery. It was this place not far from my high school where we always used to go after choir practice. They had the absolute best coffee in town, and I wanted a cup before going over to Ain't Angus's house.

I looked a mess, so I was glad that the place was basically empty. It was more of a fall and winter hangout, because of the coffee and the baked goods. Students didn't go there as much once it got hot out. I put my purse down on one of the small tables in the back, then I went to the front counter to order a cup of mocha java. Even though it was really warm outside, I needed the hot jolt of caffeine in my system. I took the cup back to my table and savored the first few sips with my eyes closed.

I was feeling abandoned and disconnected. So what else is new? Yet, with the whole Sal ultimatum bleeding at my feet, I was feeling especially disconnected. I hadn't brought a lot with me from the dorm, but at the last minute, I had grabbed a cryptic piece of evidence that seemed related to my past.

Once the caffeine had the chance to careen through my bloodstream, I opened my purse and carefully took out the manila envelope I'd brought with me. There was no writing or explanation on the front of it, and the article clippings inside were becoming yellowish-gray and wilted around the edges. I'd been holding onto this envelope since the day I left for Morgan, wondering about it but too scared to investigate it. Then, when everything went wrong with Sal, I thought I'd better take a look at its contents again. I reviewed the first clipping with relative ease. The second clipping gave me butterflies and anxiety. It was just too weird to understand. I stuffed the clippings back into their holder and drank the rest of my coffee. Five minutes later, I left for Ain't Angus's.

I never knew why we called my aunt by this peculiar name, so when I got to her house, I asked her about it.

"Okay. It was back in one of those hot summers in the late '50s, early '60s, along in there. They started to call me Angus, trying to make me out for a cow. The thing was that I never wanted to be out in the sun like the rest of them. They could get as black as they wanted, but they'd do it by they *damn* selves! Craziest thing I ever heard about—bunch of dark fools out there looking just as purple and stupid, call themselves laying in the sun. Sun ain't done nothing for our people but make us black, easier for white folks to single out and mess over. That tanning and setting out, that ain't made for us. Naw.

"And there wasn't no such thing as an air machine or blower or whatever. You know, like they got now—conditioning. I still ain't got used to them. Just a fan if you was lucky, and sometimes that didn't do much for you no way. My sister, that's your grandmama, and me, we'd stay *in* doors. Fan. Read magazines and watch TV. Wonder if we had got the television by then? I don't remember, but I do know that we kept our yellow tails indoors! So that's when folks started to calling me *Angus* instead of *Agnes*. Black Angus. To tease me and make me out for a cow. Course, I never was as black as none of them no way. Then, your grandmama started to having all those babies, and they took to calling me *Ain't Angus*. Because my name ain't Angus; it's Agnes. So, that's that. What else?"

I explained to Ain't Angus that I was getting curious about my lineage, specifically my father. At first I saw worry flush her brow, but she straightened it out quickly.

"Your daddy? That what you come around here looking for? I never knew who exactly he was. You say his people was named Mandarene or Chasinger?"

I pulled out the clippings I had swiped from the guest room over at Aunt Lette's during my last year of high school. She had them tucked inside of a large manila envelope, which was buried inside the side desk drawer, where she kept the old sewing machine. One was an obituary about Evian Mandarene, who died of cancer in early 1972. The article said he was survived by his mother, Cordial Mandarene, of Bourbon County, Kentucky, as well as two distant cousins, Della and Theresa Chasinger. They didn't say where these two cousins were located.

It was a short article, but it did show that this man that I assumed was my father was well loved. He was given a memorial service that was well attended by students and friends from the University of Kentucky. The article said my mom, her brother Albert, and two others sang at the service. It also said that Evian Mandarene had some "bizarre family struggles" just before he died.

There was no picture included with the obituary, so I had no idea what my father looked like. I wondered about that. But the other article in the envelope puzzled me even more. It wasn't exactly an obituary, but it talked about this man, Franklin Chasinger, who had been shot by his own uncle, Norman Mandarene. I recognized the last name Mandarene from the obituary about my father, Evian Mandarene. Yet, I wondered why Aunt Lette had bothered to save this article about a man who'd been accidentally shot and killed. I wondered why this man had been shot, why it concerned my aunt enough to save an article about it, and what this man had to do with my father, Evian Mandarene. I held onto the obituary, and I handed the Chasinger article to my aunt. I hoped she could shed some light on things. She had such an awesome memory; I knew that if she'd ever heard anything about the situation, she'd remember.

Ain't Angus took the small newspaper clipping that I handed to her, but she closed her eyes and squeezed her eyebrows together before she read it.

"Chasingers. Came from out there in Western Kentucky. Let's see now. What was her name? Theresa. Folks said it like this: Tray-sah. Ain't nothing but Tuh-ree-sah. She moved way out West, where her folks came from, near Tennessee and Hopkinsville, in there. She was a Chasinger. Some kinda way. Distanced herself when she turned eighteen cause she didn't like her people's ways. By that time most of them was dead and gone anyway, but she moved West just the same. Used to quilt and knit real well. Had a shop for a hot minute downtown. But she charged too much, especially for those fancy designs. After the shop closed, they say she started to selling stuff in catalogs and at the fairs during the summer. She had a nice little following.

"Chasinger. Let me think. Okay! The daddy used to be head of the Police Department out in Fayette County back in the day! Maybe he was fired or maybe he stepped down. Seem like there was trouble. I disremember. But he was married to a woman named Hester. Although she might have changed her name when she turned white...

"You see, Hester turned white. Hester had a sister named Hilary who was a little younger than Hester. Their family worked the land behind that horse farm acrosst from where your great-grannie and all us used to live.

"Nobody knew for sure, but they used to say that Hester and Hilary were both black. Had a black mama who died soon after Hilary was born. Raised by they daddy. Daddy was a dead ringer for Colonel Sanders. They say the dead, black mama still haunts the place. That's how come it can rain over there on top of that house whiles the rest of the neighborhood is just as sunny. Black mama died but never left. You ever been around there, around to the farm acrosst from where me and your grandmama and all us grew up? Remind me to take you before you go back. Part of your history. Reason you young folk don't half know where you going is cuz you don't know where you been. It's a shame."

I scooted to the right edge of the couch and spread my legs out. I could see this explanation was going to take a while.

Ain't Angus continued, "Well, Hester never was as dark-toned as Hilary. Hester had that thin, yellow hair and pale skin and behind just as flat as a pancake. Hilary had a reddish tone at the face, a wide-spread nose, and balloon behind. I don't guess they ever treated her as nice as what they did Hester, because Hilary ran off with one of the Baxter boys and lived alongside of black folks, just like she was one of us.

"And far as I can tell, she *is* one of us. But her sister, Hester, she married up with the Police Chief and moved out of town, like she was as white as he was. Wasn't until much later that she and her white husband come back to these parts, living like white folks, as if nobody remembered she was Black Hester from around there where it rains for no reason. They say it's the black mama's tears. The rain, I mean."

Ain't Angus sat in a fake leather recliner with her left foot propped up on her right knee. There were dress patterns and fabric all over the dining room table and on the floor at her feet. Her slick silver hair would have reached well below her waist if she unpinned those two braids and let them hang. She had on pants that had a flair at the end and were the color of old mustard. She'd folded one pants leg up around her knee to expose one skinny yellow calf. The blouse had orange, green, yellow, and blue vertical stripes and two large patch pockets in the front. She fished in her smock pocket for a tissue and dusted off the glass end table next to her, the one that was covered with porcelain figurines of cows. The table on the other side of her held a vase of fake yellow flowers, a set of salt and pepper shakers shaped like owls, and a greening metal rendition of the

Statue of Liberty. In the middle of the room, for no apparent reason, she had a life-sized statue of Sappho. Someone had put a red baseball cap on top of Sappho's head.

Ain't Angus held the fraying paper clipping in her hand while she felt around her neck. She had a pair of scissors strung around there as well as a pair of cat glasses on a chain. She placed the glasses on the tip of her nose, squinted down at the clipping, and said, "Let's see...

"Franklin Chasinger. Um-hmm. What they say. Shot and killed? By his own uncle. Now, that's a shame. When was this, 1971? Okay—Norman Mandarene was his uncle. Now, they the ones used to own that house out there by my sister, your Grandma Pearson. Still do, I guess.

"Bless her heart, your mama, Sister Becca, took up with those Mandarenes until way after you was born, and then the mama put Sister Becca down. Far as I can tell, this here is about the Police Chief's son. What's his name—Franklin? I don't know nothing about him, baby. Been dead for the longest. Wish you could ask your mama, Sister Becca, bout them, but she hasn't said a word in years. And your Grandma Pearson, well her memory isn't what it used to be, with the Old Timers, you know, since the last stroke."

By then, I was so tired, from the trip and from the recent history lesson, that I must have looked hopeless. I could see my aunt's brain working overtime when she recognized my disappointment.

"I know! See if you can't talk to Ruthanne, your auntie, Sister Becca's sister. Ruty, they used to call her. Cute as she wanna be, with her tiny self! Wonder if she still sews all those clothes? Had no business in to call herself a seamstress. Like she could say her name in the same breath as mine. No. But she was a cute little thing. See if you can't catch her on a good day, when she isn't too busy taking care of your grandmama, when she feels like sitting up and talking." She handed me the aging newspaper clipping.

"I betcha Ruthanne and some of them would know what went on over there. Who this Franklin Chasinger is."

When I went to hug Ain't Angus goodnight, I could feel the straight pins she had stuck inside the bra that she wore all the time, even when she was sleeping. I sat on the brown, faux leather couch that was covered in plastic and stared at the patterns until I could think of what to do next.

21

[LORD HAVE MERCER!]

After a few sleepless hours on Ain't Angus's couch, I yelled back to her that I was heading out to Frankfort to see Mercer. I had called him from the wall phone in the kitchen, while I straightened up and put away the dishes. I still hadn't told Aunt Lette I was in town. I wasn't ready to go home yet.

Ain't Angus wasn't the best housekeeper. She was a pack rat. Some fifty odd years of trinkets, gadgets, books, pictures, doo-dads, broken appliances, and who knows what all else made their home in her small, three-bedroom house. And the kitchen. Don't get me started about the kitchen! Every kind of sticky, molasses-covered, remnant of crumb cake-looking, coffee-stained something took refuge there, knowing it would never be disturbed. Let's just say I cleaned it from top to bottom when I woke up, organized the shelves and the counter space, which was limited behind the large bottles of extract, the high stack of dish towels, and the three toasters, circa 1958, that hadn't worked since 1962. Made what sense I could of the confusion she called a refrigerator, and as I dried the aluminum glasses, in multicolors, like relics from a retro, 1950s diner, I dialed up Mercer.

I had tried him at his mom's house, and she was her usual, chipper self. I was surprised to find out that my buddy had gotten an apartment off campus, and that he lived in Frankfort year-round now. I got the number from her and called him to let him know I was on my way.

"Girl, I thought you wasn't never gonna get hurr! They told you I was staying out in Frank now, right? Dawned on me that I hadn't mentioned that when you called yesterday. I still take my clothes out to Ma for laundry and stuff, so I was out there when you called. Girl, when did you get ee-yin?" Mercer spoke in his signature fast and raspy voice.

Mercer's thick native tongue had me tripping. I guess I left most of my accent behind when I went to Morgan a few years ago, so his words sounded funny to me. "I got *ee-yin*, as you say, a few hours ago and crashed over *hurr*, at Ain't Angus's. But now I'm ready to roll out." I put the glasses in the cabinet above the sink, wiped down the counters, and hung the dishcloth neatly over the sink.

"Oh, please! Now I know you aren't trying to imitate me and front like you ain't never lived down hurr and never heard of how Southerners talk! You better act like you know, Dignity! Cuz I knew you back whee-yin!" I could hear Mercer gearing up to read me like *The New York Times*.

"I feel you; I feel you! You're right! I just don't get to hear that good ole down home flavor as much as I used to. So, what else? Can I jet over, or are you up to something else?" I was already pushing into my imitation Birkenstocks, despite the fact that I hadn't had my toes done since before finals. The pink and white flowers that Kiko had painted had begun to splinter and fade. It was too hot for sneakers, and I hadn't had the time for a pedicure, in all this drama.

"Girl, you know I'm always into something! But come on out hurr! We'll get into it together. Just like always."

"Okay. I'm almost out the door. Do I need to bring anything? Maybe some tequila? I could use a head change about now." I dropped my cigarettes into my purse and grabbed my keys out of my pocket.

"Umm. Yes. Do that. I got lemon in the fridge. Yes, you better get you a head change before you come around hurr. You would want to be ready for all this..." Mercer left his sentence unfinished, which was not uncommon for him. He was all about dropping me with all kinds of drama.

"All what? What you got up your sleeve, Mercer?"

"Don't worry about it. Just bring your little shot glass and come on. You'll see when you get hurr."

I stopped on the way and bought a bottle of Cuervo Gold and a shot glass that said "The Bluegrass State" across the front, then I headed toward Frankfort, the state capital. I was never big on that place—it always seemed cramped and full of winding, sharp-cornered streets. It is close to Kentucky State, though, so I could see why Mercer would want to stay there, at least until he finishes school. Which might not be for another twelve years, the way he is going. He is on a music scholarship, and those music majors take forever to get done. He sings on every choir on campus, performs almost every week, and misses a lot of his other classes.

I am familiar with the development he lives in, which is a glorified project. Mercer's black, 7-series Mercedes was parked in front of this sea of government subsidized row houses. Mercer's uncle Jack had died of an undisclosed illness and left him the car.

Uncle Jack. They called him Skip Jack. He was Mercer's mom's older brother. Skip Jack was a dancer and choreographer who lived in Chicago. He was sort of flaming, but he was really nice to us. Only man I ever knew who set his hair on rollers. I met him lots of times over the years, and he always came to town with a flourish—drove fancy cars and wore all of the latest fashions. He would take me and Mercer out to the movies or to see a play and out to dinner, called himself giving us culture. He died just before I graduated from high school. Family never wanted to say why, but it seemed clear that he'd contracted AIDS. Anyway, he left Mercer his car, and Mercer has kept it shining and running ever since. It's his prized possession.

I pulled into the space next to Mercer's black Mercedes, which we had nicknamed Kelly, for reasons I can't go into, the day after our misbegotten attempt at sex after prom night. Pulled out my purse, the Cuervo, and a few random tapes. Then I knocked on my best friend's door.

It didn't dawn on me that he had a roommate, so I was surprised when this tall, glamorous woman came to the door. She had slender hips and wore a flowing, rose-covered dress. The dress was laced at the neckline, but the laces were undone and showed off her meager but perky bust. She was beautiful. Her nails were painted the same rose color as her dress. Her toes, unlike my own, were painted and manicured. She had soft, wispy hair that was gently curled around her face. Her makeup was subtle and romantic, just a little foundation, rose lipstick, and a slight touch of liner under her eyes. I was impressed; she was lovely.

But in that instant before I spoke up, before I asked for my best friend, I felt jealous. Am I neurotic or what?! But there it was, a heart-choking split second of jealousy. Because this woman was so feminine and beautiful. Her familiar behavior sort of bugged me. I tried to mask my feelings before addressing her through the closed screen door.

"Hey! I'm Dignity. Is Mercer around?" I slung my purse over my shoulder and waited for her to unlatch the screen door.

When I asked for Mercer, this woman seemed to have a chuckle behind her eyes, and that bugged me, too, but I ignored it. Her voice was a little raspy, like she'd had her share of heavy drinking and smoking, and I stored this implied information away as ammunition, should I find myself having to measure up against her. I did that sometimes, especially when I was feeling insecure—compared myself to women around me to see how I stacked up. Those who were manicured, well-spoken and well-dressed always got the most points. Sue me for being superficial, but I can't see their insides. I have to go by what's on their outsides. My toes weren't done and I wasn't wearing a full-blown coordinated outfit, but I had better sense than to party my voice away, like she obviously had, so in my book we were even.

"Oh, I guess he's around here somewhere, doing one of his pop visits. He knows everybody around hurr. Stays in people's business, you know. Come on ee-yin, Girl. He won't be gone long!" Had the nerve to be all familiar with his personality and habits, too. Oh, no. I wasn't all that ready for her.

She switched her narrow hips to the living room, where the walls were painted stone and the carpet was fluffy and beige. She asked me to take off my shoes, since "You know how Mercer is about these carpets, now! He'd have a fit if there was ever so much as a smudge on they-umm. Just had they-umm put in a month ago, with his own money. He couldn't stand that inside-outside mess they had in hurr before." She padded off to the kitchen, promising to bring back lemonade and an extra ashtray.

How did she know I smoked? I only took it up less than a year ago, and I had only mentioned it to Mercer over Christmas break in passing. Mercer's been spreading my personal business to this perfect, lanky-limbed woman, too. Just what I need.

I looked around the townhouse Mercer was calling home. Too cute! Soft, caramel-colored leather couches with paisley-patterned throw pillows. Shelves full of books and sculptures and photographs he'd taken in the past few years. Mainly street scenes and festivals with close-ups of interesting faces. I especially liked the series of pictures he had on his end table, all in gold frames, that he'd titled "Appalachia." He had a sound system and a large television, two floor-size potted plants, and a whole lot of paintings and pottery in earth tones. It was comfortable, appealing, and artistic. Just like Mercer.

"So, I know you must be anxious to see our Mercer! He talks about you all the time. Let's have some girl talk before he gets back—get to know each other some, shall we?" She told me her name was Elizabeth. I prattled on, in my anxious fashion, about how I'd been tight with Mercer since we were children.

"Yes, we have been all through it, all through it, me and that boy! Love him to death. Can't wait to see him." Nice as she was, I was getting tired of making happy with this woman. Something about her was strange. The awkward way she crossed her legs, that played-out scarf she had tied, a little off center, around her neck. I don't know. And the cigarette she smoked seemed practically minia-ture in her broad hands. Her countenance was encumbered and her feet were big.

"Well, you know Mercer has changed a lot since the days when you knew him. A lot has happened since thee-yin, Girl..." Elizabeth drank from her glass of lemonade like she was chugging a beer. She was clumsy! Another feather, some-how, in my jealous cap.

"Yes, Mercer has always been a rebel, so I wouldn't be surprised at anything he would do, crazy thing! And it hasn't been all that long since I seen him; I was down here over Christmas break. He hadn't gotten this place yet, but we hung out in Lex." I made sure to be clear with this Elizabeth, with her big-handed self, trying to tell me about MY best friend.

"What's the craziest thing Mercer has ever done? Whatever that is, multiply it by six hundred, and that's what he's like now!" The woman chuckled outright.

"I doubt it's that drastic, Elizabeth."

"Well, did you know that Mercer is, umm, considered bisexual?" She didn't look at me as she lit another cigarette that nearly disappeared in her huge hands.

I cleared my throat and tried not to bristle visibly. How dare this woman try to drop me and "out" my best friend without even knowing me that well! I wasn't actually surprised to hear this news, but I was uncomfortable hearing it from her. What if I didn't know? Who was she to pass this kind of drama on to me without his consent?

"Look, Elizabeth, I don't know what your relationship is with Mercer, but I know that he wouldn't appreciate you talking to me about this without his consent. So… let's just wait on him before we get too deep. You may not know him as well as you think." I lit my own cigarette and inhaled deeply, holding the smoke in as if the nicotine might lend me some kind of power.

"Oh, please, I know Mercer like the back of my hand, Girlfriend! Don't be confused!" She patted my arm with her left hand, and that's when I noticed the mole she had on the side of her pinky. Mercer had a mole like that, too. My throat closed, and I squinted closely at this woman's face. The face looked back at me, unflinching. I felt a wave of recognition.

"Elizabeth, are you…?"

"Mercer! Yes, Honey! I'm giving you full drag now, Doll!" Mercer laughed, clapped his hands, and ran over to give me a hug, happy to know he had completely dropped me.

When I realized that Elizabeth was actually Mercer, for some reason I felt overwhelming relief along with a growing nest of hysteria somewhere around my belly. I started laughing and crying at the same time, shocked, amused, and scared to death all at once. "What?! Shut up! What??!!"

"Yes, Digs. I'm a WOMAN, Honey!" Mercer rubbed me on the shoulder, chuckling, and perched on the edge of the couch, looking at me with a beam in his eyes. Her eyes?

I didn't know where to begin. "Lord, have mercy! What next?" I said.

"Lord, have Mercer! You got some time? I got some dish!"

I brought the tequila bottle over to the couch and drank a swig straight from the bottle before sitting down.

Somewhere along the line I must have missed that my best friend was struggling with his identity. Back then, and to some extent still, we were all struggling with identity. But, how did I miss something this big? Cripes, he was the Homecoming King junior year! He dated more girls than I even knew existed, and he slept with a good portion of them, too. He was voted biggest flirt during Senior Superlatives Week, when we voted on labels for all of the most popular kids in the senior class. There wasn't one girl in our school who didn't want to get with Mercer. When did this whole female thing happen?

But he told me how he had met these two friends, Jasmine and Tony, how they had this show called "Queens and Things" every other Saturday at this gay club down there. How they held this contest called "Queen of the Crop" during the club's annual Fall Ball last year, and how he entered. And won. Said he has his own show now and makes so much money that he got his own place, furnished it, and paid for school. Blew me away. I couldn't hear anymore.

"Hold up, hold up. Hold-the-fruit up! Okay, you done dropped me enough for right now—dang! Let me get my bearings for a minute!" After nearly two hours of listening to Mercer, now called *Marcy* in some circles, I finally put my hand, extended palm facing out, in his face and made him stop. Made her stop. Whatever. I rubbed the salt off the back of my hand from the fourth tequila shot I'd had, smashed my cigarette out in the ashtray, and stumbled upstairs to the bathroom.

My head and heart were throbbing. Part of it was a buzz, just the head change that I needed, but part of it wasn't. I put the toilet top down and sat on the chocolate velvet seat cover. I bent over, so that my head was down between my knees, and breathed deeply. Mercer had done an Aztec theme in there, with the same beige, tan, and yellow from downstairs. Had a nice border up around the walls and matching towels, rug, and soap dish. Smelled like sandalwood in there, and there wasn't a thing out of place. True to form. Mercer is practically more fanatical about cleanliness than I am, and that's why we always get along so well. With Mercer, everything has its place. Same with me. But this Mercer/Marcy thing had no place with me.

Sitting on that toilet, with that burning tingle of smooth gold in my belly and the spinning sensation in my head and heart, I got that feeling I get when my apartment is disorganized and out of order: flirtatious panic. Feels like a swarm of gnats is circling around my head, nipping me on the cheek, then backing away, only to come back and bite me on the neck. It's the kind of panic that taunts me. When it happens, I can fight for control and gain composure for a second; then the fluttering frantic feeling comes back for a few seconds, and the cycle continues until I correct the disorder, organize the clutter.

If I'd been at home, the solution would have been simple. I would have cleaned the apartment and cleared the frenzy in my head along with it. But this thing. How in the world was I going to organize this thing?

Thing. Thing. Mercer is not a thing. He is a person; in fact, my very best friend.

But, he was always a "he." This Marcy thing, I don't know. As I thought through the implications of this gender conundrum, I felt the swirling circle of panic seize up on me again.

I took deep breaths and stood up to splash water on my face. I looked at myself for a minute. All things considered, I didn't look half bad. I'd broken up with my boyfriend, potentially dropped out of school, traveled eight hours on sadly little sleep, lost my best male friend and had gotten, unannounced, a new female friend. I pinched my cheeks a little to make sure that I was awake and not dreaming. It also gave my washed-out complexion a little color. So, Mercer is Marcy now. Okay... How different can this be? He's still the same person, right? I mean she's still the same... Who am I kidding? Everything is completely different.

I looked at my teeth, fluffed up my hair, and decided to head back downstairs. Same theory as always: if I looked attractive on the outside, maybe the insecure panic that I had so often would disappear from the inside. I *looked* fine, so everything would *be* fine. Breathe. I traveled all this way to get his support. I don't mind listening to his drama, but I intend to get a little "love-you-anyway-here's-what-you-do" type support, too. Whether my best friend is male or female, it's still my best friend. And the whole reason I came here is because I need my friend.

When I got back downstairs, Mercer had finger-combed his hair back, so now it lay in soft waves away from his face, like it used to. He'd changed into sweats and a T-shirt. Both of us had long since tequila, salt and lemoned our lipstick away. He looked more like the person I was used to, and I was relieved. Which was strange, because he hadn't really changed that much since I went to the bathroom. Funny what a dress and a little lipstick can do for a person.

"Look, Little Miss Transgender, I gotta be me, love me anyhow, drop me and throw me for a loop when I'm the one supposed to be leaning on your shoulder, Lady! Fine! You win! Your trouble is bigger than my trouble! Always trying to top me, Mercer, Marcy, whoever!" I flung myself down on the leather couch and readied up two more shots of Cuervo for me and my lady friend. I was laughing and shaking my head.

"No you *wouldn't* give me fever over this, Digs! It's not like I planned this, you know..." Mercer stood up and went into the kitchen with an exaggerated huff. Come to think of it, he was always supersensitive and prone to fits. I knew if I didn't play this right, he'd have another one tonight. Wasn't up for all that.

Especially with him using all that dated gay lingo he'd picked up from Skip Jack all those years ago.

I licked the salt, dropped the shot, and squirted the plastic lemon down my throat. It was like water by now, being my fifth shot. "Okay. You're right. And, you know, no matter what you choose, I am on your side. But dang! Give me a chance to react, okay? I mean, I didn't see this coming, and I am… gonna have to get used to it. Give me time." I sat back on the couch, slid out of my sandals, and pulled my legs under me, Indian style.

Mercer came back with a chocolate peanut butter cheesecake, from Leiger's, my favorite bakery downtown. He wasn't smiling, and I could see that it was taking all he had not to have a hissy, telling me how I need to try to walk in his shoes (pumps?) before I complain about this situation. "Are you too dropped, Miss Perfect, to eat your favorite cheesecake? Not to mention the skinny latte I slaved over for your judgmental ass. And don't you know I paid over one-thousand dollars for that couch you're so comfortable on, and I know you better take your little grubby feet off of it, too!" He laid down a red and white checked table runner on the coffee table along with the cheesecake, a silver cake cutter, mint green saucers, and two steaming mugs of skinny latte. All my favorites. All things that Mercer alone would remember. Not even Sal knew about Leiger's and their special cheesecake and their divine skinny latte. Only Mercer knew how this same combination had helped get me through every major disaster from all through high school. Suddenly I started to cry. Not the silent tears running down the face kind of cry, but the loud, heave your shoulders and imitate the sound of dying cattle kind of cry.

Mercer first looked shocked; then he started to tear up, too. "No, Dig, don't do this! Whatever it is, we can make it work—fiercely! You know we can!" He came over and put his arms around me and held tight, like he always did, pulled my head to his chest and rubbed my back until the sobbing slowed to hiccups and then finally rolled away. When I pulled away from him, my face was pink and swollen, and his eyeliner was running all over his face.

"No. Mercer, I am not prepared to tell you that your liner is running down your face, now—no! What am I supposed to do with that?" I reached for Kleenex from the box on the end table, and Mercer wiped his makeup, boyishly, on his shirt sleeve.

"I know. It's weird. Believe me, I know. But, this is what I'm doing right now. Hiding." He rubbed his shirt sleeve and cleared his throat in a final, that's that and I can't get into it any further way. I knew he'd gone as far as he could with telling me his new dilemma. Now he was ready to hear mine. He let his long legs fall apart at the knee, scrunched down in his chair, and postured himself differently, the way he used to when he was just Mercer. Once again, my best friend was setting himself aside to help me with my trauma.

22

[MARCY, MARCY ME]

I huddled on top of Mercer's leather couch with my hands underneath my bottom to keep my thighs from sticking. Mercer was looking at me steadily, the way he always does when he wants me to spill it. His eyes are soft and stern at the same time. They remind me of an old, loyal dog. I pulled the Kleenex onto my lap and started in.

"See, you remember how I told you that I have been seeing this guy since back in freshman year, right? And we have been kicking it for years now. But, like, all this shit started to go down spring semester, right? And it all got shot to hell or something, and now it's done, only I don't know if I want it to be done, but I don't know any other way it can be. It's so messed up…" Another jag of ugly, raucous tears. I had never really spoken to anyone at school about my relationship with Sal. Maybe a little to Kiko, and real superficial stuff with Khalil, but I never get too deep with them about my personal business.

Mercer was licking the whipped cream off the top of his latte and keeping his eyes, warm and unmoving, on me. He always listened to the whole story without comment, waited until the very end to say anything. "Okay, now, calm down. Whatever it is, it ain't nothing but a thing; we can figure it out. Go on."

He had this way of cutting my hysteria at the root by encouraging me to trace the source and work through it logically.

"Remember when, umm, me and you… after prom?" Mercer nodded without a flinch or a giggle. "Okay, so, you know how we were going to like, kick it on the internal, right? And how you wanted to but I… like… panicked or something?"

Mercer blinked his eyes to show me he was listening. I knew I had his full ear, and I wanted to take my time so that maybe, somehow, we could figure out what went wrong between me and Sal. I sipped my latte and plunged on.

"Well, it's kind of like that." I couldn't speak the words, didn't want to admit the I had not changed or grown since that time we tried to do it in high school. I felt my cheeks getting hot on the inside, down along my jaw line. I ran my tongue over my teeth and swallowed hard.

"Yah. So. This weird kind of frenzy panic thing happens when I, uhh, am trying to be close to Sal. Same as that night with you. It's messing me up." I tried to look casual as I picked up my cigarette and lit it, funneling smoke through my nose just for the burning it would cause. I needed a physical distraction.

"And? What are you saying, Digs? You broke up with this dude over sex?"

"Not exactly, but sort of. I mean, not being able to actually do it has put, like, a wedge between us. And then there's the other thing. The crying and night shakes..." I needed a little space, the space of a few moments, to get into the part about Sal, his family, and his dead cousins.

Mercer stretched his long legs out in front of him and crossed his feet. He seemed a little surprised when he saw the nail polish on his toes. He didn't make a comment, but it was as if he didn't understand for a minute why the color was there, like he was surprised at his own body.

"Okay. Who has the night shakes? You or him? And what do you mean by night shakes, exactly?" He furrowed his brow a little to prepare himself. He put his right foot over his left leg and held his foot in his hand, like he wanted to cover up the nail polish.

"What's the matter, there, Marcy? That's not the right color for you?" Sarcasm was always my way of dealing with a difficult situation.

"No, Digs. Don't try it. This is not about me right now; it's about you. Now, back to the night shakes.

It is a weird dynamic Mercer and I have. We are basically peers and all, though he is a little older than me. But he has always been strict whenever we are talking about my problems. Like he's my father or something. Which is literally impossible. Yet, for some reason, I need his strictness and appreciate when it kicks in, especially in the middle of an emotional dilemma.

"Righto, Cap'n. Ever since, oh, about a year or so ago, I have spent the occasional night over at Salmon's apartment. We like to cuddle and sleep next to each other. He is so cute when he sleeps, Merc! He is so strong and gentle at the same time—I love it! But as I began to sleep over there more often, and as he sometimes slept over at my apartment, I noticed that sometimes he gets, uh, nervous in the middle of the night." I was still searching for the right words because, though I was technically broken up with him, I didn't want to paint Sal in a negative light. Mercer is real protective of me, and he will encourage me to eighty-six someone quick if he thinks they are problematic in any way, shape, or form.

"You know you're driving me crazy with this half stepping mess, right?" He lifted his left brow at me.

"Yah. Okay, he tosses and turns and, like, boxes the air and stuff. Sometimes he talks and cries out saying no, no! Used to not happen so much, but these last few weeks it happens all of the time." Tapping the ashes into the overflowing ashtray, I picked the ashtray up and went over to the wastebasket to throw the ashes out.

"Ah, ah, ah! Not in there, Dignity. I put the ashes in the bag next to the big can in the kitchen. They have to go out every day. I don't put ashes in my trash cans, so they don't stink. It's bad enough having the smell in the carpets and in the curtains."

I took the ashtray out to the kitchen. I heard Mercer clear his throat, so I knew he was about ready to speak his mind. "So, how does this night thing relate to your sex panic? Build that bridge for me." He called out to me from the living room.

Before answering, I looked around the kitchen area and noticed how there wasn't a dish in the sink, how the counters were shining and clear of everything but a spice rack, a toaster, and a coffee maker. Cabinets sparkled, floors looked as sanitary as hospital beds. Loved it! "I'm not exactly sure that they relate at all, except that they were both part of the ultimatum. See, he didn't want to take me to the Easter celebration, but he wanted me to 'work through' my sex panics. I wasn't having it!" I felt growing anger about Sal's therapy expectation, and my hunger grew as well. I realized that I hadn't had any real food since yesterday sometime. I opened the fridge to see what I could grab.

"Now, I know you're not in there meddling in my kitchen, messing everything up. You hungry or something?" I could hear Mercer's heavy footsteps coming back to the kitchen, and I quickly closed the refrigerator door. He had a pet peeve about that—people messing up his kitchen. Never wanted anyone to open the fridge or peek in the cabinets without asking. Not even me.

"Oh, so you still trip about the kitchen, huh? Remember how you were always in charge of the kitchen at your mom's house? Even *she* didn't go in the cabinets or mess with the fridge without your permission! Wonder what she does now that you are gone?"

"Worries me to death! Calls me every five minutes about what did I do with this or where can she find that. But nothing has changed. I didn't rearrange everything before I moved out! What you want to eat, Digs?" He leaned on the fridge door with his arms outstretched, as if he was guarding a rare treasure. He wasn't selfish at all; he just didn't want anybody moving things around or spilling something, or, God forbid, leaving something out on the counter.

"What time is it? Can't we order in?" I checked my watch. It was a little past midnight.

"Now I know you've been away too long! You know the only place that delivers is that pizza joint, and they stop delivering at ten p.m. If you want something, I'm going to have to make it for you." He reached into the drawer by the stove and pulled out a long butcher's apron that was stark white. Then he washed his hands and said, "Have a seat, Madame. I am at your service!" Mercer loved to cook, but he especially loved all those fancy schmancy dishes from the cooking shows. If Julia Child has made it, Mercer has, too. And it always tastes great. But me, I'm a down-home kind of girl. I don't want anything exotic or weird.

I sat down at the little kitchen table—round glass with brass-limbed chairs, all close to the kitchen window, with its crystal clear surface and two tiers of heavy gauze curtains in almond brown. I knew better than to put my elbows on the table, because Mercer doesn't go for that. Bad manners, he says, and creates smudge marks, as well.

"I don't care, Merc. Whatever is quick and easy! I haven't had a bite since I don't know when. But, yah. Sal thinks I need therapy to overcome my sex panic. He says it's not about sex but about intimacy." I pushed the chair back and rested my left arm on the windowsill. There was no one out in the parking lot, and it was very quiet. Most of the lights were out in the windows on the rest of the block.

"I don't know, Digs. He might be right. It just might be an intimacy thing. If it is, it's worth looking into." From the back, he was the old Mercer, with the broad shoulders and the well-defined butt. I could still see why he had all the girls vying for his attention. Life can be so weird.

"Why are you taking his side, Merc? How should he know if I have an intimacy issue? And so what if I do? What business is that of his? Of anybody's!"

"Just go on. What is this Easter thing about? Give me the rest of the details, and we'll see." He reached in the fridge for an onion and green pepper, pulled out four eggs and some milk. He laid these out on the counter while he looked in the cabinet for spices, in another cabinet for a small, metal mixing bowl, in still another for a whisk.

I breathed deep and gave him the details. I spared him nothing. Told him about how much I wanted to be with Sal, how much I loved him. About Sal's dad and his views on race. About how Sal wanted more time before introducing me to his family. How his night sweats are related to his dead cousins. How he wants us both to have therapy. That these were my reasons for coming home so quickly and with such a heavy heart. And maybe for not going back.

He listened, glancing up at me now and again to see the look on my face when I described my last attempt at intimacy. Nodding his head to show he was listening as he flipped the omelet into a perfect fold. Pouring off the extra grease from the bacon skillet so the meat could get crisp, like I like it. Sipped his coffee wordlessly while I ate my delicious midnight breakfast. I explained how I didn't want to lose Sal but didn't know how to address the issues surrounding our relationship. I finished the meal and let the last of my energy drain from my face. "My goodness that was good. Thanks so murch!" I said, imitating the Southern dialect we had both grown up hearing.

"Hmm. No problem." Mercer sighed with a weightiness that spelled intimacy. "I hear that." He reflected for a moment, clearing his throat again, and then he launched in.

23

[EMOTIONALLY UNAVAILABLE]

"I hate to say this, Digs, because you know that you are my best girl, and I only want you to be happy, but it does sound like you and Rocky Romano may want to get some outside help." My best friend was leaned back in the kitchen chair with his hands crossed over his chest.

"His name is Salmon Rinaldi." I knew he was getting Sal's name wrong out of some weird form of jealousy.

"Whatever. The point is, both of you have got issues..."

"What do you mean, issues? I mean, of *course* we have issues. Doesn't everyone? Tell me something I don't already know!"

Mercer slid his chair back and began to clear the table. I knew he wouldn't be able to sit with the kitchen out of order for long.

"Well, here's something you may not know, Dignity. It seems like you and your Italian stallion are emotionally unavailable. You can't get but so close to someone when your emotions are on lockdown. And that's why you may need some therapy. It really could help."

I swallowed hard and began to chew the inside of my cheek. The area was raw and had the metallic taste of blood. I had been chewing it, a nervous habit, since that night in front of the apartments with Sal. I sipped on the water Mercer'd served me to clear up the stinging. "So, you're on that whole therapy band-wagon, huh? Not likely. You know me, Merc. How am I gonna spill my guts to a stranger that I don't even know, to figure out why I don't want to be emotion-ally intimate with my boyfriend? It doesn't make sense. Become intimate with a stranger to find out why I'm not intimate with the man I love best? Get real!"

"First of all, I thought *I* was the man you loved best. But, I guess I hear you.

Still, if you want to get past this roadblock, then you are going to have to be willing to do the work. If not with a therapist, then on your own." He rinsed and dried the dishes I'd used and put them away in their rightful places. He was beginning to move more slowly, so I knew that he was as tired as I was.

"No. You're the *woman* I love the best. Hah! No competition, Mercer. You know that. But, how would I, ahh, do this on my own, do you think?"

"You can't love the fruit until you get to know the root, Digs. And if you don't love the fruit, well. Ain't much you can give to somebody else. You gotta take a deep breath and go find out." Shoulders rather hunched now with fatigue and cold, Mercer put the butcher's apron away in the drawer, motioned me out to the hallway in front of the steps, and led me upstairs to the extra bedroom.

I grabbed my purse on the way up the steps before asking, "What do you mean, know the root?" It sounded like unintelligible baloney to me, but then, nothing made much sense by that point.

"Think about it. We'll talk about it tomorrow. You can take the other bedroom, but fold the comforter down and put it in the chair next to the bed. And don't be smoking in there, neither. Go downstairs to do that. I have an appointment in the morning, but I may be back before you get up. If not, there's some bagels in there. Just leave the plate in the sink, and don't be rummaging around in my business. And if you leave, grab the extra keys on the front table. Never know when you may want to crash here again. Lock the top but not the bottom. That one's a bitch to unlock! Otherwise, make yourself at home!" Mercer laughed at his long list of requirements, knowing how bizarre he sounded, and went into the bedroom down the hall. "Love you, Babe. It'll be alright!" I heard him say from behind the door; then I heard the click of his door locking.

True to form, my thoughtful friend had left a T-shirt on the bed along with a face cloth, towel, toothbrush, and travel-size toothpaste. I slipped on the shirt, placed the toiletries on the dresser, and flung the comforter on the chair before dropping on the bed and zoning completely out.

But once again my dreams were breathless and disturbing. I kept thinking of what Mercer had said about needing to know the root to love the fruit.

What was the root, anyway? The source I guess. My personal history. But, then, I already knew my personal history, so that couldn't be it. He must mean my family history. Good grief. It would take some doing to find out about that. And the way that my family guarded its history, I doubted that it would help me so much as hurt me even worse.

24

[THE ROOT]

I heard Mercer leave out around eight a.m., and I was up, in the shower, and dressed in the T-shirt and sweats he left me before nine a.m. I grabbed my purse and went down to the kitchen. Mercer did leave bagels, but there was no cream cheese, and I was afraid to look for coffee, even though there was a coffee maker on the counter. Mercer might have a tizzy, and I wasn't ready for all that. I poured a small tumbler of water and sat down at the kitchen table. I fumbled through my purse for my steno pad and a pen.

Finding Dignity, I wrote at the top of the first clean page. *Who am I, and Where am I From* I added as a subtitle. Then, I put the pen down and began to think. I blanked out, clueless. Okay, think back to the root, like Mercer said. I skipped a few spaces and began to list the family members that I knew.

My mother is Rebecca Pearson. She is a jazz singer. She doesn't come around anymore, and last I heard she had stopped talking. She may have some answers about lineage, but obviously she's not going to give any, if she won't talk. Plus, who knows where she is. My father, now I have no idea who he was. Alls I know is he is dead and he was white. Not a lot to go on. My grandmother, Mama Pearl, had a stroke in 1990, and she is not always in the best state of mind. She's forgetful. My mama's sister, Aunt Ruty, lives in Versailles most of the time, but she comes over to take care of my grandmother a lot during the week, to help the nurses out. Apparently my grandmother is difficult, but I don't know that firsthand. I also have an uncle named Timmy who is in the service and Uncle Albert, who sings in the band with my mama. Like Mama, though, he is not very accessible. Uncle Timmy is overseas. And, of course, there's my great-aunt, the one who raised me, Aunt Lette and her husband, Uncle Sam Jackson. They gave me their last name when I was three, when I first moved in with them.

My list contained many names and many dead leads. I drew a light line through the names of those who would not be able or willing to give me any information about my parents. Aunt Lette never gave me any straight answers, always said I was a direct gift from God, sent to keep her young and happy. Ain't Angus didn't keep close enough ties with my grandmother to really know for sure. Judging from the list, the best bet would be Aunt Ruty, just like Ain't Angus had said.

When I was here at Christmas, Ain't Angus mentioned that my Aunt Ruty rented the back of a hair shop out in east end. She sews, but Angus won't give her the respect of calling Aunt Ruty a seamstress. Says Aunt Ruty can't hold a candle to her. I believe it, too. Everybody talks about how well Ain't Angus used to sew. She built all kinds of clothing, even hats. But she doesn't do it anymore. Now she just works crossword puzzles and meddles in other people's business.

Find Aunt Ruty's shop, I wrote on my bulleted list. Underneath, I indented and wrote *Call/Pay a Visit*. I closed up the book and dumped it into my purse. Stuck the pen into my hair behind my ear and slipped into my sandals. I grabbed a napkin and left Mercer a note saying I was going to move in at Aunt Lette's and to call me when he got home. I took the set of keys he left for me and hustled back out to Lex. I had not called Aunt Lette to remind her that I was finished with school for the semester (and maybe for good). She always expected me to call or show up around this time anyway.

On the way into town, I got a shiver and remembered what I'd run into last night. The whole Marcy thing. All I could do was shake my head and chuckle. I am a bleeding-hearted liberal and a true revolutionary, but even *I* didn't expect Mercer to pull this. Something about it was not ringing true, anyway. Seemed affected. But, selfishly, I didn't have time at that moment to do a close reading of this new image. I was too preoccupied with this new decision to find out about my family, namely my father.

Aunt Lette and Uncle Sam's house, where I grew up, is a small rancher in a pretty decent, mixed neighborhood. It has three bedrooms and a small, closet-sized room where she keeps her important papers and menus from all over the country. She has people bring them back for her when they go out of town. She has only been out of Kentucky a few times, to Detroit and to Chicago and once to Baltimore to visit me. But she still collects menus from fancy restaurants. If she sees something in one that she likes, she might try to find a recipe for it and fix it for me and Uncle Sam. She's a good cook, but I like her regular stuff better. Cooking is something she and Mercer have in common, and that's why they get on so famously.

I collected my baggage from the trunk and, encumbered, stumbled through the front door. The house was quiet. "Hello? It's Dignity! I'm home!" My voice echoed and went unanswered as I dragged the luggage down the hall to my bedroom.

Everything was as I left it, peach walls and rainbows everywhere you looked. That and unicorns, which I began collecting in eighth grade. I dropped the bags and plopped on my bed. It smelled like pine needles. Aunt Lette was crazy for the scent of pine, especially in the winter. I tried to explain to her that pine is not right for warm weather, but she didn't listen. I stripped down to my T-shirt and fumbled in my drawer for socks. I always kept socks and underwear at home, so that, if something were to happen and I were to lose my baggage, I would still have clean underclothes. I could see myself borrowing some of Aunt Lette's clothes, but I couldn't see borrowing *anyone's* underwear. And I would need underwear, even if I had to go to K-Mart to buy new ones. I don't believe in no underwear. Seems unsanitary. The thought of borrowing another's panties made me so nervous that I wanted to wash my hands, but I resisted the urge. I stretched out, closed my eyes and started to zone.

Two minutes later I was at Sal's apartment cuddling on the couch with him while he read the newspaper. He read me the highlights, knowing I wanted to keep informed but that I couldn't stand to read the paper, since it always left black ink on my hands. I like to keep my hands clean. The scent of Cool Water cologne was lifting my spirits, and for a second, I felt clean and safe. The next thing you know, we are kissing really passionately, our bodies hammered together even though we are fully clothed. And I'm whispering to him, urging him to undress me, when Mercer shows up wearing the gold dress I wore to the Que Jam Sal and I went to when we first met. Mercer was turning around in the dress, saying, "I'll bet she'll like this! She's gotta be in favor of this!" Even though he doesn't say it, I know he is referring to his mom. I sit up and push Sal away, ready to scold Mercer for wearing my clothes, when I hear someone calling me.

"Baby? You struggling like something's got hold to you—wake up! Come on out of that whatever it is you dreaming, now. You know it scares me when you talk in your sleep!" Aunt Lette was standing over my bed. She had on a powder blue suit with a white bow blouse and white pantyhose. Had a pillbox hat on, too, powder blue pumps, and a blue and white bag. She looked beautiful and smelled like Youth Dew. I jumped up to hug her.

"Aunt Lette! Yay! I am so glad to see you! You look awesome—where've you been?"

"Where have *I* been? I been around to the fashion show luncheon they put on every year at First Baptist. Went with Ethel and some of them. None of the clothes was that much—didn't buy anything. Question is, where *you* been? Somebody said you been in town since yesterday without coming home!" Aunt Lette pulled off her shoes, laid them on the floor next to her bag, and then sat down on the bed. She had a slightly joking tone in her voice, but I knew she wanted an explanation.

"How do you know that? Amazing! Anyways, I did get here yesterday, but, umm, it was a weird hour, so I went to Ain't Angus', first. New suit?" I rubbed my face on my aunt's shoulder and breathed her in. I needed her scent, her comfort so much.

"I know you better take your oily skin off of my suit, too, with your worrisome self! Got this two, three years ago. You've seen it and don't remember. When's the last time you ate? Look like a holocaust victim!" Aunt Lette fussed, but she was smiling. "Come on, let's go in the den. I gotta get out of these clothes before Sam Wayne gets home!"

I went to the other end of the house, to the den, and Aunt Lette hurried back to her bedroom. She used the extra bedroom as a guest room, but she had filled the closet and dresser in there with clothes. Had her perfumes all over the dresser and two or three shoe racks. Aunt Lette was a clothes horse, loved to dress. But Uncle Sam didn't like it when she went to First Baptist for fashion shows and stuff. He was strict Holiness. However, Aunt Lette slipped and went sometimes, behind his back.

I sat in the den and flipped on the television. Nothing but soaps on, and I don't usually watch soaps. I used to, when I lived at home. Me and Aunt Lette and Mercer watched the ABC shows religiously. Especially *All My Children*. It was about to come on. I hadn't watched it in a while, so I didn't know what was going on, but I wanted to watch with Aunt Lette, like old times.

"You know, I shouldn't fool with them around to First Baptist anyway. Now, the program clearly says ten-thirty a.m. to twelve-thirty p.m. Supposed to hit it and quit it! It got to be twelve and they had barely brought out the chicken, so I knew we were in for the long haul. Naw. Finished lunch and came on home. Didn't even stay for dessert. Sam Wayne'll be back from meeting soon, and I don't aim to be around to the Baptist church, waiting around for dessert, after watching some sorry dresses and pants outfits when he told me no. You got the stories on?" Aunt Lette had changed into a sleeveless housedress with two big pockets and snaps up the front. Seemed like she had lost a little weight, which she really didn't need to do. She is small and skinny, like me, but she doesn't have the behind that I have. She had on some of Uncle Sam's dress socks and pink house shoes. She sat on the couch next to the phone, where she always sits.

"Probably didn't miss much. None of them can bake like you, anyway. It's about to come on. Fill me in on what's happening. Whatever happened to Phoebe, and what about Brooke and Tad?"

Aunt Lette brought me up to speed on the latest soap happenings, and we watched together. Both of us yelled at the screen when someone did something stupid, and I applauded when Erica came on, perfect and beautiful as always. She's one of my idols. We'd been watching for half an hour when a commercial came on and the phone rang. Aunt Lette answered. I could tell it was Mercer calling by the way she was talking. She handed me the phone. He must have been watching, too, because he was also shocked at Erica's latest antics.

"Digs? I see you got home alright. So, what are you giving us this season?" Mercer was speaking quickly, trying to check in before the show came back on.

"Nothing. Made a list, though. You know. What we talked about."

"What? Addressing your emotional availability? Due to your lack of knowledge about lineage and self? What did you write?"

"Just exploring the possibilities. Thinking about, ah, my aunt and the root." I said this cryptically, not wanting my aunt to understand since she was listening to every word I said. "Call me back when this is over. Hope you're available today." I hung up the phone and went back to watching with my aunt.

"Girl, what you and Mercer up to? 'The root' and all this? Haven't been here but a minute and already y'all are up to those old schemes! What is it now?"

I wished the show would come on so I didn't have to answer. "Nothing. Just thought I might get in touch with Aunt Ruty, that's all. I haven't seen her since freshman year! And she's my family!" I regretted making this last comment. Aunt Lette was always sensitive about my mentioning other members of the family, ones who might be closer kin than herself. She was my mama figure, and she didn't want to share this space in my heart with anybody else. The thing is, she doesn't, but she never seems to recognize that. Ain't Angus is like a mom, too, but she didn't raise me.

"Mmm. Not like she's been beating the door down to see you, either, Dignity. What you want with her for?" Her brow furrowed and she looked angry or worried.

"I know. I just thought it would be nice to say hello. Chat, you know." Finally, the soap came back on, riveting our eyes to its melodrama.

"Mmm-hmm. You be careful with that. She and your mama make enough strange choices. May be better to let well enough alone." She sucked her teeth a little to show her disapproval.

"What strange choices, Mommy?" She loved it when I called her that, even though she always used to tell me not to, out of respect for my own mama.

"Auntie." She corrected me. "Shh shh shh, now. The stories are back on." She set her chin and crossed her legs to let me know she was done talking about it. I made a mental note of her comment on strange choices and decided I'd take it up with her later. I leaned over some, lying on the couch with my head in Aunt Lette's lap. She fluffed up my hair and patted my head. It felt good to be home.

The Sound of Silence

[HARRODSBURG, KY 1985]

25

[SISTER BECCA PEARSON]

Sister, or Sister 'Becca, as she was now called on the Southeastern Chitterling Circuit, walked into the efficiency apartment that came with her latest contract. It was dimly lit and poorly decorated. Sister Rebecca didn't care. She had long since stopped worrying about colors and lace and flowers. Life had killed that stuff out of her.

On this day, she had called Edward, one of the members of her singing group *Sister 'Becca and Them*, (Edward was also her husband, though she rarely acted like it), and told him she was heading out to Georgetown to take care of some business. Edward knew that a trip to Georgetown was another name for trouble, and he asked her not to go. But he did it halfheartedly because Becca had stopped listening to him years ago. So instead of pleading with her, he asked if she planned to be back in time for that night's gig. She said she would. He asked her if she needed him to go with her. She said she didn't.

Becca, Edward, Albert, and Pam were scheduled to sing that night at the lodge. They would be performing two sets every Friday, Saturday, and Sunday night for the rest of the month. Julian, the owner, seemed to have a deal with the fire department because he filled this joint past capacity every night, but he never got suspended or even fined.

Julian lived with a woman named Barbara and had for years. But his wife, Cammy, whom he never officially divorced, did all the cooking at the club. Macaroni and cheese, fried chicken, catfish—Cammy threw down. And she baked, too. Sometimes during the week, folks would come by after work just to pick up a plate to take home with them. And on the weekends you better get there plenty early if you wanted to eat *and* see the show, much less have a seat.

Julian owned a second-rate building of efficiencies right next to the lodge. As part of the contract, he gave *Sister 'Becca and Them* the whole third floor. Becca had her own apartment. Edward had the one next door, but Edward usually stayed with Becca. Pam and Albert stayed in the one across the hall. They ate most of their meals at the club, since the food was so good, but they did have their own kitchens if they wanted to cook. Mainly greens. Cammy never cooked them as good as Pam, and Albert always wanted some kale on Sundays. Small living area with a space for sleeping and surprisingly large bathrooms.

Now, a few weeks previous, a whole group of folks came over from Georgetown, a mixed bag of tricks. Most of them were white, although two of the girls looked like they might have had some Native American in them. One of them was a heavy set, blue collar redneck with a coarse red beard, bear hands, and a low slung belly. His skin was yellowish and tan. He seemed to be with one of the Native American-looking girls. Must have been about five or six of them combined. They sat at a table right up near the stage, ate plenty of pulled pork barbeque and drank pitcher after pitcher of beer.

Sister 'Becca and Them came out at nine forty-five p.m., same as always for the first set. The house band (Lips on guitar, Dog on drums, Benny on bass, and Nelson on piano) played a cover tune, usually something by Earth Wind and Fire or Stevie Wonder, and 'Becca and Them took their places on stage. No sooner had the quartet launched into their trademark version of "God Bless the Child" than that low-bellied beer guzzler started making a lot of noise. Not heckling, really, but hooting and whistling and being a real disturbance. He was calling out saying, "Look a there, fellas! That there's my next of kin!" That's where it started. They'd come in regular, each time with the bear-handed one calling out in familiarity to Sister Becca.

Somewhere toward the end of the '70s, way after Brown vs. the Board of Ed, they started forcing integration in the school systems all over Kentucky. They bussed in black folks to mainly white schools and a handful of white folks to mainly black schools. It was a disaster for a while. But long about the mid '80s, young folk had gotten rather used to one another, and it was almost a fashion of sorts to mingle with other races. Especially the ones who played sports or who were involved in the music programs. They traveled together to competitions and hung out together even out of school sometimes. It got so it was almost normal to see a group of young people, white and black, eating together or walking around the malls together, or even going to a club.

But for Julian and the folks who frequented *his* club, this interracial stuff was still suspect. Far as Julian and his regulars could tell, it always meant trouble. So, when that mixed group would come in, even though none of them looked black that was with them, per say, Julian got his back up, and the bouncer, Ray Charles, no relation, kept his hand on his club, ready.

Then last weekend, sure as rain, that group came back again, only this time one of the girls they had with them was black, sure enough. And the one with the low belly decided it was time he got to know Sister Becca up close and personal. Same as always, he was belting back the brew and boasting to his friends, "That there is my next of kin, sure enough!" But one of his buddies didn't believe him, said he was bluffing. That's when low belly decided to tap Becca on the shoulder as she came off the stage toward the bar and invite her over for a chat. To "swap remembrances," as they say.

Edward was always the first off the stage during a set, because he always sweated so much. He liked to clean up in the restroom as soon as they finished singing. And as protective as he was of Becca, he never would have let low belly near her if he'd seen him approach. But because Edward was in the bathroom, and since Sister had already managed a low-grade buzz (Sister Becca'd taken to drinking whiskey and bourbon by then), she went over to that table to "swap remembrances," as they say.

Well, Pam and Albert went out front, like usual, so Pam could get some air and Albert could have a smoke in peace, and Sister took her whiskey and had a seat with low belly and friends. Julian had his eye on them the whole time, and at first it seemed to be going fine. Then Julian noticed low belly getting loud, saying, "What am I gonna lie for? Tellin' you the truth! Come on out to the house with me, and see for yourself—talk to Della. She'll tell you!" He didn't have anger in his voice exactly. Just passion.

Sister slid back her chair and said, "Uh-uh. Naw-naw. You hush your mouth!"

Edward came out of the bathroom, and that's all he needed to see: Sister Becca upset and trying to move away from a low-bellied, bear-handed white man. He walked over, held the bear-handed man at arm's length by pressing his hand into his face, and directed Becca in a calm voice: "Becca, go on back to the apartment now, go! I be up there shortly." Soon, Ray Charles, no relation, was over at the table with his billy club in his hand, asking was there a problem. Low belly's friends didn't want the hassle, so they threw money down on the table and forced him out to their Ford pickup—three in the front, and the rest of them in the back. The truck bed was covered with dirty Mexican blankets.

Next thing you know, Becca was calling Edward on the phone saying she was going to Georgetown to take care of some business. Back in the room that night, after she'd sat with low belly, Edward drilled her to find out what low belly had said, what had made her upset, but she wouldn't say. Plus, Edward felt like he probably already knew, anyway. He just didn't want to put a word to it. Nobody did.

When Sister got back from that trip, she kicked off her sandals, changed into her stage clothes, poured herself a bourbon with crushed ice and lemon, and she didn't say a word. Not a single word. To this day she will sing, but she will not speak. Not so much as a hello to anybody. Ever. Whatever happened that day in Georgetown, it took her words from her, and she has never spoken since.

26

[HERSTORY]

Sister Becca had never really gotten away from the scarf bottoms and Danskin that colored the late 1970s. She'd patterned her life so closely after divas of that period until finally she bridged that fine line between Donna Summer and Chaka Khan. Permanently. She got away with her dated look because she was a performer. Audiences assumed she was dressing in costume. They did not recognize that Sister Becca dressed that way because she had never officially left that era. Something told her that she would not be able to survive the 1980s, so she settled back permanently into 1977, in her dress and in her mind.

Seven years past her prime but with Becca none the wiser, Sister 'Becca and Them got tired and fussy. They had been touring steadily, resting at small venues and Black-owned businesses all over the country, but toward the end of 1984, somewhere around Pittsburgh, the group decided to go home. They'd had enough. Albert contacted Jimmy, their agent, and he arranged a short-term local gig in Harrodsburg, close to their hometown in Kentucky.

The foursome had begun to chafe each other: Pam had a tendency toward tantrums and loud, country tirades. Albert, back in 1972, had become the self-appointed leader of the local (imaginary) revolution. Sister Becca, bless her heart, had never gotten over what happened in '72, when Albert gave speeches and acquired a following. The year that she gave birth to a dead man's Dignity. The year her spirit sailed off so fast it knocked the wind out of her and set her on her bottom: '72, when somewhere in her heart she was trampled to the ground and always, always needed a good, stiff drink: '72, when Edward loved Sister so richly that he sacrificed his own dreams to help Sister through her worst nightmares.

So that day, a day soon after a group of ethnically integrated hillbillies came into Julian's club, a blended bunch of pork eaters, beer drinkers; a day soon after a bear-handed fellow flipped up his pudgy finger to tap Sister on the shoulder and breathe the past into her face; that day Sister Becca put on a banana yellow Danskin dress, one that crisscrossed at the breast and had an uneven bottom, a pair of strappy, yellow, patent-leather platform spike-heeled shoes, and she picked her hair out until it flew down in feverish orange raves from her head. She armed herself with Charlie perfume. She rolled on Tussy, Jean Nate powder, Nivea skin cream, dreamsicle lipstick. Mainly, she placed a small nickel-plated flask, engraved with the name "Norman" and filled with Wild Turkey, inside of her gold space sack bag.

"Imma go 'head on and go, now," she said to no one in particular in the hallway of the place she called home.

She left early. Once the sun rose up with sherbet-mellow haze to the east, Sister Becca felt the rays on her back, driving west. Her insulated travel mug was full with coffee, light, sweet, and wild with whiskey. She was heading away from the sun.

She couldn't turn it off. That night back at Mama's, back home, back of her house, back of that field, back of her mind.

"Naw." She spat through the window, took a sip from the nickel flask.

She swallowed until the attacker's hands, popping with fat and yet sharp as farm tools, slid from her arms, down her waist, and to the ground. She swallowed two more times to escape the hot, silvery saliva he injected down there, in her middle, where it wound itself into a coil and wrapped around everything she had that was deep and internal.

She drove down the road further until the ground lay out on its stomach and wove out blue and green ribbons in equal measure on either side of the highway. She passed horses and passed cows, lazy in the meadow, tails swinging fat flies and yellow bees. Passed these and an hour further, Sister Becca began squinting and looking. Green eye shadow showing through yellow sunglasses with over-sized rims. When it got to be nearly five minutes between houses, Becca started to count them and breathe humility.

A late-model Chevy on cement blocks. A rusted basketball hoop. Brown-skin jockeys in dark pants and red jackets holding lanterns. A patch of vegetables, bronzing in the sun. Becca looked at these images separately, evenly, and none of them seemed connected or pregnant with meaning. Then she saw the house that she was looking for, a red Ford pick-up parked in front. From the flask, another long, hollow swallow.

There was cornflower on the grass out there, and so she smiled. This made Sister think of a man she used to know. A man who offered his heart like holy water in a fluted summer glass. Her precious Evian, the memory of whom had kept her alive in these last years. She propelled herself forward to the front door with the volition of lost love.

The Chasingers

[GEORGETOWN, KY 1985]

27

[DELLA CHASINGER]

D ella's place was ratty but clean. The carpets in the house had been swept bare, and they were dingy, but they didn't contain a speck of dirt. It was a shotgun house where she lived; her granddaddy had built it himself in the early part of the century, and her daddy had added the appliances, an indoor bathroom, and built a small upstairs bedroom back in the late '60s. Daniel had added the front porch in 1974. Didn't stick around much to enjoy it, though.

The house had only a few rooms. There was the front room where they recently added a floor-model television with a built-in record player and tape deck. A kitchen with built-in cabinets and a large baker's rack for a pantry. Back of that was the big bedroom with the brass bed; in the middle was the medium bedroom with the twin beds and the wood burning oven; and in the back was the small room that faced the backyard. There was a door on the side of the small room that led to the upstairs room Daddy built for a guest house when his people came to stay. They stopped coming, though, a few years before Daddy died.

In the front room, on top of the floor-model television, was the picture collection that Della started when Daddy died.

Dell never knew her mother—she died nine months after Della was born, so Dell had been raised by her daddy, her paternal granddaddy and Mum-Mum. Granddaddy and Mum-Mum got married when Mum-Mum was fourteen; he was six years her senior. And the two stayed together until the day she died. Granddaddy died a year later on the same date as Mum-Mum, but not in the same hour.

Daddy and Mama Carol, Dell's dead mother, married late, when Daddy was forty and Mama Carol was thirty-six. They had Della right off, after only four years of marriage. Since she'd had sugar since childhood, folks warned Mama

Carol against having young ones, but she was hell bent to do it. She wanted a young one, and she had one for long about nine months. Never had the strength to take care of the baby Della. Only nursed her once in the first week, and after that, Della started on cow's milk. Which Mum-Mum thought was a sorry shame, seeing as how the milk in Mama Carol's breast was made especially for Della. Never mind the fact that it had all dried up.

Mum-Mum always knew Della's daddy could do better than that for a wife. Said Carol was too "citified" and "thought she was prettier than what she was." Only lasted less than five years, but that less than marriage between Daddy and Mama Carol generated a whole lot of talk from Mum-Mum all of Della's life, and every bit of it was negative. And that's how come Della walked with her head bent toward the ground. That and the mess Daddy made of his cousin's family. She had shame circulating in her very blood.

So, there was only one picture of Mama Carol because, frankly, she came and went before the family got a camera. When she moved in with Daddy and them, only thing she bought with her was a picture of herself wearing a stiff cotton dress with a lacy collar, and a picture of her own mama.

Dell didn't know what happened to the picture of Mama Carol's mama. But she remembered the woman was fat with a heavy bust and silver-white hair piled up in a bun. She'd memorized the picture of her Mama Carol, though. The crease in her lower chin, the powder press matte finish of her cheeks and fore-head, the sausage fat curls dangling past her shoulders. The smoky flower smell that emitted somehow from her faded gray, paper smile.

All of the pictures were in white porcelain frames that had a delicate border of pink, yellow, and purple hand-painted flowers. Della had made them herself. Got the kit from the craft store. But the pictures came out of that trunk in the back room, where Daddy kept all of his treasures. And secrets. Photos, mostly of family: Daddy's brother; Uncle Thomas and Aunt Katherine; Della's cousin Theresa; and Theresa's rat bastard brother, Blister. Real name was Franklin. But the photo told the whole story of why nobody who saw him thought to call him anything other than Blister. Like someone squeezed the middle of his body until the blood, meat, and juice exploded up into his upper cavity of a head. Murdered years ago. Good riddance, Della thought, to bad rubbish. Grandma Willy,

Mum-Mum's best friend, and Willy's second husband, Fella. And that picture of her second cousin, Evian Mandarene, with his arm around Blister down at Kentucky Lake. She never understood how the two of them got to be such good friends, anyhow, Evian and Blister. Both of them were dead, so she guessed it didn't matter.

These were pictures of the old days, when they used to have fun together, roasting pork on the back barbecue and playing badminton, Della and Theresa. Blister off somewhere behind a tree spying on them or playing his guitar, when he was in a level mood. Granddaddy and Mum-Mum playing poker with the jar of nickels they kept in the kitchen to bet with. And the scent of honeysuckle so thick you could scoop it with your fingers just as sure as you could whipped cream. The good days, safe days of late spring and broad, endless summer.

Della Chasinger wiped the dustless frames on the television with a damp cloth, same as always, before stuffing the cloth in her apron pocket and sweeping the barren rugs with a nylon broom. She preferred nylon. The straw ones left remnants on the carpet, and she couldn't tolerate that. Everything had to be clean. She collected the imaginary dust that materialized in the eight hours while she slept into a metal dustpan and dumped it in the kitchen trash can. Which was sprayed with lemon-scented Lysol and transferred to the outside can every night just before dark.

She only dusted the back rooms lightly every other day and sometimes sprayed disinfectant on the furniture in there, but nobody ever slept in those rooms anymore and so they didn't require much cleaning. She herself slept in the front bedroom, the big room, which used to belong to her grandparents, and she had kept all the original furniture and many of the porcelain figurines Mum-Mum had collected. And the glass perfume spray bottles. Only thing really different was the small television on the nightstand and the crisp goldenrod bed sheets and comforter on the bed. She bought the set five years ago at K-Mart.

After her morning cleaning, Della looked at her wristwatch, a masculine, gold-plated number, with huge Roman numerals—she'd inherited from Granddaddy (informally—there was no will) and found it was heading toward ten a.m. She gave a satisfied sigh before putting up the broom and hanging the wipe cloth to dry. She kept the apron on all day, so as not to soil her clothes.

The steel fry pan she used to scramble her eggs was so shiny that she could clearly see her reflection: pale skin, relatively smooth, though, and soft, except around the eyes where she had permanent pigeon's feet, not from laughing but from squinting. Wild, coarse red hair that belonged on a horse's tail rather than a woman's head. Pastel blue eyes and long, cumbersome chin. Not ugly, but made to feel that way by circumstance and by Daniel, more so now, in his absence, than ever.

Nobody came around much anymore. Theresa, her cousin, called, but she had moved out past Paducah, not far from the Tennessee border, two years ago. They didn't see each other as often as they used to. At the time, Della'd lost her immediate family, and Daniel had been long gone. So Theresa asked her to come and stay with her and her husband, but Della wouldn't go. Creature of habit, she was. But besides those times when Theresa came to town with her husband and their new daughter, Teensy, or the occasional visit from members of the Willing Workers at the First Baptist Church, from whom she kept a careful distance, Della almost never had visitors.

So, she was surprised when she heard the pinched howl of the Taylors' dog, Buster, from way down the street. Stringy-haired mangy mutt was small, no bigger than two fists put together, but Lord how he howled. Della hated that dog and was certain such a small canine was not of God. Those Taylors were strange anyway. Never went to church, not even at Easter. She wouldn't be shocked if they had done something spiritually unsettling to produce that dog and the constant litter of cats they had running in the backyard. They were filthy.

Buster usually kept his howling for noon day, when he wanted to be fed, or dusk, when Mitchell Taylor got home from his in-town hustle (selling vegetables, shining shoes, running errands, fixing appliances—anything to earn a little money while never really committing to a 9-5. He was a heathen). It was irregular to hear the mutt howling at this hour. Della whisked a little more cheese into the bowl of eggs before sloshing them into the hot, buttered pan. Then she went out to the front room to look out the screened glass door and see what the commotion was about.

Moving slowly and creating a mist of fog in its wake was a white, late '70s model Cadillac, with a front and back end as long as a boat. She couldn't see who was behind the wheel, but she could tell that the person was not from around there and was looking for someone or something. The car had Fayette County tags, so she figured it was someone looking for the Moores or the Williams sisters, since they had people out in Lexington. Della went back to the kitchen relatively appeased and tossed her eggs lightly so they'd stay fluffy and bright yellow. Time to put the toast in the oven. She never used the toaster—seemed like the bread tasted fresher when she baked the toast a few minutes in the oven. By the time the teapot started to whistle, she could turn off the eggs, take out the toast, and make her cup of tea. A teaspoon of honey, a sprinkle of sugar, and the slightest bit of lowfat milk.

Della was deciding whether to use the gold-trimmed plates she grew up with or the sunflower-covered plates she'd ordered from Lillian Vernon last year. She'd chosen the flowered plate and matching saucer and was just about to set the hot breakfast on the kitchen table and say grace when she heard the soft rapping on the screened-in glass door. She was all prepared to give a lost Lexingtonian directions to the Moores' house down the road. Then she saw Sister Becca, behind sunglasses that almost covered her whole face, and with a heated head of spiraling curls jutting from her head and onto her slim shoulders. She had a space sack purse on her shoulder. Something in Sister Becca's countenance, in her perfumed essence, made her immediately recognizable to Della. This woman, without doubt, was the one Daniel had told her about.

Without waiting for an inquiry or giving an introduction, she led Sister Becca in and sat her down on the tapestry-covered divan while she put her temptingly hot breakfast in the heated oven so it would stay warm.

28

[DADDY'S PEOPLE]

S ister Becca felt her heart beating trouble inside of her throat. Her eyes scanned fleetingly the living room and the sofa where she sat, never resting on anything for more than a second. She noticed pictures but did not look long enough to identify faces or objects. She noticed that the place was old but clean, and in a strange way it reminded her of home. The carpets were especially clean, and she longed to take her platform shoes off and rub her tense toes.

From her seat, she could see into the kitchen, where the woman went, and she heard her fiddling with dishes and doors. She didn't pay attention but instead breathed a little before fishing in her bag for the nickel-plated flask. She was recovering from a brisk shot when the woman came back in the room, closing the door to the kitchen and sitting on the upholstered chair across from the couch. Sister rubbed the condensation from the flask. She fingered the engraved portion and hoped to draw strength from the name. Norman.

Della cleared her throat. "Hah! I can see we got something in common! Only I don't usually get started until after four p.m. You fine with that you got, or you want you a glass?" Della motioned at the whiskey-filled flask.

"This is fine, thanks." Sister held back a belch as she focused on a spot just above the woman's head.

"I guess I expected you'd come around sometime, but I didn't know when. They give you a flask, I see." She nodded again at the nickel-plated receptacle.

"Yes." Sister didn't stop to comment on the implications of this comment. How this woman recognized the flask or who it came from. She didn't come to talk, anyway. She came to listen.

"First, I just want to say that I know all about what happened, and it's shameful.

I'm shameful sorry for you. I can't imagine how you been getting on all these years. But I figured it was you in that sanging group, Sister 'Becca and Them. Always meant to get out there to see y'all perform. Out of respect."

Sister wrinkled her brow and prepared for the headache she knew would set in after she drank the next sip, the last sip, of her Wild Turkey. Sweat, like morning dew, popped up on her forehead, and she sat on her hands to keep them from shaking. "No disrespect, but what you know about me, Miss? Don't make sense. First that fella, name of Daniel is pulling me up at the lodge, and now you speak like you know my insides. S'cuse me if it seem a might strange…"

Della's eyes locked with Sister's for a blind moment followed by a second of mutual, naked exposure. Dell lifted her chin to this queer intimacy before placing her hands on her knees, lifting herself to her feet, and motioning this woman into the kitchen. "Kem on in the kitchen. I just fixed breakfast, and I specs you'se hungry, too. We's two of a kind, me and you. Might as well talk face-to-face. Might do us both some good."

Sister felt a cotton soft buzz as she slid out of her yellow, platform shoes and padded, barefoot, into the kitchen.

At the round kitchen table, Sister could see out into the front yard and a little down the street. Back from the direction she came. The smokey dirt was just beginning to settle out there, and she could hear the hungry howl of a small dog. If she squinted, she could see the outline of cornflowers that circled the driveway and boxed themselves around the mailbox. She focused on that blurring of blue as this woman brought her a mason jar and a half full bottle of Ancient Age whiskey. She also gave her fluffy yellow eggs and warm toast. Sister longed for country bacon but didn't say so. Sipped the tea the woman poured for her and added a shot of whiskey before taking another sip. When the burn came and went in her belly, Sister knew she was ready to listen. "I thank you kindly for this food, Miss. Umm, you say we's two of a kind or something?" Sister had her back to the woman, who was busy at the sink whisking more eggs and buttering more toast.

Before answering, the woman nodded her head even though she knew Sister couldn't see her. Then she trotted back to the end room to the box where Daddy kept his treasures. Pulled out the fat green album and thought about bringing the flask, but decided against it. She plopped the book down in front of Sister and went back to cooking the eggs.

Sister read the front page of the album: *The Chasinger Clan*, it read, in fancy cursive letters. The first page showed an old woman, maybe seventy, in a rocking chair with an older man towering over and behind her. The woman had no lips at all, and the man had a bottom lip and a full beard. Both had long silver hair, only the woman's was braided and pinned on top of her head. The man's was scraggly and long, past his shoulders. The next page showed a picture of the house Sister sat in, only there was no porch on the front like now. She wondered when this was taken. Must have been a while ago since it was a black and white photo.

"Specs we'll do this like a picture storybook. Might take some of the stink off it! Hah! Put a distance on things. That first one, that's my grandparents, Grandaddy Charles and Scarlet Chasinger. Always called her Mum-Mum. Everybody did, around to the church and all. Turn the page. That there is Mum-Mum and me, Della. That was round about 1953, in there, 'cause I was three years old or so. See that eyelet on the skirt? Mum-Mum loved that stuff. That and daisies. I had a piss load of dresses like that one until I was seven or eight; then she switched to plaid." Della turned the eggs out on the plate and sat down in the chair closest to Sister. Sister pushed the album over so it sat between the two of them and waited for more instructions.

Sister sat through the explanations of this woman's family, looking at Della in her daisies and later in her plaid, watched as the pictures turned color. Saw a broad-chested man named Harold, who was this woman's father; a dear friend name of Uncle Willy and her late husband, Oscar; and of her second husband, Fella. Sister tried hard not to yawn. Didn't want to appear rude. The woman had been generous with her time and her food. Even her whiskey, which both of them had begun to drink even though the woman said she doesn't do it until four p.m. But, Sister knew she would eventually have to go back to town for the show, and she wanted to make sure she got what she came for. Della had come to a picture of the low-bellied man, name of Daniel, who'd pulled Sister over the night before at the lodge. He looked a little younger and didn't have so much of a beard. Cleaned up in a suit and tie and Della under his left shoulder with too much pancake and a wide brim smile. Looked happy.

"Now, this here's the one from the lodge, what talked to me yesterday. Said we was next of kin…" Sister mustered courage to look into Della's eyes and test her reaction. The woman blanched a little but made sure not to sound fazed.

"Figures he'd say a clown thing like that. He's my ex."

"So, is it true…?" Sister kept her eyes planted on the album.

"Well. Sorta kinda. Not exactly. More like *you* and *I* are…umm…related. Skip those next few pages. Daddy and some of his army buddies. Let's see here. Yes! You know this man?"

The man was tall and handsome in a dark suit and suspenders. Hair was slicked back and came to a point in the front. He had an olive-tone tan and a smirk on his face. Both hands plunged deep in his pockets, and the shoes looked shiny and new. He was good looking.

"Naw. Can't say as I do. Who he?" Sister held the book up closer to her eyes to stare at the man's face. There was a familiar shine in his eyes, bare and honest. And his neck was thick and strong. Seemed like a sweetness came from him, even though it was just a picture. He was familiar, but she couldn't figure out why.

"That there is Norman."

Sister looked up quickly, fearful and hopeful, into the woman's eyes. "You mean…the one from…?" Sister didn't want to speak the words.

"Yep. One and the same. My Uncle Norman, Daddy's older brother. Daddy and Norman's brother, Uncle Tom was, uh, the father of my, uhh, first cousin. The one that, uhh, you know…" Della cleared her throat and turned to her eggs, started to whirl them into her mouth by the forks full out of hunger and anxiety. Sister followed the woman's lead, eating her eggs in small bites, breaking the edges off the toast and chewing them slowly. Completely blank through the face.

Dell began to jiggle her legs so bad that she almost spilled her tea. She could literally feel this woman's pain, and she didn't know what to do with it. Her own was so muted behind cleaning and whiskey and Bible verse. It had been a long time since Della had been so close to another's emotions. "So, you got a kid, right? A daughter?"

Sister blinked a few times, as if brisk wind had blown directly into her face. "Yes. Name of Dignity. She thirteen now." The words were delivered clinically, like she had read the words off a piece of paper that she did not own and did not fully understand. She smashed the last words behind cold toast. "Raised by my auntie."

The woman rose and, without asking, lifted the plate away from Sister along with her own. She washed them both and placed them in the rack to dry, and then she freshened both cups of tea. She pulled a round tray down from the top of the refrigerator and placed it on the table. Sister, as if instructed to do so silently, placed the whiskey bottle and the two tea cups and saucers on the tray, and then she held the kitchen door open while the woman passed through into the living room. Sister took her own saucer off the tray and sat again on the big couch. Della, hitching up her pants and placing one foot underneath her bottom, leaned back on the small couch and got comfortable.

"Been a long time since I spoke on Daddy's people. Real strange folk, you know. But, seems like you carrying a burden, like to break off your shoulders. I used to be like that. Not so much anymore. But, ah, you don't spose to talk ill of dead folk—I know that's true. Ain't missing no home training. But, ah, that Blister was a twisted fuck, and I ain't ashamed to say it. Twisted, messed up son of a bitch. And you and me got to let his spirit go." She leaned forward and drank a bit of tea, added more whiskey, and scooched back on the couch again.

Sister nearly choked when she heard the name. Which for her was synonymous with stomach sickness and old blood clots. "What you. What you know about him? Why you say that to *me*?" She dared Della to put a word to it.

Another sip and a whispered condolence. "I know what he done to you, Sister. Done the same thing to me. Same thing. Only you got living proof of what he done, and, miracle of miracles, I don't. I seen to that."

The woman went to the floor-model television, where she kept the family pictures, and she pulled out the one of her bloated cousin, Blister, and her second cousin, Evian. She placed it carefully in Sister Becca's hand, and when she did, Sister Becca began to cry.

Home Again!

[LEXINGTON, KY 1994]

29

[DIGNITY]

"Where's my Dignity?! Take anything you want, but leave me my Dignity!" Uncle Sam marched into the kitchen with a flourish and sparkle. He had this way of lighting up a room with his silly sense of humor that contrasted with his overbearing size and countenance. He was six feet five, had slick, coal-black hair and skin to match. Always dressed impeccably, always smelled fresh and new, and always had something ridiculous to say. This time he had picked up the magnifying glasses Aunt Lette kept on the counter for reading her mail and the Bible, and he was peering around the kitchen corner, searching for me. Having the two of them together in the same room with me felt just like Christmas. I forgot my age as I rushed into his arms.

"Uncle Sam! You big silly! Here I am!" I barely came up to the middle of his chest, but I burrowed into it, feeling like a child again.

He picked me up and spun me around. Gave me three big squeezes before setting me on my feet again. "There's my girl! You looking mighty fine, too. Mighty fine! Made the dean's list again, too, I suppose." He turned toward his wife. "She gets her head smarts from me, Lette, and her good looks from… someplace else!" He winked at me, teasing Aunt Lette like he always does. He smacked his wife on the behind and pecked her cheek.

"Yes. I did make the dean's list again, but not straight A's this time. Got one B. School can get so boring, Uncle Sam!" I sat at the kitchen table and peered up at my uncle, sort of introducing the idea that I am disenchanted with school. This way, if I truly decide not to go back, they will think back and remember that I was not happy, even at the beginning of the summer. Aunt Lette didn't let the comment go unnoticed, though.

"Boring, you say? Umm-hmm. Now, in addition to everything else, those professors got to entertain you, too? Well, naw they don't! Diggy, it isn't the college's job to make fun for you. You just get your work! You'll have time for fun later, after you done given the valedictorian speech and marched across that stage. Naw. Don't start this bored foolishness now!" She poked out her lip and scrunched her brow as she pulled the chicken out of the oven. It was crisp and golden brown, and I swooned at the sight of it.

"Now, Lette, Dignity's just a young thing. Hard for us to remember a time when spring itches at you so bad, the last thing you wanna do is be inside of four walls with some fool teacher. Natural that she be bored, swift as she is." Uncle Sam pushed his sleeves up and, getting directly in Aunt Lette's way, began washing his hands at the sink. Uncle Sam is a bit of a clean freak, too. That's where I get it from, I guess. Starts and finishes everything with a brisk hand washing. Next, he picked up the colander of grapes and brought them over to the table before sitting down with me. "What they got you learning these days, Nelly?"

Nelly is a name he calls me sometimes, never really explained why. Just said I remind him of somebody that would be called Nelly. "Not much. History. English. Math. Same old stuff. I have been taking more art classes, though. And choir." We both picked at the seedless grapes, making a small pile of vines in the middle of the table between us.

"Yep. Still doing the backdrops and things for the plays, or did you get bored of that, too, Miss Nelly?" Uncle Sam had this way of making me understand what he is thinking without ever saying it. I got the impression he was going somewhere with this line of questioning, too, but I didn't know where.

"Oh yea! That was fun! I worked on the set for the fall play last year and then again this fall. They gave me full run of the theater, too! I had a budget, and I designed all of the backdrops and had input on the set, too. I really liked that!" I got caught up talking about our production of the August Wilson play we'd done earlier last semester, how I'd gotten the idea for the color scheme looking at old pictures in the library, and how Sal had been the one to build the set and all of the other props.

Uncle Sam had a victorious smirk on his face, like he'd just been dealt a winning hand but the other poker players didn't know it. "See there! Sounds like that old Morgan State ain't such a big bore after all, now, is it?"

Should have known that's where he was going with this. What he didn't know was that boredom wasn't the problem. My ex-boyfriend was.

"Wished we could have seen that August Wilson play last year. Folks make such a big fuss over that man and his plays. I told everybody it was our Dignity did the picture backgrounds for that show. So proud of you, Baby! Always was good with colors and pictures. Stop with those grapes, now. You'll ruin your dinner." Aunt Lette swept the vine pile into the trash can and took the colander away, putting it back on the counter. "Diggy, get the cream-colored dishes out and the crystal tumblers. Sam Wayne, best to get out of those meeting clothes; we fitting to eat. And don't go getting in the shower. Just change your duds and come on."

Aunt Lette was squeezing the juice from eight lemons and had the bag of sugar out and the glass pitcher she used in the summer. I began to hum to myself as I set the table for the three of us. About then, the doorbell rang.

I opened the door to find Mercer, dressed as himself, in crisp khaki shorts, a navy boatneck T-shirt and navy deck shoes, with his hands stuck way down in his pockets and wearing a sheepish grin. "Hey! Y'all et yet?" He spoke in an exaggerated country drawl. "I done bought yee a fresh pecan pie we could et fer dee-zert if'n you ain't!" I noticed the bag he'd placed on the ground next to him.

I grabbed the bag fast and pretended to slam the door, saying, "We gave at the office!" But Mercer just pushed his way on in, calling out to Aunt Lette as he headed back to the kitchen.

"Hey there, Beautiful! How 'bout some fresh tomatoes with whatever you got that smells so good! Mama said to send you these." Mercer gave my auntie a kiss on the cheek and pulled three ripe tomatoes out of his pocket.

"Hey, Baby! Haven't seen you since I don't know when! So glad you stopped over. But I know you didn't come to see me! Diggy, set a place for him, Baby, right next to me. That way both of you got to pay attention to me. Otherwise I might get lost in the crossfire, the way you two carry on." She put the chicken on the serving platter and put the potatoes and green beans along the side of them. Pulled some muffins out of the oven and dumped them in a wicker basket.

"Make yourself useful, Homey. Slice those puppies up and put them on the table." I handed Mercer a knife and a cutting board so he could slice the tomatoes and add them to the dinner table.

When Uncle Sam came back, he blessed the table, and then we all began to eat and talk at once. It was chaos. Mercer needed to ask Aunt Lette what she used to season the vegetables; I needed to find out from Uncle Sam if he was still leading the trustees in the church and if he ever got them to change the color of the ushers' uniforms. Aunt Lette wanted to make sure we knew all about her garden club and the fund-raiser she hoped Mercer's mama would contribute to, and all of us ate like we hadn't had a meal in a while. Sure beat the spaghetti sandwiches on campus!

We slowed down for a few minutes while Mercer and Aunt Lette cleared the table. I got out the dessert plates and started dishing up Mercer's pecan pie. Uncle Sam isn't big on sweets, so he took his pipe and went on to the family room to watch *Entertainment Tonight*, which he watched faithfully. So, the three of us sat at the kitchen table with our coffee and our pie, dishing the latest dirt. It was such a familiar scene that it felt like déjà vu.

"Mercer. Now maybe you will be straight with me, since Diggy thinks I don't know and doesn't want to tell me. What happened with her and her beau with the funny name, Santa Lucia, or whatever? They still going together? Seems like they done broken up." Aunt Lette had scraped most of the nuts off the top of her pie and had made a pile of them on the side of her plate. She would later dip the nuts, one by one, in the whipped cream, finishing them off after the rest of the pie was done.

Mercer kicked me under the table, and I began coughing. I couldn't believe that she even remembered Sal, though she pretended not to remember his name, and I wondered how she figured out that the two of us were having problems.

"Well, now, Miss Lette, I think I better leave that to Digs to tell. She can get so convoluted with her stories that I can't tell what's going on with her, half the time! Digs? Something going on with that fella you took up with at school?"

Aunt Lette had never met Sal, didn't know that he was white, and certainly didn't know that our relationship included frequent sleepovers, even if they were sprinkled with night panics and anxiety attacks on both ends. I didn't know what to say.

"Salmon? Yes, we got to be good friends, he and I. I wouldn't exactly say we were going together, though..." I kept my face down, focused on my pecan pie, the crust of which was so tender and delicious it made me want to slap my mama. If I knew where the hell she was.

"See there. Like I don't know she spends all her time over there with this Salmon, whom she doesn't go with, during midterms and finals when she ought to be studying, getting a *B* when she could have an *A*. Mercer, maybe you can tell me whether or not this is why she came home with a quickness, not even waiting until clean-up day on campus, like she used to. Maybe you can confirm whether or not she got in a spat with this gentleman and come running home right fast to escape some hurt feelings." My auntie kept her eyes on Mercer, spilling all this information to let me know that she knew all about what was going on, that I could talk to her if I wanted to. I didn't want to. Not yet.

I never understood where Aunt Lette got all of her information, but she always knew what was going on with me, whether I told her or not. This time, I didn't want to get into it with her, because she would want to know all the details, and I couldn't tell this Holiness woman that I broke up with my white boyfriend because I'm too neurotic to have sex with him. Better let this information sit.

Mercer took one last bite of pie, wiped his mouth, and picked up his mug of coffee. He didn't look at me, either. "Miss Lette, now we know how peculiar and secretive our Digs can be, don't we? I just leave it alone and lift her up! She'll come clean when she's ready."

"I guess you right. Hope you'll let me know, though, if you find out there's any truth to these rumors about the spat and all that. Isn't a man out there worth a minute of heartbreak for. Hope she knows that. Let me get this dinner put up and tend to my own man. Sam Wayne brought home one of those videos he likes for us to watch. And my nails need touching up, anyway." She lifted from her seat and headed for the cabinets, where she'd find Tupperware to store the leftovers.

Mercer and I shooed Aunt Lette away and offered to clean the kitchen ourselves. I liked to color-code the leftovers—tonight I would use square containers with blue tops. That way I'd remember which of the Tupperware containers held food that I could actually eat. Aunt Lette hated to throw food away, and there were already a few containers in the fridge, left over from Lord knows when. I had to stay away from those, didn't even want to look at them, much less eat them. I am afraid of old food. Might contain bacteria or mold, or something. Once I opened a container from the fridge when I was in high school, and the contents, which were old and indescribable, scarred me for life.

With the kitchen clean, the food color-coded and tucked away, Mercer and I went out on the back porch to plan our night. Aunt Lette didn't let us smoke in the house, even though Uncle Sam smoked his pipe inside all the time. I ran and got my purse and the steno pad I started writing on that morning, and we set up in the white, aluminum chairs Aunt Lette bought too long ago for me to remember.

30

[OUT EAST END]

"That's out east end. You know where Cher and them do hair, sell incense and scarves and stuff, too? Stays packed over there, and don't try to wait for your mama to get her hair did on a Saturday—no ma'am, girl! You be over there for days! You remember? Place was called Chuckie's after that woman with the buck teeth that used to run it." Mercer was reared back in the chair, just as butch as you please, as if he never had come to the door in a dress and lipstick the day before.

"Oh—*that's* where Ruty works?! That's a good gig, then; if it's anything like it used to be, then she gets a lot of traffic and probably stays busy. Ain't Angus says Ruty can sew alright, but not as good as she can. All she'd have to do is have a needle and some thread over there, and people would probably knock her door down. Good gig." I was on my second cigarette, making up for lost time with the nicotine; I had missed smoking all day hanging with Aunt Lette.

"Yep. So, if you go down there, you know you gonna run into all kind of folk, and you know it's gonna get right back to Miss Lette, so you better get ready. No sense in hiding it, anyway, Digs." By now Merc was jiggling his left leg and sitting on the edge of his seat, anxious. He got that way when he was ready to make a move.

"Look, cool your heels already! I ain't done yet! Where are you trying to go, anyways? So, do you think I should just show up there, or do you think I should call first?" I was trying to imagine what Ruty looked like and what I would say to her when I made my little visit.

"Please! I don't have to have someplace to go to be ready to go from here! Sitting on the back porch, it ain't exactly my idea of real excitement for a summer night. No, I wouldn't if I were you." He smashed his cigarette against the sole of his shoe and put it back inside the pack. We didn't have an ashtray, and we weren't going to throw the butts down and sully my auntie's porch.

"Well, excuse me, Mr. Saturday Night! Hate to hold you up in my small town house with my small town problems! You wouldn't what, if you were me?"

"Wouldn't call first. Just show up. Make sure she is there first—maybe ask somebody what hours she's there. Then, have at it. Just go and state your business." Now Mercer was drumming his fingers and looking very distracted. I was trying not to be offended.

"Fine. I see your point. So, tomorrow is Saturday—she's bound to be around then. Will you go with?" I ignored the fact that Mercer was only half listening to me and obviously had his mind on something else.

"Umm. If it's in the afternoon—okay. But, I'm not trying to stay around there all day." He glanced at his watch and looked over his shoulder, back toward his car.

"Look, Mercer! I hate to keep you, so why don't you just go! I mean, you act like it hasn't been months since you've seen me, like we get the time to talk every single day! If it's so important, GO already!" My jealous neurosis set in, and I could no longer hide my disgust.

"I'm sorry, Digs. It's just that, I do, sort of, have a, umm, previous engagement… Do you mind?" He leaned forward and prepared to stand.

I was surprised. I really hadn't expected him to take me up on my offer for him to leave. It was out of character. It was practically tradition that we spent the first few days of my being back home together. Where was he rushing off to? "Oh. Okay, sure. I understand." We both stood up.

Mercer could tell that I was everything from surprised to disappointed. "It's just that, well, I planned this thing a while ago, and usually you wouldn't have gotten home until Sunday, and I really have to…" He didn't know what all to say. He knew he was coming off strange. I let him off the hook.

"No, really. Go! Shoo! I understand! You want to meet me here tomorrow, and we'll go out to east eee-yund?" I put on my best Lexington drawl to make him laugh.

"Of course! I'll come around two, and then we can head over there. Maybe go by and see some of the old gang after, okay?"

I told Mercer that would be fine. I needed some time to think and to rest anyway. No telling what I might find out after talking with my Aunt Ruty. I also needed to decide what I was going to say to her myself. So, Mercer shouted goodbye to Aunt Lette and Uncle Sam, and he went off to wherever he had to go. I sat out on the porch a while longer, smoked another cigarette and was halfway through with it when I realized that it was the last one in the pack.

I went back inside. My aunt and uncle were both asleep in front of the television. I knew better than to turn off the movie—this would wake them up. Uncle Sam could never admit to being asleep, even if he was snoring and cutting z's loud enough to shake a village. The second you turned off the light or cut off the television, he'd start to fuss, saying he was just resting his eyes and to stop meddling. I skipped that drama, grabbed my purse and keys and headed out.

I intended just to go to the convenience store around the corner, but something about the still, country air made me drive on. It was soothing. First I drove by my old high school. Looked the same. They still had the "Senior Circle" in front of the main door. This was a ring of parking spaces that were designated for seniors who drove to school. It was a rite of passage, parking there. The circle'd been around for years, but our class had started the tradition of drawing pictures on the spaces. Our mascot was the Bengal tiger. The picture of the mascot that I'd drawn was still smiling with its cobalt blue eyes and bright gold whiskers in space #3.

Next, I drove around New Circle road for a while, looking to see if there were any new additions to this part of town. There were a few. Then, I decided I wanted to take a look at downtown.

I passed some of the familiar spots—our old church, the salon where Aunt Lette had her fake nails put on, the office where Uncle Sam used to work. Then, I headed back toward home, planning to swing through the park before heading home.

I pulled onto the asphalt at the park, and there were plenty of other cars there, too. This was a popular place in warm weather, a place where we parked and smoked and listened to music and made out. I popped in Tony Toni Toné and was enjoying the sweet stillness of the air when I noticed Mercer's car parked a few spaces up. Without thinking, I piled out of the car and headed for his, to say hello. But, as I approached, I noticed the car windows were fogged up and Heavy D's latest was blaring away inside. The whole car was vibrating.

Now, I am not the type to sneak or spy. I think it's really tacky. Mercer hadn't told me where he was going, so I assumed that he didn't want me to know. I remembered this especially when I realized that he was inside of his car, windows steaming, music blasting. I was planning to slip back to my own car without speaking when the person he was…spending time with, rolled down the window and started giggling. She was fanning her face and combing her fingers through her short hair.

I didn't want them to think I was spying, and I didn't want to create an awkward situation for myself. I mean, what a coincidence that I would show up at the park, alone, right after Mercer left my house without saying where he was going. No way he would believe I wasn't stalking him. So, I conveniently "dropped" something on the ground and had to stoop down there for a while to "look for it." In this stooping position I could see Mercer, but he couldn't see me.

The girl he was with had a high, helium-filled voice, practically sounded like The Chipmunks. She wasn't facing me, but I could see the reddish color of her skin and the long, pinched nose; I put the picture together right away—he was with Cher! Cher Login! She went to school with us but was a year behind us. Her mother, big Cher, ran the very beauty shop we talked about earlier, the one where my Aunt Ruty was supposed to be working. Big Cher took over the shop when Chuckie, the first owner, OD'd.

I was puzzled. Why in the world was Mercer making out, Benz just a shaking, with Cher Login, of all people??? True, she did always have a thing for Merc, but then, back in the day, who didn't? And, in light of his recent, uhh, experimentation with cross dressing, I found this episode especially puzzling. But when she leaned her head against the glass window, and Mercer's head disappeared somewhere below her waist, I crab-walked back to my own car with a quickness!

Oh no! What on earth?! My first impulse was to burst out laughing. But, true to form, my next was to feel, I don't know. Jealous. I started the car and drove home feeling a block of loneliness in my stomach. Mercer, who had apparently created an alternate ego of a different gender, still had no problem having sex. I didn't have the issue of confused gender, but somehow I couldn't bear to be intimate with my (ex) boyfriend. What is wrong with me?

31

[CHER'S HAIR]

I was about to hop into bed, freshly washed and wearing my favorite flannel pajamas. I have this habit of wearing my flannel nightgown in the summer when I am at home. It is warm and comfy, and since Uncle Sam keeps the air conditioner on so high, you like to freeze back in my room. So, I sleep in flannel, just like in the winter. The only difference is that I don't wear socks to bed in the summer. I was rubbing the last bit of cucumber face cream into my chin when I heard heavy footsteps in the hall.

"Knock knock, baby girl. You decent? Can I come in?" Uncle Sam always makes it a point to allow me my privacy when I am in my bedroom. He does it to compensate for Aunt Lette, who barges in whenever she darn well pleases, whether the door is closed or not. She says there's nothing I should be doing in here that she can't see. And the day I need to do things in here that I don't want her to see is the day I need to go on and get a place of my own. She doesn't want a lot of secrets in her house, she says. Used to bug me when I was in high school, but now I don't mind so much. I said it was okay for him to come in.

He had his undershirt and sweatpants on and had his customary glass of warm milk. Helped him sleep. "Baby, where you been tonight? You and Mercer go visiting, seeing about your old friends and all?" He took a sip of his milk and sat on the edge of my bed.

I pulled my knees up under my nightgown to keep warm and leaned against my pillows. "Yea. Just driving around. I guess I should of left a note…" I didn't know if he had been worried about me or what.

"Naw, naw. You grown. 'Less you going far or gonna be out longer than a spell, no need. Just that a fella called around here looking for you. Sounded mighty troubled to find you wasn't here." He laid this information down gently, knowing it was bound to illicit an explanation, one that he was interested to hear.

Check it out! Had Salmon actually tracked me down already? I did give him Ain't Angus' number, but I didn't give him this one. I wanted to be sure before I explained this phone call to my uncle. "Really? Did you recognize the voice, Uncle Sam?" I tried to sound casual, not too interested.

"No, Sir. Didn't sound like none of your regular crowd. Had an accent, and talked soft and fast. Didn't leave a name, either." He rested the glass on his knee and belched. Looked around the room a minute before resting his eyes on my own.

Well, that cinched it. It was obviously Salmon. And it seemed typical that he wouldn't have left his name. Wonder what he called for, what he wanted to say? "Oh. I don't know. Probably a friend from school wanting to make sure I got home alright. See if you can get a name when he calls back. *If* he calls back." I pulled the covers up to my neck now, not wanting Uncle Sam to see the shiver his news brought me or the anxiety it caused.

"Yep. I'll do it, if the fella calls back. Nelly, you still seeing that rascal you told us about before, the one who lived out near you on campus?"

"Uh, not really. I never really was see—"

"Now, quit fooling, Gal. Act like I haven't known you since you was three. You were seeing him, and seeing him in a big way. I know. The way a parent knows about his younguns. Tell me, truth, you still seeing him?" He pressed on, and I knew that he wanted an answer.

I started to cry. Out of nowhere. Tears just rolling down my cheeks, and I wanted Uncle Sam to hold me against his chest and make it go away, the hurt, disappointment and panic I was feeling, that I had tried to leave at Morgan but which had followed me right back home. "Oh, Uncle Sam! I don't know! Yes, I had been with him, but then we started to have problems, and then I said I didn't want to see him, and now I just can't see not seeing him! I don't know what to do!" I boo-hooed my way onto his shoulder and closed my eyes while he stroked my back.

"Yep. Now, now. Let it out. Let it all out, Baby. Umm-hmm. Sounds like you got some decisions to make, Nelly."

I had a hard time hiding from Uncle Sam. He never seemed to know specifics, like Aunt Lette, but he vibed into my essence sometimes, and he knew when I was hurting. Sometimes I thought, when he saw me cry, that he felt the tears, too. "I guess so. But, I do like Salmon, Uncle Sam. I do. I just… I don't know…" I couldn't tell him the details about my relationship with Sal, but I didn't have to. He didn't ask me to. He just let me cry and stroked my back to let me know it was going to be okay.

"Now, now. Let those worries go, baby girl. You'll know when you know. If you not sure about this fella, may be that it's for a reason. Don't block His blessings by fretting over nothing. Turn it on over and let it work itself out. You young and pretty. Plenty time to let it work out." He gave me a final squeeze and pat on the back and stood up. "One thing I do know, though. You can't run from nothing. Far as you think you go, there you are, right back where you started. If this fella calls again, better talk to him. And I betcha he calls again." He winked at me and headed for the door. "Sleep sweet, Nelly Nelly."

I lay there for a minute and thought about what he said. About not running away. About talking to Sal. I hoped he waited a while to call again, because I wasn't ready to talk to him. I wanted to talk to Aunt Ruty first, find out more about myself before making a decision about him.

Saturday, Mercer showed up as planned, and I acted like I hadn't seen him muff diving with Cher Login in the backseat of his Benz. If I knew Mercer, he would come clean soon enough, and when he did, I was going to wear him out for taking up with Cher and not telling me right away. But for the time being, I just played dumb.

I had spent the morning trying to formulate questions to ask Ruty. I had not come up with any, except two: Who is my father, and what's up with my mother? That about covered everything I wanted to know! Worst she could do would be not to have any answers.

We took Mercer's car to the beauty shop, which was now run by the Login family. They'd changed the name to Cher's Hair, and they still did a booming business. They'd gotten rid of the counter in the back where they used to sell incense and stuff and put it in the back room. The back room, where they used to just have a small washer and dryer, now had the counter, a couple of small, round tables, two sewing machines, and random bolts of fabric, pin cushions, buttons, zippers, and a whole lot of other disorganized clutter. Looking back there, I tried to ignore the chaos and focus my attention on the two women who were sitting in the room. I spotted them as soon as I walked into the shop and knew one of them was bound to be my aunt.

I couldn't make out the features of the two women from the front of the shop. I would have to make my way to that room if I wanted to talk to my aunt. Before I could get back there, I got side-tracked by the owner, herself.

Mercer plopped down in the styling chair next to Cher and gave her a cool nod, but I could tell he was looking hard at her gracious behind, which had swollen some, but in what most men would consider an attractive way. She wore her hair in a short, curly natural, had her lips lined with dark pencil and filled in with deep, wine-colored lipstick. She had on a sleeveless sundress and was wearing thong sandals that matched her dress. She made like she was thrilled to see me, though clearly she wasn't feeling me. She never had. Most of the girls who wanted Mercer were not too thrilled with me.

"Hey, Girl! When have I seen you, Miss Thang! Let me give you a hug! You back for the summer, huh?" She came close and made the gesture of putting her arms around my shoulders but managed to barely touch me. She kissed the air that surrounded my cheek before moving back to her own space. Mercer had suddenly become engrossed in a fashion magazine, probably trying to figure out which dress he would buy next. (Let me stop). I wondered if Cher knew of his recent walking on the other side.

"Yes! Just got back a few days ago. So, you done blown up, I see! Got your own shop and all—good for you! I bet you never get any time off, the way people are lined up to get in your chair!" Which was true. There was a room full of people, and half of them were sitting in the waiting area, prepared to stay a while to get their locks coiffed. Some had brought their chicken and their pops and their magazines. It was something I never understood, women's willingness to spend whole days in a hot hair salon to get their hair done. I never had patience for it, but, then, my hair was always a wild mess all over my head. It was a trade-off.

"It's good, though. You know I'm saving to buy me a house, Girl! So, I just look at these heads and think of the white picket fence and the finished basement I'mma have before it's all said and done." Cher was bustling around her station, setting up the hot irons and putting the rollers, according to their color and size, back into the plastic organizer. "You should let me hook you up, Dignity! Trim those edges and have you looking *most* fly!"

"Absolutely! I will have to come in soon and let you do your thing! I'm trying to get someone to alter this dress I bought a few weeks back, though. See if I can get some extra room to accommodate my big behind! I heard you have a tailor, or something, working in the back?" I tried to sound casual, as if I didn't know already that Ruty rented the back of the shop.

"Oh yes, Girl! She's excellent, too. Stays busy! You know, I put on a little weight myself this year. I try to get to the gym and work some of this stuff off, you know. It's hard to find time. We should go together sometime…"

I knew that her offer was not completely sincere. Cher did have a little junk in her trunk, but she was tiny otherwise. She wasn't exactly in need of a workout, much less a workout with me. "Yes, soon as I get my strength up, I'll check you out. Mercer, let me go on back here and tell her what I need. I'll be back, okay?"

Mercer nodded again and shrugged, like he wasn't pressed, either way. But as I walked to the back of the shop, I could see in Cher's full mirror that both of them were smiling sly at each other. Oh, brother!

I kept my mind on the task at hand and planned to deal with Mercer's contradictions later. As I came closer, I could see that there was an attractive girl with a very large head, huge eyes, and a mass of small braids hanging to her waist, and she was sitting behind a half counter and talking on the phone. She was perched on the edge of her stool and had a notebook full of numbers in front of her. She looked to be around my age, maybe a little older. The other woman that I had seen was no longer in the room. I figured this girl couldn't be my aunt, since she was so young, so I motioned to her, indicating that I wanted to talk to her when she got a minute's break from her conversation on the phone. She pointed to the table across the room, letting me know that I should sit down; then she turned her back, tossed her hair over her shoulders, and kept on talking.

I had a seat in the folding chair next to the table and looked around the room. A big, confusing mess. I was wondering how in the world someone could work in that cramped and cluttered space when the other woman came back into the room. She had a tape measure under her arm and two straight pins in her mouth. She stopped in her tracks when she saw me sitting at the table.

It was like looking in a mirror, seeing this woman. Not her every feature exactly, but, I don't know. The way she came together, the way she carried herself. The shape of her body, the way her chin narrowed abruptly into an overly long neck. The way her head lorded over her narrow shoulders. Her skinny legs and ashy ankles. She looked so much like me that I gasped.

"Help you with something?" The woman inched closer to the table, looking over to the younger woman on the phone for support or confidence but finding none. "Has Kita already helped you?"

I noticed how the woman's face had begun to age but remained elastic, smooth, and pleasant, how her lips contained no denting and lay full and straight under her mouth, how her eyes at once questioned and answered. I wondered if I would look like that when I got a little older. If I did, I wouldn't mind at all.

"No, she hasn't. I mean, I didn't ask her to. I… My name is Dignity. Are you Ruty?"

The woman slipped the few inches to the chair across from me and spilled herself into it. She shook her head and looked at me, just kept shaking her head, as if in disbelief. "Lord, Lord, Lord. Umm. Lord, Lord…"

"I'm sorry. Maybe I came at a bad time. It's just that I… I wanted to…" The woman kept shaking her head.

"Dignity? For real?! Ma! She the one who, I mean. Dag! You Dignity?" The woman behind the counter had laid the phone down on the counter and come over to stare in my face. She seemed delighted, like she was seeing a movie star. She went back to the counter and, picking the phone up again, she said, "Girl, let me call you back! I got some family business to take care of up in here!" She rushed back over to me and stood between me and the woman she'd called Ma.

"Ma! Get a grip, now! Dignity done come all this way. You always said you wanted to talk to her. Now she here, and you act like you ain't got words! I'mma go get y'all some pop. I be right back!" She dashed into the front of the store, and I saw her pushing coins into the pop machine.

The woman the young girl called Ma leaned over and touched my hair, dropping her measure on the table. She took the pins from her mouth and placed them on the table. She pushed my hair off my shoulders so it hung straight down my back, away from my face. Then she squinted her eyes and smiled. "Lord. Dignity. I been waiting a long time to see you!" She rose from the table and closed the door that led to the main shop where Cher was busy doing hair.

32

[GOD BLESS THE CHILD]

We sat at that table for over an hour, with Kita as mesmerized by Aunt Ruty's talk as I was. Aunt Ruty told us about when she and her sister, my mama, and her two brothers, Timmy and Albert, had all lived together with Grandma Pearson. About the swing on the front porch they used to sit in all summer long and how my mama's best friend, Pam Elizabeth, lived in a house close by. She reminded Nakita about her daddy, Peanut, who moved away to California when she was five. Reminisced about how she used to sew, even back then, but how she never could cook. Said that my mama was always great in the kitchen. That, and she could sing better than I could imagine.

"Now, that's for real, Dignity. Aunt Becca can blow! She made three albums already, and Uncle Albert say they might do another one, too. They still singing— where they at now, Ma?"

I looked hopefully at Aunt Ruty, interested to know my mama's whereabouts, but she looked down at the table and didn't answer. Instead she said, "I bet you would like to hear *Sister 'Becca and Them*, huh? What say you come on out to the house with me? I gotta go past there on my way home anyway. Mama had some tests run at the hospital, and she be there overnight. I got to get in there and clean up before she get home, else she'll fuss. If you come around there with me, you can listen to her album, and I tell you the rest of what I know." Aunt Ruty had long, brown hair that was thick and straight, like she never had a perm and had pressed it into shape. But aside from her hair and her chocolate brown skin, she and I could have been twins.

I wanted to go to "the house" as she said, but I didn't want to go alone. I told her I wasn't driving and would ask my friend if he would run me out there. I didn't know what Mercer had planned, in light of his new alliance with Cher, so I got up to see if he would go with me.

"Girl, come! You ain't never seen where your mama live, and ain't never heard her sing, neither! And I been done heard so much about you, I wouldn't mind having you around for a taste." Kita urged me to ask Mercer so I could go out to her grandmama's house.

I went out to the main store to find Mercer giving Cher a shoulder rub while she rolled an older woman's hair in bottle-sized rollers. I could tell his instinct was to drop his hands quick when he saw me, but Cher gave him a look in the mirror that dared him not do. He kept at it but acquired a bored, disinterested stance instead.

"You do what you need to do, Digs? You took long enough!" It was after four p.m. by now, and the shop would be closing soon. Even though I knew part of it was a front, I could tell that Mercer was ready to roll out.

"Yea. I need to go out to Paris, though, and see some samples that, ah, Ruty has at home. She's gonna make me an outfit I been wanting to have. Since I don't have my car, will you go with?" I looked at him with a subtle pleading in my posture. Cher spun the chair around so that she would be facing Mercer, wanting to see what his answer would be.

"What, you mean, like now?" Though she was still rolling the last strands of the older woman's hair, Cher kept her eyes steadily on Mercer, silently imposing herself on his answer. Mercer looked from Cher to me, seeming half amused, half tormented.

"Yes, or in a few minutes or so." I crossed my arms over my chest, stared in Merc's face, and pulled rank on Cher's ass. I don't know what he has going on with her, but I know what he has going on with me, and he knows how important it is to me to find my roots, as he says. So, homeboy, tell me something!

"Yeah, okay. I'm down." He didn't take his eyes from me as he reached in his pocket and threw me the keys to his Benz. "Go on out and start the car, Digs, and I'll be right out." The look in his eyes said, *Don't push it by asking me questions; just be glad I said yes and go start the ding-dang car!*

I went to the back where Aunt Ruty and her daughter, Nakita, were folding up fabric, labeling patterns with tape, and gathering their pops and purses. "My friend, Mercer, is going to bring me. Do you mind if we follow you?"

"Oh, good! I was hoping you would bring that fine, young specimen with you! Does he belong to you, or is he with Fair Cher?" Nakita was half joking, but I could tell she was kind of interested. Some things will never change! These Kentucky women are forever sweating Mercer. If they only knew what they were getting into!

"Umm. We're just good friends. You'll have to ask *him* about the other question. I don't know nothing about that!"

"Kita, mind your business, now. My car is in the back, Dignity. I'll pull around to the front, and you can follow us out. It ain't too far from here. You can go out this side door if you want."

I ducked out the side door, and when I got in the car, I could see Mercer and Cher gesturing and talking as I peered through the glass door. I wondered how he was going to explain his strange behavior with Fair Cher, as Kita had called her.

I left the keys in the ignition and slid over to the passenger seat. Mercer would let me start his baby, but he wouldn't want me to drive it. I popped the CD into the stereo and was bombarded by loud Luther. Remnants of last night's parkside adventure, I guess. I turned it down and tried to stay calm. This trip to Aunt Ruty's combined with the whole Mercer/Marcy/Cher thing could give me an anxiety attack, if I weren't careful. I already had enough to deal with; I didn't want to have to sweat and fight for breath, too.

Mercer affected a casual stroll when he came out to the car. Once again, I ignored the whole scene in the shop and waited to see what he would share with me on his own, in his own time. At least that was the plan.

But, when he got in, and I could see a little wine-red lipstick on his lower cheek, I couldn't resist. "So, you've taken up with Cher, I see... Since when is all this?"

"Oh. What makes you say that? Hold up, though, I need to concentrate. Is that her Camry up there?" He made an exaggerated motion of looking out his window to make sure he was following the right car. It was pretty obvious, though, that the Camry in front of us, with the flashing lights and the waving, flirtatious Nakita in the front passenger seat, was the one we were supposed to follow.

Once we were safely on our way, I continued my line of questioning. "Marcy, have you taken up with homegirl, or what? You can tell old Digs, your old pal!"

Mercer's face turned a pale shade of red when I used his other name, and I could tell that he was not at all comfortable with where this was going. "Look,

Digs. A lot has happened since you went to school. A lot. That's all I can say. I filled you in on, umm, that whole Marcy thing because, well, I needed to. But umm. Let me bring this shit up when I am ready, okay? Because right now I don't know. And, yes, I mean, I guess so." He rolled up the windows and turned on the air conditioner. He kept his eyes glued to the gold Camry in front of us.

I felt a little bad for pressing him, and for acting a bit flip about what was obviously a sensitive issue. "No problem, Mercer! Really. You know me. Always joking and stuff. You guess so to what?" I pulled all of my hair into a twist on my head and fanned my neck.

"The Cher question. I guess so. You know she been sweating me for the longest, and I just started to give in. You know, she is fine!"

"Yes, she is. She definitely is that. Thanks for taking me, Mercer. I couldn't make this trip without you." I turned to look at him, but he was still focused on the road ahead of us.

"I said I would, and I don't have a problem doing it. But, fyi, your usual arrival date is not until tomorrow, and I do have plans later. So please don't trip…"

"Oh. Cool. We won't be long; I promise. Then, ahh, she's all yours." I looked out the window to keep from laughing, as I flashed on the bump and grind I had caught him in the night before.

We pulled into a short driveway in front of a small, clapperboard house that was dingy white and in need of paint. It was narrow and stacked on two levels, and the windows and lawn looked cared for and clean. I looked on with my photographer's eye. I wanted to remember every nuance so that I could reflect on it later. Kita jumped out of the car and ran over to the driver's side of our car. She waved again at Mercer before looking at me and motioning for me to get out and come in.

"Girl, this my grandmama house! I used to sleep in that room right there, see, that faces the front. Next to that was Grandmama room. She share with Aunt Becca, your mama. But Aunt Becca were gone before I can remember. And in the back was Timmy and Albert room. Living room in the front and then the kitchen in the back. Got a side door, too, that we mostly use when we stay. Don't nobody come up on the porch no more, hardly." She spoke with her mouth and her hands as she led me and Mercer up the front porch and into the living room.

We sat down on the flowered couch that sort of sagged in the middle but that still looked clean.

Aunt Ruty seemed to take her time coming in, grabbing a bucket out of the trunk of her car and surveying the front yard and steps as she mounted them. When she got inside, she said she'd be in the kitchen when I got ready to talk. She looked tired.

Nakita didn't. She made it a point to sit between me and Mercer as she pulled three records from the entertainment center in front of the couch. She explained each album, front and back, pointing out each member of Sister Becca and Them. She explained that it was pronounced "Sista Becca an' nem" since that's how everybody talks around this way.

One album cover had a wonderful mural of black art on it. Reminded me of the paintings on the show *Good Times*. It was called *Revolution*. Another had a watercolor picture of a field on the front and was titled, *ForEVer*. But the one that I couldn't take my eyes from was the one with the group's picture on the front. I listened from a distance as Kita pointed each of them out. Pam Elizabeth had shoulder-length hair turned under all around the edges in a mushroom. She held her weight mostly on one foot, wore red and yellow vertical-striped hip-huggers, and had her hip stuck out like she thought she was cute. She was. Albert was wearing sunglasses and a Big Apple hat. He had his arms crossed in front of his chest and his head cocked to the side. Edward, Pam's brother, had one arm slung around Sister Becca's shoulder, and one leg was crossed in front of the other. He was wearing a red velvet shirt and striped pants.

The woman he leaned on, the woman who was the focal point of the cover and of the group, was my mother. She had spirals of orange-red hair that was clipped up in the front and that hung in tangles down her back. She had a sunny color in her cheeks, but her essence looked tired, heavy, and sad. She had a floppy, wide-brimmed patchwork quilted hat and a half grin that looked like Aunt Ruty's. And like mine. The album was called, *God Bless the Child*. Nakita played for us the title track.

When Kita got up and put on the album, Mercer must have seen the earnest way that I looked at the cover photo, transfixed and nearly mesmerized. I was gripping the sides of the cover as if they were my own mama's hands. And when the song started, with that crackle and pop that characterizes old vinyl, and when the voices began, a capella, and when the words turned forth like spun gravel and melted candy and moonlit air, I knew, KNEW that they were singing about me.

It was the first time that I had heard my mama's voice at a time when I could take note of it and remember. I leaned forward, not wanting to miss a word. I knew that Nakita wanted to take back her original spot in the middle of me and Mercer, but I guess she also must have seen the look on my face and understood that I was having a moment. She didn't interrupt. Instead, she went back to the kitchen with her own mama and let me have a recorded moment with mine.

I didn't want tears, but they came anyway. Mercer collected me in his arms, but I still held tight to the album cover. And neither of us touched the hot salt tears that rolled, once again, down my face, as they had every day for the last few days, but now for different reasons. And when the song ended, the tears ended, too. I wiped them with my free hand, holding the empty album cover in the other, and leaned softly on Mercer. Neither of us said a word. Then Nakita came in and turned the album off. She took the record from the stereo, slipped it inside the album cover I was holding, and said softly, "Take it home with you. It's yours now."

33

[ENEMY FIELDS]

Back in the kitchen, Aunt Ruty had taken the lace curtains down from the window over the sink and put them in the sink. She was rubbing them down with a soft brush and soaking them in hot, sudsy water. She'd filled the bucket she got from her trunk with water, too, and she put the stove burner covers down in there after dumping in two capfuls of ammonia. She dried her hands on a yellow towel and sat down at the table with us—Mercer, Nakita, and me.

"Nakita probably know this story so well she could tell it to you herself. But I guess I better do it. See that old house out there?" She stood up and pulled the kitchen door open, the one that led outside. She pointed to a large house with boarded windows that sat way out across the back field. "That's where they used to live. Nobody ain't lived there for a while now, but ain't nobody come to sell it or tend to it, neither. They say it belong to your mama." She left the door opened and came back to the table to sit, but this time you could hear the bones in her legs crack when she bent down.

"Tell her who, Ma. She don't know who." Nakita looked and listened like she was watching her favorite movie.

"Let me tell this, Baby. Was white folks called the Mandarenes. Lived over there for a time. Early seventies or so. Sister switched right on acrosst that field and asked could she work for them white folks, you know. Cooking and cleaning and all. That's where it started."

"But, you said my mama owns the house. So...?"

"Yep. That's what they say. But back before that, when the white folks still live in the place, *they* was the ones that owned it. Was a white woman around my ma's age, an old man, and a young man name of Evian. He the one your mama took up with."

Mercer looked at me and lifted his eyebrow, like he already knew the story but was anxious to see how I would take the news.

"Mandarene?! I have a newspaper clipping about them! I showed it to Ain't Angus, but she didn't know much about it. Who were they?"

"Well, the mama come from Lex, but the old man and his people come from Georgetown. Used to own a horse farm, had some money. The old man died back before you were born, and the woman married off and moved away. Now, Evian. He and Sister got to be pretty close." Aunt Ruty got up again, took the brush and scrubbed the burner covers, then pushed the curtains aside and rinsed the burners off in the sink.

"Tell her about Evian, Ma." Kita acted like she was getting to the juicy part of a Harlequin romance. She licked her lips and her eyes got bigger, if that was possible.

"Yes. Well, Evian was the woman's son. He was about Sister's age. A little older. twenty or so. Had cancer. Seem like he used to be into music some, too. Least-wise, the two of them got to be friends, kissing friends. Sister never did let on about it, but I knew. Next thing you know, Sister was pregnant, and next thing you know, you was born."

Nakita clapped her hands in delight and looked at me with envy and interest. "Can you believe all this drama, Girl! Aunt Becca taking up with a white boy, way back in the day!"

I felt like I was missing a link. Not getting a piece of the puzzle. "Okay. So, then, Evian is the one who… got my mama pregnant?" Mercer grabbed my hand under the table and squeezed.

"Like I say, Sister never let on what all went on with her and Evian. But, like I say, they was real close. And she came up pregnant. And when you came out, well, it seem clear somebody in the picture was white. And it sure wasn't Sister." Aunt Ruty returned the covers to the stove and ran new water over the curtains, until the water ran clean. Then she wrung the water out of them and hung them on the back of a chair.

"Okay. So we think Evian is Dig's father. Now. Whatever happened to him? Do you know?" Mercer leaned in for the answer.

"Yes, we know. He died of cancer in 1972 or something. And the old man he lived with, that was his granddaddy. He died, too. If you ask me, he had some-thing wrong with his heart, but I don't know for sure. But, the granddaddy left that house over there to his grandson, Evian. But the thing is, he dead, too." Kita had waited long enough to give the details of this story, and she delighted in giving this last bit of information.

I swallowed sharply every time I heard the name Evian. Like the album *ForEVer* that Kita had just shown me with the picture of the watercolor field. Evian, they say, had gotten my mama pregnant. So that meant…

"I thought you said the house belonged to her mama?" Mercer sought clarity, knowing I could not.

"Umm-hmm. But see, Evian died. And he left all he had to Sister. Everything. Including that house."

I took a moment to let this information sink in. "Mind if I go look at it? The house, I mean?" I wasn't really asking so much as telling them where I was going. Mercer stood to follow me, but he must have thought better of it and reclaimed his seat.

"Lot of weeds and brush out there, Dignity. Watch your step, hear?"

"And snakes and mice, too!" Nakita hollered.

I heard their voices behind me as they were in a faraway dream. This house I approached, past all of this greenery, wild weeds, flowers, sticks, and brush, was something that belonged to my mama, that had belonged to my…Evian. Weeds came up to my hips as I picked my way through, and I could feel the tops of them brushing against the tips of my fingers. The whole picture was intimidating to me and made me feel queasy.

Across the field, the house looked large and imposing. There was a large window that faced Grandmama's house, but it was mostly boarded up. The parts that were not covered reflected the wild weeds from the fields, and the shadows moved on the windows like dancing ghosts. The driveway had begun to crack, and grass was growing up through the holes. The brick front was graying and faded. I was almost at the back door of this old house when I stopped short.

A thick wave of nausea brushed over me, and I had to hold my head together to keep it from spinning off my shoulders. I felt like I was going to be sick. The thick pollen, the smell of the grass, and the sight of the house combined, nearly knocked me over. I bent at the waist, with my hands on my knees, and breathed deep. But the air wasn't coming. It felt like I was in a vacuum, like the air was being sucked quickly from my lungs. I began to pant and to panic. I wanted to sit down, but it felt like the ground was cracking and spinning underneath me. I needed to keep my eyes closed to stop the intense feeling of vertigo.

I felt the weeds tickling the palm of my hands as I tried to keep myself from puking and fainting. But it was too late. I kept hearing "God Bless the Child" in my head as I fell to the ground.

I lay on the ground with my hands over my eyes. I was afraid to take them away, afraid that the world would still be spinning, that my skin would still be clammy and crawling, that my stomach would still be threatening to spill its contents. I sat up. Looked around. Back toward the house where I'd come from, but the weeds were too thick to see through. I looked, instead, at the house they say my mama owns. I imagined her in and around that house, cleaning, with Evian, having taken up with him. I imagined the woman in the picture and a faceless stranger in that house, singing, laughing, conceiving me. Then I heard a gunshot.

I stumbled to my feet, screaming, and then I saw Nakita shooting at the field with a BB gun. She missed.

"Dag! Almost had him, too! Ma, I'm getting as good as you with this thing! Almost hit me a mouse!" Nakita noticed me standing, looking dumbfounded, in the middle of the field, so I waved. I wasn't sure how long I had been gone, but I headed back quickly, anxious to rid myself of the spooky, nauseous feeling I had just encountered in this overgrown field in front of the house that my mama supposedly owned.

When I got back in the kitchen, Aunt Ruty was drying the bucket and putting the bottle of ammonia back inside of it. She had re-hung the lace curtains and was looking around the kitchen, obviously ready to leave. She nodded to me again and said she was going to change the sheets in the bedroom right quick. She told Kita to be ready when she got back downstairs.

Nakita was busy telling Mercer about how she was going to go away to school to study fashion design. Said she'd already sent away for the information on a school in Delaware. She said Lex was so tired, she knew she'd appreciate it more if she got away for a little while.

"Yes, a lot of people say that, about leaving. I guess I'm just used to it here. But, Kita, if you got something in your mind you wanna do, go for it!" Mercer was being his usual, charming self.

"For real! But call me Bug. Everybody else do. On accounta my eyes. You never think of leaving?"

I had to interject. "Believe me. I have been trying to convince him for years to come see me in Maryland, but he won't come. He's one of the state's natural resources, Bug. He can't leave." I put my hand on his shoulder to let him know I was ready to jet.

"Mama is like that, too." She stood up and adjusted her short skirt and fluffed her long braids. "Well, me and Ginger going to the club tonight, anyway, so I need to go and figure out what Imma wear. Dignity, girl, we still need to talk. I always wanted a cousin around this way. My daddy's people is way out in Richmond, and I only get to see them every once in a while. We should get together sometimes. Hang out." She touched my shoulder lightly, and I knew she was being sincere.

"Definitely. I'll come down to the shop one Friday, and we can hang. And umm, thanks for, ah…"

"No thang but a chicken wang! See you, Mercer." The three of us piled out the door and said our goodbyes. Aunt Ruty told me to call her if I needed anything. I said I would.

On the way back to Lex, I kept quiet. I had the album Kita gave me on my lap, but I couldn't really look at it. It makes me sick to look at pictures or try to read in the car.

"You know, your auntie said that Evian's mother lives in Ashland. Her name is Howard. Cordial Howard. I bet she's listed."

"Umm-hmm. Let's talk about that tomorrow. After all, I normally wouldn't be coming home until tomorrow, and you have other plans."

"True. True. So. Whenever you want to talk about it, you know I am right here for you."

I gave Mercer a deep hug when he dropped me off, and he promised to call me first thing on Sunday. I tucked the album under my arm and went in the house and straight back to my room. I needed time to think before explaining to Aunt Lette where I had been all day.

[OUT PAST GEORGETOWN, KY 1985]

34

[TWO OF A KIND]

Sister Becca held the picture Della gave her in her hands. She felt the old, cold splash down her spine, the tingle of salt that signaled vomit, and began swallowing and blinking. Brief pause, then she opened her eyes, diverted them from Blister, and looked only at her Evian.

"Ev used to sing and play the guitar. Sweet as you can believe. It were old hymns, but he made them sound new. And clean. Always love Ev. Always will." The tears spilled out of Becca's eyes, sharp as vinegar, and she didn't bother to wipe them away.

Della picked up the box of Kleenex and placed it softly in Becca's lap. She pulled a handful out for herself and sat down again. "Well, they were my cousins. Them and Blister's sister, Theresa. Only I never really got to know Evian. Not as an adult anyway. You know he was sick coming up, so we didn't visit his family much. Now, me and Theresa was tight. But Blister…"

"Now quit it! Not too many times I'mma here you say that word fore I lose what you just fed me—enough! Say what you got to say, now. Just say it." Sister reached for her cup of tea, then thought better of it, and dumped a hefty taste of whiskey in the mason jar before tucking it down her throat for safe keeping.

Della wasn't exactly surprised by the woman's outburst, but she did clear her throat twice before she began to talk. "Yeah. Mum-Mum used to say that if you gain something, you also lose something right away. Said it was Satan's way of keeping score. It was always true for me. I gained my womanhood and lost my, ah, innocence, all in a matter of days. Got my womanhood around my thirteenth birthday. Like to scared me to death. We never really talked about such things. I mean, Theresa, my cousin, me and her had talked a little about it, but not much. So when it happened, I was put off. Didn't want to tell nobody about it. I think

I had been planting in the garden, and when it happened, I thought I'd cut myself. Off I ran to the house to see, and found all this blood—you know. I cleaned myself up and all. But then I didn't feel like planting. Just felt like crying."

Sister nodded her head. "Don't none of us really expect it, I guess. Always come as a shock. I remember I was surprise, too." Becca ran her finger around the edge of the jar as she listened.

"Umm. Yeah. So, all that week I moped around and felt sorry. Stomach hurt me something awful, and this new blood thing. Freaky. Threw me off. But it passed, and I knew I was in the clear for a month or so. That's when I got happy and started to think what fun I could have. Being a full woman and all. Started to see this thing as a gain."

Becca kept her eyes on the picture of Evian and Blister and listened.

"'Bout this time, Blister took a special interest in my planting. He'd come around asking which seeds were what and wanna help me with the digging and the watering. Don't you know he told me there were all kinds of flowers I'd never seen, some that blossomed in the spring, others in the summer and the fall. Even told me there was one special kind of flower that came up only at night."

Della's cheeks flushed audibly when she said these words, and Sister Becca looked up, meeting Dell's eyes with a glazed glance before letting it flitter away. "Said they bloom at night? I heard of four o'clocks, but never any that bloom at night." Sister stuck the mason jar between her clenched knees and folded her arms in on herself, still holding onto the picture Della had given her.

"Yep. Said they bloomed only at midnight. Just as pretty, all pink and red, but only at twelve o'clock at night. He told me there were some of these flowers planted out back of the church, behind that row of trees out there. Said I never seen them since I never been out there that late." Della pointed toward the back of the house. "And I knew I had to see these flowers, because that was my thing back then—making things grow. So, here I am trying to figure out a plan to where I can get out back there close to midnight so's I can see these mysterious midnight flowers." She shook her head. "Figured I'd take me a bag and collect a few seeds, if I could, and plant these magic flowers in my own backyard. Seemed like a great thing to do, getting these secret flowers, especially with my being a woman and all."

Another sip and Becca shared. "Mama used to plant a lot, too. She liked vegetables, though. Tomatoes, green beans, and greens, mostly. I never had a notion to do it. Dirt never set well with me."

"It's not the dirt, per se, that you want, although I didn't mind it at the time. Can't take the mess now. But I liked the digging and the mashing down. And the flowers. That was the reward. Anyway, I was determined to see these flowers he described, and he seemed anxious to have me see them. Even offered to meet me out back there one night, if I was brave enough, so I wouldn't be all alone." The woman crossed her leg over the other, Indian style.

"Me, I never like to be out in the dark alone. Don't seem right. Used to look out the window at night, though. Had a field back of where I live full of all kind of mess. Weeds, mostly, and some flowers. Trees. Grass as high as you can believe, too. But I didn't used to be out there much at night." Sister Becca started to finger her curly hair, caught up in the memory.

Della agreed. "Me neither. But I was determined to do it this time. Such a fool. Snuck out of the house long about eleven-thirty, give me time to get out there and meet my cousin. Had my bag and my planting gloves, too. I was ready. Least I thought I was."

By this time, Sister's eyes had begun to pulse with action though she had them closed. "It were a pretty night when I were first with Evian, you know. Real close and all. Had this cousin in town, and we were setting out in the back, eating ribs and drinking some, too. It was pretty at first. But then it got different."

Della shook her foot a little as it rested on the edge of her knee. She massaged it some and kept talking. "Well, he showed up, and here I am bent over and just looking. He's pointing and pointing at this one spot on the ground where these flowers are supposed to spring up in a few minutes, like magic. But I don't see anything…"

"Got late that night I was round to Ev's. We had, umm, been close and all, and I got shy and thought I'd go on home. Mr. Norman in his room, and, uh, the cousin asleep in the guest room. Evian asleep in the bed, spread out like a gold eagle, just as peaceful as you can believe. My Ev. But it seem like I should go. Cross that field, back to my own place, way late in the night." Sister wanted to drink more whiskey to fend off the oncoming memory, but she couldn't get her arms loose from the fold in front of her, couldn't get the jar from between her clenched knees.

Della made a cave with her two hands around her left foot to stop it from shaking. "Dirt, ants, moss, but damned if I could see any trace of those midnight flowers. Son of a bitch. Next thing you know, he's pushed me over, got my skirt way up over my head somewhere. And pressing it cold against me. Felt like knives."

"Naw, naw. Not knives. Tools. Rusted tools from out the shed. And it don't seem possible that such a pretty night, all those stars and all those ribs, and you thought you was in love. All that twisted into a rough, old, rusty farm tool and pushing its way on through. Splashing that nasty spit inside." Sister Becca covered her mouth to muffle her own voice, eyes vibrating now and likely to pop straight out of her skull with the recollection.

Della's foot jiggled in spite of the handheld cave she'd fashioned around it with her fingers. "Nope. No splash, my love. Son of a bitch tricked me, and he wasn't gonna get a splash if I could help it! I grabbed and scratched until I had a good handful of that moss and slammed it across his teeth and clear into his nose, down his rotten throat. Got your nose open, Buddy? Well smell this!" She had a wry smile that Sister's closed eyes couldn't see.

"Tried to be sweet. Let him walk me home. But he want more than a walk, I can see. Jealous of my Ev and wanna spoil what we got. Naw. S'posed to be sleep, Mr. Cousin. Don't spose to be following after me, way in the night, farming me with tools out the shed! Naw!" Sister's eyes flew open to look Blister's picture dead on the eyeball. "I see you ain't new to this here! Always did wanna force what you got that don't nobody want!" She seemed to be speaking directly to the picture in her hand. And her body seethed with the words, and finally her arms came unfolded.

When her arms freed, the picture dropped to the floor. The glass frame cracked and made a Zorro's "Z" over the dead cousin's face. Sister rose from the couch to try and catch the frame, but as she did, the mason jar, once clenched between her knees, was emancipated. It drooled brown liquor all over Sister's yellow dress.

Della was shocked into action. Before the whiskey could seep through Sister's dress and onto her fresh-swept floor, Della dove for the box of Kleenex, piling several onto the carpet in front of Sister, ready to sop up the very first drop before it hit the floor. On her knees there, she waited, anticipating the flow of lukewarm liquid. But none came.

Sister peered down at her, this woman who kept things clean, and watched as she dammed up the carpet for whiskey that wouldn't come. "I think I got the worst of it, Miss. Ain't none of it on your floor." She pulled more tissue from the box and dabbed at her wet midsection. "It's all soaked up now in stain. I caught it. No need to worry."

Della came off her knees, relieved, and set the jar upright on the tea tray. Sister followed behind her with the mostly gone bottle of Ancient Age and the cracked picture of Evian and the cousin. In the kitchen, Della put the dishes into the sink and left them. Then she flopped into the wooden kitchen chair.

"Guess I better get back. Got a show to do. You ever tell anybody? You know. About Blister?" Becca put her sunglasses back on.

"No need. Threw the dress away. Cleaned myself up and went on. I didn't cry when he died, though."

"No one did. We two of a kind, huh?"

"Two of a kind. You can come back if you want." Della rose from her chair to walk Sister to the door.

"Maybe one day. You keep this. Don't look like none of my Ev no way, hugged up that way with the cousin." She handed Della the picture in the cursed frame. "I don't need a picture no way. Got a million good ones inside my head."

"I keep mine in the open, so's I can keep them clean. You know Evian was sterile, right?"

Sister blanched visibly. "Guess nothing could come from him." Her spirit sucked in and readied for collapse, but didn't. "Anything come of you and... Daniel?"

"Nah. Too messy. So. Goodbye, Sister Becca."

"Guess we's sisters sure enough. Bye." With this, Sister spoke her last words. She lumbered to the car and drove off, speechless, in a cloud of clay and dust.

IN MEDIA RES:
JUST AFTER FINALS, JUNIOR YEAR
[MORGAN STATE UNIVERSITY 1995]

35

[EASTER]

Salmon

I have tried calling Dignity once already, and I haven't heard back from her. Getting the number wasn't exactly easy, either. I had to talk to her Aunt Angus for about an eternity before she would give me the number to her Aunt Lette's place, where she lives. Not that I minded talking to her. Aunt Angus, I mean. She was funny as hell. Said young people couldn't get it together for even a minute if it would save their lives. Which might be true. My life is definitely a shambles. I haven't been able to put it together. The whole thing makes me wonder if I made a mistake with this Dignity thing; I don't know. Hard to tell.

But, Digs was putting the pressure on so tight, and there were finals I needed to ace. Not to mention Pops and that whole Easter thing, with Aunt Celia and Ma crying. Nightmare. Tears make me nervous. I just can't take it when women cry. Breaks my heart. And Pops wasn't exactly budging either, even though I stood my ground and dared him to love me, like Frankie said. But that day, it just wasn't happening.

I don't want to lose my family. I mean, cripes. It's a high price to pay. Especially with the way Ma and Aunt Celia carried on. I do love Dignity. For real. And I don't want to lose her. But staying with her would be a lot of work for me. And very hard for my family. I just figure like, if I'm working up a sweat over this thing, Digs ought to want to work along with me. She said she didn't want to do the work, so we split. But the thing is, with Digs gone, with school over, and with Khalil down in Virginia, I am miserable.

So I phoned her. Just to say hi, no big deal. But she wasn't around. And I still haven't heard from her, so I guess she's moved on. Meanwhile, I'm still stuck in limbo over here.

I keep playing the Easter tape over and over in my head. When Frankie talked me into the thing, I was actually looking forward to it, in an anxious, stomach-cramping kinda way. Because Easter is a big deal with us, and I hadn't had the chance to take part in it for a while. I missed my family.

So, on Easter, I show up at St. John's for the nine a.m. Mass, and I slip into the pew behind Ma and Poppy. The place was decked out like always with the altar full of lilies and the children wearing their white dresses and dark suits. Made me feel good. I got there early, too, because I knew that the parents would already be there holding seats for the family, which they're not supposed to do on Easter since it gets so crowded. But it doesn't work anyways. Celia and her husband, fat-ass Uncle Eddie, and their two loud-mouth kids are always late and end up standing somewhere in the back every year. Frankie always gets there just before the doors close, and I get there a few minutes before that. Least I used to.

This year was no different. I showed up just before nine, but this time I slipped in behind Mommy and didn't even say hello. Took her a minute to notice me, but when she did, she winked at me and started to nudge Poppy. Poppy just nudged her back, like he didn't know what she was nudging about. But he knew. I could tell he knew.

I loved the service. It was good to hear the word and pray. And they had those hibiscus plants Mommy loves so much, and the whole place smelled like heaven. So, when they had the congregation stand up and give each other hugs and wish each other peace, I stood up and hugged Ma while Frankie hugged Pop. Then Mommy and Poppy hugged, and I hugged Frankie. And then, just before we were motioned to sit down, Poppy leaned over the pew and gave me a quick hug across the shoulders. "Good to see you, Son." He sat down quickly after that.

That's when Ma started crying, and she kept it up for the rest of the day. Like to kill me with those tears! When the service was over, Frankie slapped me on the back, and we walked together to his car. I'd rented this tiny little Ford Focus for the weekend, and alls they had was this queer shade of purple. I remember he got a big kick out of that. "Check out Barney, over here!" I didn't mind, though.

We knew the parents were inside finding Aunt Celia and gabbing it up with the families they only see at Easter, so we stood there and talked for a minute. You know, belaboring the obvious.

"So, you made it. Proud of you, Kid. I don't want to, ah, disillusion you, though. It ain't gonna be easy. You know how Pop is, and he hasn't exactly changed his mind or nothing. But, ah, we'll see what happens, huh?" He kept patting me on the back, but the whole time, true to form, he was looking over my shoulder. Wouldn't you know, there was Darcy Hurston, with her long red hair and boobs a mighty, heading out of the church. And here I am wanting his full attention. Yeah, right.

"Listen, I'll catch up with you at the house, alright? I picked up that vino Ma likes, so we can toast before dinner. Start things out right. So, I'm out."

I watched as he made his way over to Darcy, who did look good in her sky-blue sundress with heels to match. I got in the car and started to wheel around, thinking. I remember I had this tape of Steely Dan on that I got from Digs. I don't think she owns a single tape that was made in this decade. But I like Steely Dan. I was listening to that one song where they talk about chasing the dragon and turning water to wine and it rang true. Because this whole thing with Pops, it was like chasing a dragon. I knew I was in for fire and who knows what else. But I was hoping that the wine and the fuzzy family thing might take the sting off of things. Make the silver turn to gold, I don't know.

I kept remembering Dignity. She was back at school and wanted so badly for things to go well, even though I refused to bring her with me. I said to her, "It's been a few years since I even laid eyes on Pop. Let me go alone, smooth things over, lay some groundwork first. Then, maybe."

I got home, and I could see Aunt Celia and the family were already there. I didn't see Pop's truck, though. I was relieved. Went in and said my hellos. My aunt was in the kitchen setting out the dishes and going on and on about how thin I had gotten. And all of this with a puddle of tears in her eyes. Uncle Eddie was in the basement watching the game, and the kids, Alex and Jimmy, were running around the backyard like maniacs. The whole place smelled of ripe tomatoes and olives. Business as usual for Easter, and I loved it. I loosened my tie and sat with Aunt Celia at the table while she pulled out Nanny's good china. Figured I'd better take advantage of this moment of peace while it lasted.

"They don't have food at this university, I see. All this education, and you can't find time to eat! Honestly, you're dwindled down to nothing!" She put the serving platter in the center and placed the crystal glasses next to each plate.

"Oh please! I eat enough, alright! I do miss Ma's cooking, though. That frozen lasagna ain't exactly cutting it." I wanted to keep the conversation light, and at the last minute I wished I hadn't made that comment about Ma's cooking.

"Suddenly your mommy stops cooking? I don't think so, Sallie! It's you that stopped eating! And coming by or calling, and coming to Mass with us. You could only blame yourself." She thought better of the stemware next to the children's place settings and went to the kitchen for the plastic tumblers.

I wasn't going to get into it with her. But somehow the tone of her voice pushed a button. "Aunt Celia, wait a second. You know I would come. But, ah, racist comments and all, it doesn't exactly whet my appetite. I'm here now. That's all I can say."

"So, who is she anyway, this woman keeping you from us? Has she got a golden coochie or something, what? Tell your Aunt Celia." She pulled out the chair across from me and wiped her hands on her apron before sitting down to grill me.

My stomach jolted with the vulgar comment. My aunt was always brassy and tactless. It was part of her charm, I guess. I chose to ignore the comment. "My girlfriend's name is Dignity. Dignity Jackson. She is very smart and pretty, and I think you would like her."

"And she's very dark, too, I understand." She threw up her hands with exhaustion. "What happened?! With all the schools in the world, you gotta go to *this* one. All the beautiful women out there, and you go and find a *colored* one. Why… ?" She leaned over the table and took my hand into hers. She was trying to be sincere, in her own backwards way.

I squeezed a little before dropping her hands. "Look, colored is a word you use to describe paintings and televisions. Hello! Welcome to the twentieth century, okay? There's a lot of schools out there, but this is the one that gave me a scholarship. I wasn't exactly Einstein back in high school, alright? And you don't go looking for friends, or education for that matter, based on race or whatever. It just happens. Life happens, Aunt Celia." I found myself getting hostile, and I had to remind myself that my aunt is an elder. Gotta talk to her with respect. Even when the words out of her mouth are ignorant, she still deserves my respect. I cleared my throat and softened my tone. "You gotta understand. Dignity is special. She understands me, and she's in my corner one hundred percent. She's more than just a color, okay? And I love her."

Aunt Celia pushed back her chair to stand up, and I could tell by the way she narrowed her eyes that I had struck a chord with her. "Yeah. Love is funny. You know, quiet as it's kept, your Grandpa John didn't want me with Eddie. Said he had a bad disposition that I'd be sorry for later. And he was right. Your uncle is a son of a bitch half the time. But inside, where you don't always see, he's a pussy cat. A real marshmallow. And he's crazy about me. Always was. So." She stood up and pulled the antipasto from the platter in the fridge. "I don't know, Sallie. Your poppy ain't gonna like this. He isn't good with change. It could be a real struggle. And the world ain't exactly living out Dr. King's dream, either. It could be trouble. You up for it?"

I went to the kitchen and, squeezing her shoulder, I lifted some olives and cheese from the tray. "Oh yeah, I'm up for it. I don't give up easy. Runs in the family."

36

[CRUCIFIXION]

"Our Sallie's got him a colored girlfriend, Lucille. Says her name is Dignity. I'd like to meet her!" Aunt Celia poured herself another glass of red wine and belched.

By this time we were digging into Ma's ziti and having at the homemade bread. My God, was it good. Ma had the oil for dipping, and the wine Frankie bought was the perfect temperature. Had my stomach singing. But then Aunt Celia goes and makes this comment, and the whole table goes silent. I looked over at Frankie for support or something. But he just went on eating like he never heard a thing our aunt said. I followed suit, figuring silence was golden at that point.

But she kept at it. "You know, the Mangiannis, remember? The ones who fell out at St. John's and switched last summer to St. Peter's? Their daughter, Candice, is with a color, I mean, black guy. He's a doctor or something. And they bought a place out in Potomac, too. Real posh, I hear. They didn't invite me to the wedding. Not that I would have gone or anything. But everyone's doing it these days. Tell us about your friend, Sallie." Her voice was soft and ripe from the wine, and I think she really did mean well. But, so much for time and place and broaching a difficult subject.

Finally Frankie stepped in. "I seen her. She's a real doll. I don't got a problem with her. I figure, if the kid's happy, then I'm happy."

I didn't know what to say. I nodded and kept eating the bread, soaking up the rest of the dipping oil and washing it down with wine. I needed to be drunk. I could see Pop's shoulders tighten, and his bottom lip went straight. Which only happens when he's about to shit a brick about something.

Alex piped up. "At school? In my related arts class? That's, like, this thing where you get to choose what kind of special activity you want to do? Well Jamie and me chose crafts, and…"

"Jamie and I, Pumpkin. Go on." Aunt Celia corrected Alex. Alex has this annoying way of going up at the end of every sentence, like she's asking a question. Grates my nerves. But she's a hell of a cute kid.

"Jamie and I chose crafts, cuz, like, you could make really cool jewelry. Like, this bracelet I'm wearing? I made three of them already. And you can give them to your friends, cuz they're like, friendship bracelets? Anyways, there's a kid in there whose name is Tanya? And she's black. She always sits with us and stuff. She's funny."

"Couldn't pay me to *pork* one of them! If you ask me, they're practically the missing link! Except that Halle Berry—now she's a hotty!" Jimmy reached over his sister for the gravy. Ma keeps a boat of her thick meat sauce on the table in case you want extra.

That's when I had to speak up. How old was Jimmy anyway? Twelve, thirteen? What did he know about a missing link? You don't just pick up that kind of thing; you gotta learn it somewhere. What do you wanna bet he learned it from his dad or his uncle, my father? What kind of shit is that to teach your kids? The idea of my kid cousin saying something like that knocked me out of my silence.

"What do you mean, pork? What kind of talk is that? Listen, nobody's asking you to pork anybody! You watch how you talk at the table!" I looked at Jimmy with a scold in my face, and he looked back with a wise guy smirk. So, I finally looked at my parents.

I couldn't shut up. "Is this what you guys want? Another generation of backwards ignoramuses who don't have enough sense to get to know other people? You guys, we can't afford to do that!" I pushed the dipping bowl aside and brushed the bread crumbs onto my empty plate. "Listen. I go to a black school, alright? And I learn a lot there. It ain't exactly killing me. Matter of fact, I'm gonna keep on going until I graduate next year, and then I'm gonna go a little further. Because I'm interested in urban planning, and, and I'm good at it! Furthermore, I have a girlfriend. And, yes, her name is Dignity, and, yes, she happens to be black. But she's also funny. And smart. And brilliant. And, uhh. I'm not ready to stop seeing her."

Right there, Ma started crying. A real soft, pitiful sob. And Aunt Celia leaned over to her and put her hand over Ma's. But then Aunt Celia started crying, too.

And, let's face it; none of us likes to see a woman cry, so right there the mood at the table was shot.

Uncle Eddie, with his typical chicken-shit ways, cut and ran. "Lovely dinner, Lucille. Real tasty." He left the table in a hurry and went back downstairs. Next thing you know, the kids wanted to be excused. So the only ones left were me, Frankie, Aunt Celia, and my parents.

My father waited until the others left, and then he started steaming. "Who the hell you calling an ignoramus, huh? Nobody here is ignorant! If you ask me, it's ignorant to turn your back on your family to have some fling with a black girl! What's it worth to you, huh? What? All the times I'm working fourteen, sixteen, twenty hours a day to put food on the table. And your mommy over here pulling the ends to make them meet. And this is how you thank us? It's a disgrace, Salmon." Already he was visibly shaking, but he tried to keep his voice low.

"Pop, I don't aim to be a disgrace, okay? Since when is getting an education a disgrace? I'd think you'd be proud of me! I got a plan for my life. And I'm happy. I'm not disrespecting all you done for me. Honest. I remember every little thing. But I'm not an electrician. No matter what you say, I'm never gonna be good with that stuff."

Aunt Celia and Ma kept sobbing and kept quiet.

Finally Frankie came to my defense. "Maybe he's right, Poppy. Me, I gotta natural gift—you said it yourself. But Sal over here, his gift is with something else. I think it's damn lucky you got me to carry on the family business. That's what this is about, right? The business? Well, you got that. Ain't that enough?"

"No. It's not just about the business. It's about respect and family values! I didn't raise you to go taking up with a different kind, Sal. Mommy and me worked hard to give you boys culture. *Our* culture! And you throw that out the window like it ain't good enough for you! It's shameful."

By then, Mommy started to cough. She'd started this awful coughing a few months back. She's always had allergies, and if there's too much of the wrong stuff in the air, she starts to wheeze. Aunt Celia poured her some more of the wine, which was about gone, the way we'd been drinking it. Ma sucked it down, and the cough settled down some. But sometimes her body would quake quietly, and when it did, Aunt Celia would look at me accusingly and rub Ma's back.

"Alright. If this is about culture, I got it covered! I know all about our grandparents, and their grandparents, and how they started over here in America from scratch. And I know every Hail Mary known to man. And I seen *The Godfather* at least three thousand times. I got much love for Sinatra and even Mama Celeste. I wear leather whenever it's physically possible, I gesture when I talk, and I'm thinking about buying a 'Vette. I got it all down, Pops. Really. And I love it. But just because I am with Dignity doesn't mean that I threw the rest of my upbringing away! They got nothing to do with each other! Why can't you see that?" By this time I was standing. My voice had raised an octave, and my veins would have popped out of my skull if I weren't careful.

"Salmon, please…" Ma started to talk, but my dad wouldn't let her finish.

He stood up and met my glance full throttle. His lips were like a slit across his lower face, and his eyes shot daggers at me. "I see. I see. You think all there is to this family is a lot of bullshit stereotypes from the movies. But what you don't seem to see is the *blood*. It took blood, Salmon. Blood to forge out this space in the world called The Rinaldis. It ain't all about leather and Hail Marys, Son. It's about tradition." Pop took some deep breaths, and I swear I could see steam in his nose.

"It's about blood. And in this family, the father makes the decisions. He sees what's best for the family, and he makes a decision. And he's solid about it.

"Now you get this clear, once and for all. I made a decision on this. There ain't nobody in this family so far who went and tangled with another race, Salmon. We don't *do* that. I don't know why, but we just…don't. And we don't just walk away from the family, neither. Not for any reason. You gonna be a ball breaker? You gonna be a wise guy rebel? You think you know more than your father? Well, you don't. You make these kinds of decisions, Salmon, and you make them on your own. Finished! End of story!"

"No! You don't mean what you're saying…" Mommy stood up then and tried to pull Poppy back, but he was halfway through the kitchen door, nearly out of the room.

"The *hell* I don't. Rinaldis follow the father's rules. Period. I make the rules. He don't want to follow them? He don't wanna be a Rinaldi."

"Nooo… listen to what you're saying… just listen…" Ma was trying to hang on to Pop's sleeve, but he knocked her hand away and went through the kitchen and out the back door. She came back to the table and collapsed into a puddle of tears. Aunt Celia sat there cooing and trying to soothe her, and Frankie and I just stood there, not looking at each other.

Finally I came around the table and put my arms around my mother. She was breaking my heart over there. I couldn't take anymore. "I love you, Ma. And I'm sorry for all this." Then I made for the front door with a quickness. Somewhere in my middle, I felt like I was going to be sick.

Frankie followed me out front, and we both got into my car. I told him to buckle up, and we started driving. The tape of Steely Dan was still playing. By then it wasn't helping my mood.

"So much for making the silver turn to gold...," I said to myself.

"What?"

"Nothing. Well, I'm not gonna quit school, and I'm not gonna stop seeing Dignity, so... I guess I better change my name. If I can't be a Rinaldi, maybe I can be a Kennedy. How's that sound? Salmon Kennedy." I tried to make light of the situation, but neither of us was feeling it.

"She's sick, you know."

I pulled into the parking lot over at the Safeway across from my parents' house. "What are you talking about?"

"Mommy. She's sick. Something about her respiratory system." He was looking out the window, and I knew if I even tried to make eye contact with him that we both would lose our composure. So I didn't.

"Shit. I knew something was going on, but, umm. I guess I just thought it would clear up on its own. What is it, anyway?"

"Look. That's what medicine is for. It's gonna be alright. I just think Poppy is stressed out over it, is all. Maybe he's taking it out on you. This, too, shall pass, Sal. Take my word for it."

We sat there for a while longer before I dropped him off at the house. Later that night I called and apologized to my Aunt Celia. She told me the same thing. To give it some time and let it work itself out. I wanted to know more about Mommy, but Aunt Celia didn't go into details. That's what my family does. They never want to take a look at anything that's serious. When I pressed her, she told me it wasn't fatal and that the doctors were taking care of it. She made me promise to give Mommy and Pop a few weeks to simmer down and work things out before disturbing them again with this "Dignity business." I told her I would. She promised to call me if anything happened that I should know about.

So Easter was a big drama. I went, but I didn't accomplish what I'd set out to. Not even close. I couldn't tell Dignity that things weren't any better. No way was I going to be taking her home to meet the folks any way soon. So, the pressure was on, big time. I felt trapped. I couldn't give Dignity what she wanted, and I couldn't bring myself to tell her why. So, when she gave me that ultimatum, and when she didn't want to do the therapy thing, I had no choice but to call it quits.

But, like I said, ever since we split, I've been miserable.

37

[Blood]

It wasn't until after Mommy got sick that I really understood what Pop meant about blood. It has to do with investment and commitment, a fact that I really didn't grasp until then.

I remember the night it happened. It was a typical summer afternoon on the yard: the (Que) dogs were barking. The ice cream man drove through the development every hour on the hour blaring "London Bridges" so loud until you wished they'd fall down already and shut up about it. The kids in the building were playing dueling stereos; one favored house music, and the other was on a hip-hop tip. And I was alone in my apartment, where I had been every day for the past several days. I had nothing to do but feel sorry for myself on a full-time basis. I wouldn't start up my job again in the financial aid office for another week. Dignity was in Kentucky and not returning my calls. Khalil had gone down to Virginia to work with his dad for the summer.

On top of that, Frankie was busy with the new office, had contracts up to his ears. He barely had time to breathe, much less to call me, and Aunt Celia had forbidden me to call my parents for a while, after the whole Easter debacle. I was in a bad way.

So, that night at McDonald's, when I ran *into* Stacy, you'd have thought I would have run *over* Stacy. I should have barreled her down for the way she acted at the Ms. Morgan thing with Dignity. But she was sitting at this back booth looking as bad as I felt. And when she waved me over, I went ahead and sat down with her.

We didn't say anything to each other at first. She kept to her filet of fish and I stuck with my quarter pounder with cheese. But, sick as it sounds, I was glad as hell not to be sitting there alone.

She was wiping the extra tartar sauce away with a napkin and balling the napkin up in her hand when she said, "Talked to Lil?" She didn't look at me, and I didn't look at her. My eyes were riveted to the napkin she'd placed in a ball on the corner of the table.

"Not since last week. He's down at his dad's."

"Mmm. Dignity?" She took a long sip of her shake.

"Umm. Not actually. She went home for the summer." I shoved a stack of fries in my mouth, so I couldn't say anything else.

"What's your plan for the summer?"

"Ahh. Working. That's about it. Catch up on some flicks, maybe. Get ready for the big senior year."

There was silence for a minute while I finished my burger and she discarded the rest of her fish. This was awkward as shit. I had no clue why I was sitting there eating with a woman who drop-kicked my girlfriend a few days before my girlfriend drop-kicked me. Made no sense. I was about to roll up out of there when she caught me by surprise.

"You think I'm pretty, Sal?"

Bad time to ask a question like that. She wasn't at her best, in any regard. First off, she messed over my girlfriend. But beyond that, she looked the worst I'd ever seen her. No makeup at all, which wouldn't have been so bad if her skin had looked clear. And it didn't. She had deep circles under her eyes, the color of bad grapes. Her lips were chapped. Her hair was slicked back from her face in a weird way, and it looked like she was wearing pajamas. She was pathetic. And I didn't want to answer her question, but something… I don't know. Something made me go ahead and address it. Because when chicks get depressed, they start to think they're ugly. And if they think they're ugly, it all goes downhill from there.

"Well, yeah. Most of the time. You can be real attractive. But, frankly, you got a bad attitude. And that spoils everything." I knew this comment would sting her, but, it was the truth.

Stacy dropped her head. For a minute, my stomach twisted because I thought she was going to cry. There was no way I could take another scene like that—a woman crying her face off in front of me. But she'd pissed me off in the recent past, so I couldn't actually console her. Instead, I thought the right question might way-lay her.

"What's your problem, anyways? I mean, ahh. Why are you always hating on Dignity?"

She kept her eyes closed. "I don't hate her! She's just so…perfect. It's hard to take."

I didn't really agree with what she said. But I looked at Dignity through Stacy's eyes for a minute, and I felt sorry for her. Because Stacy can be kind of classy, but, let's face it. She's no Dignity. And it's got nothing to do with Dignity's looks, either.

Stacy went and threw our trash away, and when she got back, she didn't sit down. "You doing something later? Because I rented that Tina Turner movie. And, umm. I'm not making a play, Sal. Really. I just don't want to be alone. And umm. You seem like you could use some company, too." There was pleading behind her eyes. I understood how she felt.

"Unbelievable." I shook my head and marveled that she could ask me to spend time with her. "No. I guess I ain't exactly busy. You could bring it over and watch it with me." I stood up then and walked to the door. I didn't want to look at her face because part of me was still furious with her. Another part was pitied into compliance. Still another part of me just didn't want to be left alone.

Two hours later we were on my couch with, like, five miles between us. Both of us were slumped down and leaned over to opposite sides. In the movie, Ike had just opened a can of whoop ass on Tina's behind. Wasn't exactly news because he'd been beating on her since the movie started. We hadn't said a word since Stacy got there. It wasn't because we loved the movie, but it held our attention, which was good. Created a much needed diversion for both of us. I didn't want to miss a scene, so I paused the tape before I went to the bathroom. When I came back, I was about to turn the movie back on when Stacy started talking.

"You ever hit a woman?"

Caught me off guard, and I thought surely she was joking. "No."

"Anybody ever hit you?"

"Not really. I got in a fight once in eighth grade. But I'm not exactly one of these big violent types."

"Never occurred to me that anybody would hit someone like Tina Turner." She shook her head like she really was puzzled. "She's so pretty. And talented."

"You know, Stacy. You don't hit someone because they're ugly. You do it because you're a violent punk ass who takes shit out the wrong way." She was starting to bug me.

"My sister is like that."

"Like what?"

"Real light and pretty. Smart, too."

"Good for her." She kept talking, and I was beginning to wish I had never let her come over. She could say some whack shit. What was she getting at this time?

"But he beats her up anyway."

I could tell by the way her voice quivered that she would cry if I didn't handle this thing the right way. And I couldn't go there. So I questioned her carefully. "What are you talking about, Stacy?"

"Helene. My half-sister. Called me over the other night, and her face was two shades of purple, and it was swollen like a balloon." She swigged from the Pepsi she'd brought with her.

"What happened?"

"I don't know. That jerk she's with. Treats her like a punching bag."

"Who? Her boyfriend? Tell her to leave him already! She doesn't deserve that. Nobody does." It seemed like such a no-brainer to me.

"That's what I thought. Nobody deserves that. Especially not someone like her. I mean, she's nearly white, she's so light. She's so perfect looking. Hair way down her back, good figure. I don't understand it. Why would anybody hit someone like her?"

The talk was getting to me, and I really hadn't planned on all that. Khalil told me she had a thing about light skin, but I had no idea she tripped like that. "Look, Stacy. You're worried about the wrong thing, alright? If someone is hitting on your sister, deal with that. Don't worry about what your sister looks like. It's not about what she *looks* like. It's about being with an abusive asshole—that can happen to anybody."

I turned the movie back on. I remember we were cheering at the scene where Tina and Ike are in the cab, and she finally hits the son of a bitch back. I was so glad to see this woman finally realize what a jerk she was married to. I felt happy for her. It was the best I'd felt in a few days. But then the phone rang. I paused the tape again to answer it, and when I heard it was Aunt Celia, I knew it wasn't good news.

Normally, when a personal call comes like that, I get up and take it in the bedroom. But my heart froze when I heard my aunt's voice, and I couldn't move. So, I sat there talking, and Stacy must have listened to the whole thing.

Ma was in the hospital. Her throat had swollen up so bad she couldn't breathe, and she was in emergency surgery. When I heard, my throat closed, and I lost my breath right along with her. Because I knew Mommy was afraid of doctors. And I knew she must have been petrified of having surgery. I thought if I could just sit still and concentrate, I could make this whole thing go away for her. And I wanted it to go away for her. Bad.

Everything I heard and felt must have shown in my face, because when I hung up, Stacy put her arms around my shoulders and held me for a long minute. I was so scared, so lonely, so worn down by this news that I honestly wanted to lay down and cry. But Stacy had her arm around my shoulders, so I couldn't.

I told her my mommy was in the hospital. She didn't miss a beat. She stood up and pulled me up next to her. She got her keys out of her purse and said, "Where is she? I'll take you out there." Next thing you know, I'm in her passenger seat headed toward Holy Cross Hospital in Silver Spring. The drive seemed to last a lifetime. I kept my eyes closed, but I was crying and praying the whole time.

I was the last one to get there. As soon as we got to the floor where Ma was, I saw Frankie and Uncle Eddie sitting in the waiting room. My uncle was drinking Pepsi and eating a bag of Doritos. He had his eyes glued on the television, which was playing a rerun of *Three's Company*. Frankie was leaned up in his chair and kept running his hands through his hair. He does that when he's anxious.

I introduced Stacy to them, and she said she was going to find the ladies room. I could see Uncle Eddie lift his brows when he looked up and saw Stacy, but he didn't say anything to her. Just nodded a hello and went on watching the tube.

"They only let two people in there at a time. Pop and Aunt Celia are in there now. Let them know you're here, so you can see her. She'll be glad that you're here."

"Is she... okay?"

"Now she is. But it was serious. Way serious. And if Pop hadn't got her here... I don't know."

I nodded and went down the hall to Ma's room. When I stuck my head in, Aunt Celia got up and came out. "She's still really out of it, you know. And it was close. Real close, Sallie. Go be with your poppy now. He needs you." Her eyes were the size of baseballs, and I knew she'd been crying for a long, long time. Which made me wonder. When did Mommy get sick, and why hadn't they called me sooner?

Pop was in the chair next to Ma, so close to her that he might as well have been in the bed with her. He was arched over her, like he could spring at any minute.

I pulled the other chair over, close to my father. First thing, I bowed my head and said a prayer. I crossed myself and crossed my mother. She had a tube down her throat, and her face looked almost blue. It didn't look like she was in pain.

But my dad was. Looked like he'd aged twenty years since the last time I saw him. Or maybe I hadn't noticed it before, but my pop was getting old. He had that cave in the middle of his neck, right at his throat, and then a flap of extra skin, and there were lines like a major staff across his forehead. He'd been all through it, and it showed all over his body.

When I looked at him, my own reflection caught in his eyes for a minute, and he put his hand softly on my face. Then he leaned over, put his head on my shoulder, and my poppy cried.

38

[SWEAT AND TEARS]

When my father put his head on my shoulder, when he was lying there sobbing like a baby, a big part of me froze. I didn't know what to do or say. I hoped I could just pacify him with good thoughts, calm thoughts. That's all I was up to. While he lay there, I just prayed and sent him vibes of peace. It was weird, but I hoped it would work.

After a few minutes, Pop got up and closed the door. He wiped his eyes on his sleeve and patted me on the back before he sat back down next to me.

"My son. You got grown up or something, before I could even notice it. I wish I'd paid more attention. You know your Uncle George—he missed this, watching his boys grow up. I got the chance to watch, and I didn't pay attention."

"You paid attention, Pop. You was always there for me. Always."

"Not in the middle years. When you got into trouble in high school—what was I thinking then? You messed up in school. Maybe if I'd took a bigger part, you know. Been more on top of things, you'd have done a little better in school. Had the chance to go to a, uh, different college. And then maybe…"

"You didn't mess up, Pop. I did. And I still got to go to school, and I'm happy about it. Real happy. I've had a good life so far."

"When we, ah, lost Darryl and Georgy. It was a real hard time, you know. Real hard. I felt so bad for my brother. It was a real heartache. So I figured I'd work hard, just work real hard, and build up my end of the business, you know. So he'd have something. Because I owe that to him…"

"Poppy, you don't have to…"

"Don't interrupt your father, Sallie. Let me finish. I felt like I owed him something. Because God smiled on me, and I got to keep my children. But George, he…" My father started to tear up again, and I knew he didn't want to lose his composure anymore. Uncle George moved to Philly soon after the accident, and we didn't hear from him much after that. Pop bit his lower lip and stopped for a minute. "My big brother lost everything. Last night, I almost lost your mommy, my wife. And it scared me."

"Lost Mommy? What happened? Why didn't you call me?" Hearing those words set my heart in a panic.

"Stop talking, Salmon. Listen to your father. For once."

I'd been ready to launch an argument about how wrong it was for them to keep me out of the loop when Mommy was sick, but when he said that, a switch went off, and I shut up.

"I may not be the smartest man, Salmon. And maybe I don't always make the sharpest decisions. But I love my family. *I'm* the one who takes care of your ma, not you. It's *me* that she leans on. And she can't take the stress right now of not having you around. She can't. So I need you to cooperate. Period."

"Okay, Pop. Whatever you want, I'll do it. You know I will."

"I know you will. It's hard times right now, and we need each other. Every one of us needs the other. It's natural that you should grow up, make your own way. And I guess I gotta let you do that. But I look at George over there, and he's heartbroken. He don't say nothing, and he don't come around, but I know. Because he lost his family. And ah. I ain't trying to lose mine."

"You're not gonna lose us, Pop."

"This thing with, ah, your African-American friend, or whatever. It ain't my first choice. It's different, and the world won't always understand, so, no. It ain't my first choice. But, ah, *you're* my first choice. My family is my first choice. So, within that, we all gotta do what we gotta do."

Before he could finish, Ma started to stir. Dad positioned his chair so he'd be the first one she saw when she opened her eyes. Ma couldn't talk with the tube in her throat, but she could talk with her eyes. And she seemed to be saying she was glad to see me. And she also sort of said get lost so I can be alone with your father. She didn't have to tell me twice.

Back in the lobby, my family was in a semi-circle around the doctor. I walked over and joined in. He was explaining to us that Ma got an infection that she didn't take care of. It went so far that her throat got swollen, and before you know it, she couldn't breathe. He was telling us that since Ma is diabetic, she won't always feel the symptoms of things right away. And because of the asthma, she's really gotta be careful when it comes to infections in her throat and in her head.

"Wait a minute; hold on a second! Since when does Ma have diabetes?" Once again, I was outraged.

"Fortunately, the worst of this is over. I can see you all have a lot to talk about." The doctor looked at the tension in my face and got ready to leave.

"Wait, though. What now? How long will she be in here? When can she come home?" Frankie caught the doctor on his sleeve before he slipped away.

"We'll have to wait and see. We should be able to take the breathing apparatus out tomorrow, if things go well. Then, it should only be another two days or so. I do have a few others to check on, though. Your mom is going to be fine." With that, he looked at his clipboard and walked away.

I noticed Stacy over in the corner, with her head stuck in a magazine like she'd never seen anything so fascinating. I knew this must be awkward for her. She put herself out there bringing me all the way there, and I didn't want to make things any worse for her. I decided not to carry on about being left out of the loop.

We all sat down again, and I tried my best to decompress and calm down. I was glad Ma was gonna be alright. That was the main thing. I went over and sat with Stacy. She didn't look up from the magazine. Just gave me a pat on the knee and went on reading.

When Pop came out of Ma's room, Aunt Celia and Uncle Eddie stood up. He said some words to them that I couldn't hear, but he had a smile on his face. He looked tired as hell, though. Aunt Celia and Uncle Eddie decided to call it a night, but Celia was coming back first thing in the morning. Pop and Frankie were going to the cafeteria for a while, but neither of them was going home.

Then, Pop surprised me. He came over to where we were sitting and cleared his throat. Stacy put down the magazine and stood up to meet his glance. My throat closed. Stacy can be a hard ass, and so can my father. But this time, he had something different in mind.

"I'm Sal's father. You must be Dignity." He extended his hand.

"No, not by a long shot. But I'm Sal's friend. My name is Stacy. Nice to meet you." She gave his hand an awkward shake and tried not to look at the floor.

"Oh. A *good friend*. Driving Salmon all this way. We ah. *I* appreciate your doing that. Can I give you something? Some gas money? Or, have you guys eaten anything? I could get you dinner." He put his hand in his pockets and grasped in there for words.

"No, thank you. It wasn't a problem at all. Really. I'm just glad that everything is okay."

"I think we're gonna be alright. Listen, Stacy. Thanks again. You can never have enough good friends." With that Pop turned to Frankie, and the two of them headed for the elevator.

Stacy and I followed behind them.

Frankie pushed the button and we all waited. "Look, Kid. Let me stay here with Pop. You go on back to the house and rest."

I wanted to protest about being sent home, but something told me not to. A light had gone off in my head, and I knew that what Pop wanted more than anything else was for me to listen. And to respect tradition. The tradition is that the oldest takes care of family emergencies. I'd broken enough traditions already. I didn't need to fight him on this one.

"Okay. Sure. I'll just go back to the house tonight. Let the older son do his job. But, ah, call me if… you know."

Pop smiled when he heard me acquiesce and let Frankie stay there, alone, with Pop. "You know we will. Go home now, Son."

Pop and Frankie got off on the first floor, and Stacy and I rode down to the garage where we'd parked her car. I had to direct her to my parents' house because she wasn't at all familiar with the area. I pointed out some of the landmarks as we drove by, just to lighten the air. And because, really, I was proud of her, in a weird way. And thankful that she'd been around to help me.

"You can stay if you want. We got a guest room downstairs." I tried to keep the pleading out of my voice, but I kind of wanted her to stay.

"Well. It is late, and I don't like to drive in the dark. But, I gotta get out of here really early. I got plans tomorrow. Do you mind?"

"Not at all. It's the least I can do."

I locked the front door and then led her downstairs to the guest room. I was surprised to see that they'd put a phone in there and a color television. With cable.

"Looks comfortable. Almost like a hotel!" Stacy seemed really happy with the accommodations.

"Not hardly. But, um, you're welcome here. I gotta turn in. It's been a long day, and I'm drained."

"Me, too. Mind if I use the phone later? Just to check in, let my folks know where I am. I have a calling card."

"Go ahead; help yourself. Of course."

"Sounds good." Stacy looked around and then sat on the bed, putting her purse up there next to her.

I turned to leave, but then I had a thought. "Stacy. You know that question you asked before? About, umm, being pretty? Well, you're looking better and better every day." And with that I went upstairs. Let her figure out what I meant.

So, that's when I understood what Pop meant when he talked about blood. It's not blood exactly. It's about respect. In our family, the father takes the weight, and because he takes the weight, he gets to make the rules. I'm not sure why Pop had such a problem with my going to college and dating a sister. But I was beginning to understand that it was more my not listening to him, not following his rules, that bothered him. Still, I can't listen to him when he says don't go to school and don't date outside the race. But for all the other stuff, I'm gonna try to listen to whatever he says. He's my blood, and he deserves that.

39

[RESURRECTION]

Stacy Smithe

I had to swallow my pride. That was the hardest thing for me to do, but I had to do it. See, I saw this guy on *Oprah*, and he was talking about self-preserving behavior and how so many of us are our own worst enemies. I was beginning to recognize that I was guilty of that offense.

I'd gotten home from work that day, over an hour early. Which is another story. But let's just say that I was rude to one of my boss's clients, Claudia Whitacre. She's been a pain since they took her case. Always prancing in there with her high-yellow self, with the Chanel suits and all that jazz. She expects me to drop everything I'm doing, just because she walks into the office.

She'd come in nearly an hour before, and she was in the boss's office boo-hooing over the latest run-in with her husband. Whom she clearly still loves, but never mind that. She comes storming in demanding that I give her a file that she wants my boss to revisit. Well, it just so happened that I was in the middle of a billing cycle on the computer, and I told her I'd be with her in a moment. Well, maybe I didn't put it just that way, but that was my point. It must not have been good enough for her because she went back in Litman's office. Next thing you know, he's at my desk telling me to pull the file right away and to "check my attitude" while I'm at it.

I was furious. Because I am totally in this man's corner. Going and getting his lunch. Shopping for his wife's birthday presents. I do all kinds of stuff that ain't on my job description. And there he is calling me out in front of this worrisome client. I was too through, and I told him so. He's the one that wants the billing cycle to end on the same day, every month, even if it falls on a weekend, and who do you think is coming in on Saturday and Sunday to make sure it's done? Let's just say it's not him.

And there's Miss Fancy Pants Whitacre, with her arms folded, watching him lay me out. It was humiliating! I pulled the damn file, but I also stormed out of there afterwards. I'd come in early twice that week, and they owed me some comp time. I figured it was time I took it.

But I forgot my purse. When I went to my desk to find it, I could hear Claudia back there with Mr. Litman, and she really was boo-hooing. She *did* still love her husband. That much was clear. But when I heard her talking about the way he treated her, the way he called her names and slapped her, I had to wonder. In spite of all that, the abuse and the womanizing, there she was still crying over the man. Why?

I had to wonder. On the one hand, I wondered how you could love someone who messes over you like trash. But I also wondered where he got off treating someone like Claudia Whitacre that way. Talk about perfect! She was a real class act. Had her hair done to the nines every week, and clothes and shoes from Neiman-Marcus. She drove a BMW convertible. Expensive cologne. Money to burn, and just as pretty as a picture. What was her husband looking for, anyway?

She reminded me of my sister, Helene. Fine as she is, she's with an abuser, too. And no matter what I say, she goes back to that m.f. every time. And then there's Dignity. She's so cute and so smart, seems like she'd have an easier time of things, too. But, I know the thing with Sal didn't work out because when his family emergency came up, she was nowhere around.

I'd gotten home from work early, and I had kicked off my pumps. I was doing the *Oprah* thing. I also had a pint of Ben and Jerry's, the kind with the peanut butter and the pretzels, and I was just about to start my own little pity party. No friends, no love life. And trouble on the job.

If I hadn't checked my attitude, and if I had said all that was on my mind about Whitacre and her files and everything else, I would have lost my job. As it was, I was a step away from the unemployment line. It wasn't the first time I had lost my temper at work and gotten in trouble for it. I told another client what was on my mind on the phone last year, and they wrote me up for it. Only reason why they kept me is that I'm the only one who knows the computer system, and if they fired me, they wouldn't have me to train someone else. But, I was skating on thin ice. I knew I'd better try to hold my tongue; I needed my job.

I was busy eating ice cream, feeling good and sorry for myself. Then, I started to listen to what this man was saying, and I saw how all of the women in the audience were reacting. All kinds of women, half white, like Dignity, and dark, like me. Nobody there had cornered the market on special treatment, and many of them had been abused in one way or another. This guy Oprah had on was talking about how we have to break these abusive patterns and start practicing self-preserving behaviors.

I nearly choked at first, the revelation was so strong. The man was talking about people who keep doing the same things over and over, expecting different results. It felt like he was talking directly to me. I remembered how whack the last several days had been, since my incident with Dignity and my break-up with Khalil. I wasn't getting anything that I wanted!

All this ugly behavior, as the man on *Oprah* said, and I was not getting even one single good thing out of it. I'd probably lost my chance at being Ms. Morgan. I had lost my relationship with Khalil, and that really hurt. We had spent some really special times together, and I missed him like raw hell. And there was Salmon over there, stressing big time over Dignity. Dignity had gone home. There was a rumor that she might not even be coming back in the fall.

I had finished most of the ice cream and was too full and lazy to get up and throw it away, so I sat there thinking. What did I have in my life that was really meaningful? School? Sort of, though I'd have to work if I was going to finish on time. I used to love my job, but I might have just ruined that. Not Khalil. I had to think about the last time I felt good about myself. I didn't have to reach back far, because it was that night when I took Salmon to the hospital. That was the best I'd felt in a long time. Which is strange. His mama was sick, so it wasn't a happy time. But his family was all there. They had come together to help each other through a bad time. My family sure doesn't do that. But his does. I was glad I could take him out there. And I got to see, from a weird angle, what a real family looked like. Made me feel good.

That's when I swallowed my pride. I had already gotten the number from directory assistance the night I stayed at Sal's parents', in the guest room. But I didn't have the nerve to actually call. That day, with a belly full of ice cream and a head full of psychobabble in my brain, I went ahead and dialed the number.

He answered on the first ring. I started to hang up, but when he said hello the third time, I said hello back.

"Hello. It's Stacy. What's up?"

Khalil paused like he was swallowing a brick and having a hard time making it stay down. "Oh. Hey."

"I know you must be surprised to hear from me, huh?"

"Not really. But, umm, I'm expecting another call. What's on your mind?"

"A lot, actually. Helene. You know she's still with that hoodlum. And now she's got a bruise on her face and can't go to work. And…"

"You called me to talk about your sister?"

"No. Khalil… I don't know what to say. I guess I'm sorry."

"Sorry for what, exactly?" His voice didn't soften, and he wasn't making this easy for me.

"Everything. Salmon said I had a bad attitude. Said it ruined everything. I don't know what gets into me, seriously. I just… I don't know. I mean, what I did to Dignity was wrong. And maybe I have said some crazy things since you known me. But. I guess I'm just sorry."

"*Now* you're sorry. Look. I'm not the one you should be apologizing to. I got no beef with you. It just wasn't happening, that's all. But, if you're so sorry, and all this, tell her. You want to make amends with someone, find Dignity and tell her."

"Yeah, okay. I guess you're right. Lil, I can change, you know. I'm capable of it. And, umm, I may not always have acted right. But, I know one thing. I really do love you." I was surprised to hear myself telling him that. Pride is a hard pill to swallow. He didn't say anything.

"Hello? Are you still there?" I hoped he hadn't hung up.

"Yes, I'm listening."

"I miss you, Khalil. You ever miss me?" I held my breath for the answer.

"Yes, actually. I do. I gotta go, though. I'm out." And with that, he hung up the phone.

My heart raced when I heard him say that, and I actually had butterflies in my stomach. Or maybe it was all those pretzels and chocolate from the ice cream. Either way, I was feeling hopeful. And it was the best feeling I'd had since the night with Sal.

I guess the call to Khalil must have given me a boost of confidence. Next thing, I called Salmon to see how he was doing. Thought I'd ask about his mama, find out if she was at home yet and how things were going. First I tried him at his apartment, but I didn't get an answer. So, I called out to his parents' house. His brother answered and called him to the phone. It took Sal a long time to get on, and when he did, I barely recognized his voice.

"Yep." He sounded like machinery, he was so monotone.

"Hey—the fish! How's it going today?!" I put as much enthusiasm in my voice as I could, wanting to off-set his bland tone.

"Stacy? Yeah, what's going on?" If the color gray was vocal, his voice is what it would sound like.

"Not a lot. Just checking to see how you're doing. Thinking about your mom." I was being sincere, and I hoped he knew that.

"She's okay. Thanks for asking. She got home a few days ago, and Pop's been waiting on her hand and foot ever since. Me and Frankie are staying until tomorrow, so it's really been like old times." Salmon didn't have even an ounce of energy in his voice.

"I guess you must be tired—I can hear it in your voice. When are you coming home?"

"Tomorrow. I'm gonna see if Frankie will drive me."

"Really? I can come and get you if you want. I remember how to get there." I really wanted to help him. And I wouldn't mind telling him about my phone call to Khalil, and asking him what he thinks I should do next.

"Oh, okay. Sure. I'd appreciate that. You coming after work?"

"Sure. Guess what! I talked to Khalil just now!"

"Oh, really? What's he saying?"

"Said he missed me. Sort of. Can we talk about this tomorrow? Because I'd love to get some input. In person."

"Okay. So, what? Six or so?"

"Yes. Somewhere around then. Should I call first?"

"Nah. Just come. I'll be waiting."

When I got off from Sal, my mind started racing. I wondered what Khalil meant when he said he missed me. Wondered if he thought about me. Wondered if he was thinking about me right then. I started to think about how he said I should apologize to Dignity. That was going to take some thought. I didn't know if I was up to that one. What would I possibly say to her? And, how could I admit to being wrong?

I was going to pick Salmon up that next day. Normally, I would planned a facial and made sure I had the perfect outfit. Made sure my hair was styled just right. I have this thing where I want to make sure I make the right impression, especially when it comes to men. But, for some reason, I didn't worry about it. I didn't jump up and look through the closet or set up the hot curlers. I didn't have the energy. The air conditioning was off in the dorm again, and *Martin* was coming on later. Besides, Salmon had seen me looking a fright the other night, and he didn't seem to care. I wasn't after him, anyway. It was Khalil I wanted. So, I sat there on the couch and got comfortable. Maybe I'd even order a pizza later.

While I was sitting there, I was planning how I'd get Dignity's number and what I would say to her if I called.

40

[BLIND FAITH]

Khalil Towers

an't say I was surprised to hear Stacy's voice. The way it ended with us, she was bound to call at some point. We'd put nearly three years into that relationship, and she didn't want it to end. Quiet as it's kept, I was kind of glad to hear her voice. Not that I'd forgiven her or anything. Not that I'd changed my mind about us. But, you see someone every single day for three years, and you get used to having them around.

She said she was sorry. Confused the hell out of me. Stacy is not usually what you would call remorseful. She holds on to grudges the way your daddy holds on to the last piece of chicken—relentlessly. But I heard a sound in her voice when she called. I don't know what it was. Sincerity, I guess. Or desperation.

I already had a plan for that day. I was waiting for Sheila, this Latino babe, to call. We'd hung out the night before, after Stacy called. I guess her phone call left me in bad form because I wasn't really into the date. Ended up cutting it short. We decided we'd get together the next night. She lived out by the water, and we were going to chill on the boardwalk for a while. And get into it later, I was hoping, although she didn't know that.

But the next morning, I called Sal. Hadn't heard from him since the day I left town, which was a few weeks ago. I knew he was struggling, too, after his split with Dignity. Actually, before school ended, I begged him to come down here with me—my dad can always use another hand on his contracts, especially someone like Sal; he's a smart guy. But homeboy wasn't trying to come. He did say he'd come and visit me sometime over the summer, though.

I tried him at home, and I didn't get an answer. I figured he must be at work in Financial Aid, so I called over there. But the work-study supervisor told me he'd had a family emergency and wouldn't be in until the end of the month. I was concerned right away.

I called 4-1-1 to get the number at his parents' house. I assumed he must be at home. At first I was afraid to call. He said his dad trips over colored folks. But then I remembered I'd be on the phone. Surely old pops couldn't tell my race if I put on a real proper tone. I was just about to do my best white-boy phone voice and see about my friend when the phone rang. I assumed it would be Sheila, the Latino babe. Wrong again.

"Khalil? It's me, Salmon. What's up?"

"Salmon, my man! What's up, homeslide?" I made sure to keep the enthusiasm on swoll.

"Not a lot. I'm at home, Lil. My mom is sick." His voice sounded low and even, with not even the slightest hint of emotion. Real strange.

"Oh, man. I'm sorry to hear that. What happened?"

"Well, I just found out she's diabetic, although nobody here wanted to tell me. And she was in the hospital this week cuz she couldn't breathe. She's home now, but it got real crucial for a minute." Still no inflection his voice.

"That's rough. I'm glad she's doing better, though. How are you holding up?" I asked, but I could already tell. He must have been stressing big time because he sounded like an Italian robot.

"I don't know. Tired mainly. I'm just so sick of all this bullshit, you know." His voice caught at the end. I knew he was upset.

"Dude, what's going on? Tell old Lil all about, now. I can handle it!" I put on a funny voice, like I was his old grandpa or something. I hoped it would make him laugh. It didn't.

"My folks can get so weird. I mean, we just went through this whole family drama, and everybody's acting like nothing happened. They don't want to tell me what the doctor said, you know. Like special instructions and all that. And, I found out that the night Ma stopped breathing good, Pop didn't even call an ambulance. He drove her over to the hospital himself. I mean, what if something happened and he hadn't got her there in time?" My friend was saying a lot more than the words he'd put out there. There was a lot more on his mind.

"Parents can get like that—always wanting to take care of shit themselves. I'm just glad it worked out this time…" I wanted to make sure he knew he could talk to me. If he wanted to. There quiet moment. Neither of us said anything. His breathing got erratic, and I hoped to God he wasn't crying.

"Sal, you alright?"

"Nah, not really. Depressed as hell, Man. I ain't been able to shake it."

"Is it the Dignity thing?" If he was tripping over a lost love, I could understand how he felt.

"Sort of. But it ain't just that. Did I ever tell you about my cousins, Darryl and Georgy? They died a long time ago. Freak accident. But it was this time of year when it happened. Sometimes I get sad around this time."

But he sounded more than sad; he sounded comatose. And either he had a bad case of the hiccups, or he was fighting back tears. It tugged my heart strings some. "Nah, you never told me about that. Sorry to hear that. Must be hard not to think about them at a time like this." I really didn't know what all to say.

"Yeah, but the way my dad acts, it's like, a crime to think about them. Ever. And don't even think about mentioning their names or he might shit a brick!" Finally, I heard some feeling in his voice, and it sounded like soft fury. It was getting weird.

"Sounds like he's got his own issues to deal with. Listen, I'm coming home tonight. Got some stuff to take care of and, well, I miss Moms. You busy? We could hang." I don't know where that came from. Out of the blue, I got the feeling that I should just go. And it was true about missing my moms. And her fried chicken and cornbread. Figured I'd just roll out for the weekend. Tomorrow was Friday, so I could take a long weekend.

"That'd be cool. I'm at my parents', you know. You could come here."

"Cool. It's on the way. We can roll back to your crib. Mind if I stay with you? Chill up on the yard for a minute?"

"Yeah. That's fine. Let me tell you how to get here."

I didn't want to waste time getting directions from him. I was gonna go online and send my dad an email saying I was heading home for a few days. Then, if all went smooth, I'd pack a small bag and jet within the hour.

As it turned out, though, the process took longer than I thought. After I got off the computer, my father called. He wanted me to come by the office, pick up a package, and drop it off to one of his clients before I left out. I didn't end up getting on the road until after one p.m. As always, I ran into traffic around Richmond, so it was after six p.m. when I pulled into Sal's driveway. That's when I noticed Stacy's Volkswagen. I knew it was hers because of all the stuffed animals in the back window. I'd given her most of them. What was she doing there? Did I smell a set-up?

I was just about to get really angry when the two of them came out of the house. Sal looked like death warmed over, but Stacy—my Lord! Wearing all kinds of blue, and high heels, and I could smell the Paris perfume she always wore from here. I wanted to jump out the car and jump her bones right then and there. And her butt was as delicious as ever. Big and round, but without the slightest jiggle. Halleluiah! But I had to keep my cool. Because I wasn't supposed to be glad to see her.

I got out the car and walked up to Salmon. Gave him a slap on the back, even though it was clear he needed a hug. And a good, hot shower. He was definitely not at his best. "Say, Man! You ready to bounce?" I tried to keep my eyes off Stacy, which was most hard to do.

"Just about. Stacy showed up to drive me home. I completely forgot she offered to come yesterday. Hope you don't mind. Oh, let me tell Pops I'm leaving. One sec." All this in a monotone whisper. And then he moved, practically in slow motion, back inside the house.

"Hey, Khalil. You're looking good." Stacy gave me the once-over with that sexy way she has.

Took everything I had to keep my smooth. "You, too. Most definitely."

Sal came back out carrying a large paper bag. He had no expression on his face, but his eyes were deep red, and underneath he had circles. "Listen. My mom wants me to take this over to my Aunt Celia's house. Says it's important, so it's not like I can say no. Lil, can I borrow your car and run this over to her? Because it might be easier than if we…" He dropped the sentence, and both of us knew what he was getting at. He didn't want to show up at his aunt's house with his black buddies and set off the spook alarm.

"Why don't you take my car, and I'll ride with Khalil. We'll meet you on the yard later."

"Good plan. Lil, you mind? I'll give ya the keys, in case you get there before I do. That way if Aunt Celia starts to running her mouth, you guys won't have to wait for me." The plan was too perfect. But I didn't question it.

"I guess."

Before he could give me an answer, Stacy had the keys to Sal's apartment and was getting into my car. The way she slid into the seat, waiting a peek-a-boo second before pulling her skirt over her knees, I knew I was done for. It was all this heat and energy, and then anxiety.

"Look. I do miss you. But you can be so whack, and I ain't up for all that." I resorted once more to my rhymes to hide the fact that I was feeling her in a big way.

She didn't answer with words; instead, she pulled me toward her and planted a deep one on me. The shit dipped down my legs and landed at ground zero. I closed my eyes to hide the relief that kiss gave me. I'd been missing her more than she knew. More than I wanted to admit.

"Baby. I'm sorry. Real sorry. Let me make it up to you." She was so close to my face that I could feel her breath making wind in my eyelashes. I wanted to believe her. Needed to believe her. But part of me still wasn't sure.

"I'm for real. I ain't up for tricks, Stacy. Tricks are for kids."

"I guess we're just gonna have to practice a little blind faith." We held hands all the way back to Sal's.

[FINDING DIGNITY]

Salmon

I didn't stay to talk to Aunt Celia when I dropped off the books. Really, Frankie could have taken them to her; he lives out that way. But, after talking to Stacy, I figured she deserved another shot with Khalil. I wanted to give her the time to be alone with him. I was beginning to believe she was trying to change. Plus, they were good together. Lil was always claiming to be this big player, like he didn't care that much about Stacy one way or the other. But it was for show. He hadn't looked twice at anyone else since the day they started kicking it. I could tell he missed her.

Change ain't easy. I was finding that out the hard way. Take this thing with my father, for instance. I'd been staying out there for the last two weeks, and nothing was any different. Since we'd had so much time apart, I thought we might take this time together to, I don't know. Talk. Mend our relationship, make it stronger. But I was the only one feeling like that. Pops didn't see anything wrong with the way it was, and he wasn't about to make an effort to make it different. He didn't see where it was necessary.

Not that our relationship was specifically damaged. Just the usual intergenerational stuff—me going to school and dating outside the race, mainly. But the thing with Darryl and Georgy still bothered me. A lot. Because I was the one that witnessed it. I saw the whole thing happen right in front of my face. It haunted me. Which is an understatement.

I still had the feeling that somehow, maybe without even knowing it, Pops was blaming me. Or maybe I was blaming myself. We moved from Brooklyn to Silver

Spring after it happened. Uncle George moved to Philly. I hadn't laid eyes on him in years. Still, in his absence, it felt like he was blaming me, too.

The way my family is, they don't want to talk about stuff. Period. If it's bad, then as far as they're concerned, it didn't happen. And with Darryl and Georgy, they weren't there. They didn't have to see the thing transpire, like some kind of a horror flick you want to turn the channel from and can't. They didn't experience it like I did.

I wanted to talk to my father about it. Not in depth or nothing, just touch base on it. Hear him say he remembered my cousins, my best friends. Hear him say he understands the horror I was feeling. But when I brought it up, he clammed up and eventually left the room.

Alls I was saying was, every year, in the middle of June, I think about them. Not the accident, exactly, but the good stuff. Hanging out over there in the summer. Going to the Y to swim. Eating dinner with Uncle George and Aunt Misty. Which wasn't her real name. And how I don't even know her real name because when she left after her sons died, everybody pretended she never existed. That stuff. It's like a big chunk of my life that he wants to pretend never existed. Excuse me, but I don't know how to do that.

He told me to let it go. Said my cousins were dead and buried and I had to bury the bad feelings along with them. Actually, he said something weird. "Nobody can be with you in your sorrow, Sallie. You gotta go to God alone."

So, I swallowed it. I tried hard to bury the whole thing. And with every new swallow, it felt like I was gaining about two hundred pounds. Seriously. I felt so heavy and disgusting, I could barely get up and walk. Then Pop said that thing about going to God alone, and I knew my time was up there. Because I'd decided, back at the hospital with Ma, to listen to him and follow his rules. I was beginning to realize that I couldn't always follow his rules and have a good feeling. That's when I knew it was time to go home, back to school. Back to my own life and my own rules. Time to go to God. Alone.

That night, when I finally got to my apartment, I could hear Stacy and Khalil before I even got in the door. They were yes-ing and yeah baby-ing up a storm. Good for them. I didn't blame them. But it didn't exactly help the hollow feeling I had in my heart to hear them happily playing makeup over there. I decided not to go inside.

I walked across the street and bought a bottle of Bacardi and a twenty-ounce Coke. Then, I decided I'd sit over there by Holmes Hall, under that tree where me and Dignity first got close. I needed to think.

I kept drinking because I liked the burn. I'd take a swig, and then I'd get this rush down my throat and a fire in my gut. It hurt, but it was something. It was the first time I'd felt something, anything, inside for a few days. I liked it. For once I didn't feel empty. I ignored the fact that I hadn't eaten, that I'd never been a big drinker. Just kept belting it back and enjoying the slow burn in my center. Which soon led to a light, fuzzy feeling in my head. And before I knew it, I was on the bridge, looking out at the cars passing by, and singing from *West Side Story*, "There's a Place for Us," at the top of my lungs.

It wasn't serious. I wasn't suicidal or nothing. But the guy from my French II class didn't know that. He came out of Tubman and ran into me on the bridge. I recognized him. He kept asking me if I was alright. He must not have believed I was, because he called my apartment to tell someone to come see about me. Told them I was on the bridge saying I wanted to fly. Which wasn't exactly true.

Next thing I know, Khalil is coming toward me on the bridge, trying to make me come home. But it seemed like a game to me. I started running from him. Still babbling about flying. When he put his arm around my shoulder and started walking me back across the bridge, down the hill to the parking lot in front of McKeldin, I started to sob.

We were driving back to the apartment, and I must have been crying, calling out for Georgy, begging Darryl to forgive me. Making a moron of myself and spooking my friends to their core. Next thing I know, I'm hearing Dignity's sweet voice on the phone, and I'm slobbering all over myself. And that's the last thing I remember before waking up in a gas station in Charles Town, West Virginia.

Dignity

I spent a lot of time planning for that trip out to Ashland. I had prepared a list of questions to ask. I had steeled myself for the answers, but even still, I wasn't prepared for what I would hear.

Mercer gave me the idea to go. When we were out at Grandma Pearson's visiting

Aunt Ruty, they'd mentioned my father's mother, Cordial Howard. Said she lived in Ashland and was remarried. I guess I lazed around in a daze for so many days afterwards that Mercer got worried. We were drinking tequila every night, or at least I was, and then sleeping away the days at his apartment. He took it upon himself to look up Cordial Howard's number.

I had the number for a week before I got the nerve to call her. Once I got her on the line, I knew why I had hesitated so long. It was like talking to a cold, Southern fish. Most unpleasant. I don't know where I'd gotten the idea that she would be glad to hear from me. I imagined her inviting me out to her home and giving me the welcome you'd give a prodigal granddaughter. Didn't happen. First thing she did was to ask how I'd gotten her number (as if she wasn't listed). Then she didn't want me to come to her house, claimed the directions were too complicated. She agreed to meet me at a diner off the highway close to her house.

At first I wanted to curse her for treating me like an unwelcome stranger. Then I wanted to cry and let her know how mean I thought this was and how much it hurt my feelings. In the end, though, I remembered what Mercer said about finding the root. I decided to meet her on her own level, at The Sweet Pea Diner, just inside of Ashland, Kentucky.

I was relieved when Mercer volunteered to drive me. We decided to make a day of it trip. There was an antique shop out there that we both wanted to see. Since we were meeting this Cordial woman at the Sweet Pea Diner, we decided we'd stay overnight at the Sweet Pea Inn.

You'd have thought we were going away for a week with all the stuff we packed, with our neurotic selves. We had blow-dryers and cosmetics and extra underwear and special toothpaste to beat the band—it was comical. Mercer had planned the drive so that we could take some back roads on the way out of town. We wanted to stop and take pictures. We left early in the morning that Friday, and I had called ahead so we could get an early check in. That way we could set up in the hotel first thing. Then, I could walk over to the diner and meet the Cordial woman, and Mercer could stay in the room and watch the soaps while I was gone. Depending on what happened at my meeting, we would go to the antique store, find a nice place for dinner, and maybe look around town, if there was anything interesting, before going back home.

Well, the first half of the plan went off without a hitch. We checked into the hotel about a half hour before I was to be at the Sweet Pea. I looked casual but well put together. I was wearing a navy skort set and navy deck shoes. My hair was pulled back in a neat knot at the back of my head, and I had used just a little mascara and light-colored lipstick. I'd powdered myself down in case I started to sweat, and I had my pad of questions and a pen in my bag, so I could stay on track with my questioning. From the way she sounded, this woman wasn't going to be up for a lot of meandering small talk. I was all set.

I walked into the diner at noon, as planned, and the place was moderately full. But there was one woman who stood out, and I knew that she must be Cordial Howard. She looked out of place there. Too fragile or something, not physically but mentally. She looked to be in her late fifties or early sixties, and like she'd be insulted if you said she was more than forty-five. Her hair was positively yellow. Hard and yellow, like she'd been dying it for so long that the very nature of the strands had changed, and not in a good way. Her face was round and flat. She had pancake on that was one shade too light and, perhaps, the wrong texture. So, when the sunlight hit her face directly, it looked like she'd been cooking with flour and hadn't been careful.

She had her head down mostly and was drinking from a steaming cup, even though it was nearly ninety degrees outside. She had on a flowered skirt and a round-neck T-shirt, both in tones of lilac and beige. She was hovering somewhere between full-figured and plain old fat, but she'd probably blush and become hostile if she knew I'd described her that way. I stood at the front of the diner for a moment and practiced breathing. Then, I used the deepest breath to propel me back to the table where she was sitting. She rose when she saw me coming.

"My word, you look just like your mama! Like she spit you out. I know you're Dignity! Come have a seat with me." She extended her hand and gave mine a sharp squeeze before pulling a chair out for me and then reclaiming her own.

"Yes. That's me. And you must be Mrs. Howard. I'm glad to finally meet you." I could see this woman blanch when I said the word "finally." When the waitress came over, I ordered lemonade with extra ice, and when she walked away, I quickly pulled my pad and pen out of my straw bag.

"What a lovely bag! I just love to carry straw in the summer. Don't you? Adds such a crisp touch to whatever you're wearing. Nice and crisp." She seemed to pull her own bag closer to her, against her stomach, making sure the bottom was firmly in her lap and that the handles were pressed against her middle.

Something about the way she held her mouth and her purse, coupled with the fact that she'd met me in a diner rather than in her home, made me less than sociable. I couldn't manage niceties at that moment, so I just stayed quiet.

She read the reason for my silence in my countenance, I guess, and she jumped to the point. "Yes. So, what brings you here today, Dignity?"

As if! "I, ah. I visited with my aunt recently, and she pointed out the house where you used to live. She remembered how your, ah, son had been friends with my mother." She looked at me stone-faced. "I'm working on this project at school, a senior project, and I am trying to create a family tree. I thought maybe you could help." I lied about the project having anything to do with school, but the rest of what I said was true.

Cordial stiffened. She was gearing up for something, and I could tell by the bitter way her lips met with her hot tea that I wasn't going to like it.

"Funny you should use the word family here. Your mother was a friend of my son's, I guess. But mainly she worked for us. She was our maid. And in that sense, she might be seen like family. Really, good help is so hard to find, and your mother was excellent. Truly excellent. The family loved her for that. Especially Evian." She sipped her tea, which was so light and weak that it appeared that she was drinking hot water.

"Really? I'd gotten the impression there was a little more to it than that..." I didn't want to offend her or make her stop talking, but I couldn't let her off the hook that easy.

Cordial coughed, fanned her throat, and dabbed away perspiration from her upper lip with a lavender handkerchief. "Not really. My Evian was sick. He had cancer. Sister came at a time when he was recovering, and she tended to him. She cooked, she cleaned. She was good to us, good to him. And we appreciated her for that." She began to dig in her purse then, not looking at me. I took the time to look over my list of questions. I didn't have much hope, from this exchange, of getting them answered.

"When my mom got pregnant, wasn't this around the time that she and your son... were working together?"

"You could say that." She found what she was looking for, which was a small five by seven picture in a rusted, gold-colored frame. It showed two teenaged boys, one who was pale and thin with orange-red hair, and the other was swollen and discolored like an infected flesh wound. The swollen one had his arm around the other, and both were smiling at the camera. Cordial thrust the picture into my hand.

"You can have this. On the left, that's my Evian." Her voice warmed when she spoke his name. "We lost him in 1972. That was a hard year. We lost his grandfather, Norman, that year, too." She stopped talking and waited while I looked at the picture.

First I drank my lemonade and diverted my eyes. My adrenaline was kicking up, and I knew I'd have to be careful if I didn't want to have a panic attack. But I wanted to look at the photograph. I tried focusing on the pale, thin one she called Evian. He looked sweet and simple, in a complex and artful way. His eyes were the color of cornflowers, and the corners crinkled with his smile. He must have loved whoever took the picture, because his smile was tangible, genuine.

But the other one. I didn't even want to look at him. The very sight made me frantic. He was awful. His cheeks and head were a distorted misrepresentation of the truth. Jelloing like congealed grease. And when I looked at him, I got that panic, that frenzied hysteria that I got sometimes. Whenever Sal used to touch me below the waist. I put the picture face down on the table and gulped my lemonade.

"Who's the other one?" I tried to make the words sound casual, though clearly they were weighted with horror.

If I'd met Cordial's glance, I would have seen that her eyes were also laced with horror. "Evian's grandfather took that picture. Out at Kentucky Lake. They used to love to go out there. I never could stand the bugs. But Norman, his grandfather, would take him out there. Sometimes they'd take Evian's cousin with them. He liked to fish. His name was Franklin. From what I can remember, they used to call him Blister. That's him in the picture next to my son." Mrs. Howard rested her hands, lightly folded, on top of the purse in her lap. There was a coolness in her face, in spite of the sweat on her forehead.

I nearly gagged when she called this boy Blister. The imagery nearly did me in. I remembered the name Franklin Chasinger from the envelope I carried in my purse. "Oh. Your son looks like a beautiful person. You must miss him a lot.

Were the two of them, Franklin and your son, good friends?" Looking at the picture, and feeling the terror that it, for some reason, brought to my soul, I wanted to feel guilty, but I didn't. I know you shouldn't base impressions on the way someone looks, but this boy looked like walking trouble.

"I guess you shouldn't speak ill of the dead. Franklin died that same year, too. Just before we lost Evian and his grandfather, Norman. He wasn't what you would call...a crowd-pleaser. Franklin always did have strange ideas. My son attended to him, I suppose, out of familial obligation. Yes, they did spend time together." She reached over the table and turned the picture face side up again, as if to force me to look at it.

"Listen. I know what you must be thinking. Because of the time frame and everything else. And maybe the fact that Norman left so much to your mother. But, truly, Norman was a bleeding-heart liberal; he wanted to do his part to set things straight, make things more equal. I think that's why he left your mother the house and the money." She had that tightness in her lips. The words she was saying must have worried her something awful because she barely parted her teeth to let them out.

I looked up at her then. I wasn't sure what she was talking about. "This... Norman. My mom inherited stuff from him?"

"A great deal. The house that we used to live in." I could see that this point was one of contention for her. "And a trust. For you. When you turn twenty-one." She blinked at me through borrowed eyes.

Once again, I was blown away. I was turning twenty-one next March. "My birthday's coming up at the beginning of next year."

"Then, you can expect to acquire some money. A nice little sum. But, Dignity. That's all we have for you. My son, Evian." She shook her head as if to say no. "He had cancer. He was sterile." She threw this last information at me like a rock grabbed from a secret supply she'd stashed under her skirt. I took it hard in the face and in the heart.

"Excuse me?" I thought I might have misunderstood.

"He was sterile. The idea of his fathering a child is...an impossibility." This last rock she held in her voice, across her brow. It seemed to give her comfort. It gave me none.

"Sterile. So…?" I didn't know how to form the question that was rising up out of my soul.

Cordial reached across the table and pointed to the picture of the swollen boy whose head was an injured bubble. "That's your father." In her pointed tapping there seemed to be satisfaction.

"No, you're not serious. *This* man? Franklin?"

"Yes. They had time together, your mother and Franklin. They were intimate. And… well. The rest is obvious."

"Will you excuse me for a moment? I need to go to the restroom." I didn't wait for an answer. I didn't take my purse or the picture she'd given me. I leapt up quickly and practically ran to the ladies' room.

I slammed into the first stall and started to hyperventilate. Why in the world would my mother sleep with a wretched-looking creature called Blister? It just didn't make any sense. And if this man, this Blister, was my father, and since he was also dead, how was I going to find out anything about that part of my history?

I leaned against the wall, bent at the waist, and tried to believe that the breath would come, that I wouldn't faint. I pulled a long line of toilet paper off and kept fanning my neck and blotting the spirals of sweat that were circling my face. Because that boy, that Blister, gave me a sick feeling at my stomach. And a panic. And a feeling of nausea, worry, and fear. I thought about the article I had in my purse, in the manila envelope. The one I'd stolen from Aunt Lette's desk. No doubt that the name Franklin was mentioned in it. And now Cordial Howard had mentioned the name as well.

I looked at my watch. I'd been in there for nearly ten minutes. I had to go back out there and face Cordial Howard, the woman who, apparently, was of no blood relation to me.

As soon as I got out of the bathroom, I could see that she was no longer at the table. Again, I got those butterflies in my stomach that signal oncoming frenzy. Or danger.

I noticed as soon as I got close to the table. There was a ten-dollar bill stuck through the handles of my purse. And next to that was a Xeroxed copy of a newspaper article. Cordial Howard had left these items with me and moved on. She didn't even say goodbye.

My head was spinning. Whatever it was in that article couldn't be good. And the way she told me about Franklin, the fact that she left without notice. None of it boded well.

I left the ten dollar bill on top of the check. For some reason it seemed like blood money. I slurped the last bit of lemonade from the glass. Then I stuck the article she left down in my bag and walked back to the hotel room.

Stacy

Salmon was all messed up, and it scared us. We didn't know what to do. Me and Lil were preoccupied and lost track of the time once we got to Sal's apartment. All the way from Sal's parents' to Baltimore, the heat was rising. We didn't say a whole lot. Just kept the 92.Q jams rolling. We had the windows down, and I wasn't even worrying about how my hair must be blowing and looking a fright. At least not as much as I could have. Lil had his fingers laced around mine, and it felt good. Real good.

We got to his apartment before Sal did, and we didn't plan it. It just happened. He kissed me as soon as I got inside the door. One thing led to another, and before you knew it, we were in Sal's room, blankets on the floor, going for it. Big time. We didn't take time to think about it, just did what made sense at the time.

We must have been down there for a couple of hours because when we looked at the clock, it was after ten p.m. Salmon was nowhere to be found. When the phone rang, we started not to answer it.

Khalil picked up, and it was this kid name Benny. I knew him because he was up Tubman all the time. He said Salmon was on the bridge on the other side of the yard acting crazy. Khalil raced over there to see about him. I stayed in the apartment, cleaned up the mess we had made on his bedroom floor, and prepared for the worst.

When Khalil brought Salmon in, he smelled like a Jamaican brewery. He was crying and talking and making no sense. Lil kept trying to calm him down, but he just kept sobbing. Saying he wanted his cousin. Said he wanted his Dignity. I would have stayed out of it, but once again, something told me not to. I went back to the bedroom and started rummaging through the papers on his desk.

What do you know, there was a bank statement that had Dignity's number in Kentucky written on it. I looked at the time and weighed my decision. It was almost eleven p.m., which was late, but it was also a Friday. I decided to take a chance and call her. It felt like an emergency.

I got her Ain't Angus, as Digs call her. Sal had written her name as Angus, but I figured he'd made a mistake. She answered and seemed nice enough. I explained that I was a friend from school and that it was important. She must have been satisfied with the explanation because she gave me a hotel phone number. She said Dignity had taken an overnight trip with a friend, but she didn't think she'd mind if I called her.

I was surprised when I heard a male voice answer in her hotel room. At first I thought I'd gotten the wrong room number. But I could hear Sal out there, and it didn't seem like he was getting any better. I'd heard him in the bathroom puking his guts up a few minutes earlier. I went ahead and asked for Dignity, explaining who I was.

The reception I got wasn't what you'd call warm. In fact, he covered the phone, and I could hear a heated discussion going on before Dignity got on.

"Yes. This is Dignity."

First thing, I felt furious. Or jealous. She strikes me that way. I wanted to hang up and forget about it. But that wouldn't do anybody any good, so I pushed past it. The anger didn't make sense anyway. "It's Stacy, but I guess you already know that. And I'm sorry to call you so late. I'm sorry for… everything. But it's about Salmon. He's really messed up, and we're worried about him."

"Salmon? What's the matter? What's going on?" She didn't sound so great herself. Sounded like she'd been crying, too. I wondered what I'd dialed into.

"Long story. He's been drinking. See, his mama got sick a few days ago, and I was around to take him to the hospital. She's okay, but he stayed with his parents for a while. Long story short, Khalil came home for the weekend, and we went to pick up Sal from his parents' house. But when we got to his apartment, he, ah… Started drinking. Now he's all upset."

"You took Sal to the hospital? Drinking what? Is his mom okay?" I could tell that the information I was giving her was making her upset, and like I said, she already sounded like she'd been crying. So this mess wasn't helping.

"I wanted to help him, Dignity. That's all. Honest. Nothing more. And then he helped me get back with Lil. Oh, we're back together, by the way. But Salmon is asking for you, Dignity. He's out there crying like a baby. Keeps talking about some guy name Darryl and saying he needs to talk to you."

"Oh, God. Put him on. And, Stacy. Thanks for calling me."

I don't know what all they must have said when Salmon got on the phone, but from this end it didn't make sense. Salmon did seem to calm down when he heard Dignity's voice. But then he dropped the phone and started bawling again on Khalil's shoulder. So Lil got on the phone and talked to the guy Dignity was with. He got this worried look on his face. When he got off the phone, Salmon passed out on the couch, and Khalil got on the phone with his father.

Khalil

"Daddy? I'm out at Salmon's. Yeah, sort of. Listen, me and some friends are gonna ride out to Kentucky for a minute, visit a good friend. Nah, you never met her. Probably heard me talk about her, though. Dignity. Uh-huh. Kind of an emergency. Can I use the credit card? Just a day or two, that's all. No, I won't. I promise."

I talked to my dad, gave him the number to Dignity's hotel, and hung up the phone. Then I handed the phone to Stacy.

"What's going on now?" She was trying not to get irritated.

"Something happened to Dignity. She found out about her father, and it's messing her up. And you can see that Salmon is a basket case, too. We're going out there. Call your job and let them know you'll be out on Monday and Tuesday. I'm gonna go home and get us some clothes and stuff, fill up the tank. Be ready when I get back."

It wasn't open for discussion. She wants to be with me, she gotta roll with me. Put herself aside for a change. We all gotta do that sometimes. It was sort of a test, really. To see if she was down, really for real about this thing.

I was going, regardless. Because I could hear it in Digs' voice; she was out there. And so was Sal. Her friend sounded like his hands were tied over there, and he actually asked me to come. In this case, he didn't have to ask me twice.

I didn't want to go to Mom's. I knew she'd have a lot of questions. I'd have to call her once we got there. I went to the frat house and grabbed whatever I could that was clean. Sweats, T-shirts, some boxers, and a hairbrush. I knew Stacy would be nagging me about her hair first chance she got. I went to my private stash and dumped all the quarters and singles I had in there in my pocket. Then I stopped for gas. Got some chips and some slices of pizza—my ass was hungry. A few cans of Minute Maid orange, and I was back at Sal's crib in no time.

Stacy must have sensed she'd be spending time with me when she went to pick up Sal. She had a purse the size of an overnight bag. Had a toothbrush and a change of underwear in there. I had no comment for that. I just told her to take a firm hold of Sal's left side and help me walk him to the car. She did it without question. I was beginning to think she really had changed. I can remember a time when she'd have laid me out if I even suggested she drop everything and go on a road trip mission in the middle of the night. This time she complied, and I was glad she was on my side.

It was no joke getting Salmon to the car. He was gibbering and stinking, a pile of funky dead weight. We poured his ass in the backseat, sprayed him down with Lysol, and then we were on our way.

Somewhere around Charles Town, West Virginia, Sal started to wake up. He complained that it was too hot in the back seat, that he wanted to sit up front. Stacy wasn't really feeling that, but neither of us wanted him to get sick. We stopped so Stacy and Sal could switch spots. I looked over at my friend, and his face was green. He had those circles under his eyes, and his breath was hitting. I felt bad for him.

"What's going on? Where are we headed?" I could hear the confusion in his voice; I knew he was still intoxicated. I didn't want to get into it at that time. Who knew if he would have protested or what. I just handed him a lit cigarette and told him to relax. Sal finished the cigarette, downed a whole can of soda, and went back to sleep.

Once he passed out again, I took the time to fill Stacy in on what was going on. She already knew that Digs was raised by her great-aunt, that her moms was a jazz singer who stayed gone all the time. We both knew that her dad was a white man who died before Digs was born. But Mercer, Digs' friend, told me that Digs had been trying to find out more about her father. Apparently, that's why they'd made the trip to Ashland in the first place. But whomever Dignity spoke with gave her some news that really messed her up. Mercer wouldn't go into it on the phone; he said he'd let Dignity do that herself. But I wanted to give Stacy the heads-up, so she could be on her p's and q's.

"Wow. That's all so messed up. I know what it's like to have a jacked up family situation; mine has been screwed from the word go." Stacy leaned up from the back seat to touch my hand. I looked at her in the rearview mirror and was stunned to see compassion in her face. It was the prettiest I'd ever seen her look.

[STRANGE FRUIT]

Dignity

I got back to the hotel room, and Mercer was draped across the bed watching *All My Children*. "Girl, sit down; you won't want to miss this! Miss Erica has carried on today! And looking fabulous, too, I mean to say! Girlfriend had on…" He looked up and noticed that I was visibly shaken. I saw his face drop, landing somewhere on the floor, alongside my own. "Dignity? Oh, no. What happened, Honey?" He pulled me onto the bed and sat down next to me. First he just held onto me; then he leaned himself away to look into my face. And then into my hands.

"What's this all about?" He gestured at the Xeroxed article I'd brought from my meeting with Cordial.

"Look at this! She just gives me this and goes on her merry way! Look at it!" I was thrusting it into his hands, as if relieving myself of the paper would also exempt me from its contents.

Mercer looked scared to touch the paper, seeing how it was affecting me. But, as always, he put himself aside and took the article out of my hands. "Do you need me to read this?" It was a rhetorical question.

The caption read, "Alleged Sexual Assault Leads to Family Murder." Mercer nearly dropped the page when he read the opening line to himself. Then, he looked at me, giving me strength with his eyes, and began reading aloud:

"Franklin Chasinger, son of former Fayette County police Chief, Thomas Chasinger, died yesterday from a gunshot wound. He was 24…"

The article went on to explain that Franklin Chasinger was not new to crime. He had been arrested twice for assault and battery and picked up for questioning for a series of hate crimes on the campus of the University of Kentucky in the winter of 1971. There was not enough evidence to link him to those crimes, and he was released. Mercer continued reading:

"Chasinger was shot while trespassing on private property owned by Norman Mandarene of Bourbon County, Kentucky. Mandarene also happens to be Franklin Chasinger's uncle. According to police reports, Norman Mandarene and Thomas Chasinger, father of the deceased, were half-brothers. The two had been estranged for some time.

"... Mandarene came to the aid of a young woman in Mandarene's employ, police said. Rebecca Pearson, also of Bourbon County, worked as a domestic in Mandarene's home. Chasinger was allegedly sexually assaulting Pearson on the grounds of Mandarene's estate when Mandarene approached the trespasser, brandishing a rifle to scare the trespasser away. Evian Mandarene, grandson of the alleged perpetrator, was also involved in the scuffle, an eyewitness said ..."

I had covered my ears, and tears were raining down my face so fast and furious that the whole front of my blouse was soaked.

"Take some breaths, Dignity. We don't have to do this. We can ball this thing up and forget it ever existed. Because you don't need..." Mercer was about to drop the paper on the floor, but I caught his hand.

"Just read it! Get it over with! I have to know. Whether you read it or not, I still have to know..." I put my hands over my mouth, bit my fingers, and braced myself, tried to will myself to stop crying. "Go on."

"Though it is unclear exactly how the shooting transpired, Chasinger was shot and killed, police said. It was not until Chasinger was pronounced dead on arrival at the County Hospital that the Mandarenes learned that this trespasser was their relative. Both Mandarenes were released when it was determined that the shooting was an accident..."

When Mercer finished reading, we both sat there in silence. It was surreal. In the course of one day, I had lost and gained a grandmother, lost one dead father, and acquired a new dead father, who had also been a racist, a rapist, and an all-around criminal. I was born out of an act of violence; I was a child of rape.

"No wonder." My voice was nearly inaudible.

Mercer put the article down and put his hands around mine. We both were shaking.

"No wonder what?" Mercer asked.

"No wonder my mom left me. She can't look at me. She can't look at me, Mercer! She thinks I'm so disgusting, she can't look..." I dropped the sentence and dropped my body to the floor, banging my head on the corner of the boxspring. My mind removed from the hotel room and spun in unspeakable space. I felt my soul screaming and punching, but in fact, I could not create sound. Like my mother, I was left speechless. I felt Mercer slip down to the floor beside me. He was crying, too. I reached up to touch one of his tears. Then we held onto each other, down there on the floor of Ashland, Kentucky, and cried.

❀❀❀

I must have fallen asleep down there. I woke up with my head aching from where I'd banged it on the bed. I felt old, cold, and swollen. I stayed down there for a minute and tried to remember where I was and how I had gotten there. Slowly, as I focused on the strange carpet, its odd shade of rust, the ancient television, the double beds with their matching, striped spreads, I remembered that I was in Ashland. And that I was the daughter of a dead rapist.

I pulled myself off the floor and looked around for Mercer. I didn't want to be left alone. "Mercer?"

"I'm in here, Honey." I walked into the bathroom looking for Mercer and found Marcy instead. My friend had brought along a makeup case, and in the time that I had slept, he had completely beat his face. But the foundation was ghostly white, and the eye makeup was dark and drastic.

"I'm giving you the better kabuki, Miss Thing! I'm serving you Japanese, girl!" He pursed his lips and added more pouting red to his mouth.

"Will you stop it already? What is it with you, anyway?! Like I don't have enough going on right now—I don't need this, Mercer!"

Mercer dropped his hands to his sides, showing a hairy chest underneath the green, silk kimono he was wearing. "Me so horny! Me love you long time!" He sang a song that'd been popular back in the day with an Asian accent. We both cracked up.

"You are nuts! And that song's not Japanese, anyways. That woman is Chinese. Or Vietnamese." I was laughing in spite of myself.

"Chinese, Japanese, dirty knees, WHAT ARE THESE?!" Mercer shook his absence of breasts at me. I followed him back to the double beds. He sat on his, and I sat on mine.

On the way to the bed, though, I spotted that article, that gift from my ex grandmother, Cordial Howard.

"Oh, Lord. I'm the child of a rapist, Mercer. I feel so disgusting. It sucks to be me." I contemplated suicide and ice cream.

"You're a child of God, Dignity. And truly, nobody's got it all that easy." Mercer looked down at his bare, hairy chest and pulled his kimono closed. He looked across the room at the mirror, but when he saw his own reflection, he looked at me instead.

"Why do you do it? The whole Marcy thing?"

Mercer closed his eyes and sighed. "I don't know, Girl. To be someone else. Sometimes it's too much trouble to be me." He grabbed a tissue from the nightstand and began wiping away the white foundation, revealing streaks of reddish brown underneath.

"Why? I mean, your father didn't rape your mother, did he? And both of them stuck around once you were born. What have you got to complain about?" I knew my being glib was probably inappropriate, but sue me for not knowing how to react in this situation.

"No, he didn't rape anyone. Just hated me, is all. They didn't want a little boy, Dignity. That much was very clear."

"Why do you say that?"

"Because it's true. Daddy doesn't like men. They threaten him, or something. And Mama doesn't know what to do with males, either. Grandmama, Aunt Sarah, Mama, and my uncle, who was practically a woman, God rest his fabulous soul—that's all Mama ever dealt with. She grew up with women. She never thought she'd have to deal with a little old boy." By now his face was clean, and his bed was covered with color-stained Kleenex.

"Yes, but that doesn't mean that she doesn't... love you, even if you are a boy."

"It seems that way sometimes. I mean, they never did anything mean to me. They just ignored me, in a way. I don't know; it's hard to explain." Mercer took off the kimono and put his T-shirt back on. "The way Mama carried on over my uncle. And my cousins—all girls! Neici's gone to modeling school, and Lisa's got to have a dress for the debutante cotillion, and all this. She never put on that way for me. I could bring home straight A's and be named MVP on the soccer team, remember that? Mama barely blinked an eye. But, my God, if Lisa got a new dress—please!"

"Your parents were always proud of you, Mercer! When you were accepted at Howard, the way they went on about that to Aunt Lette?" I was grasping at straws. Because, though I had never really realized it, Mercer's parents were never around to witness his victories at school. They didn't go to his games. They didn't come to most of his debates, either.

"Right. Whatever. I used to jump through hoops to get them to acknowledge me. It wasn't happening."

I wanted to protest, wanted to launch an argument to convince Mercer that his observations were wrong. And maybe they were. But, the experiences were his, and he had already formulated his version of truth. I hadn't the energy to dispute it. "I was there, Mercer. And I was also proud of you. Still am." I came over to his bed and leaned against him. He put his arm around me and touched my hair.

"I'm not gay, Dignity. I know it doesn't make sense. I love me some women. Maybe too much. But when I first put on these clothes, this makeup, suddenly all these people were looking at me, and ooh-ing and ahh-ing. I mean, I walked the ball and won! They gave me so much attention, so much love, just for being who I am."

"But, Mercer! Listen to yourself! That's not who you are! And anyways, you get plenty of attention when you don't do drag, too. Cher's Hair? Hello?"

We both giggled. "I know. But Cher doesn't give me money! When I perform at the clubs, I get paid, Girlfriend!" Mercer scooped the soiled Kleenex from his bed and dumped them in the trash.

More time passed, and it was getting dark outside. Mercer went over to the diner and brought back dinner for us, but neither of us felt much like eating. In the middle of the mashed potatoes, I started to cry.

"This is bullshit! What did I do to deserve this? My father was a criminal, Mercer! You said I had to find the root. Turned out to be the root of all evil. I feel so disgusting. I mean, the apple doesn't fall far from the tree, you know." I pushed the meatloaf around in its Styrofoam container and tried hard not to gag through my tears.

"But it can get kicked away. You got kicked away from that tree. You have nothing to do with your father, nothing in common with him. You're a whole different fruit, Dignity." He took the food away from me and threw it in the trash along with his own. Neither of us was hungry.

"You should know about fruit, Mercer!"

"True. I feel disgusting sometimes, too. Circumstance can do that to you. But I look at you, and all I see is beauty. And you look at me, and you see the same thing. Let's try to look at ourselves more through each other's eyes."

His words were so sincere that they made us both cry. We fell asleep on his bed, both of us crying, both of us wiping the other's tears. We might have slept that way all night, but then the phone rang. Mercer picked up to find Stacy Smithe, the Wicked Witch of West Baltimore, on the line.

When I found out what had happened, how Sal was so upset and longing for me, I collapsed. I wanted to comfort him, and I was afraid I didn't know how. I was afraid that he would find out the truth of how disgusting I was and never want to lay eyes on me again. But Mercer talked to Khalil and told him he should come. Before I knew it, Stacy, Khalil, and Sal were on their way to Ashland. All I wanted to do was sleep, throw a fit, and cry.

"Looks like we're going to have some company." Mercer hung up the phone and put it back in its place on the night table.

"What if he leaves again, Mercer? What if he finds out and can't stand the sight of me? I don't think I can lose one more person. Honestly. I don't think I can."

"Stop it. You're not going to lose him. He loves you! You heard how he was carrying on up there! And anyway, you'll always have me."

"That's true. And it's good because it means I can always borrow your makeup."

43

[CIRCLE OF FITS]

Salmon

It was as if I'd taken a wad of cotton, soaked it in hot rum, rubbed it in an ashtray, and sucked on it for the last eight hours. Disgusting is not the word for what I felt. I had the same clothes on that I'd been wearing the day before, only now they were full of sweat and dirt and the stench of vomit. I had sleep crusted in the corners of my eyes and a headache pounding on me like I owed it money.

When I woke up, I couldn't figure out where I was or what was going on. Lately, I'd been having these bad dreams, and I was afraid I was in the middle of another one. I looked over, and there was Khalil behind the wheel of a car, and when I looked out the window, I didn't recognize anything I was seeing. I looked over my shoulder, and there was Stacy Smithe asleep in the backseat. First I touched myself, just to see if I could feel it. I did, but it didn't convince me I wasn't dreaming. I reached out and pinched Khalil on the arm, hard. When he started bitching, I knew I must be awake.

"Ouch! What the hell is wrong with you, Man?" Khalil pushed my hand away from him with force and then rubbed his arm.

"Lil? What's going on, anyways? Where are we going? What time is it?"

"Chill, Man. I got this covered. We on a mission, alright?" He was playing a CD of some instrumental jazz. Boney James, maybe. And the sun was just coming up over the mountains. I rolled down the windows to get some fresh air, but there was none. The day was hot and clear, and already you couldn't buy a breeze. No telling what the weather would be like by afternoon.

I put my head back against the car seat. There was an empty, raging pit in the bottom of my stomach, and I didn't particularly like the feel of Lil's car rolling over the highway. I was nauseous and thirsty. I shut my eyes and wanted to go back to sleep, but it was too late for all that. Reluctantly, I opened my eyes and stared out the window. I tried to remember what had gone on before, why the three of us were together at all, much less in Khalil's car in the middle of what seemed to be the mountains.

I could remember Stacy coming to my parents' house and having Khalil show up. I know we were supposed to go out to my place, back at school. But after that, I was drawing a blank.

I spoke softly because I didn't want to wake Stacy. "Dude. Seriously. What's going on?"

Khalil chuckled. "You sound like Marvin Gaye, over here!" He imitated my accent, a thing he does all too well. "You really don't remember, do you?" He sounded surprised. "I bounced down to hang with you this weekend, went to your folks', conversated with Stacy for a minute, got back with her. Meanwhile, you got bent up the bridge at school and was acting crazy, so we got the digits to call Digs in Kentucky, and, hey, that was that. Now we fitting to roll up on her ass."

When he said I was crying over Darryl and asking for Digs, I knew he was telling the truth.

It was almost eight in the morning. We were pulling into the parking lot of a seedy-looking motel somewhere in Kentucky. I sat in the car while Stacy and Khalil got a room. They tossed me the keys and told me to go shower my ass and stop asking questions. Said they were going to take a walk and get some grub. That I should be ready to jet when they got back.

I was glad about the shower. Lil handed me a plastic kitchen bag full of clothes, and he'd put my toothbrush and paste in there. I must have brushed my whole mouth, tongue included, for a solid hour. I got in the shower and let the cool water run all over me for a while. Scrubbed up and got out. No sooner than I had put on the clothes they'd bought for me, a pair of jeans and a polo shirt that I probably wouldn't have chosen, than I heard a faint knock at the door.

I got a knot in my stomach.

"Yeah, who is it?"

"Room service." It was clearly Dignity's voice. I literally ran to the door. I stopped short before jerking it open, though. No need for her to know how anxious I was.

"I didn't order nothing." I couldn't take my eyes from her. She was so smooth, so powdered and cool, she reminded me of a glass of water. And I was thirsty.

"You didn't order nothing. That's a double negative. Which means you did order something. That's what I'm here for." She stepped inside the door, but she didn't close it behind her. I think she wanted me to invite her in.

I went her one better. I scooped her up by the waist, brought her up around my own, and she wrapped her legs around me. She felt so good to me I wanted to cry. But from what Khalil had said, I'd done enough of that already. So I just rubbed her back and wound my fingers up in her soft hair. We stayed that way a while. I didn't want to let her go.

When we finally broke ourselves apart, she handed me a bag. Inside was a bagel with extra cream cheese and four small packs of strawberry jam. It was my favorite. It was sweet she remembered.

We sat on the bed together while I wolfed down the breakfast. I was hungry as a mug. Just in time, she produced a bottle of apple juice, and I chugged that down. The whole time we had our eyes on each other, inside each other, but neither of us was saying anything.

Finally, she broke the silence. "So, Salmon Rinaldi. What brings you? What's a handsome guy like you doing in a place like this?" She pulled her legs up in a bunch and surrounded them with her arms.

I shook my head. It was just too good to see her, and I couldn't get over how much relief I felt just looking at her. "Check you out. Dignity, it hasn't been the same without you. I guess I couldn't take it anymore, or something. These last two weeks—they been rough, okay? Real rough…" I thought about being at home, with Ma being sick. About trying to talk to Pop. That thing he said about Georgy and Darryl. About going to God alone.

"Same here." There was something thick behind those words, but I didn't press her to explain what, exactly. You can't press her to talk about really emotional stuff. She'll freeze up on you. Which is weird. Because I have no problem "getting heavy," as she calls it. I want to talk about stuff, even the stuff that ain't so pleasant. I'm more like the typical woman that way. But she's like Pop and the rest of my family. She don't like to talk.

I unfolded her arms and spread her legs out in front of her. Then I took one of the pillows from the bed and threw it in her lap. I laid my head on the pillow, with my body curled around hers. It felt like heaven.

Another long silence. "I guess you heard my ma was sick." I wanted to broach the topic of my father, try to give her a feel for why I hadn't taken her home.

She was running her finger over my eyebrows. "Stacy told me. I am glad she was around to…help you out." There was a little something in her voice, paranoia, maybe, but I chose to ignore it.

"Digs, my Pop is old-fashioned; he's too old to change, really. I mean, he's making an effort, for Ma's sake, but it ain't exactly easy…"

"I know. Nothing is especially easy anymore. I'd been looking for my father. Did Mercer talk to you?"

"Wow. That's a brave step. Did you find out anything?" I asked gently. I knew that this was a hard topic for her.

"Yeah. A lot. Listen, Sal. I love you. It's not easy for me to…admit that, or something. And it's not a promise that I can always be, like, Miss Perfect for you. But, umm. I do. You mean the world to me."

"Me, too. Nobody's looking for perfect. There's no such thing as perfect. And, ah. I love you, too." I stopped talking and pressed my face against her stomach, put my arms around her legs, and breathed her in. I made sure to keep my middle away from her, in a certain way. I didn't want her to freak out on me.

Then she surprised me. All of a sudden she takes off her shirt, takes off her pants, flings them both to the floor. I just sat on the bed, stunned. Then she stood in front of me and peeled off her underpants, snapped away her bra. She's just standing in front of me, nude. She took my hands and put them on her bottom. Then she started kissing me all over, with a passion I'd never seen from her before.

That was it. I came to attention, jumping out of my fog, and I touched her, kissed her, pressed myself against her. Next thing you know, we're on the bed, both of us naked, and I'm all on top of her. She takes my index finger and puts it in her mouth. It felt so soft and sweet, I wanted to lose my mind.

She's looking up at me, and I can see where she is scared. She's breathing heavy; she's excited, but somewhere in there, I can still see fear. I rolled off of her and pulled the blanket over us.

"Let's wait on this, huh? We got plenty of time. No rush." I pulled her body close to mine and wrapped my leg around hers. She didn't say it, but I could tell she was relieved. A little disappointed, but mostly relieved. I kissed her again. I felt like I had a barrel of gold in my arms. Honestly.

"You know, my Pops is old, but he's trying. One of these days, we're just gonna go over there. Let him meet you. Let him see what I been seeing. One day he may come around on this, I bet you."

"Like you said, Salmon. We got time. I'm not in a hurry. If you're not." I looked through her eyes and saw straight through to her soul, and it was fluffy and sweet, like cotton candy. Made me smile.

We spent the next hour under the cover, just touching each other, exploring. She led my hands to her southern region. Led it all around the outside, down her inner thigh, over her ass. She held on to me gently and kept her eyes locked on mine. I never felt so close to someone; it was even closer than sex.

"Salmon," she said, "let's be together, okay? I mean, like before, but different."
I knew exactly what she meant. "Yeah. Let's."

❀❀❀

I was the last one to find out about Digs' father, and I guess I took it the hardest. Or maybe, since the others had read the article earlier, they'd had more time to digest it and react.

We were all in Digs' and Mercer's room. We'd bought a bunch of pizza and beer. Only Stacy and Dignity were each nursing peach wine coolers. I wasn't really in the mood to drink, but Mercer and Khalil were having at it with a vengeance. They got along famously. Mercer was an ace; I could see why Dignity was friends with him. I even tried hard not to be jealous when they reminisced about old times, back before she ever knew I existed.

Everybody in there smoked except Stacy and Khalil, so the place was billowing with second-hand garbage. We opened the windows, but there was no real breeze to carry the smoke away. We were all laughing like crazy and having a good time. It felt like a bar. I think we all needed the time to hang out and act stupid. Every one of us had been majorly stressed.

Mercer and Dignity are neat freaks, so I knew the mess in the room was bothering them. I took a plastic bag and started collecting up the garbage and throwing it in. That's when I saw this Xeroxed article. I read the headline, and it struck me as strange. I was about to throw the thing away, but then I didn't.

"Anybody want this?" I flashed the paper around the room, and the whole group went silent. Khalil looked at Stacy, Stacy looked at Mercer, and Mercer looked at Dignity. Nobody was looking at me. "Anybody gonna answer me on this, or what?" More silence.

Mercer nodded at Dignity, and finally she spoke. "Sal, that's an article about my real father. Go on and read it." Suddenly, there was a hanging awkwardness, and everybody pretended to be busy doing other things. Stacy and Khalil turned on the television and got real interested in an episode of *Star Search*. Mercer decided to pick up the cleaning where I had left off. Dignity came and sat next to me on the bed.

I read through the article, but it didn't make sense. Which one of those people was her father? Who was this Rebecca Pearson?

"So…I don't get it. What's this got to do with your father, Digs?" When I looked at her, she had that look of fear and anxiety she always used to wear on her face. She hadn't been looking like that since we, uh, messed around in the other room a while before. I wasn't glad to see that look return.

"Rebecca Pearson? That's my mother. You know, I go by my great-aunt's name, Jackson, since she and Uncle Sam adopted me. But my mom. Her name is Pearson." Her lips were trembling.

I looked over the article again. Slowly I was beginning to put the whole thing together. "Huh. So, this, ah, Franklin whatever. Are you saying he's your father?" My heart stopped. Because the way this thing was written, this man was a low-life, a criminal. I mean, it said he'd raped Digs' mother. Unless I'd misread it. I hoped I'd misread it.

"Yes. Sal, I never knew him, I swear! And, umm, please don't hate me because it's not my fault." Her eyes spilled over with tears, and she looked like I felt yesterday, all last week, ever since my mommy got sick. Like an orphan.

Like a lonesome rock with a sickly hot middle. It made me feel so sorry, so angry, I wanted to knock the shit out of someone.

I punched the paper into a ball with my fists and tossed it in Mercer's trash bag. "Fuck this! This is bullshit! He's a low-life bastard, okay? He's a dead, low-life bastard son of a bitch, Dignity! I don't give a shit about him!" I pulled her inside my arms and pressed her head against my chest. "Listen. This ain't your fault. You gotta believe that. We don't get to choose our parents." I could feel her whole body quaking next to mine, and it was breaking my heart. She had her hands covering her face, but I could still feel the wetness of her tears on my shirt.

"I know that's right! If I could have chosen, I'd have picked something totally different! My father? Let's not even go there! And my mother? She never said a word to me except to say why I wasn't pretty enough, or light enough, or good enough for her love. I never would have chosen that!" Stacy put down her cooler and looked toward me and Dignity with desperate sincerity.

"I heard that! I don't know that I'd trade my parents? But I know it would sure have made things easier if they'd been different. I mean, if they ever even looked at me, for once, and appreciated me, accepted me. Maybe I wouldn't be going through all this now..." Mercer set his bag of trash on the floor while he sat there, agreeing with Stacy.

"But, for real. It's like, they're just people. Half the time they don't know what the fuck they're doing. I mean, they look up one day, and they're parents. Maybe they do the whole marriage thing, maybe not. Then they start cranking out babies. Nobody tells them how to do it! Half of them don't know shit about how to be someone's mama, how to be a good daddy. It pisses me off. But, then, I remember. They're just people. They make mistakes. We got to learn to forgive their mistakes." Khalil was drunk. He was not the average drinker. When he'd had a few, that's when he'd put on his thinking cap. Suddenly, he's Phil Donahue over here. A modern-day prophet, or something. He had some good points, though.

I could feel Dignity's body begin to quiet and get still. She still had her face pressed against my chest, so we could barely hear her. "Yeah, they're people. But you're talking about choices and mistakes. My mother didn't have a choice. And rape? That's more than a mistake!"

"What did she say?" Stacy was too far away to interpret Digs' muffled words.

"She said that her, ah, Franklin, did more than make a mistake." I gave them the paraphrased version.

"Still. He was a human. He was at least some semblance of a human. And he did do one good thing in his life. He produced you. You gotta take it from there, Digs. It's your responsibility to be you." Khalil belted back the last of his High Life before crushing the can and tossing it into Mercer's trash bag. And who knew what the hell he was talking about, really. But we were all so tired and so stressed, we decided it made good sense.

Stacy said, "Exactly. We all have to be responsible for ourselves." She looked longingly at Khalil and kissed him with her eyeballs. I'd have done the same thing to Dignity, but by then she had her back to me. Plus, I didn't know how.

"Let's do a toast, everybody!" Mercer came out of nowhere with a bottle of bubbly and those plastic champagne glasses with the pull off stems. He gave out the glasses and poured equal amounts for everyone until the bottle was gone.

"Here's to Dignity!" He raised his glass.

"Hear, hear!" I shouted the loudest.

"No, for real. To dignity. To being able to forgive and make things work. To not running away." He clinked Stacy's glass, indicating that she should add to the toast.

"Yes. And. To good friends. Who help you to be the best you." She looked gratefully at Dignity, and clinked Digs' glass.

"Okay. To fathers, the ones who try hard to change. And to moms who stick around. And here's to looking in the mirror and… and trying to like what you see." She looked away before the tears came again and clinked my glass.

I spilled a little champagne out on the carpet. "Yeah. And to, ahh, those who went on before us. Because we remember them. And we love them." Mercer nodded his head in appreciation, but he still grabbed a napkin to sop up the drink.

Khalil caught his arm and stopped him from cleaning it. "It can wait, Man. Here's to cleaning up the mess from the people you love. And to knowing when to let the shit go. And to us! Because we are some bad-ass mo-fo's! We got it going on and on and on!"

With that, we clinked each other's glasses. I was standing there with Dignity and a set of good people around me. It felt really good.

The Epilogue: Senior Year

[MORGAN STATE UNIVERSITY 1995]

[STANDING UP]

Dignity Jackson

I looked over at Salmon and watched him as he slept. Peacefully. We still had some rough nights. Sometimes I woke to find him crying in his sleep. It didn't happen all the time, though. We still have our issues, but we're trying.

I remember the first time we made love. It was at my Grandma Pearson's house last summer, the week after they'd all come down to Ashland. Right after I found out about Franklin. Stacy and Khalil left for Baltimore, and Khalil went back to finish his summer gig with his dad. They both had to go back to work, so they only ended up staying through the weekend. We had such a good time together! I forced them to go antiquing with me and Mercer. We went to this hillbilly bar and sang karaoke. And it was, like, magic. I bonded with them in a way I never had with anyone before. Except maybe with Mercer.

The last night at the hotel, we were playing that drinking game, quarters, where you have to bounce the quarter into the empty shot glass, and if you miss, you have to drink. Only, in our version, you drank if you missed a shot, but you also had to tell something personal. We called it "True Confessions." The rule was, anything we said that night would stay in that room, just between the five of us.

Salmon told us about his cousins, Darryl and Georgy. He admitted that he still felt guilty that they were gone, guilty that he was still alive. And Stacy admitted that she'd been jealous of me, that sometimes she still was. Khalil confessed that he'd been a virgin when he got to Morgan, which blew us all away. Stacy and I just looked at each other and rolled. To think we had spent that time with that bet, to see who'd lose their cherry first, and there he was in the same situation. The way he acted, he sure fooled us!

Mercer told everyone that he had a flair for drama and liked to perform, but he left it at that. I just gave him a look, and he didn't take it any further. I didn't think my college buddies were ready for that. But he also admitted that he had a thing going with Cher. Which I already knew. He spent the last hour that night before going to sleep on the phone with her. That one was going to take some getting used to, sharing my best friend with Cher. Of course, he had to share me with Sal, and I guess that wasn't easy for him, either.

Fortunately, I have good aim, so I didn't miss the shot glass too often. There weren't too many times when I had to drink or confess. When I did, I told them about the article I had taken from Aunt Lette, the one I showed to Ain't Angus. In my heart, I sort of already knew about...Franklin. I told them what I knew about my mother. How I barely remembered what she looked like. I admitted that I listened to the album my cousin gave me, and I wondered where she was and what she was doing.

Even though we had two rooms, everybody passed out in the same room that night. We pushed the double beds together and sprawled out every which way. The next morning, when we were checking out, Salmon decided to stay. He didn't have to work the next week, and he wanted to see where I was from.

For the first few days, we stayed with Mercer. But around the middle of the week, I was down in the living room listening to my mom's record, which had become a daily ritual. That's when Salmon suggested we go find my mom. I explained that she hadn't come around for a long time. In fact, I'd heard she hadn't spoken a word off stage for almost ten years. But he insisted.

Aunt Ruty gave me the number. My mom's group, Sister 'Becca and Them, would be playing at a club in Louisville all week. Aunt Ruty had called my step-father, Edward's, mother, and gotten the number where they were staying. It was Salmon who placed the call. He talked to Albert, my uncle. Uncle Albert told us to come on down, that he'd tell my mom I was coming, that she'd be glad to see me.

We were going to see the first show, which took place during happy hour at a bar down by the water. It was a mixed crowd. A lot of them were yuppies who'd just gotten off from work, but there were some old heads there, too. The place was okay. Nothing fancy. It had pictures of horses from the Derby all over the walls, and the tables were arranged in the shape of a giant horseshoe. At the top of the horseshoe, in the open space, there was a small platform, and next to that there was a piano, two big amps, and a couple of stools.

I sat at a table at the bottom of the horseshoe, where we'd have a clear view of the stage. Sal went to the bar and got us some Cokes—neither of us was up for alcohol.

Right at six-thirty p.m., the lights dimmed, and they announced my mom's group over the loud speaker. "Ladies and Gentlemen, The Thoroughbred Club is proud to present the quintessential quartet of vintage, country soul. Please welcome, Kentucky's own, *Sister 'Becca and Them.*" There was a round of loud applause, and then the band came out. Just four men, one on drums, one on piano, one on lead guitar, and one on bass. They plucked out the first few chords of "God Bless the Child." I knew that song intimately, I'd listened to the album so frequently that my heart raced when I recognized the notes.

First, Edward and Albert came onstage. They didn't look that different from the last time I'd seen them, which had been years before. Edward had gained some weight in his stomach and had lost some hair. Albert had some gray in his coifed goatee. They were doowopping and snapping over the piano's bass line. Then Pam Elizabeth came out. I'd never seen her in person, but I recognized her from the album cover. She looked exactly the same. She was petite and shapely with long, thick black hair, pressed straight and flipped under all the way around. They built the chord together, oohing and doowopping. Finally, Sister Becca came out, pulled the stool onto the stage, and sat down. She had a drink in one hand, and she waited two more measures before she began to sing. The whole time, the audience was going wild, clapping and yelling out her name.

I felt every line, every note they sang, in my very core, and the words resonated again in my soul. It was like listening to the album, only better. Sister Becca kept her eyes closed most of the time, but she hit those notes rich in the center, and she never missed a beat. Her voice reminded me of s'mores, those graham cracker, marshmallow, and chocolate sandwich treats we used to make at summer camp. So much sweet, succulent texture, your ears couldn't get enough.

I knew Sal had been sitting beside me, and I knew I was in a room full of people, but somehow it seemed like we were all alone, like Sister Becca was singing just for me. And, it didn't feel like it was my mother singing. It sounded like a CD that I would listen to over and over again. Because the melodies were so unified, so heavy with experience, so tight, so masterfully spun. I understood why the room was packed, why people had rushed over after a long day of work to hear this group sing. They were saying something that all of us really understood.

I couldn't even clap when they finished that first song. I didn't cry, didn't move. I just sat there staring at them, all of them, but mainly Sister Becca. Sal kept his hand on my leg, under the table. But I stared straight ahead, star-struck and completely engaged.

Finally, after two more songs, Sister Becca opened her eyes. She looked to the back of the room and motioned subtly to the bartender. Then a waitress came around to the side of the stage and handed her another drink, taking the empty glass from her hands. Sister Becca took a sip of it. Then she looked out into the audience and found my face, my eyes. She held them in her own for a moment. She put her index and middle fingers to her lips gently and blew me a kiss. I caught it in my stomach and welcomed the butterflies it caused there. Then she spoke. "This next one's for my Dignity."

"*When the world is cold/it takes the words away/stills the sun and kills the light of day/freezes up your heart and keeps you old/makes it hard to hold/to keep hold/of your Dignity…*"

She sang alone, a capella. She kept her eyes open and gave them to me, like they were all she had left. I knew she'd written this song for me. And I accepted it from her, unblinkingly, hoping there would be more, something more, later, after the show.

But there wasn't. Uncle Albert rushed offstage after the set and gave me a big hug. He was genuinely glad to see me. He sat down for a minute and told me what they were up to, how they'd be at that club for the rest of the week. How they were going to Ontario the next week and would be gone for a month. He fumbled in his pocket and pulled out a double cassette. "It's got some of our tracks on it, and some old stuff, you know. Make sure you stay familiar with the old school jams, Kid. Part of your history."

Edward came over, but he was clearly uncomfortable. Like he wanted to be forthcoming but didn't know how. He shook Sal's hand and gave me a peck on the cheek. "You've really grown up, huh? You look beautiful." He left after a minute and went to get Pam Elizabeth.

There was a mesh railing of pity in Pam's eyes, and she didn't know what all to say. She hugged me for a long time, though. "She wrote that song for you. It's really popular, too. Everybody loves it. She doesn't sing it all that much, though. But people request it like crazy. She's gotta be in the right mood." They had an hour before the next set, and Pam Elizabeth went back to the dressing room to freshen up. I hoped Sister Becca would come out and see me. She never did.

Sal and I waited until just before the group was ready to sing again. He'd have stuck around if I'd wanted to, but I didn't. We stopped at a McDonald's on the way out, and then we went back to Grandma Pearson's.

Of course, I was disappointed. I'd been reluctant to go and see my mom. I knew she wasn't really emotionally available to me. And hearing them sing, it was so completely awesome. I wouldn't trade that experience for anything. But when she spoke my name and looked at me, when she sang that song, I guess I hoped. That she would put her misery aside for a minute and come and tend to me. But she didn't. She couldn't. I was disappointed.

Aunt Ruty let us stay at Grandma Pearson's because my grandmother was staying in the nursing home full time by then, and the house was usually empty. They couldn't decide what to do with it. Uncle Albert didn't want to sell it, since he thought he'd stay there when they stopped touring. Aunt Ruty had her own place, and she wanted to stay there, so she didn't care if Uncle Albert kept Grandma Pearson's. But in the meantime, the house was just sitting there.

That night, when we got to the house, I was mostly quiet. It was emotional, the whole experience at The Thoroughbred. I needed to mull it over and decide what to do with it. We went to bed early that night. Upstairs in the room where Uncle Timmy and Uncle Albert used to sleep. It was in the back of the house, and the window in there overlooked the backyard, that huge, overgrown field, and the house where Cordial Howard used to live. And Evian. The man who should have been my father. And who wasn't.

That's when we first made love. I hadn't said two words to Salmon since we left Louisville. And he didn't press me. Just stayed nearby, in case I needed him. I sat looking out the window for an hour or so, before going to bed, and he laid on the bed and read the newspaper. I remember he fell asleep with the sports section spread out on his chest. He looked so adorable, and I was overwhelmed with the emotion I had for him. For coming to Ashland. For staying with me in

Kentucky. For taking me to see my mother, and for being there when she wasn't really able to see me. I loved him, and I didn't know how to say it; the words would have been empty. I wanted to show him.

I pulled up my nightgown and straddled him. He woke up to find himself underneath of me, inside of me. We didn't say words. But there was an inaudible flow between us of wordless, powerful consent. It was the most beautiful thing.

The next day, I got out of the shower and went down to make breakfast. The place didn't have air conditioning, so we had the windows open, and the back door in the kitchen was open, too. I was lingering over my coffee, and Sal went back upstairs to watch television.

That article, the one Cordial Howard had given me, was still on my mind. I stood up and went to the back door and looked out over the field, over to the house they say my mama owns. I wanted to work out the logistics in my head. Where had it happened? What was going on when... When that man raped my mother?

I put the coffee mug on the counter and walked out into the field. I reminded myself to keep breathing, not to panic the way I had the first time I'd been out there. Somewhere in the middle, between Grandma Pearson's and Cordial Howard's ex-house, I sat down. I sat sideways, so that I could see both of the houses. I noticed that someone had taken the time to mow the grass since the last time I'd been there, so it wasn't nearly as tall. I ran my hand along the blades and tried to picture my mother, with her big quilted hat, like on the album cover, with Evian, that skinny boy with the orange-red hair.

That's when I heard the car pull up. I could see that it was a big, old Cadillac coming into the driveway, but I didn't recognize it and could not see who was inside. I assumed it would be Nakita, stopping by in hopes of seeing Mercer. I was easy to spot out there in the open, and I didn't feel like moving. Whomever it was, they'd see me and come out there to me.

The car door slammed, and I could see a woman getting out of the car. But she was too thin, too graceful to be Nakita. She had on a flowered sundress, and she carried a pair of sandals in her hand. She had a mess of sherbet-colored spirals piled up all over her head. As she got closer, her face was expressionless, but she smelled sweet, like roses.

It was my mother. She sat down carefully on the grass next to me. She kept a little space between us, but not a huge gap. She didn't say anything, and neither did I.

I looked at her from the corners of my eyes. She seemed so delicate, so fragile. The tips of her eyes turned down at the ends, and there were permanent creases in her forehead. Her shoulders sloped downward, as if she carried bricks inside herself from her shoulders down to her elbows. Her skin was the color of warm chocolate. She looked worn out but pretty.

We sat like that for the longest time. She pulled the grass up, blade by blade, and made a pile of it in the center of her lap. Then, when the pile got big, she'd fan her dress up from her lap and let the grass fly down around her. After about an hour of this, she reached for my hand. We sat that way for another block of time, both of us looking up at the sky.

Much time had passed, and I had to go to the bathroom. I was afraid to leave, afraid she'd be gone when I returned. Still holding her hand, I said, "I'll be right back." She released my hand and nodded reassuringly. I ran all the way to the house, went to the bathroom quickly, and ran for the door. Then I thought about it, and I grabbed the quilt Aunt Ruty had on the living room couch. My legs were starting to itch from the grass.

I got back outside and found my mother where I'd left her. She'd pulled a nickel-colored flask out from her big side pockets. I could tell she was about to drink from it. When she saw me, she decided against it and put the flask down next to her white sandals instead.

She stood up, and the two of us spread out the quilt, making sure the edges laid smooth against the grass. I noticed Salmon looking at us from the bedroom window. I didn't wave. I kept my attention focused on my mother.

We sat down once more, now on the quilt, and soon my mother rolled to her stomach, putting her hands together up under her chin. I followed suit, and we lay there and looked up at the clouds.

"I see a castle."

I was shocked to hear her speak, knowing she'd only spoken while performing for almost ten years. But I didn't want to make a big deal of it, and I didn't want her to stop.

"Where?"

She pointed up to this one big cloud in the sky.

"I see it! And look, there's a unicorn next to it. See where the horn sticks out? Looks like it's moving." I pointed it out to her, but she didn't comment. Just nodded her head. More silence.

My mom sat up and pulled her dress around her knees. She kept the expression on her face even. "Over there, that where me and Evian got to be close. Use to take chairs out there, and he would play his guitar. He play real good, too, and I would sing." She motioned toward the boarded glass doors in front of the crumbling driveway by Cordial Howard's ex-house. "Back there, that were his room. They got the windows covered, I see." She stopped talking and seemed to look at the nickel flask with longing. She didn't pick it up, though.

"Use to walk this field every day, twice a day, before you was born. Back and forth from work. Had a lot more weeds, then, and more grass. It were not as safe out here back then." She put her legs out in front of her and began massaging her legs.

I looked at the places she pointed out and tried to imagine, tried to see it as she had seen it.

"Long about here, where we sitting, this where it happen. Me and Ev had been close, you know. And I left out to go home. He followed me. The cousin." She stopped short, and I wanted her to know I understood, that I already knew. But I couldn't get up the nerve to speak the words. So we just sat there a minute, once again in silence.

Mama turned and looked at me. "What they say is true. Part true. My Ev was... He couldn't be your father. But he your daddy. No matter what they say. He your daddy."

Already the tears had come, and I didn't bother to prevent them. They'd been second nature to me in those past weeks.

I wanted her to keep talking, but she couldn't. She reached for the flask. She screwed the top off and started to take a sip. Then she didn't. She turned it upside-down, emptied the contents into the grass on the other side of the quilt. She put the top back on and turned the flask around, so I could see the inscription. It had the name "Norman" engraved on the front. I remembered the name from the articles I'd read. I knew he was Evian's grandfather. I knew he was the one who… took care of Franklin.

She put the flask into my lap and pointed to the engraved name. "He loved us, Dignity. He the one who thought up your name. Norman told me to give you something you could hold all your life. I knew it had to be Dignity. Only thing you can hold on to. Plus, he gave me a home." She pointed to the house across the field. "Gave you that money, for when you get old enough. And Ev. He didn't get the chance to see you. But he your daddy. And Norman, he your grandfather. He would want you to have it." She pointed to the flask.

Mama looked at the watch on her wrist and stood up. She looked completely drained. I knew she was about to leave. She wrapped her arms around me and gave everything she could to me in that hug.

I didn't want to let her go, but she pulled away. "So, when…?" I questioned her through childish eyes, wanting desperately not to need her, wanting her to need me.

"Let me stand up first. Give me time." She released her arms from me and bent down to grab her sandals. She grabbed the corners of the quilt from her side, and we folded it between us. She handed me the quilt and the flask. "You way ahead of me, Dignity. I got to catch up. Give me time."

I followed her to her car, wanting to stand in front of the door and refuse to let her enter it and drive away. But as I walked behind her, I could see it took everything she had to empty that flask and to keep walking. For my mom, it was a struggle just to stand and keep moving.

She got behind the wheel and started the car. I just stood there, looking. At my feet. At Grandma Pearson's house. I decided not to watch her drive away. I headed for the back door.

"Always love you, Dignity. Always."

I didn't turn around but heard her back out of the driveway, and away from my life once again. That was almost a year ago. I haven't heard from her since.

[GRADUATION]

As we walked together across the Welcome Bridge, I thought about the last four years. It seemed like a lifetime ago when I stood there with Stacy, when we first met Khalil and Salmon. Hard to believe that I would actually have slept with Khalil, just to lose my virginity and win a bet! I smiled to myself when I thought about being with Sal now. How sharing myself with him was becoming so natural, so ordinary, and so crucial.

After finals, we'd spent the last week packing up my stuff and moving it to Sal's place. We made the decision to move in together some time after my birthday in March, around midterm. I wanted to wait until after graduation, to make it official.

I wanted to savor the last few weeks of independence. I'd started spending time again with Kiko. She was going to be moving to Michigan with her sister at the end of May. The last time we talked, I remember, she reminded me about her locket, how she chooses every day who she wants to be. I realized I'd learned from her, that I'd be sorry to see her go. I tried to give her a big tip after she did my nails that day, but she wouldn't take it. She said that whenever I thought about myself and who I wanted to be, I should think of her. And I do.

It was going to be weird not going home, to Kentucky this summer, but the idea of being without Sal was even more strange.

It's a funny thing. Just a few months ago, I really believed that there was no hope for my relationship with Sal. I wasn't all that optimistic about relationships in general. Somewhere along the line, there's always a deal breaker; an obstacle that you just can't get past. I thought I'd met my deal breaker when Sal refused to take me home to his parents, when I refused to work through my intimacy issues. But, this world is too stormy—you got to build safe harbors. That's what friends are for. Friends like Sal, Stacy, and Khalil, even Kiko. They're safe because you make them safe. Safe because you choose them, unlike your family and your history, which are thrust upon you, even without your consent.

Even still I get afraid sometimes. I think about that thing about my real father, how it completely ruined my mom's life, how it sometimes threatens to ruin my own. And I get this instinct to drink, or go completely crazy, or just run away from school and go back home. Then, I think about Salmon and how much we've been through. About Stacy and Khalil, and all that they've overcome. About the four of us, our true confessions, and our pact to support each other. I think about these things, and I realize that I *am* home. Home is not a place; it's a person and a feeling. And, let's face it, a relationship is only worth what you put into it. If you have to run away from it, then maybe it wasn't worth having after all. Who knows?

We decided we'd go down for Mercer's graduation two days after our own and spend a few days in Kentucky. Stacy and Khalil were going with us. We were calling it the "True Confessions Graduation Reunion." Mercer thought of that. He loved to have a working title for special events. Cher was having a big party for him right after graduation, with the parents and family and all that. (Was it a coincidence that Mercer's parents weren't throwing the party? That it was his friend who planned the celebration?) Then later on we were having another set out at Grandma Pearson's house. Some of our other friends from high school would be back in town by then, so I'd have the opportunity to introduce them to my Maryland posse and sort of say goodbye before starting my life with Sal in Baltimore, whatever it would be.

The sun was blaring down on us, but it felt good. For a second I worried that I might be sweating or that my makeup might be streaking, and that everyone might be laughing at me.

I thought back to when I was getting dressed for the day. I had only used one all-over body cream, and I'd spent only one hour in the bathroom—that's nearly half the time it used to take. I was making progress! I was getting tired of all of my neurotic rituals; they were so time-consuming! With the Quiet Revolution, finals, and ColorKind, I had too much to do to be wasting time in the bathroom.

I was doing my best to realize that I didn't need these procedures in order to feel acceptable and secure. It wasn't easy, but I was making progress. This time, before the panic started, I turned the process off and thought of something else. The scent of fresh roses and the texture of ripe plums. This was my favorite piece of imagery. When I get really freakish, I try to think about pleasant things. I learned that technique in the women's talk group I joined last summer. It's the best I can do in the way of therapy for right now. I still can't picture myself spilling my guts to some German analyst on a brown leather couch or anything like that. But, hopefully, I can work out some of my issues on my own.

The women in my group, I don't mind talking to them. They don't know me outside of the group, so I know I can drop whatever's on my mind if I want to, without having to worry about running into them later. Not that they'd mention anything I'd said if they saw me. We have a pact not to tell what we've heard, just like with True Confessions. I don't imagine that one of them would see me in the grocery store and be like, "Hey, aren't you the abandoned one with the rapist father?" Even still, I am glad that I chose a group out in Owings Mills, where I don't know anybody.

Salmon started going to therapy last fall, but with classes, it got to be too much for him. So he started journaling. And when stuff was really bothering him, he'd talk to me. I couldn't always give him any answers, but I did listen.

As we got to the end of the bridge, in front of Soper, I thought about the whole Morgan experience. I learned a lot, not just in terms of academics. I learned that I have something to offer this world, in spite of my history, maybe even because of my history. I learned that nobody has it that easy. I thought about the friendships I'd made over the last four years. In some ways, my friends were closer to me than family. We'd grown up together. When you're dead broke and you've got ten chapters to read and a project due by the time the sun comes up in the morning, and the only people who really understand what you're going through are the people around you, either you kill yourself, kill each other, or you make friends. There really isn't any other alternative.

I could hear all the girls' heels clicking over the gravel as we walked toward Murphy, the Fine Arts Center. I looked behind me and waved at Stacy. I will always think of her when I pass by Murphy, where we finagled an empty room from the SGA and established the ColorKind office. She looked so beautiful on graduation day. She'd shaved her hair down to the quick and was wearing it short and natural. It was so flattering. She had the most gorgeous skin, and the black, scoop-neck dress she was wearing that day clung to her in all the right places. I was proud to have her smile back at me, proud to know that we had worked through some of our differences.

Stacy would be managing ColorKind the next semester. She still had a semester of Spanish to finish before she could get her diploma. Because she only needed four credits to graduate, they let her march in the big ceremony even though she wouldn't technically be finished until the following December. I'd handed my Ms. Morgan project, ColorKind and the ColorKind Journal, over to her gratefully. I knew it would be in good hands.

She had so many excellent ideas. When I was crowned Ms. Morgan, I was so overwhelmed I thought I would have a conniption and die. But she worked with me from the very beginning. It was her idea to get a faculty sponsor, Dr. Wright. And it was her idea to do Full Spectrum during the first week of classes last fall. She had this plan where we would do an exhibit out in front of Murphy. We got students to display and sell their photography, paintings, and sketches. The theme was "Living the Rainbow."

Each piece was supposed to depict some aspect of African-American culture. We had one student who did a photo essay on the Juneteenth celebration down in Texas, where he was from. We had paintings of women doing each other's hair, some sketches of our great leaders, like Martin, Malcolm, and Marley, all kinds of really wonderful stuff. Those who contributed their work agreed to donate 50fifty percent of their proceeds to ColorKind. It was an overwhelming success. With the money we made, we were able to put together a newsletter that we distributed four times over senior year. We could only distribute a limited amount of copies since we wanted to give them out free, so they always went quickly. But that was a good sign.

Between Stacy, the QR, and the ColorKind staff, we'd made a fair showing that year. We had a few poetry slams on the steps of Holmes Hall during the first semester, and with some of the leftover funds, we helped sponsor a guest speaker on campus during the spring. I was glad that I could donate five thousand dollars from the trust fund my grandfather, Norman, left me to keep ColorKind going for another year. With Stacy running things, I knew the money would go to good use.

As we got close to the fences that surrounded the stadium, I could see out onto the open field. Looked like miles and miles of chairs out there on the grass for us, the class of 1995. And friends and family from all over the place had come to witness our big day. When the time came for us to leave the inside of the stadium, to march out there onto the field and into our seats, I had mixed emotions.

I was excited. No doubt about that. I'd worked long and hard to get through my program, and it was never easy. But college is, like, this false reality. The parameters are set for you. You follow the prescribed program, and if you keep at it, eventually you'll get to the end of it with a degree. But, the next step, the future, that part was a little scary. There would be no adviser to tell us which class to take, which direction to turn. There would be no papers and no tests, but there would also be no syllabus to follow. After this, we would be on our own. I wondered if I was ready.

Salmon was in the School of Engineering, and his class was seated toward the back left of the field. I looked for him as we marched by to our own section toward the front of the field. He was there, winking at me. And his wink still gives my heart a quiver. I love that guy. Khalil was in the same school, in the row behind Salmon. Seemed like he'd grown about four inches since the day I met him, and he was tall then. I waved at him, and he gave me the peace sign. I scanned the audience, but there was no way to pick out my personal cheering crew; I couldn't see them, but I knew they were out there. Somewhere.

As the other communication majors made their way to their assigned section, I continued past them to the very first row, right in front of the stage. I would be making my farewell remarks, along with Mr. Morgan, before they introduced the keynote speaker. I held my hands together forcefully in my lap and willed them not to shake loose from my wrists. When Dr. Wright signaled me, I walked onto the stage and stood next to the podium with Mr. Morgan.

Mr. Morgan was a big wig in his fraternity, so we had to wait while his brothers screamed and cheered. He reflected briefly on his time in office and admitted that he was somewhat sad to be leaving. I understood completely. The moment came for me to speak, and I thought first that I would melt into a puddle of sweat and anxiety. But then I looked out there, and somehow I saw Salmon. And Khalil. And Stacy. And I smelled the scent of roses and the texture of ripe plums. And just when I thought I would pass out, I didn't.

I told my classmates how proud I was to be among them. I reminded them of how much we'd lived, how much we'd learned in our time together. I implored them to remember our Fair Morgan when they stepped out into the community, to give back cheerfully and faithfully. I reminded them that, as African-Americans especially, we still had to fight to end oppression. And I reminded them, reminded myself, that the bonds we created at Morgan were priceless and worth holding onto.

"*It will never be easy, Morganites. We are sharp, and we are vital, but the world will not stop turning because of us. Just remember, like the Nobel Prize winner, Elie Wiesel, said, that silence never helps the victims of oppression; it only helps the perpetrators. So, when you walk out of this stadium, with your well-earned degree in your hand, and when the going gets tough, get going. Go to a rally that furthers the cause of your choice. Go to a church, or a synagogue, or a mosque, and keep your faith strong. Go to a therapist or a class, and learn more about yourself. Go to great lengths to stand up for what you believe in. And when the day is done, and when you're too tired to keep going, have faith, and stand. When you can do nothing else, remember that you are among the elite; you are an alum of the finest university on the planet. Keep standing. My name is Dignity. Thank you for listening.*" When I got to the end of my talk, I was so full of nerves that I'd barely remembered my own name.

I could see the fans they'd given to the graduates waving and hear my classmates cheering. I looked out into the sea of faces and smiled back at them.

After the choir sang, and after the Keynote Speaker finished, the time came. Finally we were told to stand up and move our tassels to the other side. We had graduated. The girls were squealing and the guys were yelping. The dogs were barking and the AKAs were skee-weeing. It was total madness! I had this rush of adrenaline, and I ran two rows behind me to hug Stacy. We stood there, with our heels sinking into the dirt, holding onto each other and screaming at the top of our lungs.

I'd planned to meet Aunt Lette and Uncle Sam out in front of the bridge. I didn't want to fight to find them in the crowds out on the field. Salmon's parents and his brother Frankie had come to the graduation, which was a big accomplishment, in light of his father's negative stance toward formal education. Salmon and I knew that we would be spending time, separately, with our families. When Aunt Lette and Uncle Sam went back to the hotel, and his parents and Frankie had gone back home, we would celebrate together.

I wore the heels as long as I could, but once the ceremony was over, I pulled off my sling backs and let the straps dangle from my fingers. So many families were clustered around taking pictures of their graduates and offering congratulations. I was picking my way through carefully, making my way to the fence and out toward the bridge when I felt someone tap me on the shoulder.

It was Salmon's father; I recognized him right away. He looked like my Sal, but he was a little taller, a little broader, and he had hard lines pressed into his forehead. He was holding a silk, orange-colored rose with a navy ribbon around the stem. Our school colors. From the stiff way he held his shoulders and his tendency to look over my head, I knew that this meeting wasn't easy for him.

"You did a nice job up there. I was impressed. This is for you." He extended the fake flower to me with an embarrassed grin.

I took the flower from him carefully, and I let the appreciation for it show in my face. "How thoughtful! Thank you very much!" I brushed it over my nose, even though it was clear that this fabric blossom would not carry much of a scent.

"Yah. So, ahh. Congratulations. Have Sallie bring you out to the house sometime. To celebrate."

"I'd like that a lot, Mr. Rinaldi."

By then I could see Salmon and his mom with their arms around each other in a huddle with Frankie just outside the gate. Salmon's mom had her back to us, but Salmon was looking at me over her shoulder. He winked at me. Again my insides quivered.

Mr. Rinaldi was starting to sweat. "No problem. I better be going. Got my family over there." He backed away toward Salmon and the rest of his family. Then he stopped like he'd forgotten something. "I'm sorry. Tell me your name again?" he asked.

I saw Khalil holding Stacy's hand while his mom took a picture of them. I saw Salmon and Frankie slapping each other's backs and smiling all over each other.

I saw my mother dumping out her flask and struggling to stand up. I saw myself, with a rose in one hand and a degree in the other, in another state, standing with her. I looked him in the eyes and answered him.

"My name is Dignity," I said.

And I meant it.

Author Bio

J. Marie Darden, a graduate of Morgan State University, holds a
Master's in English education from Johns Hopkins University.
She is currently a professor of English at the Community College of
Baltimore County, Maryland. She splits her time between Columbia,
Maryland and London with her family.

EXCERPT FROM

ENEMY FIELDS

By J. MARIE DARDEN

AVAILABLE FROM STREBOR BOOKS

CHAPTER ONE

No in between here. That what Grannie use to say. Everything either black or white. Me, I'm black.

When I'm on the porch sometime, or up in Timmie and Albert room, I think about my Grannie. Seem like what she say always running through my mind. Stories she would tell and all. Mama say she make most of them up. Grannie say Mama claim that so she don't have to think about truth. But Grannie say ain't no sense in to run from it, and ain't no in between with it, cuz truth is truth.

The weather miserable today. Didn't have much winter before the weather turn plain hot. The air hot and thick as cocoa. Feel tight around you like outgrown sleeves. Hard to breathe. You could smell it, too. Smell solid. Seem like a mess of dirt, damp clothes, syrup, sweet honeysuckle, and rain all mix together. Real sticky.

Nobody feel like doing nothing but fan and drink lemonade. Wasn't no wind neither cuz the air too stiff and stubborn. But, bad as it was inside, seem like it was worse outside. At least you stay dry inside. Outside the air melt on your skin and stick to you like butter. Dribble down your legs like they cobs of corn. The fan don't help none. Those blades have to struggle to stir the thick air, but they can't move quick enough to make a breeze.

Pam Elizabeth come running down my street. She kick up dust that stick to the molasses air.

"Ooh, Sister! Sister, you not gonna believe! You wait!" She holler when she get excited. Then a smile rip across her face to show white horse teeth. She still pretty, though.

"What you got good to say, you simple fool? Screamin' like you crazy," I tease her. Pammie and me can joke because we close.

"Girl, you won't believe!" Pammie leap up the porch steps and plop down on the wooden swing Papa make.

"Naw, I sho won't believe less you tells me already!" I'm anxious since Pammie looking tickle at whatever it is.

"You know that big ole house? The one cross the field back of your house? Political man own it or somethin'. Well, my brother Edward say he hear from his boy Skeemo that folks is fixin' to move in Friday!" She smiling like she ain't said it all.

"That your news?" I play like I don't really care, but really I'm curious. That house so big and mysterious. Been empty ever since I can remember.

"Here's what else." She hitting me with the punch. "They's white folks, what's fixin' to move in!" She beam, satisfied that she drop me.

"Naw, sure enough? They's *white?*" I pronounce the word real clear, and my eyes get wide because I'm sure enough surprise. No white folks never come to our part of town even to visit. But to live?!

"And they rich, too. Got to be to afford that ole place. Skeemo say it need some work, but it real big. It got something like eight or ten bedrooms in it. And land for miles and miles. They say part of that field back of your house really belong to that house. Wonder how they gonna tend all that land, Sister?" The swing is old and the paint is chip and crack away. Pammie use her long skinny fingers to peel away layers of the paint.

"Quit pickin', Girl! Spose they ask some of us town folks to help them. Wonder what they comin' here for? Plenty of fine houses closer to town. Why they gonna live near us? Grannie say white folks is trouble."

"Spose she was right. I reckon we have to wait and find out for sure. You miss your grannie?" Pammie lift one foot up on the swing and use the other to sort of push and make us go.

"Yeah. Sometime it don't seem like she really gone. So much of what she say always runnin' round in my head. But she better off now, I guess." My Grannie pass last winter. She was 86.

"I miss Daddy, too. Seem like the people you love the most the ones that die first. Least he got to see me finish school. He always want for us to finish."

"Grannie, too. But she pass before I finish."

"Do your mama ever cry about Grannie? Mama, seem like she cry all the time. She a little better now that she teach piano again. Use to be she just sit around and cry. I guess she lonely."

"Mama don't cry. She pray. Me, I use to cry, but not no more. I still get lonely sometime, though."

"Why you lonely? Your husband ain't pass."

"Yeah, but Grannie pass. And your daddy pass. I ain't got no daddy. And people pass. And I ain't got no husband. I don't know. Just seem like maybe somethin' missin', I don't know." I finger my springy-coil hair.

"Right. That's why I wanna get away from here. I don't think there anything here for me."

Pammie and me talk a little longer. She always saying she going but don't go nowhere. Pammie ain't even got a job yet. She don't know what she want. Say she got a cousin name Bluff live in Detroit. She say she going and stay with him.

Me, I ain't press to go. One thing I do know is I wanna sing. Ever since I's little, I be writing down words. You know, like catchy phrases. Then I add a melody to it. Call myself writing songs. When I go to Pammie house, I play piano. Her mama play at the church and she teach some, too. I never had the patience to take from her. She wanna make you study theory or some mess. I just wanna play what I hear and sing what I play. I do like to sing in church, though.

Soon Pammie get on her going-to-Detroit kick, and I get bored. I say I'm going in the house, and she walk on down the street to hers.

CHAPTER TWO

It cramp at home. Whole bunch of us in one little house. We got a kitchen, bathroom, living room, dining room, and three bedrooms.

It ain't that bad. But it do get crowded. It me, my mama, my older sister, Ruthanne, her baby, Nakita, my younger brothers, Timothy and Albert, and sometime Ruthanne boyfriend, Peanut. Ruthanne and Nakita in one room, Timmie and Albert in another, and me and Mama share one.

Mama getting old, so she go to bed all early. She want the light out by 10:00. I can't read or write or sing in there. Sometime I can sit in the living room and write. Then sometime Albert come in with some fast girl from cross town, acting like they grown. Else Ruthanne down there with big-headed Peanut and don't want me around. Timmie only five, so he usually sleep. Sometime I go in his room and look out the window and think.

Timmie and Albert room face the back, so the window show the back yard and way out into the field. Sometime it real pretty out there. The grass all soft and plush like crush velvet. When you walk barefooted out there it feel kinda cool and wettish, and the air smell real nice. I like fall best. Then you can see the leaves on the sycamores blended in different patterns. Green, red, and gold all together. Look like the patchwork on some of Mama quilts.

When the moon bright and in the right place, kinda hazy and yellow-like, it make the meadow look like maybe ghosts is back there. It spooky. Sometime I pretend they really is ghosts back there, and I imagine what they like. Is they black ghosts or white ghosts? Do they come from the dead folks in our town or from that big house back there? Probably they's all kinds. I reckon don't nobody care what color you is when you dead.

In their room you can see the back of that house Pammie say white folks moving into. Ain't nobody live there since I was real little, and whoever they was, I don't remember them.

Not long after I hear the news from Pammie, I seen the new people moving in. Everybody in the neighborhood talking about it. Only time white folks come around is if someone take some of they property—they stuff or they women. Don't nobody here do that. We got our own stuff, and the men here ain't too particular for white women. Least that what they say.

One night I'm in Timmie room and I could see clear into those people house. Why they got windows all over the back? They don't want privacy? I could see the dining room and one of the bedroom. I seen three people in there: one old man with white hair, a fattish woman look like she Mama age, and a boy my age with wild red hair. Seem strange to put those few people in that big ole house whiles me and Mama and all of us is pile up in our house cross the field. White folks is crazy. That what Grannie use to say. I ain't really known none of them personal-like. Just some of the teachers back at Dunbar, but you can't count them. They ain't there to get to know; they just try to teach you.

The lights was dim in the dining room, but I could see into the bedroom where the boy stay. I can't see all that well, but I can tell he got a guitar. I couldn't hear him play, but it seem nice that he try. Wonder if he good? I use to wish I could play one of them guitars, but I don't got one. Plus it seem kinda hard—all them strings.

All week I hear people talking about them white folks. They say the boy sick or something. That his mama and granddaddy he live with. They name Mandarene. Say the mama got the house left to her by her dead uncle. That may not be true. Folks around here often make up what they don't know for sure.

People saying they looking for someone to keep the house and cook during the week. Don't nobody want to ask about it because don't nobody trust white folks. I'm thinking about going cross the field and see if they maybe take me. Maybe they pay good. And anyway, I ain't scared of no white folk no how.

CHAPTER THREE

Grannie say white folks is crazy. They can be as crazy as they wanna be when they pay me $75.00 a week to cook and clean they house. Mama figure these people must got money to burn.

The old man over there is name Norman. He don't spose to smoke, but I find his butts all over the back porch and in the yard, too. Mama is name Cordial. She say don't call her Miss cuz it make her feel old. She is old, so I call her Miss. Cordial a strange name anyhow.

Her son sick or something. He got cancer. Pale skin and wild red hair. Calls hisself "Ev-ee-in." His mama say "Ev-yin." But he always put that extra sound in the center. Me, I didn't call him nothing at first. No need. If he come up on me, I just answer his question and go on.

Cordial, she one of them artsy types. She set up a board by the window in the dining room and call herself painting. First few weeks I come, all I see her do is mix paint together, sometime with a stick, sometime with her hand. Then she wanna "get her own lunch." What that mean is she gonna leave oily prints and a big mess in the kitchen. I say, if she wanna get her lunch, what I come for? Never mind. She still pay me.

Mainly she want me to wash the windows. That and the baseboards. That what she call the thin wood that stick out at the bottom of the wall. Twice a week she got me using vinegar and newspaper on the windows and Pine Sol on the baseboards. I never seen such clean windows. Good thing they clean, too, cuz Miss love to stare out them. Some days she just stand and look for hours, seem like. Make me chuckle. If I had time, I stare out them, too. Me, I'm too busy cleaning them to stare out of them.

One thing I do know, white folks ain't much for work. Miss hire somebody to do everything. She call it sending things out. Use to be I clean the sheets and they clothes, but for long she send them out. Sure enough on Wednesday morning, I gather up the laundry and set them by the door. Then Jefferson son come from the cleaners and pick them up, return them on Saturday. I ain't around on Saturday. Least not at first.

Evian, as he call hisself, talk on the phone a lot. He talk in a high-pitch voice real slow and drawn out. It don't sound like Kentucky, neither. More like Tennessee or something. But when he laugh, he cackle. Whoever he talk to must really tickle him, because he always laughing. That and play the guitar. He sing some, too. Singing don't sound like his speaking, though. Sound more like cranberries: sweet, cold, and tangy. I hum along sometime. Sometime I don't know the words.

One day I'm cleaning his bathroom and he in his bedroom playing Marvin Gaye and Tammi. Where he get Marvin, I wonder? He playing it real loud, so I start singing Tammi part. This time I know the words. Next thing I know, he at the door singing Marvin part real strong. We sound kinda good, but I act like I don't notice. Just keep singing.

When the record go off, he spin me around and say, "Hey, now! I never knew you could sing like that, uhh...ahh...What is your name again, I'm sorry..." Evian look shame.

I answer quick. "Don't make no difference. Folks call me Sister." I don't look him in the eye.

"Sister, you got a mean contralto! You like to sing real low, don't you?" Evian lean against the sink. His wild red hair matted in the back.

I'm surprise he interested. "Yea. I can sing up high or low, but I like it best when it settle somewhere in my chest."

Evian get real excited, start talking with his hands. "Cool! I love to harmonize. I love the way you people sing! I wish I could emulate it."

Right there I start tuning out. What he mean "you people?" I maybe clean the house and cook the food, but it 1971, and I'm 18 years old, a full women, and King done died, and I don't feel like conversating as one of "you people." I turn away and sprinkle Comet in the tub.

He don't take the hint. "...I have so many records. Old stuff. Newer stuff. You like Ray Charles? Oh, oh, and how about James Brown? Double threat— dances and sings! Aretha, the Beatles..." Evian chatter on, don't notice I ain't hardly listening. "Who are your favorites, Sister?" He cross his feet while he lean on the sink.

"I disremember. I...I think I better finish this here tub." I try not to be rude. He ain't worth losing my job over or nothing. One hand, I wanna talk to him. Don't nobody love Aretha and music like me. Other hand, what he wanna talk music with "you people" for?

Evian turn to leave. "Oh yeah. You're busy. Like my mom is too busy to clean her own toilets. I'm in my room, mostly. Come by and say hey some- time. I wanna know who your favorites are." He scratch his head in the back as he leave. He need to comb his hair.

He puzzle me. You people. Cracks about his mama. He setting me up? And I don't see him rushing to clean his own toilet.

Soon after that, Evian get sick. Miss leave me in the house some days with the old man. She say Evian be going to the doctor a lot for a while. She say I don't have to clean his room or his bathroom, neither. Okay with me.

But I still gotta vacuum. So, I hear him in his bathroom being sick. I'm out in the hall with the vacuum. I go in the room next to his and pull the door to. Don't seem right to have someone hearing you be sick. So first I sort of dust. But really I'm finish in there, so I turn on the vacuum and just sit a minute. Next I hear him go in his room and shut the door.

While I'm vacuuming the hall outside his room, something sort of sink down low in my stomach. He so young to be so sick. Next thing I know, I hear Dinah Washington singing "Unforgettable." Something jump up in me then, same thing that had sunk before, and I knock on his door.

Hear him rustle on the bed. "Yea?"

"I like her, too." I say through the door.

"Come again? Sister...?" He turn the music down a little.

"I say, I like Dinah Washington, too." My heart pounding some.

"Sister. Come in. Open the door." He sitting on the edge of the bed, hair breaking off and skin more pale.

I scan the room slow, like I don't never seen it before. It got carpet, but he also put down these wild color rugs on the floor. He got a painting of a bird over the bed, got its head stretch up and its wings half-spread.

Evian half-laugh, half cough. "She is my absolute favorite. Gotta be in the right mood for Dinah, though. She's better than some of them, I spose, like Billie Holiday." He not looking at me. He looking at the bird.

"Yeah. She take you down some place you don't intend to go." I sing along to "Willow Weep for Me." Evian sort of hum along, too. Then the record stop and all you hear is breathing. Mine shallow and his seem like water running through it.

"You ever get tired, Sister? Sometimes I'm so tired." He lean against the back board of the bed and cross his feet Indian-style.

"Sure. After working all day or walking around with Pammie." I answer without thinking.

"Yea, but I mean deep down in your bones tired. And sick. And sick of being tired. I mean, what is this about, anyways? All these trips to the doctor and therapy. Doesn't seem like I'll ever get better. And it makes me tired." He rest his head against the back board. Small tears run down his cheek.

I don't know what to say. What I got to be tired for? Sometime things get on my nerves, like when it crowded at home and I wanna write or just think. Or the way white folks look at you in Woodsons downtown like you dirty. I gets tired of that fast and want to go home. Bone tired? I don't know.

I notice a pile of Negro spirituals on his desk. "Precious Lord" and "Deep River." They two of my favorites. These the ones they always let me lead at church.

"At home, it ain't no room to breathe. They's a bunch of us in there. I get sad sometime for my grannie. She pass a year ago. Those times I sing. You know. Out on the porch, just swing a little and sing till the heavy part slip away. You know this?" I hand him "Precious Lord."

Evian take the page. "Hand me my guitar, will you?" He let his right leg dangle off the side of the bed.

First he tune. He put the music on the bed in front of him. Then he strum soft. Close his eyes and strum around the melody. I don't never hear nobody play spirituals on the guitar before. Sound so soft on the outside, like when raindrops fall off the tree in the front yard and bounce on the window.

He rock a little and strum. Seem like some of his sick and tired, some of my dirty looks from Woodsons, and some of Grannie's "no in between" splash together and land at my feet. I start to sing.

I start at the center and move out. Through the storm. Through the night. By the time I'm back at the beginning, pleading to the Lord, Evian singing, too. We sound kinda sweet together.

Printed in the United States
By Bookmasters